The Temptation Of The Miracle Weaver

Roberto Rosas

PublishAmerica
Baltimore

© 2002 by Roberto Rosas.
All rights reserved. No part of this book may be reproduced in any form without written permission from the publishers, except by a reviewer who may quote brief passages in a review to be printed in a newspaper or magazine.

First printing

ISBN: 1-59129-598-x
PUBLISHED BY PUBLISHAMERICA BOOK PUBLISHERS
www.publishamerica.com
Baltimore

Printed in the United States of America

†
In memory of
Fr. Joseph Norbert Deddens,
a true friend in Christ.

To MARIA GUADALUPE CRUZ

I HOPE YOU ENJOY READING THIS PARABLE

XBIC

Roberto G. Rosas Jr

06 12 09

Acknowledgements

This book would not have been possible without the inspiration and the life God gave me, without my parents, Roberto and Cata, my brother, Luis, my sisters, Leticia, Patricia, Rocio, Martha, and Janie who have had an impact in my life from the beginning, or without my wife, Arcelia, my sons, Roberto III and Gabriel, my daughter, Maribel, who are all gifts from the eternal. I recognize that I owe what I am to all the relationships I have held throughout my life, and consequently this story is the result of my experience and my life in relationships. Some of the scenes described here actually have a been based on real events, but this story is just the product of mixing many experiences, mine and those of others who shared them with me, not intended to portray any real person. With this in mind, I wish to thank all those who have contributed to my life and my work by the sharing of their friendship and perspectives. Let me mention a few persons who had a direct contribution in the process, Det. Pablo Gonzalez for his personality suggestions, Maura Ciarrocchi for helping with editing, Sgt. Rene Rodriguez for referring me to PublishAmerica, Ernest Huizar for telling me he "could not put the novel down." Dr. William Peche for his sincere encouragement, Joseph DeMuoy for his writer's suggestions, Richard Mendiola for taking my pictures, Deacon Jerome Ciarrocchi for his advice and Fr. John Makothakat for his support and input. Thanks to all those other unnamed here but who helped me by reading the manuscript and making comments on it. May God bless you for your kindness!

"Amen, amen, I say to you, whoever believes in me will do the works that I do, and will do greater ones than these, because I am going to the Father. And whatever you ask in my name, I will do, so that the Father may be glorified in the Son."   (John 14:12-13)

~ The New American Bible / United States Conference of Catholic Bishops

Scripture excerpts are taken from the New American Bible Copyright (c) 1970. Confraternity of Christian Doctrine, Inc. Washington DC. Used with permission. All rights reserved. No Part of the New American Bible may be reproduced by any means without permission in writing from the copyright owner. Permission to use the New American Bible does not signify the endorsement of the Confraternity of Christian Doctrine or the United States Conference of Catholic Bishops.

Chapter I
Satan's Challenge

It was 4:30 a.m. on Tuesday, August 31st, when the sound of a piece of Mozart's violin music started playing on the radio/alarm clock. "Time to start another exciting day" was the thought in the man's mind as he stretched his six-foot frame on his single bed. As usual, he felt "splendidly well." He was almost thirty-eight but was in great shape, like a college athlete. He got up, went to the restroom, came back to his bed, turned the light on and reached for his little black book, "The Liturgy of the Hours." He knelt at the foot of his simple bed and began reciting the morning prayer of the day. When he finished his prayers, he kissed his book and put it on his night table, made his bed, and put on his running shorts, shirt and shoes. It was 4:50 a.m. when he left his house. The morning was warm, typical of South Texas; there would not be daylight for another hour. The church and Catholic school of the Holy Trinity on the West side of San Antonio looked peaceful at that hour of the morning. Gabriel Infante, the parish pastor and principal of the school, began stretching and warming up his muscles to go for a run.

Father Gabriel waved hello to a couple, the Mendozas, who passed him in a truck delivering newspapers. A little dog came to the edge of a house fence, barking as ferociously as his tiny size allowed him. The priest ran fast towards the Chihuahua, intentionally, and sent the little beast running towards the house, yelping scared. Once the danger had passed, the dog came back to the fence to bark at him again. A light wind picked up some papers in front of the athlete. His alert eyes caught sight of a familiar form among the blown papers. He caught it in the air and checked it under the street lamplight. He had guessed right; it was a ten-dollar bill! Maybe he could buy himself a nice big breakfast that morning after the 8:00 a.m. Mass. He slid the ten-dollar bill between his shorts and t-shirt and kept going at an eight-minute-mile pace.

On a bus stop bench, the priest saw a man slumped over. He looked like a "wino" sleeping with his head hanging off the side of the bench; he was going to wake up with a pain in the neck for sure. Father Gabriel decided to stop for a moment and straighten him up. The man woke up when he felt the hands of the stranger moving his body.

"Whatta hell are you doing?" shouted the homeless man as he struggled with the runner.

"I am sorry! I thought you were passed out drunk, and I wanted to rearrange you, so you wouldn't get a pain in your neck," said the priest backing off.

"Drunk? I don't even have money for food, much less for beer or wine," explained the man.

He was a skinny guy, around the same age as the priest but looked older. The man's long hair and beard reminded the minister of St. John the Baptist. Gabriel was moved looking at the sunken eyes of the man.

"You got any money you could loan me for something to eat, buddy?" the skinny man begged the stranger.

"Well…" the priest was going to say "no" because he usually did not have any money, but then he remembered the bill he had just found five blocks away.

"What would you do with ten dollars?"

Gabriel put one hand on the man's shoulder and covertly pulled the bill from his own shorts with his other hand.

"Ah, with ten dollars, I could eat for a whole day!" the man said, smiling at the thought of having that much cash.

The athletic minister picked the skinny man up from the bench grabbing him by the shirt. He managed to put the bill in the man's shirt pocket without him noticing.

"Well, if that is the case, I think you have enough to eat for today. Why are you asking me for money when you have ten dollars in your pocket?" he said, pretending to be angry with the beggar.

"Hey, let me go, man! You don't wanna loan me money, that's O.K., but you don't have to abuse me!"

Father Gabriel smiled and winked at him to let him know he was playing.

"Always check your pockets first, my friend!" the priest told the man and began running away.

The puzzled man put his hands on his chest to fix his pulled up shirt and felt something inside his shirt pocket. He had been looking at the stranger running away, not knowing what to make of their encounter. Then he pulled the money from his pocket and realized that the kind stranger had put it there and did not even wait for him to say thanks. The homeless guy looked at the money and then looked for the stranger, but the runner was out of sight in the dark morning. It was already 5:30 a.m.

THE TEMPTATION OF THE MIRACLE WEAVER

The beggar was very happy and looked around for someone to share his happiness with. The Mendozas were coming around throwing the newspapers as he was holding the ten-dollar bill.

"Hey! Did you see that big guy that took off running?" the beggar asked Martin Mendoza as they drove close to him.

"Yeah, what about him?"

The Mendozas stopped for a moment to see what the man wanted.

"Well, he's pretty cool. He gave me a scare at first; I thought he was going to kick my ass. Then I realized that he gave me this ten-dollar bill and didn't even wait for me to thank him. I wonder who he is."

The beggar searched the dark street again, but the generous stranger was gone.

"That's an easy one! It was Father Gabriel, the pastor of the Holy Trinity Church, and you're right. He is a pretty cool guy. He cured me from a malignant tumor three months ago. The doctors couldn't believe it. They wanted to operate on me, or else I was supposed to die. Look at me now, healthy as a kid! He is a man of God; people know him as 'The Miracle Weaver.'" Martin told the beggar before driving off to continue his business.

The man saw them going down the street and thought about the last time he had gone to a church. That was five years before, at his sister's wedding. Maybe he needed to go back and this had been a sign from God for him to return to his original faith. The beggar felt a warm, soft wind caress his face as if The Almighty had accepted his thoughts and approved of them. The man crossed himself, closed his eyes and prayed an Our Father to thank the Lord before going to eat his eagerly anticipated breakfast.

Father Gabriel was working out at the Wild West Side Boxing Gym. He had been practicing boxing since he was in middle school. He won the city golden gloves competition when he was a middle-school-youngster weighing 120 lbs; by the time he was in high school Gabriel preferred football to boxing but returned to it during his seminary days. There he had a couple of seminarian friends, Raphael and Michael, who were the same size as he was (185 lbs. by then) and got into boxing to let off steam and relieve the stress of young men committing themselves to a celibate life in the priesthood. Because of their names, they were known as the three Archangels in the seminary. They also liked to get together and sing. Gabriel sang best and played guitar, Michael was the organist and Raphael the bass guitar player. Those two were like the brothers Gabriel never had.

The priest was a very close friend of the boxing gym owner, Jaime Bravo, who let him come and work out for free. "Father G," as the kids in the barrio called him, worked on his waist and did some sets of pull-ups and push-ups. Then he started working out with the heavy bag. He moved like a middleweight even though he weighed an even 200 pounds of solid muscle. When he was all pumped up in the gym, it was hard to imagine he was a kind minister of the Lord. Gabriel looked like the Hercules from the movies with his trimmed beard and well defined physique. He also could bench press 300 lbs. and squat 400; he was, no doubt, a strong man.

The amateur boxer finished his workout and went to take a quick shower before proceeding to celebrate the morning Mass and face another busy day at the school. While taking his shower, Gabriel felt inspired to sing a Spanish song about a little bird, a nightingale. His powerful voice resounded throughout the gym as he sang the verses that spoke of a little bird foretelling that happiness was about to arrive. It was an almost-religious song inviting the listener to thank God for all his goodness. The other men in the gym looked at each other smiling as they listened to his song and kept working out, almost as if they were dancing to the beat of the melodious sound.

Gabriel's first language had been Spanish because his parents came from Mexico. His own birth was miraculous. His parents had been married for several years, wanting to have a child, but Maria De La Luz, his mother, was unable to conceive. She had an infection that rendered her ovaries barren while she was a young woman. Her husband, Jose Arturo Infante, was very understanding. He had suggested adopting a child, but the woman had faith that God would grant them a child of their own. Ten years after they got married, Maria had a dream about the Angel of the Lord announcing to the Virgin Mary that she would conceive the Son of God. The next day, Petrita Martinez, a neighbor, invited Maria De La Luz to a healing service in their church. The neighbor suffered from arthritis, although she was only 30 years old; she knew about Maria's infertility. A priest that was said to have healing power from the Holy Spirit was the celebrant that evening. Father Xavier, the healing priest, talked to Maria in the church and touched her abdomen; she felt hot, happy and excited at that moment. Her husband noticed that her cheeks were blushed, and that she looked radiant when she came home from the church. That was the night their only son was conceived. He was born on his mother's 30th birthday. His mother knew he was a special gift from God and named him Gabriel in honor of the Archangel. Maria de la Luz thought the baby was God's birthday gift to her. Petrita had been healed from her arthritis too, and later she became the boy's godmother at his baptism. Petrita and her husband Felipe Martinez owned the corner store on Guadalupe Street.

The miracle boy grew up on the west side of the city with a strong Mexican-Catholic influence. His father, Jose, was a moderately successful and very skillful carpenter who had his own shop. His mother, Maria, took care of the home and of her two men very well. She managed their home and stretched the money her husband made, so that all needs would be covered. Gabriel grew up as an only child, but he had a happy upbringing in a loving family.

The reverend had a large glass of grapefruit juice as his regular breakfast while reviewing the latest news in the daily paper. Nothing new was going on. The city was still celebrating the National Championship won by the Latigos (whips), the local professional basketball team. He had done his part too in bringing the trophy to the city that year. Ivory Peterson and Daniel Williamson, two of the star players on the team, had met Father Gabriel at a fund raiser a couple of years before and had heard about some of his miracles. They asked him to pray for them to make it all the way to the finals. The priest agreed because he liked the two Christian athletes and thought it would not hurt to ask the Lord for a thing like a championship even if it seemed to be so banal. At first his prayers seemed to have backfired because the Latigos actually had a terrible year. Williamson got hurt, and the team ended at the bottom of the table. This, however, allowed them to win the league lottery and get Tom Lincoln as the latest addition to the team. The talented rookie took them all the way to where they wanted to be. Once they got to the play-offs, the Latigos invited the priest to watch the home games courtside; he was there in the front row when Shawn Scott scored the winning three-pointer at the buzzer for their division. He knew then the Latigos were going all the way because his prayers were being answered. Gabriel remembered how he and Ivory were commenting on the strange ways God grants us the things we need but on His own terms, not ours. Father Gabriel looked at his watch: it was almost eight o'clock, so he dropped the paper and ran to the church. The regular parishioners were there waiting for the Mass to begin as scheduled.

Looking at the priest in the church, celebrating the Mass, preaching the Gospel, one would think that this was Jesus himself, with a haircut, talking to the audience. He spoke with power and conviction; his actions revealed his strong faith in God. People felt at peace just listening to him. He was well known in the neighborhood because he had, indeed, performed many miracles. He always dismissed the credit due to him and told everyone that it was their faith and their God together that granted the miracles. He tried to keep it a secret as much as possible to avoid the crowds overwhelming him. He had no explanation himself as to why a miracle occurred in one particular case and not in others, or why things happened like in the case of the Latigos. Because of the weave of rumors about his miracles being real or not, the people knew him as "The Miracle Weaver." Not everybody knew about the miracles, and not all the things he did were miracles. Many people did not believe he performed miracles at all.

From the church, the priest moved forward to the school across the street. He was always busy, having the responsibility over the parish and the school. He knew how to delegate authority and trusted his vice principal with most of the work at the school while a deacon assisted him greatly in the management of the lively parish.

Life for Father Gabriel was good; he was a fulfilled man. People loved him, and he loved all people. Some thought of him as a living saint; some criticized him for his lifestyle. He was a flesh-and-blood guy who liked to have a drink or two although no one had ever seen him drunk. He also had the "reprehensibly bad habit" of smoking cigars. Some people did not approve of his boxing skills, which he was known to have used in several occasions to beat up a wrongdoer or two. Others had problems with his passion for the arts. Gabriel painted and enjoyed singing and dancing. His nude compositions and his female dance partners were usually a target for gossip among the people of the community. Gabriel had a good sense of humor and did not let any of the gossip stop him from doing what he liked. Another cause for some people to have a problem with the priest was his political stand. He was openly declared a Republican and listened to conservative talk radio every chance he had; this was not seen well in the typically Democrat Hispanic community. All in all, the man was not perfect, but he was very content.

After school and some parish business, Gabriel went to eat dinner at the religious sisters' house that evening. He had four sisters teaching at his school. Kathryn Cabrini, an Irish sister, was in charge of the first grade. She was a very sweet middle-aged, skinny and tall woman who enjoyed poetry and beer. Kathryn was also the music minister at the parish. Magdalene McKay, another Irish sister in charge of the third grade, was a jolly senior-aged full-figured short woman who had a passion for all kinds of food, drink and classical music. She was the superior of the sisters' community and a consummate organist. Carmen Armienta, an Argentinean sister in charge of the fifth grade, was a very pious middle-aged medium-sized woman who had trouble handling discipline matters in her class. An inspired singer, she loved Gregorian chanting and all kinds of sweets. Mary Daskalos, of Greek descent, was the youngest of the sisters, only twenty-eight, and in charge of the seventh grade. She was an energetic, petite woman whose passion was education. An excellent guitar player, Mary was into pop music for worship celebration. Although not one of the sisters was particularly athletic, they all had developed a common taste for watching baseball on T.V. Their favorite team was the Texas Rangers.

Father Gabriel had an enjoyable golden dinner with the four sisters. They had chicken fried steak with mashed potatoes and corn, accompanied by a beer for Father, Magda and Kathryn, iced tea for the rest of them. A cup of coffee and pecan pie with a scoop of vanilla ice cream was the dessert. Gabriel, Magdalene and Carmen cleaned their plates; Kathryn and Mary just had a bite of the pie claiming they had no room for more although they had just eaten half of their servings. After thanking the Lord for their dinner, the group moved to the music room and enjoyed singing and playing some Christian music to praise the Lord. Kathryn played the violin while Magda played the organ and Mary the guitar. Gabriel and Carmen sang the hymns; they spent a whole hour with music. Father closed the evening with a joke about a Texan who went to hell. He knew about the sisters' interest in baseball. He said:

"A man from Texas died and went to hell. When he got there, he found everybody complaining about how hot it was in there, 80 degrees and 80 percent humidity! The Texan felt so well in that environment that he was always smiling. The devil noticed the newcomer with his cowboy hat and cowboy boots just walking around very comfortable in the damned place. He asked the Texan if he was not hot. He answered, 'Hell, no! This is just like Texas in May.' The devil immediately went and cranked up the heat to 90 degrees and 90 percent humidity. When he saw the cowboy again, he found him still smiling, with his cowboy hat in his hand. The devil asked him once more if he was feeling the heat yet. He answered, 'No, no! This feels just like Texas in June.' The devil went and pushed the thermostat up to 100 degrees and 100 percent humidity, but he found no great change in the Texan's attitude. He had only removed his cowboy boots and was fanning himself with his cowboy hat saying, 'Man, this is like Texas in July!' The devil thought about it for a moment and decided to change his strategy. He went back to the thermostat and lowered the temperature all the way down to 20 degrees. Icicles started appearing everywhere! The devil ran to the chamber where the Texan was and found him jumping up and down shouting with great joy, 'The Texas Rangers finally won the World Series!'"

The sisters broke down in laughter; Magda excused herself to go the bathroom. Father Gabriel then thanked them for a wonderful evening and went home on foot.

It was ten blocks from the sisters' house to the church, where he had his assigned residence. He lit up his cigar and walked slowly, taking in the last vestiges of light on the western horizon. Another successful day was coming to an end. He was talking to God as he walked, thanking him for the great day he had enjoyed. An old lady was bringing the trash to her sidewalk for the garbage collectors to pick up the next morning. She heard him talking alone as he walked up her street. She thought he might be crazy, or drunk, talking to himself. She decided to hurry back into her home to avoid the stranger that was approaching her home. Gabriel noticed her behavior and smiled to himself. He then started singing a song about a drunk singing a serenade to the object of his affection. The woman looked out the window and hearing him sing concluded:

"A singing drunk, but he sounds pretty good!"

The troubadour's voice faded down the block with his passionate Mexican song.

As the priest was approaching the church, he noticed an old, elegant lady talking to a man by the main entrance to the temple. She seemed desperate and was sending the man, obviously her chauffeur, to go ask something. She was pointing in the direction of the rectory. Father Gabriel asked if he could be of assistance. They noticed his clerical collar as he came under the light and out of the dark alley. He recognized the old lady as a new parishioner he had seen for the first time in the church that morning at the eight o'clock Mass. She might have been an attractive beauty queen 50 years before, now she was just a rich old lady full of herself.

"Father Gabriel. I am so happy to see you!" she said, walking up to him to shake his hand with both of hers.

"I see that you don't have the walker you had this morning, Alice. What happened?"

Someone had convinced the woman to come to the priest to cure her of a back pain that had tormented her for years. She had great difficulty walking and needed the support of a walker or had to be wheel-chaired by her driver. She was also very forgetful and that was why she had to come back to the church that night.

"Oh, Father, I am so happy to be able to walk without that horrible thing. I should have come to you as soon as I started having this problem," she exclaimed.

"What did I do?" asked Father Gabriel, interested in knowing the details.

That morning, Alice Silverstone had asked him to pray for her to be healed of her affliction, but the priest sensed that her faith was non-existent. He agreed to keep her in his prayers, which he had done throughout the day, but due to her lack of faith, he did not expect her to be miraculously cured. He had, however, recommended seeing a chiropractor friend of his who had an office on the north side of the city. She claimed she had seen the best doctors already, but all they wanted was to operate on her without any guarantee that she would get better.

"I went to see the chiropractor you suggested. I had never tried one of those before, but it worked! I got really scared when he cracked and popped my back; however, I felt the difference immediately! The pain left me as soon as my spine was back in line."

"I am so happy for you, Alice. God works in mysterious ways!"

He looked into her eyes and grabbed her by the shoulders.

"I don't know about that, but your advice was worth a lot to me, whether God had anything to do with it or not," she said, adding, "What brings me here at this time of the night is another issue. I lost a ring this morning. For a moment, I thought someone had stolen it, so I reported it to the police. Then I had a flashback of memory. You know my memory is not as good now as it used to be when I was younger. Anyway, I recalled that the last place I had my ring on me was here at the church this morning. I think I was fiddling with it during the service and probably lost it where I was sitting. You were saying something that touched my heart in your sermon, but I cannot remember what it was. I would like to search the church to find that diamond ring. It's invaluable to me because it was my grandmother's wedding ring. It's worth at least 50,000 dollars."

Father Gabriel looked at the old lady and felt pity. By the looks of the woman, the value of the ring was really nothing that would send her into poverty. She came in a limousine with her chauffeur and was wearing an expensive dress. She also had on jewelry worth three times as much as the missing ring. Jewelry and money were not things that excited the pastor of the Holy Trinity parish.

"Let's take a look inside. I think you were sitting on the left pews, about the middle," the priest said, opening the door to go inside the church.

"No, I think I was up front on the right," she argued, very sure of where she had been, and started heading in that direction while the priest went to turn the lights on.

Alice ordered her chauffeur to start searching all the pews from the front to the back on the right side. The employee, a middle-aged black man, complied with his boss's order immediately without saying a word. Gabriel wondered if the man actually spoke. It looked as if the old lady did enough talking, and he just had no chance to say anything. Gabriel thought, "50,000 dollars for a piece of metal and a little stone!" The priest wondered how much could be done with such amount to feed the hungry, or clothe the naked, or educate the ignorant. He went to assist the two in their search. As he was heading in their direction, a lightning bug flew across his face. Gabriel stopped and followed the little insect's path with his eyes. The firefly stopped on one of the pews on the left side. The priest felt something like a tiny fire inside his chest and decided to follow the insect.

"Over here, Father! I told you I was sitting on this side. You can check towards the wall in case it fell and rolled away or if it got kicked. I hope no one found it and decided to keep it for themselves!" the old lady ordered the priest to assist them on their side.

He ignored her order and looked at the firefly, which had taken off in flight again, shining its tiny light. It flew down to the floor under a pew in the middle of the left set. Gabriel smiled and knelt where the bug had landed. The five-karat diamond shined back as the lightning bug lit the corner under the pew, next to the ring.

"I knew it. Thank you little creature. Thank you, Lord for sending me this guide to help Alice in recovering her ring!"

The pastor got up with the ring in his hand; the little bug went to rest on his shoulder.

"Alice, we found your ring!"

The old lady was smiling like a happy little girl on Christmas morning and walked as fast as she could toward the priest. The driver followed her, relieved because earlier he had been named as one of the suspects that could have stolen the ring. Alice took the ring and thanked Gabriel. Her driver was happy and, still without pronouncing a word, shook his hand.

"Father, let me give you a reward for finding my ring. I will write you a check for 500 dollars. How is that?"

The woman pulled her checkbook from her purse and a pen to write the check.

"No, no. I cannot accept it. It was my pleasure to be of service to you."

Father declined the reward thinking he had not really done anything extraordinary. Philip Sanders, the chauffeur, noticed the firefly on the priest's shoulder and decided to swat it off. Although the priest moved back like a boxer and picked up his guard, he could not avoid the contact between Philip's hand and the little bug. Father grabbed the man's hand firmly and then let it go.

"Oh, no!" Gabriel said, looking down at the dead little insect.

Then he looked at the startled face of Philip who was wondering what he had done that was so terrible. He was just trying to help get rid of a pesky bug from the priest's clothing, and the minister had reacted as if Philip had killed a child. The reverend picked up the dead firefly and put it in his palm.

"It is funny how we value a thing like that ring at 50,000 dollars, a thing with no life, a creation of man, an object of luxury and a status symbol, yet a firefly, a living work of God, a little creature that can fly and give out light, can eat, breathe, digest food, and reproduce itself, we assign no value at all."

Philip was contrite listening to the minister. He mumbled:

"I am terribly sorry, Reverend. I never thought..."

"I know. Most of us never stop to think about these things. We take the gift of life for granted. I know you were trying to be nice to me and didn't think about the little bug."

Father Gabriel put his hand on the chauffeur's shoulder and smiled at him kindly. The old lady handed him the check.

"Accept this money, Father, if not for yourself, for your parish needs."

The pastor took the check under those circumstances as a donation to the church. Then he walked with them outside and saw them leave in the limousine. He hoped that maybe their encounter would help them reflect a little bit on their relationship with God. Gabriel went back into the temple with his dead little friend still in his palm. When he turned off the lights, he felt a burning sensation in his chest again, as he had experienced before when strange things happened around him. The priest went down to his knees and faced the altar. His back got goose bumps all over as if he had been touched by an invisible power. He closed his eyes and started to pray. The burning sensation spread throughout his body; he felt turbocharged. Father Gabriel was glowing in the dark church, kneeling in front of the altar. He raised his right hand to heaven and made the sign of the cross over the palm of his left hand where the firefly lay lifeless. When his right index finger touched the tiny bug, a spark of light went into its body and it moved its wings. Gabriel stopped glowing and extended his left hand towards the altar.

"Thank you, Lord, for granting me this wish! May your name be praised forever!"

The firefly flew off his palm and into the recesses of the sanctuary letting its little light shine in the darkness. The priest crossed himself and got up. He walked out of the church singing one of the songs they had sung at the sisters' house. He locked the place and went into his house to read a book for a while and prepare for bed.

Although it was a tranquil night, suddenly a strong wind came around the church picking up dirt, leaves and trash. The lights around it went out, and darkness surrounded the place. A stray dog that was walking by felt an evil presence and started growling at the whirlwind, which was moving around the church on the alley side. The dog's hair stood up on his back, and he ran away howling in terror. The devil was paying a visit to the place. He growled at God from outside the temple:

"Why do you grant Gabriel, a mere man, all he asks of you?"

"Because he is faithful!" a soft answer emanated from the sanctuary.

"That's because you are always with him and never let him have a chance to taste me," the devil retorted.

"That is not true, and you know it! Gabriel is good, and we are pleased with him," the voice of the Lord answered.

"How about a little test of his 'faithfulness' since you are so sure?" the devil growled in disgust.

God paused for a moment, then agreed.

"Very well, We will let you test him in one way, whichever way you can think of, but do not kill him. You will see that he, a mere man, is faithful."

The devil laughed a low, macabre laugh and asked:

"How much time will you give me to put your boy to the test?"

"Three months!" the Lord said.

"You are partial to the number three. I don't think that would be enough time. You have been working him for many years already. Give me a whole year," the devil complained.

God granted him a little more time.

"Not a year, We will give you only six months since you are partial to the number six and that is twice as much as We were giving you initially."

"If I prove to you that he is just another unfaithful mortal man, if I make him renounce his promise to serve you as a priest, may I have him?" the devil inquired.

God paused for an instant again before answering:

"If Gabriel abandons his ministry for your temptation, he is yours, but we give you only six months, from now until the last day of February. Now off with you!"

The whirlwind vanished, and the lights came back to the street outside the church. Another dog started barking in the alley; then an ambulance passed by drowning the dog's bark. Father Gabriel looked outside his window, not knowing what was about to befall him. The EMS unit went south on the avenue with its red lights flashing, just another typical night on the west side of the city. The priest got in bed and turned the light off. The last day of August was coming to an end.

Chapter II
The Encounter

The night after they had Father Gabriel as a guest, the four religious sisters were cleaning up after dinner when the phone rang. Sister Magdalene gave the phone to Sister Kathryn. It was a long distance call from Ireland from her cousin, Joseph McKloski. All the sisters knew that it was bad news just by looking at Kathryn's expression when talking to her cousin. Sister Kathryn hung up the phone and sat down crying. Sister Mary brought her a glass of water. Magdalene and Carmen put their hands on her shoulders to let her know they were ready to support her. Mary held Kathryn's hand and asked her what happened.

"My mother is very sick in the hospital. She is actually dying of a heart problem. The doctors don't think she has much more time," Kathryn explained.

All three sisters expressed their sympathy and offered to pray for her recovery. Sister Magda, the superior of the group, offered:

"Why don't you go and see your mother?"

Kathryn's eyes opened wide with hope, but then remembered her many commitments.

"I wish I could, but we have work to do here and at the school. I would need some time to make arrangements for someone to take over."

Magdalene picked her up from the chair and put her thick arm around the skinny sister.

"The only thing you need to do is prepare your suitcase, Sister. We will take care of everything for you, so that you can board a plane tomorrow and be with your mother."

Magdalene took Kathryn into her room to get started. Then the older woman came back to the living room and told the others,

"Mary, get on your computer and get her a ticket to Ireland on the first available flight. You are good at handling those things. Carmen, I want you to review Kathryn's work schedule and let me know what we will need to continue her work in her absence. I will take care of the music ministry in the church for her and will talk to Father Gabriel tomorrow about getting a substitute teacher for the first grade."

The team of religious women went to work right away and had Kathryn on a plane the next morning with the hope that she might still find her mother alive.

Sister Theresa Reynolds, a 37-year-old religious sister with a Masters Degree in Education, was having a chat with Sister Rebecca Sterling in a convent in Ireland. It was a cool, dry morning, perfect for sitting out in the patio of the convent and enjoying a cup of coffee with an old friend. Rebecca told Theresa:

"I am sure things happen for a reason, Theresa. The Lord probably needs to send you somewhere. I am just happy that you got out of Africa alive!"

Rebecca had entered into sisterhood with Theresa fourteen years earlier, and they had stayed in touch despite having always been sent to different parts of the world.

"So am I!" Theresa said. "It was horrible! One day everything was normal: I was giving classes in school; the next day, civil war erupted. Shots were fired all over the place; buildings were burning. We were ordered to leave; the new regime did not want any religious influences in the country. We could have easily been killed. I am sorry for the children there, who still are going through that terrible experience."

Sister Martha came over and asked if they would be willing to go pick up a sister from America who had flown in to see her mother that was dying in the hospital. Rebecca agreed to go; Theresa declined saying she had a doctor's appointment that morning.

Everything fell in place rather quickly. Kathryn's mother got a little better in the hospital; she was overjoyed to see her family together. She knew that her end was near but cherished the company of her oldest daughter. The mother superior at the convent decided to send Theresa to substitute for Kathryn in Texas, for as long as was necessary to allow Kathryn to stay with her family. The mother superior had spoken to Father Gabriel and Sister Magdalene, and they had agreed to do the temporary replacement and keep the shaken Theresa occupied in a stable environment while she recovered from the trauma of civil war in an African country. By the end of the week, Theresa was flying across the Atlantic Ocean to return to her native land. The woman had been born in Ft. Bragg, a military installation in North Carolina. She had grown as an "Army brat" and had moved with her U.S.

Army officer father and her fiction-writer mother to different countries and Army posts all over the United States as an only child. By the time she was a junior in high school, her dad had achieved the rank of major general and was commanding an Army post in San Antonio, Texas. Theresa had sweet memories of the city to which she was now returning after twenty years of traveling around the world. Her parents had been killed in an airplane accident after her dad retired from the Army. She had found a life filled with activity in the service of the Lord as a Catholic sister. The lady was looking forward to her new assignment in the city of her youth. She thought about the boyfriend she had in high school and wondered if he still lived there, probably married and with teenage children. She had lost contact with him since her parents took her to Germany without warning; he never answered her letters. It was probably just a youth affair for him, but she still felt her heart skip a beat thinking about him.

Sister Mary came in the sisters' old van to meet Theresa at the international airport. Mary liked Theresa at first sight. Although the new arrival was ten years older than she, Mary got the impression that Theresa was a dynamic teacher. She looked fit and smart; the way she smiled so easily and the way she spoke revealed her loving and warm character.

"Did you have a good flight, Sister Theresa?" asked the younger woman.

"Excellent! Just a little long, but it gave me a chance to catch up on my reading."

Mary was an avid reader herself but skipped asking her what she had been reading, to move on to another subject as they drove out of the airport towards the sisters' house.

"Did you have a chance to meet Sister Kathryn in Ireland?"

"No, I am sorry to say. The day she arrived, I had a doctor's appointment and could not go to receive her at the airport. Then she was busy with her family, and I got busy getting my things ready to come replace her, temporarily."

"Welcome to San Antonio, Sister! Is this your first time here?"

"Oh, no. I used to live here, right over there at Ft. Sam Houston." Theresa pointed in the direction of the military base nearby and explained, "My father was the post commander when we were here."

"Then you must have lots of friends in San Antonio!" Mary exclaimed.

"Not really. It has been a good twenty years since we lived here. Everyone I knew is probably gone. I went to that all-girls' Catholic school there, (They were driving by it) but I didn't get to graduate with my classmates. My dad got an assignment in Germany, and we had to go a couple of months after I started my senior year."

Mary nodded in understanding and then switched the theme of their conversation.

"I heard that you barely got out of Africa alive."

She covered her mouth to stop her inquiry as she remembered what Sister Magdalene had advised her earlier.

"I am sorry! I am not supposed to ask," Mary apologized.

"It's O.K., Sister. I am getting over the shock. Maybe later I can tell you more details about my adventures in the third world countries. The Lord has protected me everywhere I have gone to do what he has prepared for me."

Mary felt relief with her words.

"You have a Masters in Education, right?" asked the younger sister who had a similar degree.

"Yes. How did you know?" said Theresa.

"You came highly recommended. I have my Masters in Education too. I think that education is the basis for overcoming most of the problems in the world. I try to give my students a real appetite for learning and hope that they will spread it around."

The newly arrived teacher smiled in admiration and nodded in agreement before inquiring, "How is the principal of the school?"

Mary's face lit up upon hearing the question.

"Father Gabriel? You will love him! He is a great man, a saint. He is very sweet and energetic. He is also the pastor of the parish, so he is quite busy, and Sister, he sings like an angel! Father is very charismatic, and has performed a lot of miracles."

Theresa opened her eyes wide, surprised by the description.

"Wow! I am already anxious to meet him. What kind of miracles are you talking about? Does he have the power to heal the sick?"

"Oh, yes, that and much more. Nobody is sure how many he has performed because he always tries to keep them secret. The Holy Spirit is with him."

The replacement teacher wondered what the priest might look like; she pictured him like Saint John Bosco. Theresa looked up to the evening sky and wondered why she had been sent to work with such a holy man. The sun was already out of sight on the west, and darkness was beginning to overcome the light of day.

As Sister Mary proceeded through an intersection when the green light came on, a pickup truck ran the red light coming from the right side. Mary slammed on the brakes and swerved to the left to avoid colliding with the truck. The driver of the truck honked his horn and made an unfriendly hand signal up in the air as he sped away.

"Are you all right, Sister Theresa?" asked the driver to her shaken passenger.

"Yes, thank God for safety belts!" said the passenger, still holding on to the dashboard.

"And that man still has the nerve to honk at us, as if we were at fault!"

Sister Mary drove her van out of the intersection. The vehicle had ended up facing to the left. As she regained the right position to go on, Sister Theresa said:

"Forgive him, Sister. He thought he was right in not stopping because his red light is out. You see? He probably felt he had the right of way and we were the ones that should stop. Now, I must say that your quick reflexes saved the day for us."

Theresa pointed at the burned out traffic light not working for the crossing street. Mary nodded in agreement and said:

"Well, thank God nothing happened. Imagine that, escaping death in an African civil war to come and die in an accident in San Antonio. We are almost home. Let's go!"

Theresa smiled, leaned back on her seat looked out at the city streets and commented:

"I am looking forward to a peaceful stay with no more complications than those the children in my class may bring me."

"Oh, I am sure you'll get your hands full with those kids, but I don't think you should have any serious complications while you are here."

The other two sisters came and received Theresa as if they were old friends. She felt really welcome in their home, which would be her home for some time. It was already dark. After getting her installed in the room with Sister Mary, they all got together for supper, their night prayer, and singing before going to bed. Theresa slept like a baby after her long, tiring flight.

Early the next morning, the new teacher went to the Saturday morning Mass at the Holy Trinity Church. The priest was an older gentleman, way too old to be the pastor she had been told about. Theresa waited until the end of the Mass to go introduce herself to him. He informed her he was not the pastor and that Father Gabriel was at the boxing gym down the street. The religious sister thanked him and walked in the direction he had pointed towards the gym.

Theresa felt the warmth of the South Texas morning as she walked. A dirty whirlwind came out of an alley and surrounded the religious sister. The warm wind got under her religious habit and raised it, exposing her legs and thighs. Theresa quickly pushed her habit down and walked briskly out of the whirlwind. She heard a muffled laughter but did not turn to see who was laughing. There was no one else around on that block, only the dirty whirlwind where the evil presence watched her with interest. There was a nasty smell in the air, and the woman felt a chill run down her spine. She crossed herself as she continued walking towards the gym. Theresa looked through an open window inside the boxing gym. There were several men working out. Her eyes stopped on a muscular man punching the heavy bag with a lot of energy. His skin was shiny with sweat. He moved like a lion; she could not see his face because he had his back to her. He moved around the bag to continue punching it, so the bag got in the way and covered his face. She trembled a little at the sound of the heavy punches, shook her head wondering why men liked boxing, and moved on to the entrance. She went in and looked for someone to ask for the priest. She figured the pastor was making a social visit there. The man she had seen punching the bag had disappeared. There were others, mostly young men, some black, and some Hispanic, only one white boy. They stopped working out to look at the pretty arrival. When they noticed her distinctive religious sister clothing, they continued their exercises. A young Hispanic man, who looked like a trainer, came to ask if he could help her. He was the assistant manager.

"Good morning, Sister, may I help you?"

"Yes, I am looking for Father Gabriel. They told me he would be here."

Sister Theresa looked around, not finding any man that looked like a priest there.

"Oh, yes. He was just here. He may have gone in the back," he told her in a gentle tone, and then he startled her by calling out in a loud voice:

"Timmy! Go get Father G. Tell him someone is looking for him in the front."

The assistant manager recruited the help of a child that was working there, pushing a broom to clean up the place. The nine-year-old boy put the broom to the side and ran into the back to go get the priest.

"Father G... Father G... You are wanted in the front immediately!" the boy said.

The sister thought the child was putting a higher demand in his voice than necessary. He sounded as if there was some kind of emergency. The man who had been hitting the heavy bag hurried out of the locker room. He was getting ready to take a shower, so he came out wearing only a jockstrap to see what was so important. He stood at the locker room door, a few steps away from the woman. She tried to cover her eyes but stopped her hand before it got there and placed it on her mouth instead.

The priest recognized that beautiful face from twenty years before. She had matured a lot, but her pretty face was the same one he had fallen in love with when he was in high school. The light brown eyes like two drops of honey were the same ones he had in his dreams so many nights.

"Theresa Reynolds!"

"Gabriel Infante!"

Sister Theresa also recognized him. He had matured a lot too. He had grown a beard and had gained muscular weight, but the magnetism of his dark brown eyes and his luminous smile were the same that had caused her to fall in love with him from the moment they met in high school.

"Ha-ha-ha... Father G is naked!" said Timmy, pointing at the man standing there in front of the religious sister wearing only a jockstrap. Both had been paralyzed by the surprise until the boy's laughter brought them back to the present time.

"Excuse me."

Gabriel turned around and ran into the locker room a little embarrassed. He shouted:

"I'll be right out!"

Sister Theresa's face changed colors from pink to a pale cream and then to red. She did not expect to see so much of the pastor, yet she liked what she saw.

"I will wait for you at the rectory, 'Father G!'" she called out to him and left the gym in a hurry.

Her heart was beating rapidly; she was actually running away from the gym and almost got hit by a guy riding a bike as she was crossing the street. The rider avoided hitting the sister, but lost control of his bike and fell over the sidewalk. Theresa did not turn to see the fallen bike rider as she headed for the church. The unfortunate bicyclist mumbled something at her as he got up from the sidewalk shaking the dust off his pants.

She went into the temple and knelt, praying to get her thoughts and feelings in order.

Gabriel for his part, realizing that she was gone, stepped into the bathroom.

He needed a shower badly, and he needed a cool head. He opened the cold water only and stayed there for a few minutes wondering what was going on in his life. This was not going to be an ordinary Saturday.

"Theresa is a nun, and she is here! Why? Why now after all these years?" he asked himself.

He felt happier than usual and hurried to get dressed. He scolded little Timmy for not warning him that it had been a lady who was looking for him. The boy just laughed and ran away.

Father loved the little boy, Timmy, in a special way. He had found him in a shoebox, abandoned, under a bridge; the boy had just been born when his mother abandoned him. Gabriel had been walking by when he heard the tiny voice crying under the bridge. He picked the baby up and reported the finding to the authorities. His mother was never found. Timmy ended up being adopted by the gym owner and his wife when Father Gabriel told them about the boy. The priest had seen him grow up into a mischievous but smart boy. Timmy was in the third grade in the Holy Spirit Catholic School; he was the boy's godfather for first communion.

The priest walked fast to his church hoping that it was true that Theresa, his high school sweetheart, was there wanting to talk to him. He wondered again about the complications that their former relationship could bring them, but he decided to dismiss those thoughts and just see why she was looking for him. She was waiting at the entrance of the church, looking gorgeous even in her religious garb!

Gabriel thought about acting professionally, but she spoke first with the same intention:

"Father, I have been sent from Ireland to substitute for Sister Kathryn Cabrini whose mother is very ill."

Father Gabriel led her into his office in the parish rectory. There was nobody else in the house.

"Sister, you are most welcome. I am looking forward to working with you. If there is anything I can do to help you settle down, please, do not hesitate to ask."

"Thank you, Father. I have a list here, which I had prepared before, of the things I would like to have and that Sister Kathryn was not using in her class."

Gabriel took the paper from her hand, and they both got a light static electricity discharge as they touched, ever so lightly. He smiled at her and asked:

"Well, this is truly a shock! How long have you been a religious sister, Theresa?"

The man sat back behind his desk looking at the woman in disbelief.

"I decided to enter religious life when I was convinced you had forgotten about me."

This statement broke his heart; she sounded as if she was still hurt but was hiding it.

"But I never forgot about you! You just disappeared one day and never again contacted me. You knew my address and phone; I didn't know where you went. Why didn't you call me, or write to me?"

The formality had dissipated quickly and he was talking to her as his long-gone girlfriend. She tried to explain what had happened:

"My parents took me away to Germany with the excuse that my dad had been assigned to an important post over there. They didn't want me to have any more contact with you. They said that you and I were not of the same class."

"And you believed that?"

"No, of course not! I tried writing to you, but I think my mother intercepted all my mail and never forwarded it. I concluded that since you didn't write me back, it was true what she was saying, that you had another girlfriend already and had forgotten about me. I thought she was on my side when my father prohibited me from using the phone to call the States; she warned me about you but told me that I could write to you and see what response we got. Now I see that she never sent my letters."

It was as if a heavy curtain had fallen and let the sunlight into a room that had been in darkness for years. There was a moment of silence as the former lovers brought their feelings under control. They had to repress an intense desire to embrace. Gabriel tried to be polite:

"How are your parents doing now?"

Theresa looked down, avoiding his eyes, as she informed him:

"They died in an airplane accident a year after Dad retired, sixteen years ago."

"I am truly sorry to hear that."

Theresa looked at him again and smiled, accepting his sympathy; then she looked up to the ceiling, containing a tear.

"Now I understand that my mother thought she was doing me a favor by letting my love for you die out with the time and distance. In her mind that was the best for me."

"Did your love for me actually die out, Theresa?" Gabriel asked.

The sister got up from the chair and went to look out the window. She pondered his question, and came back to say:

"I am not sure, but tell me about you. When did you decide to become a priest? I thought I would find you happily married and with a lot of children."

"The only woman I ever wanted to marry was taken from my life, so I looked for a new direction and found God in my search," Gabe explained, adding: "One day I felt his presence like an invisible force that without words called me to the Church. Do you remember how I applied to be accepted at West Point so that I would impress your dad? Well, I turned that down and went into the seminary instead! I discovered the key to everlasting happiness and decided to devote my full life and energy to it. I have discovered that the more I give, the more I get. It is like an unending treasure that I feel compelled to share with all the people around me. I may not have married, but I do have a lot of children to educate and take care of. They call me 'Father!'"

He kept talking and trying to convince himself that it was the best thing that could have happened in his life. She looked into his eyes and whispered:

"Did your love for me die when you decided to become a priest?"

Then it was his turn to get off his seat and go look out the window to ponder that question. He turned to look into her eyes and trembled realizing that his love for her was very much alive.

"No, I don't think so. It just went to sleep. It became like a beautiful dream, part of my past life. I had to struggle with your image in my memories, but I thought my destiny was to become a priest. I didn't have the means to search for you around the world. I too was advised that you probably had forgotten about me, as just a youthful affair, and that you probably had married into high society, as your parents wanted you to."

"We both were lied to and misguided; however, God apparently had other plans for us and that was how He called us to His service," Theresa said.

"Yes, you are right! Are you happy, Sister Theresa?"

"Yes, I have a very fulfilling career. I feel useful and blessed. Are you happy, Father Gabriel?"

"Yes, but I am especially happy to see you again, my old friend. I think this is a blessing, a gift from above, at least for me."

"I agree, Father Gabriel. It is good to see you again. I am looking forward to working together. They told me great things about you and the miracles you perform."

"Don't believe everything people say. You know how they tend to exaggerate things, but God is great, and He does perform miracles even to this day, in mysterious ways."

Sister Theresa got up and gave him her little hand. He shook it, welcoming her as the new first grade teacher. She pulled his hand up to her lips and kissed it in reverence to his official position as pastor of the parish. Theresa declined a ride back to the sisters' house, claiming she needed to walk and get reacquainted with the city. She also felt she needed to be alone for a while. Her heart was accelerated as when she was a teen. She walked away fearing he might see how disturbed she had been by their meeting. He followed her with his eyes until she turned at the corner. Then he went into his office to meditate on the meaning of their encounter. A glass of wine helped him to moisten his throat that had ended up very dry after the encounter.

Sunday morning, Father Gabriel found Sister Theresa in the church ready to play the organ for the first Mass. He was delighted to see her again. Theresa had turned down Sister Magdalene's offer to do the music for her and let her sleep a little late. She wanted to attend Father Gabriel's Mass and see him in action. Looking at Gabriel serving at the altar was very inspiring. Hearing him preach, one could imagine Jesus himself talking to the congregation. The Gospel spoke about the Kingdom of Heaven being like a treasure in a field or a rare pearl which, when found, a man would leave everything to possess. Theresa enjoyed that Mass like no other before. Then when it was time to share the peace, Father Gabriel went around shaking hands and hugging the people closest to the altar. He found Theresa sharing the peace, not far from him, so he approached her and hugged her for a second that seemed to last a long time. It felt as if time had stopped at the instant he embraced her and told her:

"The peace of the Lord be with you, Sister Theresa!"

She felt charged with energy and went to play the communion hymn with gusto, although her knees were trembling. She concentrated on the music trying to avoid paying attention to her mixed feelings. It had felt so good to be embraced by him again!

Father Gabriel finished his service, shook hands and exchanged words with the parishioners as they left the church while the organist finished the last hymn. One of the couples, a chubby man and his chubby wife, both younger than the priest, asked:

"How do you manage to stay in such good shape, Father?"

The pastor looked at Sandra and Eric Jones, both of short stature, who weighed 200 pounds each.

"I have not quit exercising since I was young, running, swimming, weights and a little boxing to keep me going."

"Sandra and I are going to start a workout program together. What would you recommend? Do you think it is too late for us to start?" Eric asked.

"I recommend you two start walking together, then introduce some running if you can, and then add the swimming. You will have fun and improve your health. It is not too late for you to start, but be careful. My grandmother started running when she turned 65, and nobody knows where she is now!"

The couple of heavyweights left laughing; Gabriel loved to make people laugh.

By the time he went back to the sacristy, the sister was gone. He looked for her, but she had disappeared. He wanted to thank her for the beautiful music she provided; actually he just wanted to see her again. Perhaps he could give her a call later. He saw a plastic doll's leg in one of the pews and picked it up. Then he rearranged the hymnals and missalettes in other pews. A woman came back in the church with her little girl crying because her doll was missing a leg. Father Gabriel winked an eye at the young mother and signaled for her to bring the child to him. He squatted down to her eye level and asked her what was wrong. She was no older than five.

"Elizabeth lost a leg. She won't be able to play soccer now."

"Let us ask God to heal your little friend."

The priest took the doll in his hands and had the mother and child close their eyes

"Lord, God Almighty, grant that Elizabeth may recover her leg, so that she may play soccer again. We ask you this in the name of Jesus, your beloved son."

"Amen!" the child and her mother said in response to his prayer.

When the woman and her daughter opened their eyes, they saw the doll with both of her legs. The little kid was happy then. She went and gave the priest a kiss on the cheek.

"Thank you, Father Gabriel!"

"You are welcome, child. What is your name?"

"Tammy!"

"Well, Tammy, take good care of Elizabeth from now on."

"Thank you, so much, Father. Tammy was really distressed over it because this is her favorite doll," the mother said.

The woman took the priest's hand in both of hers. She realized that he had found the leg in the pew they had been sitting in and put it back on the doll as they had their eyes closed in prayer, but she appreciated what the gesture meant for her child. Gabriel winked at her.

The priest stayed busy giving the next two masses as usual. In the afternoon he went to the hospital to visit a parishioner who had an accident at work. He took communion to him and visited with the family. The man was going to be all right; it was just a matter of time for him to recover from his injuries. To make the injured parishioner feel better, Gabriel told him a joke.

"A man once counseled his son that if he wanted to live a long life, the secret was to sprinkle a little gunpowder on his cornflakes every morning. The son did this religiously, and lived to the age of 93. When he died, he left 14 children, 28 grandchildren, 35 great-grandchildren, and a 15-foot hole in the wall of the crematorium."

His injured parishioner complained that it hurt to laugh, so Gabriel said he would save his jokes for later.

By the time the priest was heading back home, it was dinnertime. He was very hungry because he had skipped lunch. Gabriel did not like the idea of having to cook his own dinner on Sunday evening. He was trying to decide what to eat. Anything that came to mind sounded good but would require some work in the kitchen. The housekeeper, Ms. Black, was off on Sundays; she was an old Thai widow who had married a service man in the Army and came with him to the United States after the Vietnam conflict. She was an excellent cook and a very neat and wise person. Her husband had passed away ten years before; he died of lung cancer.

As the pearl-colored, very old sedan rolled down the street where a group of boys were playing basketball, one of them recognized the vehicle as Father G's. There was no one else in the barrio with a car as old as that one, or as well kept. The mechanics shop students at a technical high school had managed for several years to restore and maintain the priest's car known as "The Priestmobile." The instructor, Mr. Ramiro Vega, was a personal friend of Father's from their all-boys Catholic high school days. Ramiro knew the story of the old sedan and was part of it himself. A man named Joseph Smith who worked for the postal service had bought that car new from the dealer in 1935. Joe kept the car in mint condition for the 20 years that he had it, following the manufacturer's instructions on scheduled maintenance. He died and left it to his surviving wife, but she never drove. Old Mrs. Smith gave the car to Jose Alfredo Infante in payment for a new set of cabinets that he made for her house in 1960. The car had not been driven in five years, but it did not need much to get back on the road. Jose and Maria Infante were just establishing themselves in San Antonio. They bought a little house on the West Side; Jose set up his carpentry shop. They got the 1935 sedan, which at the time was metallic blue, when they were expecting Gabriel, their only baby. Jose maintained the car as well as Joseph Smith had done before, so when Gabriel graduated from high school, Jose gave him the old, but well kept, car as his graduation gift. Young Gabriel loved to drive but did not like to mess with mechanics. Fortunately for him, his friend Ramiro Vega was an excellent mechanic even as a teenager. Ramiro wanted to buy the car from Gabriel, but he did not want to sell it because he feared his dad might not like him selling the gift he passed on to him. They made an agreement that if Ramiro could help with the maintenance of the old car; he was entitled to borrow it any time he needed to go out. Ramiro had driven that car with at least twenty different girlfriends throughout his youth. He stopped using the car when his wife demanded he got his own car and let Gabriel, a seminarian then, be the only driver. Ramiro went on to become a teacher and used the car to give his students training in auto mechanics. They also took care of the tires, battery, lights, body, interior, everything. They had installed a nice stereo system donated by one of the students. They added modern hydraulics and chromed new parts to replace the worn out ones. The engine was new and much more powerful than the original. A tire store owner, a friend of the priest, donated the sports wheels; Gabriel had miraculously returned her health to the man's only daughter who suffered from continuous and intense headaches; all it took was the laying of the priest's hands and a prayer for the headaches to disappear. The old car was awesome! It was the only valuable possession the priest had.

Jerry Collins jumped in front of the Priestmobile waving his arms up and down.

"Father G, Father G, you gotta help us!"

Gabriel stopped the car and got out wondering what was going on.

"What's the matter, Jerry?"

The priest looked around, scanning the area for trouble. There was nothing but a group of teenagers, boys and girls in the basketball court apparently getting ready for a game.

"These guys say they are going to whip us in a game. One of our players was taken home by his grandma, so we need a replacement. Could you play with us?"

"Let me park my ride. Count me in!"

Gabriel got back in his car and pulled over to the curb to park it there. He opened the trunk and pulled his tennis shoes from it. Then he took off his shirt to the delight of the teenage girls who started whistling and joking about being hot. Once he was ready in his black pants, white muscle shirt and tennis shoes, he proceeded to the court. Father G was well known in the barrio as a man of action. Most of them respected him, but he had made some enemies as well. The opposing team had a couple of known white druggies/thieves in it, whom Gabriel had helped put in jail once before. They smiled at their opportunity to put their hands on the priest during the basketball game. They also had assistance from a big Hispanic guy, about 6 feet 4 inches, and two black boys that moved like they were good in the court. Father G had mostly average height Hispanic guys in his team. Jerry Collins was mixed black, white and Hispanic who looked like a Puerto Rican and was the shortest man in the team at 5 feet 7 inches. The other three were so much alike you could say they were Mexican triplets, 5 foot 9 inches, slim and fast. Javier, Jacinto and Jorge. Father Gabriel was the tall man in his team at 6 feet even.

"What are we playing for?" the priest asked Jerry as they were practicing their shots.

"Dinner! If we beat them, we were planning to go for some barbecue."

"How much did each one have to pitch in?"

"I got you covered, Father G. You just give us your blessings and do the best you can in the game. I don't think we can lose with you on our side."

The game started. Father Gabriel knew that it would be tough; those guys usually got very physical in their games. He crossed himself and got the ball from Jorge. The first team to make 30 points would win. Gabriel passed the ball to Jacinto who passed it to Javier. Javier drove all the way under the basket with two opponents on him. He bounced the ball on the floor behind him for Jerry, who was clear for a ten-foot jumper. The shot went in; the priest's team went up 2-0. Damian, the big center for the other team, hit Father G with his shoulder in passing by to get in position. Antoine, one of the black players that looked like Ivory Peterson of the Latigos was handling the ball up the court. Walter and Clint, the two white thieves, got on the sides asking for the ball. Antoine passed it to their best player, Scottie. The wiry black player dribbled the ball like an all-star between three opponents and drove all the way in to even the score 2-2. The boys began running their mouths bragging they were better than the other team. Father G clapped his hands and encouraged his team to play on.

THE TEMPTATION OF THE MIRACLE WEAVER

It was a very even match. Father G got 10 points in a combination of driving to the basket and shooting from outside. He got two three-pointers and two lay ups. Jorge got only one basket; Jacinto had two, the same as Javier; Jerry had one basket and four free throws for a combined team score of 26 points. The thieves' team had 27 points already; Scottie was tearing them up with 17 points. He was a very selfish player who liked to create his own plays and rarely passed the ball but was always demanding to receive it. Antoine had 6 points, Walter and Clint only one basket apiece. Damian had no points but had accumulated five fouls already; he was a bruiser. The priest had been hit by all five opponents but had also provided them all with a taste of his shoulders, elbows and knees to keep the game fair and not let them think they intimidated him. He was hard as a rock, so the boys opted for playing a little cleaner.

The thieves decided to finish the priest's team with a three-pointer. They were going to let Scottie be the shooter. They had the ball and began moving towards the opponent's basket. Clint passed the ball to Antoine. He dribbled around Damian and passed the ball to the opposite side where Walter caught it. As soon as Walter got it, he passed it to the back where Scottie was waiting at the three-point range. Gabriel left Damian alone in the center and sprinted towards Scottie; the black player was already bending his legs and aiming for the basket. Scottie went up in the air with confidence. The ball left his hand in the exact direction of the basket. The priest's hand blocked the shot three feet away from Scottie's hand. The ball went up in the air and behind Scottie. Gabriel continued running and caught the ball he had blocked. There was no one between him and the opposite goal. He drove in and dunked the ball to put his team up one point, 28-27. The thieves still had a chance because they had the ball again. Father G was yelling at his players to tighten up on the defense and raise their arms. They covered each player, man-to-man, whole court. Antoine dribbled the ball away from Jerry who was marking him. Gabriel saw that Antoine was going to go for the basket, so he got in front of him to keep him from shooting unobstructed. The younger guy passed to their center, Damian, who was left alone under the basket when the priest went to cover Antoine. The big guy slam-dunked the ball to his teammates' delight, and for a moment, they thought they had won the game and started raising their hands in victory. Jerry reminded them that they still needed one point; the score was 29-28.

Jerry pulled Father G close to him and told him something in a whisper. Jerry served the ball to Javier. Scottie got a hand on it and almost stole the ball, but it went out of bounds. Jorge sent it back in from the sideline to Jerry. He gave Gabriel a signal; the priest sprinted all the way to the right corner of the opponents' side of the court as if getting ready for a corner shot. Damian and Antoine covered the priest at the corner, but Jerry gave the ball to Jacinto on the left corner. Scottie and Clint jumped in front of him to keep him from shooting. Jacinto threw a short pass to Jorge; he dribbled the ball towards the basket where Walter was waiting for him. Jorge bounced the ball between his legs for Father G who was running across the court from the right corner to the left. The priest pulled his markers in that direction and passed the ball to Jerry who was in the back alone. Jerry got up in the air and fired a three pointer; Scottie got there too late but pushed Jerry anyway, causing him to fall on his back as his shot went through the basket. Jerry bounced back from the floor, all excited that he made the winning shot for a final score of 31-29. After the usual bragging and exchanging insults, the two teams shook hands. Jerry went to Trisha, Antoine's girlfriend, and collected the money they had won for the dinner. The four players and their girlfriends asked Father to go eat with them at the barbecue restaurant to celebrate their victory. Father asked them to join hands in a circle and thank God. Before he started his prayer, he called on the other team to come and join the circle; only Clint turned around and left the court deciding not to join them. The priest was saddened by Clint's attitude.

"O Heavenly Father, we thank you for the life that you have given us, for all the blessings you have granted to us, for our families, for our friends. We ask you to keep us safe and united to you all the days of our lives. Guide us and watch over us as we continue the journey that you have prepared for us. Allow us to enjoy the games as much in victory as in defeat because ultimately, the only victory that matters in our life is having found you and accepted you as our God and Jesus as our Savior. We thank you. We bless you. We praise you forever and ever."

All the young people responded:
"Amen!"
"All right, let us eat. I am starving!" Gabriel exhorted them.

They all got in the Priestmobile. Jerry and Sandra in front with Father G. Jorge with Jessica, Jacinto with Rita, and Javier and Tina. The girlfriends sat on the boyfriends' laps. Gabriel told them to open the windows for some fresh air because they were all sweaty. Sandra asked the priest if he could put on some music. Father G turned on his CD player with the William Tell overture, which took them all the way to the restaurant.

They had a good time talking about the game during dinner. The couples were on their best behavior because the priest was with them. Gabriel was thankful that he had been able to satisfy his hunger and share some time with the youths. Sandra liked the priest very much, not as a priest but as a male. She asked:

"Have you ever had a girlfriend, Father G?"

"Yes, when I was your age, which was like a century ago," Gabriel answered.

"How about now?" Sandra inquired with a mischievous smile.

"No, I don't have one, I have many! And you are one of them, right?" was the priest's reply.

"You know Jerry is my boyfriend," said Sandra, putting her arm around Jerry.

"That's OK, I am not jealous," said Gabriel smiling and winking an eye at Sandra.

Then the minister got up and turned to Jerry telling him:

"You better take good care of my little girlfriend here, OK? I've got to go, but I'll see you guys later."

Jerry stood up and shook the priest's hand.

"Thanks Father G, you are really cool!"

Sandra came over and gave him a hug and a kiss on the cheek. Jerry smiled and signaled for his friends to shut up when they started making fun of him for "losing Sandra to the priest." Gabriel raised his hand and gave them his blessing before leaving.

When Gabriel got home, the phone was ringing. He picked it up and heard Theresa's voice. His heart jumped in his chest.

"Father Gabriel?"

"Yes. Who is this?"

He pretended not to recognize her voice, but had a joyful, wide smile on his face.

"Sister Theresa."

"O yes, yes, how can I help you, Sister?"

"I just called to tell you I enjoyed your Mass very much. You are a great preacher."

"Thank you. You are very kind! I looked for you after the Mass to thank you for the music. You are a great musician. People were commenting on how lively the Mass had been with you at the organ this morning."

"I had some things to do, and I knew that you are very busy on Sundays.

I didn't want to interfere with your schedule; that's why I left. I'll see you in the morning."

"Wait!" Gabriel begged her.

"Yes, Father?"

"I wanted to tell you that..." Gabriel struggled searching for some theme to make their conversation a little longer. He said: "I played a game of basketball with the barrio kids. I was coming back from the hospital – I went to see a parishioner that fell from the roof of his house – He is going to be fine I was starving on my way back and thinking what to eat. I didn't want to cook anything for myself on Sunday evening. Then Jerry, a young guy that works at a gas station and always gives me free gasoline, jumped in front of my car to recruit me for his team in a game against some tough guys. They bet a dinner for the winning team, so I helped them win and sat with them for some barbecue. The game was a little rough; I will probably be sore tomorrow. Now I really need a shower, but I had a lot of fun with the kids and their girlfriends – One of the girls asked me if I had a girlfriend, and I told her about you–"

"That I am your girlfriend?"

"No! That you had been, about a hundred years ago."

"Wait a minute. I am not that old! It was twenty years ago, not a hundred."

"Yes, you are right. I still cannot believe you are back in my life."

"These are very different circumstances now, Father."

"You are right again, but it is nice to see you and talk to you again."

"I like talking to you and hearing your voice too. Do you still sing those romantic Spanish songs that you used to sing to me?"

Father Gabriel closed his eyes and checked his repertoire of songs for one to sing. He took a deep breath and started with one that came to mind. The song spoke of the poet having been a passing bird, a butterfly of a thousand flowers who finds himself nostalgic for his true love's arms and eyes, a love of the past. He comes back asking for forgiveness for the wanderer who now returns to give his heart, and so on. The priest sang with special inspiration over the phone while his former girlfriend captured the emotions and feelings of the song on the other side of the phone line. Gabriel sang the entire song, and when he sang the end, he heard Theresa's voice say:

"Thank you!"

Sister heard someone coming into her room and hung up on the priest. She felt like she had almost been caught doing something wrong.

"Who were you talking to, Sister Theresa?" inquired Sister Mary.

"An old friend of mine! If you'll excuse me, I need to... go to the bathroom."

Sister Mary sat in front of her computer and turned it on, not paying attention to the blush on Theresa's face as she headed for the bathroom.

On the other side of the line, Father Gabriel was looking at the phone, puzzled, as it gave him a dial tone after being disconnected. The priest wondered what happened, but he hung up thinking that it would be a good excuse to engage the sister in conversation the next day. It was time for his evening prayer and a good shower. He ran his hands on his sides and discovered a couple of tender spots where he had been elbowed during the game. He laughed by himself remembering the evening, opened his prayer book and began praying in front of his crucifix. Sunday, September 5th was becoming history by the time he went to bed. How different life had turned for the priest in less than a week! He thought he was happy the Sunday before, but it could not compare to how happy he felt this Sunday. Gabriel was convinced this was definitely a gift from God, so he thanked Him for it and went into deep sleep in a matter of minutes.

Chapter III
The Kidnapping

Theresa's first week at school went smoothly for everyone. The first grade kids were happy to get her as replacement for Sister Kathryn. Magdalene, Mary and Carmen were very glad to have the new sister in their home. Without trying to compare them, they found that Theresa was a superior teacher, worker and musician than Kathryn ever would be. Theresa had great energy and enthusiasm while Kathryn was a tired, sweet, older lady, with many years of teaching to her credit. Kathryn was good; Theresa was excellent. Father Gabriel was happier than usual and looked forward to seeing the new teacher at lunch or in the staff meetings. They had not mentioned to anyone that they already knew each other: it was their little secret. They seemed to act differently with each other when they were alone than when someone else was present. Neither one had planned it so or had even mentioned it; it just happened that way.

Thursday evening, Father Gabriel was driving home from a fund-raising dinner downtown where he had spoken in favor of the Texas governor seeking the Republican candidacy for the United States Presidency. Gabriel was thinking how good it was that he could not get into the nasty world of politics and was instead working in the spiritual field. As a Catholic priest, he was prohibited from seeking public political office, but he concluded that he already held a public office in his capacity of pastor of a parish. His political views, however, were clearly conservative and more in agreement with the Republican Party. This angered some people in his mostly Mexican-American and traditionally Democrat parish, but the priest defended his views without trying to impose them on his flock.

Gabriel finished his cigar and crushed the leftover piece in his car ashtray. He came to a stop at a traffic light; there was one car in front of him with a girl at the wheel. She was about twenty-three years old and on her way to a date. The girl was talking on a phone while listening to loud contemporary music; she was also looking at herself in the mirror, applying an extra coat of lipstick on her big lips and playing with her hairdo. The light changed from red to green, but the girl, submerged in her own world of gossip and beauty did not seem to care. Father was going to honk at her to get her going, but something caught his attention from the corner of his eye. Six gangsters were carrying a young woman into an abandoned house. The poor girl was kicking and trying to scream, but they were covering her mouth. One of her little shoes fell off her foot in the struggle. The group disappeared into the darkness of the house. Father Gabriel knew immediately that the girl was in great danger, and that he must do something to help her. The priest got out of his old car and ran towards the driver in front of him. He took the phone off her hand; she gasped in fear when the man grabbed the phone. Gabriel told the person on the other side of the call that the girl would call him back. He then hung up and dialed 911 quickly. The female driver thought about driving off, but she realized that this man was a priest when she saw his white collar. Then she heard him making the emergency call to the police.

"This is a police emergency! There is a kidnapping in progress at 666 Calaveras (Skulls)... A girl was taken by force into an abandoned house by several men. Please send officers quickly!"

The priest returned the phone to the girl and ran back to his car looking for something, a weapon of some sort. The only thing he had in the front seat of his car was a good size metal crucifix, about ten inches long. He reached in and grabbed it. Gabriel looked towards the dark house where the men had taken the girl; his chest began burning with fury. He hated crime, especially violent crime. The priest crossed himself and started running towards the abandoned house, with the cross in his hand, reciting a prayer based on a psalm.

"Though the evil ones spring up like grass and all the wrongdoers thrive: their destiny is to be ultimately destroyed by your justice. Lord, you are forever on high. Look at the enemy perish; all the wicked shall be scattered."

The female driver pulled over and re-dialed the number of the man she had been talking to earlier, to tell him what was going on. She sat there waiting to see what happened. The priest approached the old house, still reciting the psalm:

"Father give me the wild-ox's strength; anoint me with the purest oil to prepare my hands for battle. My eyes shall look in victory on my foes; my ears shall hear joyfully of their demise."

He heard the sound of a struggle inside, crying, slapping, clothes tearing, evil laughter, and several voices arguing. The priest entered the house and ordered them:

"Stop, in the name of God! Let the girl go, and you will not be harmed."

"Who the fuck are you? You better get the fuck out of here or you are going to get it too!" was the response he got from the one who appeared to be the leader.

There were three holding the girl, naked, on the floor.

"I am not leaving unless you hand over the child," he declared firmly.

The biggest one of the red-eyed gangsters charged against the priest with a knife in his hand. There was some light coming from the bare windows; Father Gabriel saw the reflection of the light on the approaching blade and quickly prepared himself for the battle.

The priest used the crucifix to block the blade coming at his chest. The cross caught the knife; Father G twisted the cross and wrestled the knife away from the gangster. Crucifix and knife fell on the floor. With the palm of his open hand, the boxer-priest hit the gangster, a really big guy, right on the chin; the criminal went up in the air and fell flat on his back, unconscious. The furious priest stepped forward and looked to his right; there was one coming at him with a baseball bat. Another one came from his left and grabbed the intruder from behind in a hug, wrapping his arms around him. Father G could see evil in their reddened eyes. The one with the bat approached ready to swing at the priest; Gabriel slipped down from the arms of the one holding him. The bat struck the gangster's head instead of Gabriel's. Father G was on the floor and kicked the batter on the knee with great violence. The pain of a dislocated knee made the criminal drop the bat and scream as he fell to the floor holding on to his busted leg. Father G jumped up to continue against the other three, who were still holding the girl, watching in disbelief. One got up and pulled a switchblade knife from his pocket; he lunged at the priest. Gabriel sidestepped and grabbed the armed wrist as it passed by his side. He spun around holding on to the arm and threw the assailant through the window, out into the front yard. The minister continued his spinning move and kicked the gangster who was holding the girl on the head as if it were a soccer ball. That one went down to the floor like a sack of manure. The last one got up to face the priest; Gabriel picked up the baseball bat. The terrified thug turned around and ran out the back.

The priest took his shirt off and covered the naked, trembling young girl with it. Her eyes were wide open, but she could not say anything. He took her by the shoulders.

"Everything is going to be all right, child. It's over; you're OK."

Father G bent down to help the girl get up from the kneeling position she was in; at that moment the police entered the house.

"Freeze! Get your hands up where I can see them!"

Gabriel complied with the order knowing full well that the officer was aiming a gun at him. He heard something in the back of the house. Apparently they got the one that was trying to escape through the back door.

"What the hell happened here?" the officer asked, looking at the four gangsters on the floor lit by the policeman's flashlight, one whimpering and holding his leg, the other three knocked out on the floor.

"I got one out in the front yard!" said another officer from outside.

The girl hugged the priest who still had his arms up and was waiting for the officer to realize he was not one of the bad guys.

"I am the one who called you, Officer. Here, ask the girl. She can tell you what happened. Talk to the officer girl!"

Father G tried to get the victim to help him clarify the situation. She could not speak a word and was changing color. The priest spanked her one time, hard.

"Breathe, baby, breathe!"

The girl started crying loudly on the priest's chest. Another officer came in and recognized the minister. The second officer pulled his partner's arm down to keep him from aiming his pistol to the priest and told him that it was OK, to holster the gun.

"You did a number on these dudes, Father G!" The second officer told him and patted him on the back.

"Well, they were trying to do a number on this girl. I just couldn't let them. I tried to stop them without violence, but they wouldn't listen."

The officers handcuffed the prisoners, and the priest took the girl out to his car wearing his shirt. He asked the officers to get an ambulance to have the girl examined.

"What is your name, child?"

"Aurora... Aurora Fuentes, Father."

"Are you OK now, Aurora?"

"Yes, I think so. Oh, Father, thank you so much. I thought I was going to die tonight!"

She started sobbing again and held on to him. He caressed her head and straightened her long black hair.

"Thank God that we were in time to stop them. You are going to be just fine now. Are you injured anywhere?"

"No, I don't think so, just shaken up. I feel weak and sick, like I am going to throw up."

"Lie down in the back seat and raise your feet. Here, I will cover you with my coat to keep you warm. Breathe in and out deeply, say a little prayer and try to relax."

Father Gabriel explained to Officer Vega that the girl did not really need a trip to the hospital because she had not been sexually assaulted. She would need some counseling, but that could be accomplished out of the hospital; however, the suspects would need to be seen at the emergency room. One had a fractured skull, other a dislocated knee; one needed stitches for several deep glass cuts he sustained going through the front window and two had concussions from the hits the priest gave them. All of them were charged with aggravated kidnapping. Father G stayed with the girl throughout the initial investigation until both of them gave their statements to the night detectives. Aurora's family met her at the police station and brought her clean clothes to wear; Aurora returned Father Gabriel's shirt. She hugged him and kissed him to thank him again for saving her. Aurora's boyfriend, James Woodland, also gave him a hug and shook his hand. James was a successful contractor in the construction business.

"Listen, Father, anything you need, you just say the word. I don't know how we can pay you for what you have done for Aurora tonight."

"Don't mention it! It was the hand of God that led me to that place. I am nothing but an instrument of the Lord. He is the one to be thanked and praised."

"You are right! You know, Aurora and I were thinking about getting married. Would you be willing to marry us?"

"It would be an honor; however, there are some requirements that you must fulfill before the wedding may be celebrated. Give me a call next week and we will go over them to get you two ready."

The priest was hugged by the father and mother of the girl before he left the police headquarters. It was midnight by the time Gabriel made it home, too late to call Sister Theresa and relate his little adventure.

Friday was a busy day at school. Sister Theresa tested the kids in all the subjects and prepared a program for her children to act, sing and dance in a little play for the fall festival. She did not see Father Gabriel at all; she missed him at lunch. The priest had several appointments on parish related business, but he went and obtained all the materials Theresa had requested so that she could review them over the weekend.

It was already after school hours when Gabriel returned with the school materials for Theresa. All the sisters had left the school for the day, so before dinner, the priest went to their house to deliver the goods. Magdalene and Theresa were the only two left at home because Mary and Carmen had gone to Austin for a weekend-long conference. Magda said she was going to pick up some fried chicken for dinner. She had found a restaurant owner who had been educated by nuns and who provided her with free chicken any time she wanted it. The place was a good thirty minutes away, but Magda considered it worth the drive. The little trip provided her with an hour of listening to classical music on the local public radio station. She also loved talking to the owner, Francis Schott, a successful businesswoman who was considering joining the order after ten years as a widow. Francis had three daughters and one son as well as seven grandchildren; she was looking for a greater challenge in her life, something more meaningful than the business she and her husband had run for thirty-three years. They owned seven restaurants in the city by the time her husband passed away. As Magda was getting ready to leave the house, Theresa was in the bathroom taking a shower after an unusually hot day at work. She did not know that she was not alone in the bathroom.

If Theresa had looked out, she could have noticed the shadow of an evil entity that was causing some pre-calculated mischief. It pulled down her bathrobe from the hook on the door and then scratched the little hose under the toilet tank, causing it to tear, flooding the bathroom floor and soaking the bathrobe. The showering lady realized that she only had brought one towel in but would need two because she was washing her hair. She asked Magda if she could bring her a second towel from her room, but the older sister was already gone and did not hear her request. Magda was thinking about the delicious fried chicken as she headed for the van. Theresa dried her hair and wrapped the towel on her head. She called for Magda again but heard the van engine getting started outside. She realized Magda was out of the house already. When Theresa opened the shower curtain, she felt very cold. She also felt that she was being watched. The skin of her arms and back got covered with goose bumps; she braced herself and looked around the room. There was no other human being there, and there was no other towel either.

Father Gabriel arrived at the sisters' house in his car as Magda was driving out of their driveway. The priest made a sudden, exaggerated maneuver with his car as if trying to avoid impending collision with the sisters' van. He turned away and slammed on the brakes; he also raised his arms to cover his face pretending to panic in front of the already safely stopped van. Magda knew he was just clowning around but laughed anyway and honked back for him to get out of the way. The priest came out of his car and approached the van.

"Shalom, Magda. I brought Sister Theresa the materials she requested for her class."

"Well, she is taking a shower right now, Father. I will take the stuff for her and put it inside. I can let Theresa know that you are here."

Sister Magda was going to turn the engine off to get out of the van and return to the house. Father Gabriel stopped her saying:

"No, that won't be necessary. I don't need to talk to Sister Theresa. You go on to wherever you are going, and I will just leave the box at the door."

"If you want to take it inside, the back door is not locked. I am going to get some fried chicken right now. Would you like to eat with us?" inquired Sister Magdalene.

"No, thank you, I don't want to intrude. I have my own dinner already waiting. I'll take the box and put it in the dining room then."

Sister waved and drove off. She turned the radio on and listened to Brahms as the first composer in her hour-long concert on the road.

Theresa looked around the bathroom noticing that the water was still running somewhere even though she had closed the shower. Her bathrobe was soaking wet on the floor; the little hose under the toilet tank had busted open, and water was flooding the bathroom floor. She went and closed the valve to stop the flooding. That house was old and in need of repair. Her bathrobe was on the floor, apparently because the hook on the door came loose. The toilet would need to have that hose replaced, and the hook on the door needed to be reinforced with some screws. Theresa thought she could call the school maintenance man, and ask him for assistance with those things. He had offered his help when they met and seemed to be a nice gentleman. Theresa still needed a second towel to dry off. She decided to go get it herself since she was alone in the house, or so she thought. Concerned with the problem at hand, she did not pay any more attention to the sensation she had of being watched. The shadow of the invisible entity slipped under the door and out to the hallway lightly touching the woman's bare skin; Theresa got goose bumps all over again but thought it was due to her being wet in the cold bathroom.

Gabriel went in the kitchen and wrote a small note for Theresa about the materials she had requested, hoping that she would find everything as she needed it. He started to leave through the back door of the one-story old house. When he got to the hallway, Sister Theresa came out of the bathroom wearing only the towel around her head. She turned towards her bedroom and found herself face to face with the priest in the hallway. They froze for an instant as they had in the gym the first time they had met in similar circumstances. Before either one could say anything, Theresa ran into her bedroom and closed the door.

"I ... I am... sorry, Theresa," Gabriel stammered. "I just came in to drop the materials that you asked for."

"Thank you, Father. I didn't know you were here. I thought Magda had left and that I was the only one in the house. I didn't mean..."

"I had not planned to see you at all either. I left you a note on the table with the materials."

They were talking on both sides of the bedroom door. Then there was an embarrassing moment of silence. Gabriel decided it would be best to leave.

"I am leaving now, if you want to romp around the house nude, just close the curtains. It was nice seeing you again... especially in your very nice birthday suit!"

The priest left. Theresa smiled inside her room. She grabbed the towel she was looking for and went to the window. Gabriel was getting in his 35 Chevy. The curtain was open. The priest turned his face towards the house and saw her at the window. She waved good-bye to him. He pretended to take a picture cupping his hands in front of his eye. Theresa already had her towel around her body then; she just smiled and closed the curtains.

"I guess this makes us even, my friend!" she said, musing over the incident and remembering what happened at the gym.

The evil entity was standing near her. Theresa felt the invisible presence and turned around suddenly but only saw her own image reflected on the mirror against the wall. She was startled by her own reflection first, and then laughed it off.

"Silly me!"

Theresa stood in front of the mirror and took her towels off. She had not paid much attention to her looks in a long time. Suddenly she wondered if she was still attractive. She definitely was! She looked no older than 30 although she was almost 38. Being a dance instructor in school provided her with a great aerobic workout and maintained her muscle tone. Most sisters found it practical to maintain a short haircut; Theresa had decided to keep hers long, although she usually had it wrapped in a bun. It was reddish brown, smooth and straight. It came down to the middle of her back. She felt satisfied with the way she looked – the way Gabriel had found her in the hallway. She thought he probably got a good impression of her. The woman lay down on her bed wondering why she was feeling like a teenager in love, excited, wanting to call him on the phone and hear his singing. Why these feelings if she had been so sure of her calling for the past decade or more? She was a mature woman, a fulfilled woman, an intelligent, educated, positive and spiritually rich woman. Could there be anything wrong with falling in love with a man again, a priest, at this stage in her life? The invisible entity was blowing in her ear to incite her sexuality. She started feeling ashamed and guilty of some sin. She went down on her knees by the side of her bed and began to pray, asking God for direction. The invisible evil entity left her at that moment, but her prayers did not bring her any answers. Gabriel's smile reappeared in her mind.

Father Gabriel had dinner and went out for a walk. He stopped at a bar and looked inside. An old friend from his childhood, Mario Arambula, was there with his own friends drinking, celebrating the beginning of a weekend after a long week of hard work as roofers. Gabriel walked in and raised his hand in greeting.

"Shalom, Mario! How is it going?"

"Father G, how good to see you again! Come sit with us and have a drink," Mario responded getting up from his chair and going to meet him halfway, shake his hand and hug him.

Mario introduced him to his roofer friends, Jay Sanders and Phillip Johnson, a black guy and a white guy who shared the Hispanic's job and low economic status living on the west side. All of them were married with children; Friday evening was their time to relax and have a drink or two, or three, and forget a little about the poor man's life and its problems.

The group of men was playing dominoes and drinking cold beer. The minister joined them for a game and a beer too. The two friends had heard Mario talk about the priest.

"So Reverend, I hear that you perform miracles. Is that true?" asked Jay, the big black guy, about 6 feet 2 inches and weighing 240 lbs.

"Come on, Jay, what kind of a question is that for our guest?" protested Mario, feeling embarrassed by his friend.

"It's OK to ask; I don't mind," interrupted the priest putting down his cigar on the ashtray. "God performs miracles all the time. I have been lucky enough to be used as His instrument in some cases, so the answer is, no, I don't perform miracles. It is God who does," he explained.

"But how does that work, Father? Do you just ask Him and it happens?" asked Phillip after taking a gulp of his beer.

"You will have to ask God about that. All I can tell you is that the faith of the person who seeks the miracle is what makes a difference. When there is a miracle coming down, I feel turbocharged with electricity. I get numb. I don't even feel like I am myself or that I am there at the time. It is very hard to explain, but it is a great feeling. I can hardly go to sleep after something like that happens. It is more intense than the high that marathon runners get after running for a long time and winning the race; I feel hyper, excited, wanting to sing and dance."

Father G drank some of his own Long Neck, excited just recalling the feeling.

"Wow, that sounds great! Hey, now that you mentioned singing. Would you sing a song for my friends here? I have told them how good you sing," said Mario grabbing the priest's muscular arm.

All three men were raised in the Hispanic side of town and spoke Spanish as well as English despite their different colors and ancestry. The mariachi band had approached the table to see if they would hire them for a song.

"Sure! Why not? Hey, mariachis, let's sing a pretty song."

Gabriel got up and talked to the mariachi group; he also borrowed one of their hats. The band began playing an old romantic song, and the men screamed with joy listening to the traditional Mexican sound of the mariachi. The group members were familiar with the priest and had sometimes played for his Masses. The song relates the composer's questioning of his situation, feeling at the same time as a slave and as a master of the universe because of the passionate love he feels for his beloved. In one of the verses the poet asks God for help to forget the object of his affection every time he goes to sleep at night, only to wake up the next day realizing he must adore her even more.

Father Gabriel was singing with special inspiration that evening. The image of Sister Theresa stayed in his mind while he sang. The whole roomful of patrons at the bar exploded in applause for his rendition of the romantic bolero. He thanked them, gave the hat back, and sat down to start a game of dominoes with the trio of friends.

"Man, you sing real good, Reverend! You sound like a man in love," Jay commented as a compliment.

"I am in love, with life, Jay. Thank you!" replied the priest.

"Hey Father, I also heard Mario talking about you being good with your fists," commented Phillip picking up his guard and moving his torso like a boxer.

"Yeah! Do you want to step outside and check it out, Phillip?" said the priest getting up as if ready to fight.

"No, no, I believe!" answered the smaller white man, only about 5 feet 6 inches by 150 Lbs.

"Reverend, if you are as good with your fists as you are with your voice, you ought to be a world champion," said Jay as he raised his beer in a playful mood to toast the new friend.

"Come on, Father G. I told this guys you were like Jesus Christ himself, and here you are ready to kick their asses," Mario protested also in a playful way. He knew the priest was just pretending.

"Well, even Jesus had his moment of fury," Gabriel reminded them. "Do you remember that passage of the Gospel where they talk about the time Jesus got mad at the money changers in the Temple in Jerusalem? He overturned their tables and whipped them out of there. He told them that His Father's house was a house of prayer and that they had transformed it into a den of thieves. He was madder at the church leaders of His day than at the actual moneychangers because they were the ones responsible for the corruption of the Jewish faith. As for me, I try to be as patient as I can, but this temper of mine sometimes cannot be contained; that was why I took up boxing, to release my energy punching something without hurting anyone. I can truly tell you that I never beat on anyone... that didn't deserve it."

Jay and Phillip looked at the priest amazed that such a man, a minister of the Lord, would actually get into fights, but they could understand him.

All four drank at the same time and began their game of dominoes. While they were playing, Gabriel remembered a little joke and shared it with them.

"One day at our elementary school, the teacher was telling the children to be kind and generous, she said: 'remember, children, that it is better to give than to receive.' One of the kids raised his hand and told her very proudly: 'that's what my dad always says.' The teacher smiled and said: 'obviously, he is a kind and generous man. What does your father do for a living?' The child replied: 'he is a professional boxer!'"

Father had more than one beer, and he beat the trio in the games they played. He had collected a hundred dollars from each player by the end of the evening. That was almost half of their weekly salary. When they all left the bar, the priest gave the money back to all of them. They refused to accept it saying he had won fair and square, but he told them that it was a gift he wanted to send to their families.

"Next time, make sure you give your wives enough money for the week before coming here to bet it away. Remember all of you have little ones to support; that should come before your visit to this temple of temptation."

All three men bowed their heads in shame and took the money the priest was returning for their families.

"May the Lord bless you and keep you forever. I hope to see you again, at our Father's place, this Sunday."

The priest gave them his blessing and began walking back towards his house. He was feeling good but was not drunk. His step was steady, his mind clear. He liked drinking but never in excess. As soon as he felt that he had reached his limit, he would switch to plain iced water.

When he arrived home, Gabriel reached for the phone and dialed the sisters' number without thinking twice. He realized what he was doing and thought about hanging up, but Theresa picked up the phone on the first ring.

"Hello, Father Gabriel!"

"How did you know it was I?"

"It is known as 'Caller ID.' It shows the number and the name of the caller."

"Ah, that's right! For a moment I thought you were waiting for my call and had telepathic powers."

"Do you know what time it is, Father Gabriel?"

"One o'clock, according to this thing around my wrist, known as a 'watch,' it tells the time, and also the date."

"Any particular reason to call at this time of night?"

"Well, I just came home from a bar where I met some friends, and were having a few beers over a game of dominoes," Gabriel stammered the words looking for a theme of conversation that would justify such a late call.

"You are drunk!" said Sister Theresa, sounding like a wife.

"No, no, absolutely not. I don't know what being drunk is; I mean I have never experienced it myself. I just felt like I needed to call you when I came in my house."

"It is a good thing that I was awake and near the phone. Magdalene is asleep but you could have woken her up."

"How come you were not asleep yourself?" asked Gabriel, sounding like a husband.

"I was waiting for your call. I wanted you to call me. I could not sleep until I talked to you. Don't ask me why. I just knew you would call."

"Then I was right! It was telepathy. You sent me the message, and I had to pick up the phone. Do you remember we went through this several times when we were younger? You would call me at Mario's house even though I had not told you that I was there."

"Yeah! And one time you called me at Barbara's house when I didn't know where you were and wanted to talk to you very urgently."

"Hey, we still have that connection. Maybe we don't even need a phone," said the priest in a playful tone.

"It is weird... anyway, I wanted to apologize again for my display today, actually yesterday. It's already Saturday morning."

"Oh, please, it was a pleasure to see you like that."

Gabriel closed his eyes to revisit that moment in his mind.

"You were not shocked?"

"I was gladly surprised. You look great! Listen, I am used to nudity. You know how we artists routinely practice drawing from live models. I keep my artistic skills up by attending some figure drawing sessions about once a month. Perhaps you could be our model next time. I would make a great portrait of you."

"Not at all! I would never be able to strip in front of a group of people for them to take my picture, draw me or paint me. That's just not me."

"I am just kidding, Theresa. I would not like to share you with the rest of the class."

"Now, for you alone, I might be willing to pose one day," she spontaneously whispered in a mischievous tone.

"Are you serious? That would be so great!" Gabriel said, excited with the idea.

"I am just kidding, Father Gabriel. That was just an accident; I was shocked to find you in the hallway like that." Theresa pretended to get serious.

"How about the other day, at the gym?" Gabriel taunted her.

"I was shocked too, but for different reasons. I never dreamt that I would meet you, especially wearing only... what were you wearing?" she closed her eyes to revisit the moment she had well burnt in her memory.

"Practically nothing, a jockstrap. I was about to shower when they called me out."

The mischievous tone returned to her voice as she declared:

"Well, you looked very well yourself. I liked what I saw."

He told her about his day and the song he sang at the bar thinking of her. She thanked him for the materials he had brought Friday. They went on and on for a couple of hours talking about things that they had in their memories.

They were transported by their conversation to the time they went to their high school prom and how they danced almost the entire evening. Both had been sore the next day after so much dancing. Finally, Gabriel looked at his watch and saw that it was three o'clock already. He had not made his night prayer. Sister Theresa needed to sleep as well, so he decided to finish their conversation with a silly joke.

"There were two men who were going to be executed the same day in certain third world country. The authorities brought the first condemned man and offered him an option. He could choose if he wanted to die by hanging or in the electric chair. The prisoner thought that hanging would hurt his neck a lot, so he opted for the electric chair that at least offered the comfort of sitting down. They strapped him down and turned the power on, but the chair did not work. They switched the power on a second time, but the chair failed to even tickle the man. Apparently the circuit was not working, so they let the prisoner go. On his way out, he mumbled to the next prisoner: 'the electric chair is busted.' They brought in the second prisoner to be executed, and to be fair; they offered him the same option between hanging and the electric chair. The condemned man said: 'I guess it is going to have to be hanging because I heard that the electric chair is busted.'"

Gabriel was rewarded with Theresa's laughter, which to him sounded like pure music.

"Good night, I mean, morning, Gabe."

"Good morning to you too, Terry. Get some sleep."

Neither one of the two was able to sleep at all that night, going over their conversation time and time again. They felt a little guilty feeling so happy to have found each other, but both of them rationalized that it was God's will which brought them together again.

That following Sunday, during the noon Mass, Father Gabriel was giving his homily. As he was walking in front of the congregation and explaining the word of God to them, he felt something like a light headache. His nose caught a smell of something burning. He continued his sermon while looking around for any signs of a fire or smoke in the church. As usual, there was only the fire of the candles. His eyes rested on a woman and her two children in the middle of the congregation; he felt a chill go down his spine looking at them. He finished his sermon and looked at them again. They were charred corpses in a vision that lasted less than a second. The woman looked at him, wondering what he was seeing in her and her children that made him look so alarmed. Father Gabriel went on to do the preparation for the Eucharist, trying not to look at the mother anymore. He knew he was having a vision about her, but he still did not understand what exactly he was supposed to do. He prayed in silence for the wisdom to interpret the sign and at the same time perform the Mass without interruption.

During the singing of the Our Father, the whole congregation joined hands so that no one was with an empty hand. Everybody was touching two persons, one with each hand. The priest closed his eyes as he sang with the choir and the parishioners.

"Our Father who art in heaven hallowed be thy name."

The energy from the woman and the two children came to him through the human chain they had formed; Gabriel felt something like a light electric shock. He opened his eyes and found those of the mother staring at him.

"Thy kingdom come. Thy will be done on earth as it is in heaven."

The woman's face was burning and blackening with the fire, so were the faces of her two children, a boy and a girl of seven and eight years of age.

"Give us this day our daily bread, and forgive us our trespasses."

The minister closed his eyes and had a vision of a house burning in the night with the family trapped inside while two men ran away from the scene.

"As we forgive those who trespass against us. And lead us not into temptation, but deliver us from evil."

The guitars kept playing, waiting for the celebrant to sing his solo part before the conclusion of the prayer. Father G shook his head to escape the vision and recover his perspective. Finally, to the musicians' relief, he started singing his part.

"Deliver us Lord from every evil, and grant us peace in our days. In your mercy keep us free from sin, and protect us from all anxiety, as we wait in joyful hope for the coming of our savior, Jesus Christ."

All the people raised their hands together for the conclusion of the prayer-song. The priest closed his eyes and felt again connected to the woman in the middle of the assembly and to her two children.

"For the kingdom, the power and the glory are yours now and forever."

Father Gabriel opened his eyes after the end of the prayer as if he finally understood the message. He prayed:

"Lord, Jesus Christ, you said to your disciples: 'my peace I leave you, my peace I give you.' Look not on our sins but on the faith of your church, and grant us the peace and unity of your kingdom where you live forever and ever."

After a brief pause, the priest told the congregation:

"The peace of the Lord be always with you!"

The people responded:
"And also with you!"
"Let us offer each other a sign of God's peace!"

All the parishioners turned to each other to hug, kiss or shake hands, wishing each other peace. Sister Theresa walked towards Father Gabriel to hug him, but he walked to the center of the church where the woman and her kids were. Theresa saw him walking away and felt ignored by him although she noticed that he also ignored several other people that tried to give him their hands as he walked towards someone in the middle pews. She shook hands with the people around her and observed the priest hugging a good-looking young woman, no older than twenty-five. Gabriel told her something close to her ear, and the woman seemed to be alarmed. Father hugged both of the children and placed his hands on their heads before returning to the altar. Sister Theresa got behind the organ and played for the choir to sing "Lamb of God."

Before the end of the mass, Father G said:
"The Lord be with you!"
The people responded as usual:
"And also with you."

The priest smiled and related to them something that came to his mind before giving them his final blessing.

"The archbishop, Trinidad Rosales, was going to read the Gospel at the cathedral one Sunday, but the microphone was not working. He approached it and checked it, tapping on it and switching it on and off. He said: 'there is something wrong with this microphone,' and the people responded: 'and also with you!'"

The congregation laughed at his joke. He gave them a few seconds to recover and then gave them his blessing to end the Mass.

When the celebration ended, Sister Theresa saw the pretty woman conversing with Father Gabriel at the entrance of the church. Father got down to the children's level and kissed both of them. He hugged and kissed the woman too and gave them his blessing. The young mother kissed his hand and left with her children in tow. The religious sister waited for the priest to come back.

"What was going on between you and that woman back there?" she said in a jealous tone.

"I had a vision about her," he responded nonchalantly.

"Who is she? How long have you known her?"

She shot a couple of sharp questions at him.

"Her name is Gloria Vasquez, but I never met her before," he responded in an innocent way.

Father walked to the sacristy to change out of his vestments; the sister went with him to know more about the "vision" he claimed he had.

"What was the vision about?" asked the sister.

"I had to tell her to move out of her house today and go stay somewhere else for a few days. I had a premonition that if she does not do it, her entire family is going to die a horrible death," explained the pastor hanging his vestments in a closet.

"Do you think she believed you?"

"I think she did, the problem is to convince her husband. He is not a man of any faith and will probably not accept a priest's suggestion," said Gabriel with a concerned look on his face.

"Oh, good!" exclaimed Theresa apparently relieved. "By the way you hugged and kissed them, I had the terrible idea that those kids might be yours and that she may have been a secret lover you had."

Theresa looked down, a little ashamed of her own words.

"I forgive you and absolve you, in the name of the Father, and of the Son..."

Gabriel smiled and played as if he were hearing her confession.

"We will see you tomorrow morning in school, Sister Theresa."

She headed for the door and stopped before leaving.

"Yes, Father, have a great day!"

She paused and then asked:

"Are you going to call me tonight?"

"I will think about it," he responded as if he had not considered the thought at all.

He smiled at her and winked. She knew he was going to call her. They were finding a lot of pleasure in their nightly phone conversations.

The next day in school, Theresa heard some ladies who came to drop their kids at the school commenting on a house fire that happened on Sunday night. Some men had started a fire intentionally to get revenge on a man that had been involved in a fight a week before. Fortunately, the family had decided to spend the night at the brother's house in Austin, so no one in the house was injured. They said that it had been the Vasquez family home that was burned. The police were looking for the men responsible for the arson. One of the ladies mentioned that she knew the woman of that house, her name was Gloria Vasquez; she had two little kids. Theresa turned towards the church across the street and saw Father Gabriel coming over to the school. She smiled at him, took him by the arm and pulled him close to tell him what she had just heard.

"Good! I am happy she was able to convince her husband to leave the house."

"What if she had not been able to do it, Gabriel?"

"Then we would be holding a multiple funeral, Theresa."

"You would not have tried to stop it from happening?" she said, amazed.

"I saw it coming. It was going to happen. I was advised to warn the family because it was not their time, I think," he told her shrugging his shoulders.

He went inside the building while Sister Theresa stayed out welcoming the children. She wondered how those supernatural things worked and why her friend was not worried about them. He was enjoying the day as if nothing extraordinary had happened, but then again, to him this was simply another one in a series of supernatural events. He was used to them by now and did not seem to be looking for an explanation. It was Monday the 13th of September. In just a few days, Theresa had found herself jealous of all the women who had access to Gabriel's friendship and kindness. She dismissed her own feelings and decided to immerse herself in her work instead of worrying about her relationship with the pastor.

Chapter IV
The Birthday

Everything was going just fine in the school, but Magdalene started noticing the way Father Gabriel looked at Sister Theresa and also the way she looked at him. Magda dismissed the idea of a romance starting between the two religious. They were a very loving and lovely pair; their conversations seemed to be very polite and professional. Father was known to be a prankster and a joker all the time, so making Sister Theresa laugh was not unusual. He made all the sisters, teachers, staff and students laugh as well, yet something in her feminine perception told her that what was going on between the priest and the sister was more intense than the relationships he had with the rest of the people in school or in the parish. For a moment she pictured Theresa and Gabriel as a couple; they looked very well as such. Magda thought that she would like to have had a daughter like Theresa, and if that were the case, a man like Gabriel would be a great son-in-law to have. The religious sister shook her head to erase the image and crossed herself thinking she was offending the Lord with her thoughts. She picked up a slice of pizza from the cafeteria to give it her approval for the children's lunch that day. One of the cafeteria workers, Irma, looked at her intently, waiting for her reaction.

"Not bad! Let me have the crushed peppershaker and the Mozzarella cheese to make it better."

The cook gave her the two shakers.

"I don't think the children will like adding the hot pepper, Sister," said Irma.

"Too bad, it tastes much better with it. Now if we could only have a beer to go with this pizza, it would be just perfect."

"Sister!" exclaimed Irma looking at the chubby religious as if she had suggested something sinful, but she knew the sister was just kidding about having beer in the school, not about wanting one with her pizza.

"You see, Irma, the kids don't use the hot pepper, which is for the adults. We could also have beer for the adults only!"

"I can see all the teachers drinking during lunch," snorted the cook.

"Sometimes, with these kids, you feel you could really use a drink with lunch!" explained the teacher.

Father Gabriel felt compelled to see Sister Theresa for any little excuse. They were talking on the phone every night by then. There was always an explanation for their frequent conversations, music for the Masses, developing the school festival program or implementing some changes in the first-grade teaching techniques. Theresa also took over the Bible study group that Kathryn had been leading before. They met in the rectory one evening each week. This gave her another opportunity to come see the priest in his house. The new sister got more and more involved in the parish life as the days went by. Both of them were rationalizing about their relationship and how good it was that they could be old friends working together and enjoying each other's company in the service of the Lord. They still did not share with others in the parish the fact that they had known each other before; it was still their little secret.

One day while Sister Theresa was teaching her class how to capitalize words, Father Gabriel paid the class a visit as the principal, checking on the progress of the new teacher. The sister had her class stand up to greet the priest.

"Good morning, Father Gabriel!" said all the little voices in choir.

"Good morning, boys and girls, shalom! Please have a seat," he told them.

All the kids sat down and paid attention to the visitor. Theresa went to a chair in a far corner to hear what he had to say.

"Well, how do you like your new teacher, lovely Sister Theresa?"

The voices said all kinds of different things at the same time, apparently in approval.

"Is she too hard on you?"

"Nooo!" They replied in unison, shaking their little heads.

"Does anyone of you have a problem?"

One little girl, a six-year-old redheaded, raised her hand right away. Father raised his eyebrows in surprise. Theresa covered her face with one hand, smiling underneath because she knew Amanda Southwell always raised her hand and wanted to say something even if it was unrelated.

"What is the problem, young lady?"

The girl stood up and put her hands to the sides of her body like a soldier at attention.

"I am afraid of the devil. He is real bad and scary."

"I agree with you, thank you for sharing that with us, please have a seat," said Gabriel patting her red head lightly.

Father smiled and looked around the classroom to the little faces of the children that started wondering about the devil. One boy was putting his fingers on the sides of his forehead to pretend having horns as he mumbled to his friend nearby what the devil looks like.

"I meant, problems with your new teacher. Anyone have a problem with the new teacher? Be honest with me! I am the principal and can have her removed if necessary."

"Nooo!" all screamed, to prevent even the possibility of removing Theresa.

"So you are happy with her?" asked Gabriel pointing at Theresa in the back.

"Yeeesss, Father Gabriel!" replied the choir of voices.

"Very well then. Let me tell you a story about the devil, for you not to be afraid of him."

Father Gabriel closed his eyes for a moment to review a passage from scripture in his memory. He then started talking to them about chapter two of the Gospel according to Mark where it tells the story of a man possessed by a demon who came to the synagogue one Sabbath when Jesus was teaching in Capernaum. He put the story in simple terms for the children to understand and demonstrated that Jesus was able to expel the unclean spirit from the possessed man. He affirmed to the children that Jesus was with them and that they could always count on him to defend them against the devil.

The kids seemed to rejoice with his words. One little girl with glasses asked him if he could sing a song for them because she liked his singing. He looked at Sister Theresa who was smiling at him and winked an eye in approval for him to sing.

"I think you know this one, so join me if you want."

His powerful and melodious voice resounded in the classroom to the delight of all the kids and especially of Sister Theresa. His song spoke of the mercy and power of God; it gave confidence to the small believers that no evil could overcome them with the Lord at hand. The students and even their teacher joined him in the chorus parts of the song.

All the kids applauded along with Sister Theresa at the end of his song. Father G took the eraser from the blackboard and thanked the audience in Elvis's style.

"Thank you. Thank you very much! Well, it is time for you to get back to work."

Gabriel put the eraser back and looked at the teacher in the back corner signaling for her to come forward and take charge of her group. A little hand was raised between them. The priest acknowledged the black boy who wanted to say something. He stood up at attention and said:

"Father Gabriel, can you tell us a joke before you go?"

Father looked at his watch and then at Theresa; she sat back down to hear his joke.

"Sure! Let me see which one I can remember that you may have not heard yet. Oh, I know! There was a Mexican peasant on the side of the road not too far from a village in Mexico. He was standing there with a fat cow by his side, asking for a ride from passing motorists. No one would stop to give him a ride because of the fat cow. Along came this American tourist traveling into Mexico in his little convertible sports car for two people. He stopped and asked the man what he needed. The peasant told him he would like a ride to the next village, a few miles away. The tourist told him he could give him a ride but he could not take his fat cow. The Mexican hopped in the little car and told him not to worry, that the cow would follow them on foot. The American was a little puzzled but drove off at a slow rate of speed, 10 miles per hour. The cow, just as her owner had said, was following behind the car. The driver started picking up speed, 20 miles per hour, but the cow was right behind them keeping pace. The tourist was amazed at the speed of the cow when he hit 30 miles per hour, and he could still see the face of the cow, cool as a cucumber, in his rearview mirror. The driver wondered how fast the cow could go, so he pushed it to 40, still there, 50, still there. The Mexican peasant was all smiles enjoying the ride and holding on to his hat. At 60 miles an hour, the American driver was full of joy when he looked in the rearview mirror and saw that the cow was sticking her tongue out. 'Ah!' he said. 'Your cow is getting tired, Señor. She is sticking her tongue out.' The peasant asked the driver: 'what side is she sticking the tongue out to, patron?' The American said: 'to the left, in and out, to the left.' The Mexican told him: 'then pull over a little because she is about to pass us.' Broooom! The cow went past them and beat them to the village."

The little people cracked up with the corny joke, imagining a fast fat cow passing a sports car. Theresa came to the door to let the priest go and thanked him for the visit. They froze for an instant when their eyes met. A light shock went though their hearts and caused them to smile with pleasure. The teacher shook her head, remembering her class was watching them. She dismissed the principal saying:

"You are welcome any time you want to drop by, Father."

"It was a great pleasure to be with you and your class, Sister. Keep up the good work!"

As Theresa was leaving the school that afternoon, she was met outside the school by a very nice black couple. They asked to see Father Gabriel; Theresa knew that he had gone to visit the prisoners in jail and would not be back until later that evening.

"Is there something I may be able to help you with?" Sister Theresa asked them.

"We want to see the reverend because we want to thank him for healing our son, Johnny," the beautiful black lady explained to Sister Theresa as they stood in front of the school.

"When was this?" asked Theresa walking them under the shade of a big tree, out of the hot sunlight.

"Last year," said the black gentleman wearing the white clerical collar of a Protestant minister.

"I know we should have come a long time ago, but we were not sure. You see, our son suffered epileptic seizures since he was very little. There is not much you can do with that type of condition or whenever an epileptic goes into a seizure. We suffered thinking that our son was going to have to live with it for the rest of his life," Janie Atkinson related to Theresa, sharing their joy.

Her husband took over telling the story to the seemingly interested religious sister.

"Last year, we met Father Gabriel at a soccer match. I was coaching my son's team because the other coaches did not want to have the responsibility of an epileptic in the team. Father Gabriel was coaching the team that was playing against us that day. It was a close game. We were tied 2-2 in the second half. My son was the best player on our team, but suddenly he collapsed in the field with a seizure. I knew he was going to recover from it, but the referee stopped the game. I went in and held my boy. I carried him to the sidelines and got another player to go in until my son recovered. Sometimes it takes longer than others. I thought he was not going to be able to return to the game because there were only about ten minutes left. He had never had a seizure during a game. As I was holding him on the sideline, out of the field, and raising my eyes to heaven for help, I noticed that the coach of the other team, Father Gabriel, came running across the field before the referee started the game again. Father Gabriel told me that my prayers had been heard. He laid his hands on my son. I felt something like a shock of electricity going through my son and shocking me too when he laid his hands and prayed over the child. I felt weak and fell on my knees still holding on to the boy. Father Gabriel told Johnny to get up and gave him his hand. There I was, on my knees, watching a miracle happening! The boy recovered as if he had never gone through a seizure. He turned to me and asked me why I pulled him out of the game. He looked bright and alert, not sleepy and confused as he usually was after a seizure. I thanked the priest for his help, but, to tell you the truth, I didn't want to believe that it had been a miracle. Johnny had seizures before and then would go on living his life like any other boy until a new seizure came up. It took us a year to be completely sure that Johnny was definitely cured. We had him examined by several doctors. They found absolutely nothing wrong with him. He used to have a seizure about once a month, but since last year, he has not had a single one even though we stopped his medication."

Theresa noticed John Atkinson's eyes got teary remembering the incident.

"Now I realize that I was actually jealous that God gave Gabriel the power to heal and not me. I wanted to have been the one that touched the boy and healed him, so I didn't want to concede that the boy was healed by Father Gabriel's touch."

"But, John, didn't Father Gabriel say that your prayers had been answered before he laid his hands on the boy?" asked Sister Theresa, trying to give credit to the man's own faith.

"Yes, he did. As time went by, I was aware that God was working in mysterious ways to open my eyes. I became more aware of my faith and my own ministry. I am a preacher, not a healer. This is my call. I am here to thank Father Gabriel for his help. We got this gift certificate to SoccerPro for his team, as a token of our appreciation."

"How did your game end that time? You said it was a tie when Johnny went down," Theresa asked.

"That was the funny thing. When I saw that Johnny was ready to play again, I sent him back in, and he scored the winning goal. Father Gabriel's players were not happy with him because he had healed the one that scored on them. As we were leaving the field, I heard him talking to his players and parents about the love to our enemies. But he explained that we were not enemies, even though we were on different teams and belonged to different denominations, we had a lot more in common than the differences that divided us. He told them that something more important than a game had taken place on that field that day: God had been present and had brought health and joy to a family."

John put his arm around his wife's shoulders, handed Theresa an envelope and said:

"Could you give this to Father Gabriel for us? Maybe we can invite him to dinner one of these days, and you too, Sister."

"I have a better idea," Theresa said. "Father Gabriel's birthday is coming up in a couple of days. Why don't we prepare him a surprise party where you can have him to dinner and give him the gift? I have been looking for someone to help me in doing this."

"That sounds good, Sister; you can count on me! John, do we have the hall available?"

Janie asked her husband.

"As a matter of fact, we do," he answered with a big smile. "The only reception we had has been cancelled. The bride decided to run away with another man before the wedding."

"Let's do it then. What did you have in mind, Sister Theresa?"

They went over a general plan to organize the surprise party. Theresa went with them to their church and visited their nice hall where they could hold the party. Both John and Janie were very faithful to their creed. Theresa could easily relate to such spiritual people. They, too, found much to love about the religious sister. They invited Theresa to their place and shared dinner with her before taking her back to her own home.

That evening Theresa was thinking she and Gabriel could be like the Atkinsons, a happy, married couple, with three lovely children, serving God. Janie was very active in their church. The only difference was that they were Protestants; in order for Gabriel and Theresa to do likewise, they would have to renounce the Catholic faith. What could be wrong with that? Theresa slapped her forehead trying to get rid of that kind of thinking. She went to her room to pray a rosary and get her mind clear of what she considered sinful.

On the day Gabriel turned thirty-eight years old, Thursday September 30, he acted as if it were an ordinary day. He got up early, went running and swimming, celebrated the morning Mass and worked at his office on parish and school business all morning. At lunch, he had Deacon Andres Garcia come and join him at the priest's house for some salad and soup. Theresa showed up asking if she could have lunch with them. She wanted to prevent Father from going back to the school where all the staff was making plans

THE TEMPTATION OF THE MIRACLE WEAVER

for his birthday party that evening.

"It will be our honor and pleasure to be graced by your presence, Sister," said Father Gabriel pulling out a chair for Theresa.

The priest took his seat and told the two religious friends a joke that came to mind.

"The deacons of a Protestant church were interviewing a prospective young preacher, who had applied to become their pastor. They asked if he knew the Bible; he said he knew it fairly well. They asked what part of the Bible he knew best; he said that he knew the New Testament best. They asked if he had a favorite part of the New Testament, and he said his favorite part was the story of the prodigal son. The deacons asked him to tell them the story, so the young man told them: 'There was a leprous, blind and deaf man of the Pharisees named Nicodemus who went down to Jericho by night and fell upon stony ground, and the thorns planted by an enemy choked him half to death. He fought them off with a jawbone of an ass until he injured the sciatic nerve in his hip. The next morning, Sodom and his wife, Gomorrah, came by and carried him down to the ark for Moses to take care of him. But as he was going into the Eastern Gate of the Ark, he caught his hair in a limb, and he hung in there for forty days and forty nights. He afterward hungered, and ravens came and fed him manna and quails. He watched the angel stir the waters as he ate. The next day three wise men came riding on a herd of swine and parted the waters near the tombs with a plague of locusts. They took the man and carried him down to the boat dock where he caught a ship to Nineveh. When he got to Nineveh, he found Delilah sitting on the wall selling her flour and oil. The man called out: 'Chunk her down, boys! Chunk her down!' They said: 'How many times shall we chunk her down – seven times seven times?' And he said: 'No! Seventy times seventy times.' They chunked her down 4,900 times, and she burst asunder in their midst. They picked up twelve baskets full of the fragments. 'And in the resurrection of the just on the last day, whose wife shall she be, prodigal son?' The deacon chairman said: 'fellows, I think we ought to take him. He is awfully young, but he really knows his Bible!'"

Theresa and Andres were cracking up with laughter throughout the joke. The deacon regained his composure and declared to the other two:

"I've got to eat and run. My wife is flying back from seeing her sister in Las Vegas. She should be here in about an hour."

Theresa loved the opportunity of sharing some time alone with Gabriel.

"Oh, no problem, Deacon Garcia. You better be there on time to pick up that woman. You know how we don't like to be kept waiting," said Theresa looking at Gabriel as they sat together and prepared to eat their lunch. It consisted of cream of mushroom soup, shrimp salad, toasted black bread and a small glass of white wine. Gabriel caught the meaning of her words as they applied to him, but he just smiled back at her with an innocent look.

After lunch, Theresa picked up the dishes from the table and went to wash them in the sink. Gabriel walked the Deacon out the door and came back to the kitchen.

"Oh no, please, Theresa leave those dishes there. I will take care of them later, or Ms. Black will do it. You don't have to; besides, you have to go back to your class."

Gabriel put his hands on her waist as if trying to pull her away from the sink. She held on to the edge of it, refusing to move but enjoying his grasp.

"I am not going back until I do this. Now, if you want to, you can rinse them while I scrub them. My class is in P.E. at this moment, so I have time."

She placed her hands on his, still holding her by the waist from behind, turned her face up to look at him as he stood behind her, and softly blew her words at him:

"Plus, I would like you to sing me a song, a pretty, romantic song."

The priest rolled up his sleeves and approached the sink ready to assist Theresa. He finished what was left of his glass of wine and cleared his throat to start his song. The lyrics told of the things the beloved would learn once she found out about the poet's love, that she was his life, his heaven and his God.

Theresa turned to see Gabriel with her light brown eyes wide open.

"That is sacrilegious!"

"It is only a song, Sister. I didn't write it; I only sing it. If you don't like it, I'll stop."

"No, I love it, but I have a problem with the being-your-God part," Theresa explained.

"Then think that I am singing the song to God and not to you," Gabriel said.

"Now that makes more sense! Finish the song, please," Theresa told him as she went back to the dishes in the sink.

The singer repeated the last verse to conclude the song as they finished doing their chore. She thanked him for lunch; he thanked her for doing the dishes. She thanked him for singing; he thanked her for asking him for a song. They looked into each other's eyes, standing at the door and smiled happily.

"Now get out of here and go back to work!" Father told her with a big smile while opening the door to send her back to the school across the street.

Theresa hurried up to get there at a fast pace; Gabriel followed her with his eyes until she disappeared inside the building. The priest went into his room and got himself a new cigar. He lit it up and walked around the outside of the house, looking at the kids playing in the schoolyard. It was a great day; it was his 38th birthday! Nobody had mentioned it to him yet, and he was not about to tell anyone. He felt that he had already enjoyed his birthday just sharing that moment alone with Theresa.

A publisher's representative came to meet him outside. He had been waiting for the priest at the school office because they had an appointment with the principal to check out some texts he wanted to order. Father apologized for having forgotten about the appointment and took the man into his office to deal with their business.

That evening, Father Gabriel went to visit an old lady in the housing projects. He parked his car near a playground. There were some kids playing basketball there. The priest went into the basketball court and stole the ball from a boy. He dribbled and went in for a lay up. The kids knew him and laughed with him. He asked them to keep an eye on his old ride and to keep practicing their sport. One of the boys got the ball and threw it hard towards the priest. He caught it and jumped up for a long shot.

"Nothing but net!" he said proudly as he watched the ball go cleanly through the hoop.

Martin Davis, the boy with the attitude, went to get the ball again. He seemed to be the only one in the court that did not like the priest interrupting their game. He was no older than 14.

"Let's get on with the game guys!" the teenager screamed, dismissing the priest.

Gabriel decided to walk away and do what he was there to do. The other boys told the mad one to calm down because "el padre" was "cool." The priest knew they were juvenile gangsters but hoped to make friends with them and save at least one from their risky gang activities.

The minister prayed with Dona Mariquita and gave her communion. He listened to the old lady talk proudly about her grandson, Henry, who was in the Marine Corps. The old lady was confined to a wheelchair and lived alone. She had raised the boy and kept him in school. His mother had died of a heroin overdose; his father, who never really acknowledged being his father, was still in prison for murder. Mariquita herself had been a victim of retaliation. On a drive-by shooting one night, she was hit on her lower back as she slept on the couch of her living room. A group opposing the friends of Henry had decided to retaliate after Henry's friends had shot one of them. Henry was just an associate and had never been initiated in his friends' gang. The other gang did not know and did not care either. Henry was not even in the house when Mariquita got shot. That day he decided that he was going to join the Marines and get a better place to live for his grandma and himself. He was still working on it; Mariquita hoped he would take her with him to San Diego, out of the housing projects.

As he walked back to his car, Gabriel heard some screaming coming from an apartment building on the other side of the complex. He also smelled smoke coming from a big fire. The priest looked up and saw the evening sky become lit with the roof of a building burning up. He quickly got to the burning building to see what he could do. There was a woman wearing only a slip who was being held by her teenage son, the same boy that had thrown the ball to him in the court. The woman was screaming and crying, saying that her baby was still inside the burning apartment on the second floor. Her son was holding her back to keep her from going into the fire. The priest evaluated the situation. The building was half in flames already. He was filled with pity for the woman and thought about the baby. He heard the baby crying inside the apartment and decided to go in. He started towards the door and pulled out his little bottle of holy water. He mumbled a prayer, crossed himself and poured some of the blessed water over his head and shoulders as he made the sign of the cross. He was reciting a prayer from memory.

"O Lord, by your name protect me. Grant me strength to defend your cause. God almighty listen to my prayer. Attend to my supplication."

The priest got in the apartment. The flames seemed to make way to let him in.

"The evil one has risen against me; the ruthless one seeks my ruin."

It was hot and dark in the place. The priest heard a low, deep laughter in the fire; he continued with his prayer.

"You are always present as my helper; it is you who sustains my life."

The priest felt an evil presence observing him in the fire; the hair in the back of his head stood up as if attracted by magnetic energy. Gabriel prayed louder.

"Protect me from the evil foe; by your faithfulness, keep me from harm."

Some smoke got to the priest who started coughing. He went down to a crawl looking for the stairs and heard something like a deep voice in the crackle of the fire.

"You... are... mine!"

Gabriel looked around. The door he came through was now on fire. He started going up the stairs on his hands and knees, quickly, when he heard the baby crying again.

"I will offer you as my only sacrifice, my humble and contrite heart, and I will give praise to you, O Lord, because you have rescued me from every danger."

A tongue of fire surrounded the ankle of the priest as if a claw of fire was grasping the man. It burned the pants leg and sock. Gabriel turned to see his ankle on fire and heard the deep voice coming from the fire again:

"You are mine, Gabriel."

The priest sprayed his ankle with the holy water he had left in his bottle. The fire receded, and his leg was refreshed.

"In the name of Jesus I command you; get away from me, Satan!" he called out.

The baby was coughing and crying inside the bedroom. Father Gabriel crawled in there and located the toddler under his crib. The fire was now all the way to the bedroom door; there was no way they could go out the way he came in. Gabriel wrapped the baby in a blanket from the crib and saw that the curtains were burning on the window. He got up and threw a dresser through the bedroom window. The people outside screamed in fear when the dresser came out. It almost hit a man who was watching the fire, and the semi-nude mother. Gabriel dropped to the floor and covered the baby with his body. The wind draft sent long tongues of fire out the now broken window. The people watching outside screamed some more. The priest got up with the baby in his arms and jumped out the window head first like shot out of a cannon. The people screamed a third time watching him in flight. The trip down was a good thirteen feet. He curled his body to land on his upper back and roll on the grass with the baby safely tucked between his powerful arms. The firefighters arrived as the priest flew out the window. Gabriel's shirt was on fire; a firefighter approaching with a hose in his hands showered him on the grass. The priest got up and handed the baby over to the distraught mother, Violeta Ojeda.

"My baby! Thank God, my baby is OK! Thank you, sir, for saving my baby! Blessed be the Lord, blessed be God!"

The mother was checking the little boy who was crying but not hurt. She hugged the baby and put him on her left arm to come and hug the priest with her right arm, crying with joy to see her baby alive. Gabriel was still emanating some vapor from his partially burned and wet shirt.

"Blest be the Lord, indeed, daughter. He is the one that saved both of us in there," the minister exclaimed.

Father Gabriel kissed the woman on top of her head and also the baby's head. He looked at Martin, the older brother, standing behind his mother and little brother. The boy finally came forward, hugged the priest and thanked him for saving his baby brother.

"You can thank God personally by coming to church this Sunday," he told the teenager.

The priest put his hands on the young man's shoulders to look him straight in the eye.

"Sure, we'll be there, Father G... You know; you really are a cool dude!" the boy replied.

Gabriel smiled and slapped the boy's shoulder acknowledging their new friendship.

"That's my man! Take your mom and your little brother with you, OK?"

A paramedic came to check on the priest while the firefighters battled the flames to keep them from spreading to the other buildings.

"How are you feeling, Reverend?" asked the paramedic.

"Oh, I feel like a champ who just won a world title, sore and tired, but very happy."

Father G took off his black shirt and looked at it; it was unusable now. He balled it up and threw it in a nearby open dumpster. The wet rag of a shirt went into the trash.

"Nothing but net!" said the fourteen-year-old boy, Martin Davis, winking an eye at the priest as he held his baby brother in his arms.

"You know, what you did back there was very stupid; walking into a house on fire, like you did, without any equipment is never recommended," the paramedic commented to the hero.

"You are right, and you are wrong, my son," the priest's replied.

"Why do you say that?"

"You are right in saying that walking into a house on fire is very stupid; however, saving a baby's life is not," Gabriel explained, adding: "as to not having any equipment, this is all that I need to face any problem, any enemy, anytime!"

THE TEMPTATION OF THE MIRACLE WEAVER

The minister showed the paramedic his cross hanging from a chain around his neck. The firefighters were beating the fire, but when Gabriel looked at it, he could hear a voice coming from the fire, mixed in with the noise, that told him:

"Next time, priest."

"Anytime, Satan. I am not afraid of you because the Almighty is on my side!" Father G said and turned around.

He walked away quickly towards his car before the media could come to try and interview him. The paramedic looked at the priest puzzled, thinking the hero had been talking to him when he answered to the devil's threat.

When the priest got home, he found a note stapled to his door that read:

"Father Gabriel, Please come to see me at 2815 Delgado St. It is very important. I must see you tonight!"

It was signed by "A Desperate Soul." The minister wondered who that person could be, but decided that whoever it was, really sounded desperate and in need of help. He would skip supper until after he found out. He went in and changed clothes. He brushed his hair, refilled his bottle with holy water and put his things in order in case he needed to hear confession or give the anointing of the sick. He got back in his car and left.

The address was that of a Protestant church hall, which was all dark. The priest checked the number again on the note and on the building. He decided to knock on the door and see if anyone was there. To his surprise, the door was not locked and there was a sign stapled on it that read:

"Come in, if you dare, Father Gabriel."

Gabriel looked into the building through the slightly open door. There was only darkness and silence inside, but this was the place. The handwriting on both notes was the same. He remembered his recent encounter with the evil one and wondered if it was a trap by him. At that time Gabriel heard a muffled cough; he stepped inside saying:

"Hello! Is anybody in here? I am Father Gabriel; I got a request to come..."

The lights came on at once, and a stereo system began playing "Happy Birthday."

"Welcome, Father Gabriel, and happy 38th birthday to you!" Sister Theresa said on a microphone and began leading the congregation in singing.

"Happy birthday to you."

Gabriel looked around and found a lot of familiar faces from the parish and the school, some unfamiliar faces, and a family he remembered well from a championship soccer game a year before. The song ended, and everyone came to hug him. The last person was Theresa who asked him:

"Where have you been? We have been waiting for you for an hour! You smell like smoke."

"Well, obviously, as you can smell, I was in hell, fighting Satan for the life of a baby."

"You are kidding as usual! No, really, what happened?" Theresa insisted.

"That is the truth. Would I lie to you, Sister?" Gabriel responded with a great smile.

John, the host, grabbed the priest to lead him to the place of honor. A group of ladies began bringing plates of food to all the tables. Soft instrumental music began playing in the background. Theresa was still wondering what could actually have happened to Gabriel. She would question him later over the phone before going to bed. He obviously could not have been in hell and back that night! Or could he?

The dinner was excellent, steak and baked potato with vegetables on the side. No alcoholic beverages were served; however, the punch and iced tea were good. Although they had a stereo system playing lively music, it was obvious that there would be no dancing because the tables were filling the space. There were some banners on the walls reading "God bless you Father G!" "We love you, man!" "Happy birthday old man!" "May God keep you another 100 years!" Then, to begin the presentation of the gifts, Reverend John Atkinson took the microphone to thank the birthday boy for having healed little Johnny of his epilepsy by the power of God, even if that cost his team the championship. He presented the Miracle Weaver with the gift certificate. Father G got showered with personal gifts, books, shirts, sweaters, tennis shoes, gym bag, punching gloves, weight lifting gloves and a tiny black Speedo for his swimming, which raised eyebrows. Some people followed Deacon Garcia and his wife in chanting for the priest to put on the Speedo. Father G took it and put it on his head; someone snapped a picture of him. He then moved on to open other gifts, a white cowboy hat, a black briefcase, a CD collection with Beethoven's music, an electric shaver with adjustable head for beard trimming, a black leather jacket and some dark sunglasses! He put the jacket and sunglasses on then grabbed the lifting gloves to complete his tough-looking outfit.

"Did anyone buy me a motorcycle that I can go ride? I am ready!" he called out.

Gabriel mounted a stool and pretended to take off riding it; then he returned for his last gift.

Sister Theresa gave him a multicolored stole from Mexico. He had always wanted one like that but had never bought it or had anyone think about getting it for him. She knew what he liked and wanted, even before he said it.

After the party, when most people had left the hall, Gabriel and Theresa stayed for a little while to help the Atkinsons. Sister Theresa told Magda that she would stay back to help with the clean up since it had been her idea to hold the party. Theresa declined to use the other sisters' help saying it was not that much anyway. Either Father Gabriel or the Atkinsons would take her home later. John and Gabriel compared notes. Both were pastors of a congregation and had a small school under their supervision. They were only a couple of years apart. John was already 40. Theresa and Janie had similar duties. Both taught the first grade, led a Bible study group and had the music ministry. The difference was that the Atkinsons had been married for 18 years and had a boy, Matthew, in high school, a girl, Rebecca, in middle school and the former epileptic boy, Johnnie, in elementary school. Janie made the comment:

"You two look so good together. I think you would make a lovely couple!"

"Come on, honey! Catholic religious people are celibate; they cannot marry." Her husband quickly interjected in her comments to Sister Theresa.

"That's right, we are married to our Lord and to our ministry," said the religious sister looking in the direction of the priest.

"Well, I can respect that, Sister, but I am sure glad I am not Catholic and can serve the Lord and be married with children at the same time," said Janie triumphantly, obviously happy of her position as a preacher's wife.

"There are different paths in life. We just have to be able to identify which is the one God has reserved for us," Theresa explained, adding: "some of us are luckier than others, or so we think. To every blessing, there is a responsibility. The important thing is to let the Spirit of God guide us in our journey and accept both blessings and responsibilities as they are granted."

The two couples were walking to the door as Sister Theresa said:

"It has been a great pleasure to meet you, Reverend John and lovely Janie. I hope we may be able to share some more time together in the future. Maybe you can bring your choir to one of our celebrations!"

They were walking out to Father Gabriel's car.

"Man! How old is this thing?" asked John, looking at the old but well-kept vehicle.

"It is older than you or I. It is a 1935, not a classic. It is like a mutant. The boys at the technical high school auto shop have made it into what it is; they call it the Priestmobile. Look at the interior renewed by the upholstery shop in my parish, the sports wheels donated by a friend of mine, the stereo system donated by a converted thief. Listen to the powerful engine the boys got from a wrecked car in a junkyard," Gabriel said with pride.

Father G turned on the engine of the Priestmobile and stepped on the gas.

"It sounds good. How much money have you invested in it?"

"Not a penny! It is maintained by the grace of God and the goodness of my many friends. Another friend provides even the gasoline to me, free. It is true what they say: 'he who has friends does not suffer; the ones that suffer are his friends!'"

They laughed and waved good-bye as the Priestmobile disappeared into the night.

Gabriel had time to relate his little fire rescue adventure to Sister Theresa on the way home. She was amazed at the things her friend got involved in and how he always came up triumphant. When they were talking about the Atkinsons on the way home, the priest remembered another little joke and shared it with Theresa to make her laugh and see her sexy smile again:

"At one of the latest Theologians conferences at the Vatican, the group came up with three undisputable truths," he began saying, quite seriously.

Theresa looked at him with interest, thinking he was sharing some important theological insights with her.

"First, they concluded that the Jews will not recognize Jesus as the Son of God. Second, it was agreed that the Protestants will not recognize the Pope as the true successor of Peter, and third, Baptists will not recognize each other at a liquor store," Gabriel said without looking at her.

Theresa repeated the last two sentences and realized he was joking. She slapped him on the shoulder but had to laugh at his joke.

"You had me thinking for a moment that you were sharing some serious information with me and then I realized that his was another one of your jokes. It was funny though."

"I love to see you smile, Terry. I love to hear you laugh, to see you near, hear you talk, smell you, feel you close to me. I just love to have you around, my dear Terry," he told her.

"I feel the same about you, my dear Gabe," she said in an intimate tone.

They looked at each other for a long while. They had already arrived at the front of the sisters' house. The front light came on to illumine the entrance, so they realized the sisters inside had seen them arrive. He got out and opened the car door for her.

"Thank you so much for the surprise party. It was just great!" Gabriel told her.

"I am glad you enjoyed it. How did you like my gift?" she asked as they walked to the door.

"Oh, that Mexican stole was my favorite!"

"I thought it had been the leather jacket," she commented disdainfully.

"Maybe I can wear both at the same time! What do you think?" He declared with a childish expression on his face.

"Good night, Father Gabriel!" she said smiling as she headed for the door.

It was the end of September, the first of the six months allowed for the Devil's test, and everything was going just fine so far. The two lovers had no idea of the dangerous situation. They were enjoying falling in love with each other all over again, unaware that Gabriel's soul was at stake. After all, what could be wrong with it? They were perfect for each other, and they were not hurting anyone by their romance. They pretended that it was no such thing as "romance"; it was just a very "close friendship" from old times. The dirty whirlwind ran across the front yard and disappeared behind the Priestmobile as it turned at the corner.

"What's that horrible smell?" asked Theresa of Magda as she came in the house.

Magda closed the door behind them saying:

"I don't know, but it is coming from outside. It smells like rotten eggs, uggh!"

Chapter V
The XXV Wedding Anniversary

One day, Father Gabriel was discussing the details for a XXV wedding anniversary Mass with a couple and their children in his rectory office. It was all set for that Saturday evening. The couple did not ask for a special Mass but wanted to celebrate it with the congregation that came to the Mass regularly attended by the couple. Gabriel had not had a chance to sit down and talk to the family at length before. This was his opportunity to get to know them a little better and learn something he might be able to say during the celebration. They had two sons and two daughters. The oldest son, Peter, and the two girls, Leticia and Patricia were present at the meeting. The youngest son, Paul, was the "black sheep" of the family and was not present. Gabriel noticed that when the parents started talking about the situation with Paul, Peter excused himself and left the office to go smoke a cigarette outside.

The year before, Paul had stolen some money from the family business. They had a trucking business that was managed mainly by Peter; he had acquired a business degree for that purpose. Paul got addicted to drugs, started keeping some very questionable friends, ran up several credit cards, took one of the trucks and sold it without permission, then fled to California and lost contact with the family. The parents were concerned that he might be in some serious trouble or might even be dead. Don Santiago Cordova, the Father, had diabetes, and Peter blamed Paul for it, saying it was from the tremendous shock and disgust that their father suffered upon learning of Paul's activities right before he fled. The mother, Dona Angelita, said she kept praying to the Virgin to watch over her son, for him to still be alive and return home one day. The sisters were on the older brother's side and had also dismissed their younger brother from the family. For them it was as if their brother had died when he left. This problem concerned Father Gabriel who viewed it as a "cancer" in the Cordova family.

Sister Theresa took over the responsibility of providing the music for the Mass and organized the choir of children from the school. The family insisted that both the priest and the sister attended the reception after the Mass at the parish hall; they accepted to attend the social event so that they would be together.

When the Cordovas left his office, Gabriel called his friend, Detective Pablo Hernandez of the police department, and begged him to check on the whereabouts of Paul Cordova.

"Has he committed a crime here?" inquired the detective before accepting the request.

"Yes, he has been using cocaine with his friends. He ran up charges on his family's business credit cards, and he also stole a big truck and cash from them before fleeing to California," explained the priest to the officer over the phone.

"Well, the family apparently is not pressing charges. There is no pending case or report of the thefts. I see that he was arrested in possession of controlled substances, but the charges were dismissed. He probably got a good attorney. He is clean here. I will run a nation-wide check and will look him up on the Internet. Why do you want to find him, Father G?"

"His parents are going to celebrate their twenty-fifth wedding anniversary this Saturday, and they lost contact with him. I wish to talk to the boy to try and make him attend the celebration, maybe work out their differences and make peace with each other."

"Come on, Father! What makes you think that a guy like that will listen to you?"

"We will not know until I talk to him. That's where you may be helpful; just tell me where I can find him, since you are so good at finding people. He is probably in Los Angeles."

"O.K., Father Gabriel. I will do it for you since I owe you one."

Pablo was talking about one time when he was on patrol on the west side and the priest assisted him during a struggle with three "spray heads." One of them got Pablo from behind, one started punching him and the third took the officer's revolver. Father Gabriel ran to them and grabbed the two men by the neck before they could use the weapon on the policeman. The priest smashed their heads together and knocked them out. Pablo tripped the one that was holding him and fell on top of him, knocking his wind out. Then the officer handcuffed the assailant and called for backup to come and assist him in taking all three prisoners. Pablo had been grateful to the priest for saving his life that evening.

"Do it because you are my friend and care; you owe me nothing," Gabriel told him.

"All right! My friend, I will do it for you and because I do care," said the detective.

"That's the spirit, Pablito! I will wait to hear from you," exclaimed the priest and hung up the phone thanking God in silence for the help the old friend would provide him.

About an hour later Detective Hernandez called Father Gabriel back with the information. The rumors were right. Paul Cordova was in Los Angeles County jail, for prostitution. He did have a criminal record in California accumulated just in the last year; the last one was his fourth arrest already in that state.

"He doesn't look like a man that's worth your time, Father G," said the policeman.

"Pablito, you are prejudiced against criminals. You have to learn to give people a second chance. They are still children of God," commented the minister.

"You forgive them and give them a second chance. I will forgive them but still put them in jail to let them reflect on what they did wrong," said Pablo.

"Good! I guess you would not last long in your job if you forgave all criminals and let them go every time, eh?" the priest told him.

"That's right, my friend, but I am going to let *you* go. I have a statement to take from a witness who just arrived to the office. I'll talk to you later," the detective responded.

"Thank you, my friend. May God bless you and protect you all the days of your life."

As soon as he hung up the phone, Gabriel started planning how to get in touch with Paul Cordova in the Los Angeles County jail. There was no way he could cross the country and bring him back before Saturday. He would need to send a messenger to represent him. He remembered Father Raphael Sanguedulce, one of the three "Archangels" from his seminary days, who was working with the gangs in Los Angeles. He was the perfect man for the mission. Gabriel pulled out his Rolodex and looked up his old friend's office number in L.A. to call him right away.

Father Raphael was leaving the office when the church secretary called him back about an important phone call.

"Who is it? I am running late for that presentation I have to give at the St. Anthony's School. Get their number and tell them I will call them this evening," the priest said.

He turned towards the door again as if he had made up his mind about not taking the call, but he froze when he heard that it was a "Father Gabriel" from San Antonio and that it was urgent. He turned around and went to his office with a smile on his face. Suddenly he had forgotten about the presentation he was running late for.

"Gabriel, old man! I had not heard from you in..." Raphael began saying.

"...3 years, 3 months and 3 days!" Gabriel said to complete the sentence.

"I thought it was... Forget it. It's good to hear from you! What's going on?" said Raphael.

"I need your help," explained Gabriel in a supplicant tone.

"Yeah, as usual! You need help. God won't listen to you; then you come to me, right?"

"Something like that. I need you to go to jail."

"Hey, what did I ever do to you? That last fight we had, I won fair and square!" the priest in Los Angeles said.

"If I recall correctly, my friend, you were the one on the canvas the last time we got in the ring." the priest in San Antonio reminded him. "Seriously," he continued, "I need you to go visit a guy in jail and talk to him for me."

Father Gabriel went on to explain the situation with the family and what he needed to hear from the boy in jail. Raphael understood perfectly what his spiritual brother wanted to do and promised him he would take care of it that same evening. Gabriel related to his old friend a joke he had just heard among his fellow priests.

"Four Catholic mothers are having coffee together discussing how important their children are. The first one tells her friends, 'my son is a priest. When he walks into a room, everyone calls him "Father."' The second Catholic woman chirps, 'well, my son is a bishop. Whenever he walks into a room, people say, "your Grace."' The third Catholic woman says smugly, 'Not to put you down, but my son is a cardinal. Whenever he walks into a room, people say, "your Eminence."' The fourth Catholic woman sips her coffee in silence. The first three women give her this subtle 'Well...?' She replies, 'my son is a gorgeous, 6' 4", hard-bodied, male stripper. Whenever he walks into a room, people say, "Oh my God!"'"

"I think they came up with that joke after someone saw me in my Speedos," said Raphael laughing.

The priest in L.A. then looked at his watch and stopped laughing. The conference he was supposed to attend should be starting in ten minutes, and he was at least thirty minutes away.

"Oh my God, I will never make it to that conference at St. Anthony's school! I've got to let you go, but I'll call you back tonight with the results of my interview with Paul."

"Raphael, don't go to the conference; it's been canceled. Go to the jail instead."

The priest in California froze before hanging up the phone even though he was already standing and ready to run out to his car.

"What do you mean canceled? How do you know?" he asked Gabriel.

"Was it at St. Anthony's high school that you were going to give a presentation?" Gabriel inquired.

"Yes!"

"Trust me on this. Go to the jail and forget the conference. If you don't believe me, just turn on the TV news. Talk to you later. Ciao, bambino!" the friend in Texas told Raphael.

Gabriel left him in suspense. Raphael was puzzled not knowing if Gabriel was kidding or not. He turned on the TV in his office and flipped through the channels until he found the news. It was true! There had been a fire at the school and all the activities had been canceled.

The firefighters were still trying to put out the fire that had started in the cafeteria. All students were sent home. No one had been injured.

"How did he know?" wondered Raphael.

Meanwhile in Texas, Gabriel turned off his own TV set. He had learned the news as he was talking to his friend. Gabriel's phone rang, and he picked it up.

"You were watching the news... weren't you?"

It was Raphael. He had to make sure Gabriel did not fool him with prophetic visions.

"I should have let you rush to the canceled conference," Gabriel told him, "but I didn't want anything to happen to you before accomplishing the mission I assigned you. Of course I was watching the news and learned about the fire! What did you think? That God sent his angel to inform me?"

"You! You got me puzzled for a moment. I remember how you had some visions before, and they were always right," Raphael explained.

"This is modern technology, not clairvoyance. Now go on, and may God guide you on the right path, with the less traffic jams," Gabriel retorted.

Raphael and Gabriel laughed, hung up their phones and shook their heads at the same time remembering each other. Raphael was a Philadelphia native, a couple of years older than Gabriel, and the oldest of the three "Archangels." All three were the same size, six feet tall and two hundred pounds in weight. He had brown hair and blue eyes; his main characteristic was his thick mustache that made him look like a famous TV private investigator. His ministry was with the youth and young adults.

Raphael had been inside the jail many times before, visiting his flock of stray young men and women. He had developed good contacts in the judicial system and was also well known by the officers in the gang-infested areas. He met many detectives investigating cases involving people he frequently dealt with. His boxing skills had also come in handy more than a few times in his ministry. He was respected as a man they could trust on both sides. His power to hear confessions had placed him at odds with the authorities many times; however, when possible, he tried to talk the criminals into giving up and turning themselves in to the proper authorities. His approach was to tell the penitent that their encounter was a sign from above, that God was calling them to repent and change, to put a stop to their life of crime and turn to Him, for themselves and their families. It worked most of the time, but he did not push it when the criminals refused to change their ways.

The priest with the mustache met Paul Cordova in the visiting cell. The nineteen-year-old man looked at the priest. He was perplexed because he had not requested to talk to any clergy, and he had never seen this priest before in his life.

"Paul, I am Father Raphael Sanguedulce. I have news from your family," he explained.

The priest reached under the dividing glass between them in the cell to touch the young man's hand. It was cold compared to his own warm hand.

"Do you know my family?" the young prisoner asked.

Paul sat down and opened his eyes obviously interested in what the man had to say.

"No, not personally. I am a messenger of Father Gabriel from San Antonio."

"Ah, Father G!" smiled Paul.

The young man knew of the priest in his city although he never went to his church.

"Yes, 'Father G' asked me to come and have a talk with you. Your parents are going to celebrate their twenty-fifth wedding anniversary in his church this Saturday. He would like you to attend the ceremony," said the priest in a matter-of-fact tone.

"Yeah, that would be nice! How in the hell am I going to go if I am locked up here?" Paul shouted angrily. "Besides, my family does not want me around. I did some pretty stupid things. I don't blame them for not wanting to see me.

You see. My brother knows I am here, but he would not help me at all. They will not accept my calls either. I made life rough for them," Paul's voice faded to a sad whisper.

"You look like you have gone through some rough times yourself, son," Raphael told him.

"Well, I think I hit rock bottom, Father Raphael. Sometimes I feel I would like to go home and ask my father to take me in as an employee, washing the trucks or sweeping the office, whatever! Here, I think my days are counted. Let me tell you, I killed a guy... in self-defense, last month. His family is into gangs and drugs; they want me dead. I hear that they offered money to have someone do me in here, so I am not safe even in jail. My attorney said he was going to get me out and probably get me probation for all the charges I have pending, but I am sure that as soon as I hit the streets, those guys will be looking for me."

Raphael studied Paul's facial expressions; he seemed sincere and was very afraid. The priest was moved with compassion for the young man and thought about helping him, but he needed the boy to work with him in getting his troubles taken care of.

"I might be able to help you get out of town and return home, but you must work with me, be real honest and don't let me down."

Paul's eyes got big, filled with hope, and he promised the priest he would do whatever he needed to do to get back home to his family. They had a long conversation. Raphael heard his sad story and then absolved him of his sins to encourage him to start anew.

The priest then went to a judge friend of his and arranged to have the boy released and transferred to the Bexar County Probation Department to save his life. Raphael called Gabriel that night with the good news. He would get Paul a bus ticket and send him on his way the next day when he was to be released. The boy would be able to get to the city on Saturday afternoon for the anniversary celebration.

Father Gabriel finished his evening prayer and went outside to enjoy the warm night and be in the presence of God under the starry sky. The sound of police sirens and the flash of emergency lights reflecting around the neighborhood broke the peace of the moment. Then the police helicopter passed flying above the church and school grounds with its searching light. By the number of cruisers involved, the priest thought something serious must have happened. A K9 unit approached the church on the alley side sniffing around. The officer held on to his dog and asked Father G if he had seen anyone running across the area.

"No, not at all. I have been out here for the last ten minutes or so, Officer."

"We are looking for a suspect in an aggravated robbery who is armed with a handgun and should be considered very dangerous," the officer informed the priest.

"I will make sure all our buildings are locked," said the minister.

Gabriel stopped talking when the officer's radio started giving out information on a possible suspect being chased on foot by another officer about three blocks away.

"Excuse me, Father, we got to run."

The dog and handler went west towards the creek and left the priest alone again.

"I hope they get him," the priest said to himself.

Gabriel decided to go check the buildings anyway to make sure no door was left open. To his surprise, the side door to the church was unlocked. He opened it and looked inside. He did not see any movement inside the church or hear any noise, but he felt the presence of someone in there. He stepped inside and closed the door behind him. A very light sound of something falling on the floor alerted him. He walked towards the confessionary and opened one of the doors. There was a man inside about to shoot some heroin in his arm. The noise the priest had heard was the needle cover now lying at the man's feet. The intruder, a Hispanic guy in his thirties, reached for the gun that he had by his side.

"Finish what you were doing, my son. Don't handle the gun; I am no threat to you. The police already left. I will sit over here and wait for you. We have time," Gabriel told him calmly.

The priest went into the old confessionary as if to hear the man's confession. The fugitive had bloodstains on his pants. He opted to believe that the minister was not going to turn him over to the authorities and went on to shoot the drug into his vein. Gabriel thought it would be best to let him calm down by shooting up because he had the look of a desperate man. The drug would relax him enough to stay and talk to him. Father sat back in silent prayer, wondering what to do with the man. He felt inspired and started singing a church song about bringing to God all that we have while asking Him to give us all that we need. The verses seemed to be directed to the criminal who was listening attentively to the song as the drug began to calm him down.

The heroin addict, a fugitive from justice, just sat there listening to the words of the song from his side of the confessionary. He had been a practicing Catholic until the age of twenty when he joined the Navy. He started doing marijuana there. He was kicked out of the service with a general discharge after getting himself in trouble for not being able to follow orders. When he returned to Texas, he started partying with the neighborhood "tecatos" who introduced him to heroin. He had been to prison a couple of times for theft and burglary. His marriage had not worked out; he had two small daughters who lived with their mother. He and his wife had split up a couple of years earlier.

"Father, I want to go to confession. Will you hear me?"

"Yes! I knew you would. Can you see? God brought you here for a reason. You could have gone and hidden under the bridge or in someone else's house, but you came to your Father's house. He brought you here because He wants you to put an end to the miserable life you are living right now, and to start a new life from now on. This is your chance my son, to turn your life around and come back to God, start over!"

Father Gabriel heard the man's confession and absolved him of his sins. He convinced him to give him the gun and talk to the police. He told him not to be afraid of going to jail to pay for his crimes against society, to take advantage of that time in confinement to make peace with God and himself, to get cleaned up from the drugs and get away from his old life. He challenged him to be a real man and face the consequences of his actions, but he assured him that God would be with him every step of the way until the end of his days. The man, Eleazar Gutierrez, thanked the priest and promised him he would come to visit with him when he got out, to show him that he had changed with God's favor. The priest took Eleazar into his house and called the police from there. A minute later, a couple of cruisers were there. Officers jumped out of their cars with their guns in their hands ready to get the criminal. The priest asked them to put their guns away because Eleazar was going to go with them peacefully. Gabriel walked the man out to the first police car and turned him over to the officer. Then he gave the police the gun Eleazar had been carrying.

"I don't know how you do it, Father G, but thank you for your help!" said the police officer looking at the dangerous criminal go into the patrol car peacefully.

They thought for sure they would have to fight Eleazar to take him in. Father Gabriel gave him his blessing as the patrol car left. The priest went to sleep satisfied.

The Holy Trinity Catholic School was holding its picnic Friday on the school grounds. Sister Theresa's first graders entertained the audience with a small play that included acting, dancing and singing. Sister Magdalene tasted most of the different foods being offered. Father Gabriel played a little soccer game with the middle-school boys. They enjoyed Bingo and children's games.

Gabriel and Theresa put their legs in a sack for a three-legged race, which they lost because they fell before getting to the finish line. Sister Magda almost choked on a piece of cake watching Theresa rolling on the grass in Father's arms after falling during the race. She quickly gulped some soda and calmed down realizing that it had been an accident. Everyone was laughing about the fall of the two religious. Since Sister Magdalene had not caught but the last part of the incident, she became suspicious as to what was going on. The older sister took Theresa to the side and told her:

"Sister Theresa, we should be a little more prudent. I know that you are an outgoing person, but we are expected to be more... proper," the superior whispered close to Theresa.

"I don't think I am acting in an improper manner, Sister. What have I done that you think is not right?" said Theresa in a defensive way.

"Well, it is not one thing specifically; it is the whole impression that you cause. Look at you in those sports shorts, and running around like a little girl. Then you seem to be getting too close to Father Gabriel. You know how people tend to start gossip right away at the slightest sign," advised Magda taking Theresa by the arm and walking away from the crowd.

"I appreciate your concern, Sister, but I can guarantee you that there is nothing going on that is improper. People will always look for any reason to gossip," retorted the younger sister.

"Let's not give them a reason, Sister Theresa," said Magda, making a cutting signal with her hand at waist level in disapproval.

The superior closed their conversation and turned around to greet some older ladies that were arriving to the grounds. Theresa looked at her shorts and then at Father Gabriel running after some kids in the playground.

"Maybe Magda is right. Some people might misinterpret my behavior, but I am sure that we are not doing anything wrong... are we?" Theresa mumbled to herself.

She then noticed three teachers talking among themselves and looking at the priest, who caught a little boy and, to the child's delight, lifted him up in the air. The teachers then glanced at Sister Theresa but turned away when they realized she was watching them.

Theresa decided to change into her religious outfit, promising to try and distance herself from Gabriel, to avoid scandal. When she came back the pastor was telling the teachers another joke.

"There was an old lady reading her bible while traveling in an airplane. The man who was sitting next to her noticed it and decided to question her since he was a non-believer. 'Do you believe all that is written in that book?' he asked with a smirk on his face. 'Yes, sir, I do because this is the word of God,' she proudly and quickly responded. 'How about Jonah and the big fish? Do you believe he was inside a big fish for three days and three nights?' the man inquired. 'Yes, sir, the bible says so, and I believe it,' was her quick response. 'Well... what do you think he ate and drank while inside the fish? How could he breathe in there?' the man cornered her with hard questions. 'That is a good question. I will ask Jonah that when I meet him in heaven,' she responded satisfied and pretended to go back to her reading. 'What if Jonah didn't go to heaven?' the man asked the old lady. Without taking her eyes off the bible, she quickly responded, 'then you ask him!'"

The old ladies, the teachers and the sisters laughed out loud at the pastor's religious joke Theresa did not go with the students to the baseball game that evening in order to avoid spending too much time near the principal. The game was good; the local team won that evening. The kids had fun. The religious sister's attempt to stay away from her beloved friend was going to be only a useless, feeble attempt. She was feeling more passionate every day; she realized that she needed to see him almost as much as she needed air to breathe.

Saturday afternoon, the bus arrived to the downtown station with Paul Cordova. He was filled with hope and had already prepared a little speech he had thought of on the way back to San Antonio. He was going to talk to his family and ask for their forgiveness. He would also ask them to take him back as an employee to let him repay what he had taken. He was going to stay clean and work hard to regain their trust. With his last coins, Paul called the house. Peter picked up the phone.

"Hello, Peter, this is Paul... I am back in town... I want to talk to you guys."

"Hold it! We don't want to hear a word from you. You have caused this family enough pain already. This is a very bad time for you to show up. If there is any decency left in you, don't show your face around this home. You know you are not welcome here anymore. You took your part of the business and squandered it on drugs and whores. There is nothing left for you. Consider yourself no longer a member of this family. If I see you around, I will personally see to it that you are thrown back in jail."

Peter, angrily, hung up the phone. He looked around, hoping that his parents had not heard him talking. They were outside already getting in the car to go to the church. He lit a cigarette and headed for his own truck. His fiancée was in there waiting for him.

"What happened? You seem to be upset, honey," she asked.

"It's nothing!" Peter shouted back at her.

He did not want to tell her about the call, but she knew it had something to do with his brother. He always got that way just talking about him. The truck followed the car to the church for the celebration. The girl did not ask Peter anything else.

Paul sat down in the bus station, frustrated. Why was his brother treating him this way? He needed to talk to his parents and hear it from them. He searched his pockets and found no more money. He asked a lady if she could spare some change for a phone call. She looked at him with disgust and ignored his request. The woman walked towards an officer that was in the bus station; she started talking to the officer and pointing at Paul. The young man decided to leave the bus station before he was arrested for panhandling. He ran away and looked back from a block away. The officer was coming out looking for him; he looked to both sides but apparently did not see Paul, who quickly walked into an alley. He felt good walking free and decided he could walk home and face his family instead of calling them. It was going to be a long walk, but he had come a long way to be discouraged by his brother. He strapped his backpack on his shoulders and headed home at a brisk pace. It was good to be back in his hometown!

Paul arrived home and found no one there. He remembered that they were celebrating the anniversary at the Holy Trinity church, about ten blocks away. He started walking faster although he was tired after his long walk from downtown. When he got to the church, the place was closed already. It was 6:30 p.m.; the Mass had been at 5:00 p.m. according to the sign outside. Paul did not know that the reception was in the hall, around the block. He sat by the front door, tired and frustrated. He raised his eyes to heaven asking for help.

"May I help you, young man?" a tall guy that reminded him of Jesus, with a haircut, asked him.

"Do you know where the reception to the anniversary of the Cordova family is?" Paul asked.

"Sure. You must be Paul!"

Father Gabriel offered his hand to help Paul get up from the floor.

"Yes, I am Paul Cordova. How did you know? Who are you?" said the young man.

"Your mom showed me your picture. You look a little different now. I am Father Gabriel Infante, the one that sent you Father Raphael in Los Angeles."

"Oh, thank you Father G! I heard about you before. I really appreciate you sending me that cool priest. He was the one that made it possible for me to come."

Paul shook the priest's hand and walked with him towards the hall.

"Does your family know that you are in town?" asked Gabriel.

"Well, I called and talked to my brother, Peter, but he told me not to come or he would make sure I was thrown back in jail."

Gabriel stopped and thought for a moment, rubbing his trimmed beard and appearing concerned. He looked Paul right in the eye and asked him:

"What do you want to do?"

"I have come to ask my parents to forgive me, even if they don't forgive me. I have to talk to them and tell them that I am sorry for all the things I have put them through. I know my brother and sisters won't forgive me, but I have to talk to my mom and dad."

The priest perceived a contrite and sincere heart, so he decided it was worth trying to help.

"I will help you! Come with me," he said.

Mr. and Mrs. Cordova were at the entrance talking to some relatives and inviting them in. Paul saw them and ran towards his parents. Father G observed the scene from a short distance. Before Paul could get to embrace his mother, Peter pulled him away by his shirt. They struggled in front of their parents who tried to separate them, and an argument ensued. Leticia and Patricia came out to support Peter in his scolding of Paul. The parents were filled with anguish at the scene. Father Gabriel approached them and intervened to put an end to the argument.

"Please, please! Stop this nonsense, all of you!"

Everyone stood there in silence waiting to hear what the priest had to say.

"I heard enough bickering! Come with me into the office. I have something to tell all of you."

Father G took Paul by the arm and led them all into the small office by the hall entrance. He closed the door behind them and asked them all to have a seat. Dona Angelita was crying. Don Santiago was restraining tears himself, blowing his nose to disguise it. Peter, Leticia and Patricia were obviously angry and tight-lipped. Paul was teary-eyed and contrite.

"You may think that this problem of yours is too great to overcome. You may consider that your brother is the worst man that ever walked the earth. You may believe it would be best if he had stayed away and saved you this bitter cup. You may wonder how this came to be. Well, let me tell you that I was the one who brought him here to face you and your hearts of stone."

"Father, I can't believe that you'd do that to us," protested Peter stepping forward, not wanting to believe what he had heard.

"Silence! Sit down and hear me out, Peter," he said it with such conviction that the younger man had to comply without a word.

"There was a man who had two sons..."

Gabriel went on to relate the parable of The Prodigal Son as they sat and listened. When he concluded the parable, the priest said:

"Now, Paul, tell your parents, sisters and brother what you came here to tell them, son."

Paul fell to his knees and began sobbing. He asked his parents to forgive him for all he had done to the family. Both of them picked him up and embraced him; all three were in tears. The priest took Paul from his parents and turned him to face his sisters; they caved in and embraced him as well, with the encouragement of their mom and dad. Lastly, Father Gabriel stood Paul facing Peter.

"Forgive me, Peter. I know I hurt you and the family. I am very sorry."

Peter tightened up his lips and swallowed hard looking into his baby brother's eyes. Gabriel told Peter close to his ear in a low voice:

"What would Jesus do, Peter? What does He want you to do? How many times has He forgiven you?"

After a brief moment, Peter hugged his brother very tightly and told him.

"I forgive you, Paul. Welcome back. Forgive me for being so stubborn."

Now all the family members were crying and joined in a group hug around Paul. Father G also got teary eyed and hugged the whole family.

"It is your fault that you have my whole family here crying," Paul told Father G, laughing and crying. All the Cordovas agreed, filled with joy.

"I know," Gabriel said, smiling. "Let me make it up to you. Dry your tears and wipe your noses. We have a party to attend to! I hear the mariachi band out there already. Let's go out to face the guests, and I will sing you a nice song for your anniversary."

With red eyes and full smiles, led by Peter, all the members of the Cordova family came out of the little office. Paul came out with his dad on one side and his mom on the other. Leticia and Patricia were behind them with one hand each on Paul's shoulders. Father Gabriel called the mariachi band to ask them for a certain song while the family took the place of honor to the applause of the invited guests. Gabriel went up to the microphone with the mariachi trailing behind him.

"Brothers and sisters, today is a very special day in the life of the Cordova family. Not only are Angelita and Santiago celebrating twenty-five years of marriage bliss, but also they have just gotten the 'prodigal son' back. Let us join them in rejoicing and give thanks to God, who has granted them such blessings. I want to dedicate the following song to the bride and the groom, from the bottom of my heart."

He turned to the mariachi and borrowed a sombrero from the biggest one. He put it on as the music filled the hall. Gabriel found Theresa sitting at a table in the middle of the hall. He winked an eye at her and started singing a song about the passing of the years and how things have changed. The poet and his beloved stand now side by side like two speechless adolescents, as they did the first time they met. Gabriel's potent voice tickled the ears and hearts of those listening to his song.

The old couple was getting the full sense of the song dedicated to their lasting love, but Theresa was also interpreting the song as being sung for her and their old relationship made new. The song claimed that despite time having past, their love could not be hampered by the years. Theresa remembered the prom, twenty years back, when they made promises to each other that went unfulfilled. She let out a sigh and looked at Gabriel pulling Angelita to dance a few steps with him before singing the last verse of the song. He returned the "bride" to the "groom" and finished the song to the applause of everybody in the hall. Gabriel let the mariachi band continue entertaining while he came to sit by Theresa's side. She smiled and welcomed him to her table. He sat and placed his warm hand on top of hers on the table, giving her goose bumps on her whole arm. They said nothing, just locked their eyes on each other for a long minute.

Then came the toast. Peter was the best man and pronounced a few, well-chosen words. The family asked Father G to also say a few words. The minister blessed them and wished them happiness. Sister Theresa lauded them as an example of fidelity and love for the new generations. Everybody drank the champagne, and the dance started. A disc jockey provided a variety of types of music to accommodate all ages and tastes. As soon as the bride and the groom opened the dance, Father Gabriel pulled up Sister Theresa and took her to the middle of the dance floor. She resisted a little, but ended up giving in and began dancing to a slow melody. People were giggling looking at the priest and the religious sister dancing, but then joined them on the dance floor and stopped paying attention to them. The music was very loud although the rhythm was slow. The lights were dimmed to allow for a more intimate ambiance.

"I want to congratulate you on your latest miracle of 'the prodigal son,'" said Theresa close to Gabriel's ear.

"It is the work of God; I am just a humble instrument," answered Gabriel into her ear, exciting her with his breath.

"If you have everything so well figured out, tell me, why did God bring us together now, under these circumstances?" she asked.

"The moment we think we have figured out God, have made a big mistake. Why do some things happen? We may never know in this life. I don't claim to know why we are here, like this. I want to believe that it is God's gift. All love comes from the Eternal; He wants us to love one another, right?" he explained.

Theresa nodded in agreement, trying to follow his discernment of their situation. He continued:

"Well, I love you, Theresa. I never stopped loving you! Whom can we hurt by loving each other now? Who can oppose this love of ours? What can be wrong with it?" Gabriel asked her.

The religious sister felt her face and chest burning up. Maybe it was the effect of the champagne, or feeling Gabriel's hands holding her, or his warm breath blowing on her ear as he declared his love for her. It was truly liberating to hear him say those words and confirm that she was not the only one feeling in love like a teenager. The music stopped. Theresa excused herself to leave the hall. The music started again with a Tejano piece. Theresa asked Gabriel not to go out of the hall with her, to avoid gossip spreading. Before he let go of her hand, Gabriel asked her in a whisper:

"Do you still love me, at least a little?"

She squeezed his hand and barely said:

"Yes!"

He let her go. She grabbed her purse, thanked the family for inviting her to the reception, wished them lots of love in the future and left the hall to "go to bed early." She felt she was walking on a cloud all the way home and did not even realize how she got there. Theresa did go to bed early but could not sleep at all, thinking about Gabriel. She got up, took a cold shower, and prayed a rosary before going back to bed.

Gabriel remained in the hall after Theresa left. He did not want anyone to suspect that she was the only woman he cared about as a woman, so he danced with as many of the ladies in the hall as he could, Tejano with Dona Angelita, Cumbia with Leticia and Salsa with Patricia. He enjoyed Waltz with old Raquelita, Rock-n-Roll with Dorothy, Country with Alice, Polka with Maria Fernanda and Tango with Amparito. Even though he was dancing with different ladies, Theresa's face stayed in his mind. He felt as happy then as he had been the first time she told him, twenty years before, that she loved him. He danced and danced in secret celebration of their renewed and passionate love.

The priest was so happy that he did not notice a dark, tall man with a mustache and goatee drinking in the darkest corner of the hall, watching him dance. Despite the darkness, his eyes could be seen like lit charcoals, but when someone turned to see him, he would look down, and his black hat covered his face. Two "horny" women sitting across the dance floor drinking and waiting for someone to dance with them noticed the mysterious character dressed in a black tuxedo. They giggled looking at him while drinking their margaritas. Then they both got up and walked across the dance floor when a new song started. They decided to invite the handsome stranger to dance with either one or both of them. The dark figure noticed them coming among the dancers and smiled. He gulped the last of his drink. When the "horny" ladies arrived to his table, he was no longer there. He had vanished in the dark! The women looked at each other puzzled and then searched the hall with their eyes. There was no way the man could have left without them seeing him. They went back to their chairs laughing and blaming each other for scaring the mysterious guy off. Saturday, the ninth of October, came to an end.

Chapter VI
The Gift

On the night of Sunday the 10th to Monday the 11th of October, Gabriel had a strange dream. In his dream he was dancing with Theresa, as he did at the wedding anniversary reception. There, they were free from intrusion, so they embraced and kissed passionately. They smiled and declared their love for each other. Suddenly, they started walking down the aisle towards the altar as bride and groom. He wore a black tuxedo with his white clerical collar; she was wearing an all-white religious outfit. At the moment the celebrant declared them husband and wife, the altar caught on fire! They looked at the burning altar and the celebrant laughing as he was caught in the fire himself. It was Satan who had married them!

An alarm went off, and the people in the church started running out. The fire surrounded the wedding couple. The alarm kept ringing. Father G woke up in a sweat. His alarm clock was going off; it was four a.m. He usually had it set on classical music. He thought that maybe he moved the button a little too far and selected buzzer instead of radio the night before when he set it. Gabriel had planned to go fishing that morning. A visiting priest would take care of his morning Mass. It was a school holiday, Columbus day, and he had no appointments. Gabriel got up wondering about his dream, but he dismissed it as just a crazy nightmare. He recited his morning prayers and got ready for his field trip.

Father G went fishing with a couple of teenagers he was trying to get away from a gang. One of the little gangsters, Martin Davis, had become his friend after the priest saved his baby brother from their burning apartment. Shawn Aguilar was Martin's best friend and distant cousin who lived on the east side. The three enthusiastic fishermen caught nothing after two hours, but Father G had talked to the two teenagers about Jesus and his Apostles who were fishermen. He related to the boys the passage where Jesus went fishing with some of the Apostles and helped them catch so many fish that their nets were almost bursting. The boys asked the priest if he could pray to God, as Jesus did, and help them catch a lot of fish too.

"I think that would be cheating," he said. "Let's see if our skills and patience help us catch something first. I am not that desperate to ask the Almighty for a miracle."

"Do you think God would give you anything you ask Him for?" inquired Martin who did not have much faith in the existence of God.

"Anything! If you ask Him with true faith," said Gabriel as he put his hand on the youth's shoulder and looked him straight in the eye.

"I'd want some money to buy my mom a gift on her birthday that's coming up," said Martin.

"You expect money to come from heaven and hit you on the head?" Shawn told him, making fun of him. He did not believe in anything.

"Our Lord has different and mysterious ways of working, Shawn," the priest explained. "He is a funny guy, like you. Let me tell you about a time when the collectors of the temple taxes asked Jesus' disciples if their master didn't pay taxes. This is in chapter 17 of the Gospel by Matthew. They were in Capernaum. Peter was asked if his master paid taxes; he told them that He did. Peter went to tell Jesus about it, but even before he could speak, Jesus asked him what was his opinion. Who had to pay tolls or census taxes to the kings, the subjects of the king, or foreigners? Peter told Jesus that they taxed the foreigners, of course. Jesus then said, 'then the subjects are exempt from paying those taxes! But so that those people don't get offended, go to the sea, cast a hook, and take the first fish you catch, open its mouth and you will find a coin worth twice the amount required for the temple tax. Give them the coin to pay for me and for you.' Peter did as Jesus told him, and, sure thing, he caught a fish with a coin inside its mouth right away."

"That's a great fishing story, Father G. How did Jesus know that there was a fish that had a coin and that it was going to be caught by Peter?" Martin asked.

Father G shrugged his shoulders saying:

"That, I cannot tell you, but it happened! Jesus is God and knows everything."

Making fun of him for believing what the priest said, Shawn told Martin:

"If we catch anything, you may want to check inside the fish's mouth for money."

"At that moment Martin's beeper went off. It was his mom who wanted him to call home. Martin rolled his eyes and made a face, assuming his mother was worried about him, although she knew he was with Father Gabriel and Shawn in the lake.

"I think my mom's heard many bad things about priests molesting young kids. She is probably paging me to check on me already."

"Call her," suggested the priest. "There is a public phone over there near the bait store. Do you have change to make the call?"

Martin said he had money, left his pole and took Shawn with him to call his mother. Father G stayed back watching the three fishing poles in case something bit.

A moment after the boys disappeared from his sight, Father G turned around to see his pole shaking as if a fish were biting. He picked the pole up from the pipe it was placed into and began to work the catch. It was a big one, all right! He felt that he had it and started pulling it in. It was too bad the boys had missed it! Then, to his disappointment, the line went limp. Gabriel sensed that the fish got away. Unhappy, he reeled in his line. To make matters worse, the line got stuck half way back. The fisherman pulled wide to the left and right, up and down until finally it came loose but dragged some weed along with it. The sun was coming up on the eastern horizon. The disappointed fisherman grabbed the weeds to untangle the line from it. There was something shiny in the weeds reflecting the first rays of sunlight. It was a beautiful ladies' gold watch with diamonds. He thought it must have been lost in the lake recently, for it was still working and in good shape since it was designed to be waterproof. Gabriel noticed the date. It was Theresa's 38th birthday!

Gabriel had a memory flashback. It had been 20 years since this happened. He had been saving money earned doing yard work in the neighborhood to buy his girlfriend a nice watch for her 18th birthday. That was when he learned that she had left town, so he did not have a chance to give it to her. When he found out that she had been taken to Europe deliberately by her parents just to get her away from him because he was only a poor Mexican-American from the west side, the son of a carpenter and a housewife from Mexico, he became very angry and walked for a long time, wandering throughout the city. He ended up on the shore of a lake near a Catholic university. Out of frustration, Gabriel pulled out his gift and threw it as far as he could into the lake.

Why in heavens had he caught a ladies' wristwatch on this particular date, 20 years later, out of another lake? Was this an encouraging sign of their new destiny together? They both had been tormented in the last five weeks with thoughts about abandoning their ministries to devote their lives primarily to each other, renouncing their vows.

The excited voices of the two kids running back to the spot pulled him out of his thoughts. He placed the watch in his pocket.

"Father G, Father G, my mom said that a guy named Mr. Peters wants to take us to work on his ranch for the weekend paying us 6 dollars an hour!" said Martin pulling his line in, getting ready to go back home.

"I guess that means our fishing trip is over. Good, we were not going to catch anything anyway, but there is the money you were asking for, Martin," Gabriel told the boy.

Martin and Shawn looked at each other amazed.

"Yeah, but we are going to have to work to get it, Father," argued Shawn, wanting to put the event down as not-God-related.

"Yes, indeed. I told you that He works in different ways than you or I can imagine. The fact is, you have some 'dough' coming up, which you will be able to appreciate more than if you found it. The best way to get money is to honestly work for it!" said the priest.

Father Gabriel had spoken to David Peters a week earlier about getting some work for the two boys to get them away from the gang during the days they did not have to attend school. The big rancher, 6 feet 7 inches tall and weighing 320 pounds, had promised the priest he would try to get them something to do in the ranch as soon as he could. David liked the idea of helping Father G straighten up those boys. Apparently the rancher had called that morning looking for Martin, to pick him and Shawn up and take them with him to work on a new fence. He told Violeta Ojeda, Martin Davis's mother, that he could be there to pick up the two boys at 7 a.m. That was why the woman had paged her son. David offered to hire them that Monday and the following weekend as well.

Father Gabriel was taking the two teenagers back home. They were happy, thinking of all the money they could make working those three days, and they were already thinking how to spend the money they had not yet earned.

"How much is three days times eight hours?" Shawn asked Martin, trying to figure it out.

"24 hours!" said the priest seeing that they had problems getting the answer.

"So 24 hours at 6 dollars is... how much?"

Martin looked at his fingers, but there were not enough fingers! Shawn closed his eyes and regretted not paying attention to his math teachers during class.

"144 dollars!" Father Gabriel told them, puzzled by their ignorance of simple math problems.

"Wow! Over a hundred bucks for the three days for each one of us!" exclaimed Martin.

The boys started mentioning the things they could buy with that much money. Gabriel made a suggestion:

"Remember to give ten percent of what you earn to the church. Then I suggest you give fifty percent of the remaining money to your mothers. You can put some money in savings, ten percent of that, and spend the rest in whatever you want."

"Shawn and Martin looked at each other and decided they would not even try to tackle the problem of figuring percentages."

"Do you have a calculator handy?" asked Shawn, looking at Martin and then at the priest.

"We will see you after we get paid, and then we'll decide how to split the cash, Father," said Martin, taking the easy way out.

Father laughed at their inability to work with numbers and their ability to spend what they had not yet earned. He thought about tutoring the two in math some evenings to motivate them to learn more about math, science, religion, English and the like. This was a start of his relationship with the boys; only time would tell if it could actually have an impact in their lives. He remembered a silly joke that he related to the kids.

"A guy was walking by the side of a mental institution. There was a tall wall dividing the property from the sidewalk outside. As he walked along, he heard some chanting on the other side of the wall, 'ate-ate-ate-ate-ate-ate-ate!' The guy was puzzled by the chanting; it sounded like a group of mental patients was having fun on the other side of the wall. Luckily, the young man noticed that there was a hole in the wall, so he decided to take a peek. The rhythmic chanting continued, 'Ate-ate-ate-ate-ate!' As soon as he positioned his eye on the hole, someone from the other side, one of the crazy guys, poked him on the eye with a stick. The curious guy quickly retreated covering his eye and crying in pain while on the other side the chanting stopped for a moment and then started again but with a new song. 'Nine-nine-nine-nine-nine!'"

They arrived at Martin's apartment still laughing. Violeta came out to receive them and approached the priest on the driver's side before he left. She kissed his hand and thanked him for helping her son. He blessed her and drove away with a smile of satisfaction. Things were working out very well as usual. Violeta let go a sigh as she saw the priest leaving.

"Why couldn't Martin's father be like Father Gabriel, even just a little?" she asked herself as the Priestmobile disappeared down the west side street.

On his way back, Gabriel parked his Priestmobile and walked to Don

Pedrito's pawnshop nearby to say hello and ask the shop owner something about the watch he had fished out of the lake. Pedro Mireles was happy to see the priest and unlocked the door for him. Although the pawnshop was still closed at that hour of the morning, the old man liked to come early and read the newspaper in the office. He then had coffee and tamales or pan dulce (sweet bread) before setting up the displays for the business day. Don Pedrito loved to argue with Father Gabriel about politics. While the old guy claimed to be a pure Democrat, the priest would have nothing but Republican ideas to defend. This morning, Pedro had some barbacoa tacos for his breakfast, so the unannounced guest agreed to share the meal with his old friend.

"Come in, Father G; it is so good to see you! What miracle is this that you may descend to visit with the poor?" asked the pawnshop owner jokingly.

"You know I have to continue doing these miracles for you to keep a candle lit under my statue! Actually, if you are one of the poor, then I will have to add Bill Gates, Steve Forbes and Donald Trump to the same list!"

"Come on, Father! You know I hardly make a living in this wretched business," replied Pedro.

"I didn't come here to ask for donations this time," Gabriel said. "I just wanted to say shalom and ask you a professional question about something I have."

"Well shalom to you too. How can I help you, my holy friend?"

"Cut out the 'holy' stuff, I am a sinner almost as big as you! Check this out and tell me what would be its worth."

The priest pulled the ladies' watch out of his pocket and gave it to the jeweler. While Pedro went to get his jeweler's magnifying glass, Gabriel poured himself some strong coffee and grabbed a taco from the friend's desk.

"Hey, where did you find this baby, Father G?" asked the business owner taking a close look at the diamonds to make sure they were real.

Gabriel was adding some hot sauce to his taco.

"I fished it out of a lake this morning. I went fishing with Martin and Shawn, a couple of kids from the housing projects that I am working with, to get them away from their gang. We caught no fish, but I caught that little watch. My two young friends were called back to go to work for another friend of mine. You know him, David Peters."

"Yeah, yeah, the big cowboy; he bought a hunting rifle from me last month. This watch is not too bad. I would give you 500 dollars right now for it, Father."

The priest knew then that the watch was worth at least 5,000 dollars if Pedro was willing to give him only 500. Gabriel took a good gulp of his black coffee and said:

"I am not selling it. How much would you charge me for cleaning it up?"

"Ummm! For you, how about 25 dollars? Unless... you took me on, and beat me, in arm wrestling, in which case it would be free. If you dare, I'll even throw in a nice case for it."

The sixty-year-old man started rolling up his sleeve as the minister pondered on the wisdom of taking on such a challenge. Pedro had arms like a gorilla because he worked out with weights everyday. Gabriel decided to take him on; he had nothing to lose anyway. They positioned themselves on opposite sides of the corner of the table after pushing the remaining breakfast tacos to the side. They grabbed each other's right hand, counted to three and began pushing the other's arm with muscular power. Pedro was really strong and began gaining on Gabriel; the old man was the barrio arm wrestling champion. The priest gathered all his might and brought his arm back up with a scream. Pedro was surprised to see that he was not able to finish the priest off as quickly as he thought he would. Both of their arms were getting filled with blood, their veins sticking out. For several seconds, the hands remained interlocked and static at the top. The arm wrestlers looked each other in the eyes with great determination.

"Are you ready to give up, Father?" said the older man.

"Does that mean that you are tired already and cannot hold it anymore, Pedro?" replied the priest.

They smiled at each other, both faking ease in maintaining their position. The arms were trembling from the great effort. Pedro's forehead began to show some droplets of sweat. One of them rolled down and got into his eye, causing him to blink and break his stare on the priest's eyes. Gabriel roared like a lion and pushed the old man's muscular arm down to the table.

"You blink; you lose, my friend!" Gabriel said, getting up and at the same time rubbing his arm as if it were hurt. "Old man, I think I should have paid the 25 dollars. I didn't know it was going to be so hard to beat you. Are you made of steel or what?" the priest continued saying in honor of his worthy opponent.

Pedro Mireles flexed his muscular arm and said with pride:

"I manage to stay in shape. You never know when you might need to wrestle a thief or some other evil-doer."

"Amen to that!" said the priest in approval.

After breakfast, Gabriel placed the shiny watch in the nice red velvet case that the old man gave him as a prize for his victory in arm wrestling. He put it in his pocket and left the shop heading back towards his house. A pickup pulled up to his side on the street as he walked.

"Hey, Father Gabriel. How are you doing? I heard you went fishing this morning."

It was David Peters with the two boys already in the truck.

"Shalom, my friend. Thank you so much for giving these guys a job," Gabriel said.

After exchanging a few words, the driver of the pickup pulled a pair of theater tickets from his shirt pocket and gave them to the pedestrian.

"Here, Father, take these two tickets as a token of my appreciation for getting me these two workers. They seem to be eager to do some hard work."

"Oh, no, you don't need to give me anything. It is I who owe you for your kindness to my friends," Gabriel told the rancher.

"Please, Father, take them. You see, my wife came down with some type of virus and will not be able to go to the play. Me, I am not much into theater, you know. I heard that you like the arts and this kind of stuff, so go ahead and have a good time. I just ask you that you pray for my wife if you would."

The rancher placed the tickets in the priest's shirt pocket and drove off waving good-bye and smiling at him in his rearview mirror. Gabriel raised his eyes to heaven and asked God for the health of Mrs. Peters. At that exact moment the fever left her. She got up from her bed and was surprised to see that she no longer felt sick, had no pain to her throat and her voice was back to normal. She poured herself a cup of coffee and wondered what had happened for her to recover her health from one moment to the next. She had not taken any medication. She picked up the phone and called her husband's cell phone to share her joy. David could not believe it, but he told his wife about his request that the priest pray for her. She confirmed the time at which she had been healed, which was right after David left the priest. They had heard about Gabriel's miracles but had not believed until that day. Martin and Shawn looked at each other amazed listening to Mr. Peter's phone conversation with his wife. Shawn just shrugged his shoulders.

Father G got into his 35 Chevy without thinking too much about what he was doing. He was going out for a ride to listen to some classical music and enjoy the beautiful day, his day off, before someone came over and grabbed him for something. He meandered around the parish greeting people as he passed by. He saw a big black guy reading a story to some children outside a corner store, under the shade of a tree. It was Dominique Watkins, the "Bull." Father G honked at him and waved at the group. Dominique gave the priest a very wide and white smile.

"Yo, Father G. How you doing?"

"Splendidly well, Nicky. I see that you are becoming a storyteller. Good for you!"

"Yeah! You know you had a lot to do with me doing this now. Thank you, my friend!" the man responded

"Any time! I will see you guys later; I am cruising and jamming."

Gabriel drove off while the heavyweight sat back down to continue reading the story to the elementary-school-aged children around him.

It had been a few months since Nicky had changed his ways from the neighborhood bully to the neighborhood protector. Gabriel had heard about him beating up on people. Dominique was a very strong young man who used to play football in high school before he dropped out, to go into business by himself, pimping, selling drugs, and terrorizing the area. Father G recalled learning that Dominique was using little kids as runners to deliver crack cocaine in the neighborhood. The kids delivered the stuff hidden inside their bikes handles. Timmy, James Bravo's adopted son, was recruited to do the same. The minister caught the boy as he was making a drop near the gym and asked him what was going on. Timmy explained to the priest that he was just doing a little work for his friend Dominique. He would get paid well if he delivered the stuff, and he would get beaten if he did not do it. Gabriel felt his blood boiling, thinking how low can a bully get, using an eight-year-old to help him sell his poison. The bull was aware that if the boy got caught with the drugs, he could not be charged because of his age, so he liked to use children under ten to distribute the drugs. The priest asked Timmy where the bull was and headed in that direction to find him. At that time he had a couple of his girls and a couple of his male companions with him inside an apartment in the public housing. Father G knew that they were armed, but he was not afraid.

"This is the end of the road for you, Dominique!" said the priest, pushing his way into the place to confront the drug dealer.

"Who the fuck are you? What the fuck are you talking about?"

Dominique had raised his big hand to signal his gunmen to hold off on pulling their automatics when he saw that this was a religious minister. Gabriel was wearing his white clergy collar. The two girls pulled down their short dresses and crossed their legs in the sofa trying to appear "proper." The priest looked at them and felt pity at their obviously sinful and misguided way of life.

"I am Father Gabriel, pastor of the Holy Trinity Church. I know what you do for a living, and I have come to tell you that you must stop now, or face the consequences."

The muscular black man got up from the sofa and defiantly blew some marijuana smoke in the priest's face.

"Who the fuck you think you are to come and tell me what to do, man? I ain't even Catholic. What makes you think you can just stop me from living my life as I see fit?" Bull's fist tightened as if ready to hit the intruder. He went on saying, "You come, uninvited, into my house, insult me in front of my friends, and threaten me. I think I ought to kick your reverend ass right here."

Dominique grabbed the priest by the shirt and got him close to his face trying to intimidate him. Although the Bull was a little bigger than the athletic minister, the smaller man kept his stare and showed no fear. It was Dominique who felt ashamed looking into the priest's calm eyes. His four friends were all smiles thinking they were going to witness another beating by their tough leader as they had other times.

"You know I can have you killed right here? What do you want with me?" the younger man said, releasing the priest.

His followers were surprised to see him step back and drop his arms.

"I want you to change your way of life. You are dragging my people into the sewer. Today I learned you recruited my little friend Timmy Bravo, the gym owner's son. I will not let you corrupt him, or anyone else anymore," Gabriel told him.

One of the men pulled his gun and put it to the back of the priest's head.

"Do you want me to do the priest, Bull?"

The girls got scared thinking Joshua would pull the trigger; he had killed three men already at his tender age of eighteen. Bull looked at the priest's face. He certainly was not afraid. Gabriel kept looking at Bull intensely, and ignoring the man with the gun to his head.

"What makes you think I would listen to you?" he growled.

There was something in Gabriel's intense brown eyes that, just by staring at him, got to the marrow of the young thug's bones. It was as if the minister could see Bull's soiled soul. He felt a chill run down his spine, so he turned away from the priest's stare.

"I tell you what, priest. If you can beat me in a fight, I will listen to you."

For some reason, Bull thought the holy man would never accept that challenge and would retreat to his church business.

"OK, let's go to the gym. I don't want to be arrested for fighting you out in the street," was the immediate answer from the priest.

He turned around and headed back to the gym, totally ignoring the gunman who put his gun away as if he were ashamed of it. The Bull's followers looked at him and asked:

"Are you serious? Why do you want to beat on the minister, man?"

The girls encouraged him:

"Yeah, daddy. Whip his ass to show everybody that you are the man."

The gunman had heard about the priest, so he warned the Bull:

"You better be careful, Bull, this ain't no ordinary priest."

Bull finished his marijuana cigarette and took off his shirt.

"You just watch me handle this mother fucker. I own this turf, and no one's going to come tell me what to do!" he shot back.

His bulging muscles looked as hard as a rock on Dominique. He walked fast with his four friends behind him. The girls invited people to come and watch the Bull kick some ass at the gym.

Gabriel threw some gloves at Dominique when he entered the gym. The priest was already in the ring without his shirt. He did not look like a priest up there. He had a chiseled body that looked just as powerful as the Bull's. Dominique put on the gloves with the help of his friends and got on the ring staring at his opponent. Gabriel stared back showing no fear; Dominique turned his eyes to avoid those of the priest's. The gang leader felt mad that the older guy would not give in to his menacing looks. It was Bull whose legs felt weak looking into Gabriel's calm eyes.

Timmy, Gabriel's protégé, rang the bell.

"The fight is over when you give up or get knocked out," announced the priest moving around gracefully like a consummate fighter.

"No, the fight is over when you give up, after I beat you senseless, priest," was the bull's confident reply.

Bull threw several punches with all his might. Gabriel avoided all of them by sliding, sidestepping, and moving his body up and down, or side to side. Bull got even angrier seeing that he could not connect. He was used to tackling and pushing but not boxing. The priest danced around the bigger opponent and threw a couple of jabs that immediately opened the Bull's lower lip and caused him to begin bleeding.

"Shit, I am going to kill you now, mother fucker!"

Dominique charged towards the priest who simply moved to the side to let him go and avoid his push. Bull tripped on the minister's right foot and fell on the canvas. He jumped up, angrier, and swung with the right and the left. Father G blocked one and ducked to avoid the other one. Then he launched a jab and a hook that shook the Bull's head. The younger man hugged the priest to avoid falling again after the two solid punches. Father Gabriel pushed him away from him and against the ropes. As he bounced back from the ropes, the Bull's face met both of his opponent's fists three times, drumming his head at high speed. Everything turned black in the gym for him. He felt nothing else. The Bull's followers could not believe how easily the priest had done away with the tough gang leader. No one else in the neighborhood dared to even talk back to the Bull, and he had beaten everybody he had fought in the street. Now the tough guy lay flat on his back.

His followers left him and went back to their homes. Father Gabriel helped Dominique to recover.

"Are you back, Nicky?" the priest asked him, slapping his face lightly as he sat on a stool in a corner of the ring.

"Yeah...what happened?" the still-dizzy thug asked the priest.

"The power of God has touched you, to bring you back home where you belong," was the priest's answer.

At that precise instant, Father Gabriel's back felt as if on fire. He knew something was about to happen, so he placed his hands on the young thug's head and prayed over him.

"Oh, Heavenly Father, I ask you to open the eyes of this child of yours, so that he may see the future that awaits him on the road he is following."

Dominique had a vision of hell. His father and mother were there. His prostitute girls were there. His drug friends were there. They were extending their arms and trying to grab him to sink him into the dark with them. The place was dark and frigid although it was on fire. Bull heard lamentation and deep, sorrowful cries. He experienced the greatest fear he had ever felt in his life. Then he heard Gabriel's voice again.

"Thank you, Lord! I beg you to open your arms and receive Dominique back into your kingdom. Touch his heart and call him to you, so that he may live to praise your name and do your will for the rest of his life. I ask you this in the name of Jesus, your son, who lives and reigns with you and the Holy Spirit, one God, forever and ever, Amen."

THE TEMPTATION OF THE MIRACLE WEAVER

Dominique fell from the stool down to his knees on the canvas at Gabriel's feet.

"Forgive me, Father!" he whispered.

The bully broke down and cried, hugging the priest by the waist. Gabriel hugged his shoulders and placed his hand on the young man's head.

"Welcome back, son!"

He helped Dominique get back on his feet and accompanied him out of the gym. Little Timmy had watched it all from outside the ring; he was speechless and ecstatic about the outcome of the fight.

"You know what to do, Nicky. Go now and do it," Gabriel said to the recovering fighter.

He then patted Dominique's muscular back and sent him home without any more instructions. Gabriel was sure the Holy Spirit would guide the reformed man.

Returning from that memory, Father G found himself driving in the direction of the sisters' house. When he was a couple of blocks away, he stopped his car and wondered where he was going. He questioned his subconscious and realized that he wanted to give the watch to Theresa as a birthday present, the present he meant to give her twenty years before. This was the day to do it! He let go of the brake and continued approaching their address. He stopped the car again dismissing that idea as silly. He thought he should make better use of the valuable watch to feed the hungry with the cash it could bring in. Again he convinced himself that all the signs were right for him to give Theresa the watch and invite her to the theater with those tickets. He had not even planned it; it was meant to be this way! He put the car in motion again very sure that he should just do it, but he stopped again half a block away from the sisters' house. The driver behind him got tired of his frequent stops and passed him, honking his horn and shooting the finger at the priest. Gabriel smiled and sent the irate driver a blessing in return. He was definitely going to drive away, but suddenly Sister Theresa came running towards his car. She had been outside watering the plants when the horn of the irate driver called her attention to the Priestmobile.

"Father Gabriel, what are you doing over here today?" she questioned him.

"Well, I am cruising around the parish and listening to classical music," he claimed.

"Oh, that's very nice! Listen, it's good to see you. I need to go buy the groceries, and the sisters took the van to Corpus Christi for a conference over the weekend. Could I ask you to give me a ride, please?"

Sister made the most angelic little girl's face, pleading for his help. He could not refuse.

"Hop in, Theresa. It will be my pleasure to help you get the groceries," he said, acting as if it were an unexpected burden that he must bear.

"Great! Let me get my purse and turn the water off."

She ran back into the house after cutting off the water. Father G got out of the car.

Theresa came back wearing a flowery sundress that made her look like a beautiful flower herself. Gabriel opened the door for her to get in his car; he enjoyed smelling her perfume as she passed by him to enter the vehicle.

"How come the sisters didn't stay to celebrate your birthday?" asked Gabriel as they drove away from the house.

"Oh, I didn't mention it to them. I stopped celebrating birthdays a while back," Theresa replied, dismissing the event as unimportant.

"Well apparently it is working out for you. You look gorgeous and young at... 28?" said the minister with a smile.

"Yeah, right! You know my age, so I don't have to pretend with you. We are both getting kind of old. I remember when my mother was my age; I thought she was an old lady. Now that I am here, I feel that the 60s would be old, not the 30s, but thank you for the compliment."

They spent two hours at the supermarket buying groceries like any regular couple.

Father G found a little girl lying prone on an aisle of the supermarket, coloring a horse in a book. She had taken down the book and some crayons from a shelf. He stopped to check out the young artist's work; she got up with a lollipop in her mouth and showed the man her piece of art.

"This is very nice! Hey Theresa, look at this!"

The priest called the sister away from the mushroom cans to show her the colored horse. The girl continued sucking on her lollipop, enjoying the positive critique.

"Oh, wow! Did you color this horsy yourself?"

Theresa squatted down to the girl's eye level; the little artist beamed with pride and nodded her head admitting she did it.

"What is your name?" Theresa asked the child, brushing some hair off her face and behind her ear.

"Dorothy."

"Well, Dorothy, it is nice to meet you. I am Theresa and this is Father

Gabriel."

The priest extended his hand to shake Dorothy's little hand and said:

"I think you are a great artist. Keep practicing so that you may give the world lots of nice pictures of horses and flowers and all kinds of colorful things."

At that time, an assistant-manager-in-training came to the trio with an open box of cookies and a torn bag of lollipops like the one Dorothy had in her mouth.

"Please, don't let your daughter run around unsupervised. Look at this!" he said.

Dorothy got scared because the man sounded so serious; she hid behind the two new friends and peeked around Theresa's dress to look at the angry man.

"I hope you are going to pay for those crayons and the coloring book as well," the man exclaimed.

The employee put on a more serious face as if he had caught them committing a major crime. Father Gabriel put his hand on the man's shoulder and explained they were not the parents of the child. He invited the clerk to ask the child, since he seemed not to believe him.

"Come here, kid. Tell me, who are these people?"

Dorothy hesitated to approach the man even though he was trying to smile at her. Theresa helped her by lightly pushing her forward, to tell the man who they were.

"She is Theresa, and he is Father..."

Dorothy ran back behind Theresa's dress. Gabriel looked at Theresa; then both of them looked at the store clerk who was shaking his head. Gabriel was wearing black jeans and a white pullover shirt; Theresa had her sundress and sandals. They certainly did not look like a pair of religious ministers.

"Man, I can't believe you would deny your own child," the store clerk said.

Gabriel was going to explain, but at that moment the real mother came running after her child. There was both relief and anxiety in her voice.

"Dorothy Marie Parker! Why won't you listen? I told you to stay in the restroom with me."

The woman looked at the three people by her child and asked:

"What did she do now?"

The assistant manager trainee apologized to Theresa and Gabriel and turned to the mother to show her the packages the girl had opened. The clerk and the mother walked towards the registers. Dorothy turned to wave goodbye and sent her new friends a little kiss. Gabriel pretended to catch it in the air and planted it on Theresa's cheek, to the delight of the girl.

"Well, that was an adventure!" commented the religious sister going back to the mushroom cans.

"Yeah, it was nice for a moment to imagine that she was ours. She kind of looks like you, the same color of hair and cute smile," Gabriel told her.

Theresa did not say anything but thought that it would have been nice if the girl were theirs and they were buying the weekly groceries for their home. She wondered what life would have been if they had stayed together as they planned when they were in high school. Eventually they finished the grocery shopping and returned home.

When they got back to the house, Gabriel helped Theresa bring all the groceries in and put them on the kitchen table. As they came in, the front screen door lost its upper hinge and came loose. The gentleman offered to fix it while the lady put the food away. She told him to look in the closet for some tools, and he went to work right away. The sisters had a decently equipped toolbox, which Gabriel brought out to repair the loose top hinge, and the bottom one too because it was also coming loose. While he was working on the carpentry repair job, he remembered a song and began singing loud enough to be heard inside the kitchen. His strong, melodious voice reverberated throughout the house and touched Theresa's heart. In the song, the poet called his beloved guilty of causing all his anguish and broken heart, of filling his life with sweetness and bitterness at the same time. One of the verses claimed the poet would give his life to overcome the fear of kissing her. He enjoyed telling her those things in song; she enjoyed very much hearing them.

Gabriel whistled a melodious intermission and peeked inside the kitchen. Theresa was already cooking something. The delicious smell of tasty food entered his nostrils and tickled his stomach. He repeated the last verse of the song and finished his repair job. After he put the tools away, he brought Theresa back to the door for her approval.

"Wow! You did a fantastic job. You have been blessed with many talents," she said, opening and closing the now steady screen door.

"Remember that I am the son of a carpenter. I learned a thing or two from my dad," he reminded Theresa.

She smiled and looked at him, then she said:

"Ah, yes! You should have been named Jesus, son of a carpenter, miracle worker."

"You know, it is funny. My dad's name is Jose Arturo, and my mom's name is Maria de la Luz, Joseph and Mary!" Gabriel told her. "But they are not Jewish."

They laughed and walked in towards the kitchen. He washed his hands and was going to excuse himself and leave; however, Theresa announced that lunch was served already. She said it was the least she could do for him after all his help.

"If you don't mind eating leftover lasagna that I cooked yesterday."

"I love lasagna!" he said, knowing that if it had been cold black beans she was going to feed him, he would "love" cold black beans.

Their lunch was relaxed but started slightly formal. He acted as the pastor and principal of the school parish while she acted like the first grade teacher and music minister. They kept a polite conversation about the weather, the school, Europe, food, music, art and theater. She remembered seeing "The Lady from St. Louis" advertised on the paper.

"I have wanted to see that show. I read that it is going to be in the city all this week."

Gabriel gulped the last of his red wine and smiled.

"Sister, I think you should pray for our Lord to let you go see that musical for your birthday."

"Oh, come on, Father," she laughed, dismissing the idea as silly with a hand gesture.

"Please, believe in miracles, Theresa. Let's close our eyes for a moment of silence and ask God for what is in your heart on your birthday."

She complied with his request. Gabriel made sure she was not looking and pulled the two tickets from his pocket to place them on the table in front of the woman.

"Open your eyes child. The Lord knows what you want even before you ask Him."

Theresa picked up the tickets in disbelief.

"But Father... How?"

He put his finger over his lips signaling for her to be silent and stop questioning him.

"Say no more. Happy birthday, Terry! Accept the tickets and also this gift."

He pulled out the red case and opened it to let her see the watch. She was truly surprised because it was so unexpected. She actually needed a watch because she had given hers to Rebecca Sterling before departing from Ireland. She hesitated to take the expensive-looking watch, although she liked it at first sight.

"Please, accept it, Terry, it was meant to be your gift today. I waited twenty years to give you a watch. I hear that if you want to have a good time, you ought to have a good watch. Listen, I did not even have to buy these tickets or the watch."

"Did you steal them, Gabe?"

"Ha, ha, ha! No. I am just the delivery boy. God sent you these gifts, Terry."

All of a sudden they were calling each other by their juvenile sweetheart names, Terry and Gabe. The formality of lunch was broken away. He was sitting on a chair next to hers helping her put on the gold watch which fit her wrist perfectly.

He went on to tell her about how he fished the watch out of the lake and had to arm-wrestle Pedro for the case and cleaning. Then he explained the tickets that David gave him for the workers he got him.

"All right, all right! I accept them, but with one condition."

She grabbed Gabriel's hands and looked into his dark brown eyes.

"What condition, Terry?" he asked her.

"You will have to take me to the theater tonight because I have no one else to go with. I don't even have transportation, and I know that you will enjoy the show."

"Your wish is my command, your highness!"

Gabriel kissed her hand as if she were a queen and got up to leave.

"I am going to take a shower and change. I'll be back to pick you up in a couple of hours, or do you need more time... to romp around the house nude as you like to do?"

Theresa covered her face remembering the time he found her coming out of the shower, but then she picked up a napkin and threw it at him playfully.

"No, I don't need more time to 'romp around the house nude.' I will be ready in two hours!"

A black cat with red eyes seemed to smile from the window where it was sitting watching the two religious walk towards the front door. After Gabriel drove off, Theresa turned to see the cat as she was coming back in. The cat jumped down from the window outside the house. Theresa went to the open window to take a second look at the black feline, but it had disappeared. The religious wondered if she had actually seen red eyes on the animal or if it had been just her imagination. Thinking about the cat, she felt goose bumps on her arms for a second, but when she rubbed her left arm, she found her new watch on her wrist and admired it with great pleasure. Gabriel was so sweet to her and so good at knowing what she needed! She picked up the dishes from the dining room table and went to get ready for their date. Theresa was very excited with the idea of going out with her former boyfriend on her birthday. She wondered if he was still her "former boyfriend" or if they could just drop the "former" part. As she got into the shower, Theresa thought that they were playing with fire and that it might be better to call it off, but then she remembered Gabriel's song and convinced herself there was nothing wrong with loving him so much. Humming the song he had sung, she turned on the shower and got in, having decided to go through with their plan.

Chapter VII
The Date

Gabriel Infante went back to the Theresa Reynolds' house too soon. Although she was ready to go, the play was not going to start until three hours later. They decided to head downtown and kill some time there. The couple passed by the central library and drove around the main plaza by the old cathedral and the county courthouse. When they were passing by the Rivercenter Mall, Gabriel remembered a good place where they could go spend a couple of hours before the play, the Museum of Art! Theresa liked the idea and agreed they should go.

"Have you painted anything lately?" she asked him remembering he used to paint as a youth.

"I hardly have any time. You know, taking the teachers out to the theater and dinner does not leave me much time for my art!" he said.

"Oh really? You mean to tell me you take all your teachers out like this?"

"Of course not, I am exploring new territory here with you!"

They arrived to the museum and agreed it was always interesting to visit such places. Theresa was attracted to an abstract painting and stopped in front of it, trying to understand it. She claimed it was nice but there was something strange about the piece. Gabriel got behind her to have a similar view; he got his face so close to hers that her hair caressed his ear. He inhaled the violet perfume emanating from her neck. She felt her personal space invaded but did not object.

"Let's take a very close look at it, as close to the painting as we can," Gabriel suggested.

He held her shoulders and eased her forward, slowly, until she almost touched the painting with her nose.

"Relax your eyes in front of it and see what impression you get at this range."

Still with his hands on her soft shoulders, he started pulling her back a tiny step at the time, stopping and taking another look at the whole piece. He explained the fine points of the composition and rhythm of the painting, talked about the meaning, the relationship of the media and the title of the work. Meanwhile he was getting inebriated with her aroma and her proximity. She felt excited herself, so to break the spell she felt she was falling under, she turned around to compliment him for his deep artistic perception and his understanding of the abstract painting.

"You do know a lot about abstract art!" she said.

"Actually, I was reading you this critique from the information brochure I got at the front desk. I personally think it's a strange piece too," he told her with a big smile.

"Cheater!" exclaimed Theresa, playfully punching him on the shoulder.

They continued their tour of the museum until it was almost time for them to go to the theater. When they were going down the stairs, one of Theresa's heels got caught in the carpet. She tripped and lost her balance. Gabriel caught her in his arms quickly.

"Thank you! I thought I was going to roll down the stairs and break my neck," she said.

"I couldn't let that happen because the theater tickets are only good for tonight. I would hate to waste them! Also, just imagine having to be in the emergency room instead, that wouldn't be much fun, would it?" Gabriel told her without releasing the sister from his arms.

A security guard looked up at them from the lower level and cleared his throat. Gabriel let Theresa go and just held her hand as they made their way to the first floor. Theresa did not mind having his arms around her but was content with just holding hands.

The couple of long-time friends enjoyed the musical from beginning to end. It was interesting and well performed, but mainly, they were in each other's company. This fact made a simple walk down the street an enjoyable experience. After leaving the theater, Gabriel and Theresa went down to the river walk to stretch their legs a little and look for a place to have supper. The other sisters would not be home until the next day, so there was no reason for Theresa to return home early.

Gabriel felt like walking on clouds, but he thought about what they were doing. His conscience questioned his behavior. They were out on a date like any other man and woman. His conservative side ordered him to put an end to it to avoid further temptation, but he found himself wanting to smell her perfume, to breathe her breath, to touch her face and hair, to listen to her laughter, to hold her hand and walk all night like that. His weak human side dismissed his conscience and rationalized that there was absolutely nothing wrong happening between them. He decided to keep enjoying the evening and give Theresa the best possible time. Theresa was thinking exactly the same thing. Both came to the same conclusion, to let things fall where they might and enjoy their evening out. They looked at each other and smiled, standing in a dark area of the river walk, wondering what to say to break their momentary silence. Theresa said she was craving some Mexican food and would like to go to a restaurant where they had live music. He told her he knew a good place, not too far away.

Suddenly, a dark figure emerged from the shadows and grabbed Theresa's purse. She instinctively reacted by holding on to it. The purse-snatcher gave it a hard tug and took off, knocking her down to the ground in the process. Gabriel, filled with loving concern, helped her to her feet.

"Are you all right, Terry?"

"Yes. I am all right, but he took my purse."

She straightened her skirt and looked in the direction in which the thief fled. Like an Olympic sprinter, Gabriel took off after the criminal.

"Noooo! Gabe, let him go!" Theresa called out, worried that he might get hurt.

The thief was well ahead of the priest. To make matters worse, a drunkard came out of a bar stumbling in front of the running minister. Father G made a spinning movement to avoid pushing the drunk into the river. Gabriel rolled over a table on his back and landed on his feet to continue the chase. The drunkard spun around looking at the runner and wondering what was going on. Gabriel saw that the thief went over a bridge across the river, and then came back but on the other side of the river heading for the stairs to the street level. The priest looked at him angrily as the young bandit waved the purse and taunted him. There was no time for Gabriel to run to the bridge and catch up with the thief before he reached the street and got lost among the crowd. The thief laughed and started going upstairs towards the street. Father G raised his eyes to the night sky and asked God for assistance. He crossed himself and started running full speed over the waters of the river without sinking! Sister Theresa saw him and put her hand on her mouth in amazement and disbelief. Gabriel raced up the stairs three at the time and caught up with the criminal.

The thief felt a strong hand grabbing his ankle as he was stepping out of the stairs and onto the street. He tripped and fell, face first, losing a couple of teeth upon impact with the sidewalk. Two bicycle policemen standing a block away saw him hit the ground. Father G was jumping on top of the thief. Gabriel grabbed the purse-snatcher and picked him up from the ground with fury. The officers rode their bikes towards the two men and advised the dispatcher there was a fight in progress.

The priest slammed the thief against the wall and demanded to have the purse back. Gabriel was holding the young thug up, feet dangling in the air, his body pressed against the wall. The thief felt real fear feeling the great strength of the man holding him. He pulled the purse out of his shirt and dropped it.

"Please, please, don't hurt me anymore!" the thief said as the two officers jumped on Father Gabriel and grabbed him by the arms.

Seeing that these were law enforcement officers, he relaxed in their grasp. One of the officers pulled out his handcuffs to hold the big guy. The thief, at that instant, saw his chance to escape and took off running to disappear down the alley.

"Thank you, very much officers. You just let a purse-snatcher escape!" Gabriel informed them.

The officers looked at the purse on the floor, then looked at each other. They unhandcuffed the priest, got on their bikes to give chase and started putting out the thief's description on the radio.

Theresa came up the stairs looking for Gabriel and was relieved to find him as soon as she emerged from the river walk onto the street.

"Gabe, are you OK? Oh, you got my purse back, thank you! Where is the boy that stole it?"

"Yes, I am OK. I got the purse back, and the boy is running around the downtown area, playing hide and go seek with the police," Gabriel reported giving her the purse back.

As they started walking toward the parking lot, Theresa had to ask him, "Did I just see you walk on water?"

"No Terry, Jesus walked on water; I had to run over it, ha, ha, ha! I could not believe it myself, but it worked! I asked God to help me catch up with the thief to get your purse back, and He answered my prayer. Let's go to the car. I got really hungry from all the excitement."

They went to one of the popular Mexican restaurants on the shallow west side, at the edge of downtown, to eat and have margaritas while listening to the live mariachi band. The hostess gave them a booth in between two others. There was a big crowd eating, drinking and having a good time there. The smell of mouth-watering Mexican food floated around as traditional Mexican music filled the area.

"Thank you for bringing me here. The whole day has been a pleasure in your company," said Theresa placing her hand on his as they reviewed the menus.

"Terry, the pleasure has been all mine. Never in my wildest dreams did I imagine that we could be like this, having fun together at this stage of our lives."

He looked deep into her eyes while holding her hand.

Gabriel turned to see a little boy who was standing on a chair and tilting it backwards, making it stand on the back two legs. He was trying to keep his balance on the chair while his parents decided what to order. The priest smiled at the boy and then had to reach out quickly and catch him as the child came down when the chair tilted too far back.

"Whoa! I got you big guy. I think you have to turn around and sit down. Save the acrobatics for home," he advised the little fellow.

The priest picked up the chair with the boy hanging on to his neck like a monkey. Gabriel placed him back on his chair and smiled at his parents.

"Thank you, sir!" both of the parents said to Gabriel in unison and then turned to the boy.

"I have told you before not to be playing at the table, Justin. You could have hit someone or hurt yourself!" the mother said, scolding the boy.

Father Gabriel turned his attention to Sister Theresa and, inspired by the little incident, told her another one of his jokes.

"There was an acrobat who worked for a circus. He was very good, but he had a weakness for wine. One day in a certain small town, the circus held a one-day show. At the end of the performance, the acrobat, named Duffus, went to check out one of the local bars. They only had one school and one church in the town, but half a dozen bars thrived in the little place. Duffus found that all their wine was excellent and their prices reasonable. He drank until he ran out of money and lost consciousness. The circus manager was tired of his constant drinking and disappearing, so he decided to move the circus that night and move on to the next town on schedule, leaving Duffus behind to fend for himself..."

Gabriel interrupted his joke because a waiter brought them iced water, some tortilla chips and hot sauce to keep them occupied until their orders were ready. Theresa ordered a strawberry margarita; Gabriel ordered a regular frozen margarita. She asked for some green chicken enchiladas while he asked for a beef fajita plate. The waiter took their order and left. Father G continued his story after chomping a chip with sauce.

"Well, the next morning, our friend Duffus the acrobat woke up with a splitting headache, hungry, thirsty and sore outside the bar, lying on the hard sidewalk. An old lady was sweeping the street and looked at him with disgust. Duffus asked if she could give him something to drink. She raised her broom to shoo him away. Duffus got up and ran away from the old lady before she could hit him with the broom. He realized he knew no one in town. He had no money left in his pockets. Duffus noticed that the field where the circus had been the night before was empty; he knew where the circus was going. All he had to do was catch up with them, but he also needed money for the bus fare. He heard the church bell ringing and thought that the priest, being a man of God, would have mercy on him and lend him some money. Duffus got to the church as the priest was leaving his house to hear confessions. The acrobat begged the minister for his help, explaining his situation. He needed only a little money for the bus fare. The priest felt pity on him and gave him the money. He also asked his housekeeper to feed the man with the hangover and let him wash his hands and face before he left. Duffus was very happy. He had the money he needed; he ate and drank some water, juice and then coffee with a little brandy until his thirst went away. He washed his face and hands and felt like a new man once it all settled down. He experienced a deep gratitude towards the kind priest and decided to go thank him before going to the bus station..."

There was another interruption in his story as the waiter brought them their drinks. Sister Theresa took a sip of hers right away because the hot sauce was a little too hot for her, but good! The cold drink alleviated her burning lips and tongue.

"You are not even waiting for the toast!" said Gabriel as a reproach, although he was well aware of her situation.

"I am sorry; that hot sauce is hot!" she apologized, blushing a little.

"We could ask for a 'cold' sauce, but I don't think it is quite as good," he suggested.

"Oh, get out of here! You know what I mean," she told him laughing.

"Yes, well, let us toast to our friendship, and that the Lord may grant you many other happy birthdays," said Gabriel raising his Margarita to touch hers.

"To our love! May the Lord bless it and make it everlasting!" she responded, to his delight.

"So what happened with Duffus, Gabe?" asked Theresa dipping another chip in the hot sauce.

"Where was I? Oh, yes! Duffus walked into the church and saw long lines of people, mostly old ladies, on both sides of the confession area. He could not wait for the priest to finish with so many penitents, so he walked right up to the confessional in front of the priest. People looked at him and thought he was starting a third line in front of the priest; however, they just watched him approach the confessor as he finished with the person he was listening to. Duffus said to the priest in a hushed voice, 'Father, I am very thankful for what you have done for me. You saved my life! I would like to show you my appreciation by performing a couple of tricks that I do in my line of work.' The priest, of course, told him that it wouldn't be necessary and dismissed him with his blessing. Duffus begged him to let him do it, and the priest decided to agree so that he could continue with his work. The confessor called the next person to his right. The circus performer looked around and decided to do his act right in front of the priest so that he could watch without interrupting his confessions. Duffus did a handstand on the pews. He then spun his legs together under his arms, switching from arm to arm like an Olympic gymnast. He then did several somersaults and, to finish his show, executed several nice cartwheels over the pews. Two old ladies watched him with eyes wide open in amazement and concern. One of them said to the other in a whisper, 'I think I better go home. Father is really strict today. He is giving somersaults and cartwheels as penance, and I am not wearing panties!'"

Theresa broke down in laughter. She covered her mouth and shook her head.

"Where do you get all these corny jokes?" she asked.

"Hey, this is a true story! Well, the drunken guy who told it to us, at Rosita's Cantina, claimed that it was true," Gabriel said lightheartedly.

"So that's what you go to the bars to do, to learn new material for your homilies?"

"That, and drink some beers, look at the girls, sing a song or two, play cards or dominoes, talk to the people, do a little dancing," explained the priest.

"What kind of priest are you? Where did you learn that this is the way to live as a priest? Was it part of the curriculum at the seminary you attended?" Theresa asked playfully.

"Yes, ma'am," he replied seriously. "This is the way Jesus lived. He was a 'party guy' who enjoyed life with his friends. Some people don't think of me as a role model to their kids, but I don't think I am so bad. Do you think I am bad?"

THE TEMPTATION OF THE MIRACLE WEAVER

"How can a man who runs on water be bad at all?" Theresa answered.

They clinked their glasses again and drank in agreement. The food was served. They continued enjoying their conversation and their dinner.

When they had finished eating, the mariachis came over and asked if they would like a song. Father Gabriel asked them to accompany him singing Las Mananitas (A popular domain Mexican birthday song) for the lady at the table. He got up and borrowed one of their charro hats, as was his custom, to begin singing.

"*Que linda esta la manana en que vengo a saludarte.*
("How pretty is this morning in which I come to greet you.)
Venimos todos con gusto y placer a felicitarte.
(We all come filled with joy and pleasure to congratulate you.)
El dia en que tu naciste, nacieron todas las flores.
(The day that you were born, all the flowers were born too.)
En la pila del bautismo cantaron los ruisenores.
(In the baptismal fount the nightingales were singing.)
Ya viene amaneciendo. Ya la luz del dia nos dio.
(It is already dawning. The light of day is upon us.)
Levantate Teresita. Mira que ya amanecio."
(Get up little Theresa. See the dawn has turned to day.")

Gabriel took Theresa's hand and pulled her up to dance the musical intermission; then he continued the song, still dancing with her in front of the band.

"*Quisiera ser un San Juan. Quisiera ser un San Pedro.*
("I wished to be St. John. I wished to be St. Peter.)
Pa' venirte a saludar con la musica del cielo.
(To come and greet you with music from heaven.)
De las estrellas del cielo, tengo que bajarte dos,
(From the stars of the sky, I got to bring you down two,)
una para saludarte, la otra para decirte adios.
(one to say hello, the other one to say good-bye.)
Con Jazmines y flores hoy te vengo a saludar.
(With jasmines and flowers I have come to greet you today.)
Hoy por ser tu cumpleanos, te venimos a cantar."
(Because today is your birthday, we have come to sing for you.")

All the patrons around clapped in approval of the singer's rendition of the traditional song. Gabriel paid the band and returned their hat. The musicians demanded in choir that the birthday lady pay the singer with a kiss. She obliged and gave him a kiss on the cheek to the applause of the merry mariachi group. Gabriel gave her a tight hug and wished her a happy birthday softly in her ear. The mariachi sang "happy birthday" on their own before leaving the couple alone.

News reporter, Linda McCoy, of one of the local TV stations was filming footage at the restaurant for a program she was working on. She was interviewing tourists and visitors about their impression of the city and if they agreed that a new sports arena should be paid for with a tax hike on hotels and car rentals. A cameraman was following her and recording what was going on at the restaurant. They had filmed the activities of the couple in the middle booth, the eating, drinking, singing, dancing and kissing was all caught by the camera without their being aware of it. When the mariachis left, Linda approached Gabriel and Theresa to interview them.

"Are you two newly wed, or celebrating an anniversary?" she asked.

"No," they both said, surprised by her sudden questioning.

"Are you visitors from out of town? Or are you regulars to this place?" Linda continued.

"Neither one," said Gabriel wondering how to, politely, cut the interview.

"Well, we are asking people what they think about the county paying for a new arena for the Latigos by charging a higher tax on hotels and car rentals. What is your opinion?"

Linda extended the microphone to them. Theresa told her:

"We have no comment. Please, we would like some privacy if you don't mind."

Linda was not pleased with her answer, so she tried to open a different line. She asked:

"OK, would you at least like to say hello to anyone while we have you on our camera?"

Gabriel got a little upset, so he covered the camera lens with his hand and got up. The cameraman stepped back and tripped on the extended leg of another patron sitting in the booth behind them. As he fell, the cameraman tried to hold on to something and pulled a tablecloth with all the dishes, drinks and utensils from a nearby table. Neither the camera nor the man were seriously hurt; however, it looked as if the priest had pushed the man down to end the interview. He tried to help him up, but the man got upset and said not to touch him. Linda was happy the way things turned out and knew they could be used for a little spice in the report. Gabriel asked Theresa to leave the restaurant with him at once.

Theresa was laughing all the way to the car. Gabriel opened the door for her and asked her what was so funny.

"Why did you have to beat up on the poor cameraman in there?" she asked him.

"I did not beat him up. It was an accident, and you know it! I can just see the news, 'Catholic priest and nun found fooling around at local restaurant and engaged in a brawl that resulted in a broken camera and two injured men. The station and the reporters are suing the archdiocese for unspecified damages.'"

"That would be wrong!" said Sister Theresa as the Father Gabriel went to the driver's side and got in the car himself.

"Yes, but it could happen," he said seriously, starting the engine and driving out of the restaurant parking lot.

"I mean it is not 'a priest and a nun.' I am a religious sister, not a nun. Nuns stay in the confines of a convent; sisters go out in the community to serve," Theresa explained, throwing him off.

"You know, Sister Theresa, you are a very funny girl. I am surprised to see how cool you are about the whole incident," said the priest turning to face her and smiling.

"Bah! Don't worry about a thing. I am sure it won't have any serious consequences," Theresa told him, dismissing the whole incident with a hand sweep.

The woman lowered the car window to feel the night breeze blowing her auburn hair. Gabriel turned the radio to a classical station and drove to the sisters' house at a deliberately low speed. Theresa glanced at him as he drove. She decided she liked him much more then than twenty years earlier. She sighed and leaned her head on his shoulder.

"What's the matter, Terry? Are you out of air? Or are you in love?"

"I am in love with you, but I wonder where we are going with this."

"Right now, we are just going to your house," he answered.

"You know what I mean, Gabe."

"Yes, I know what you mean, but I don't know the answer to that," whispered Gabriel shrugging his shoulders. Theresa was a little upset by his evasive answer.

After they finally got home, Gabriel walked her to her door. She thanked him for a wonderful evening. He admitted they had a lot of fun together and suggested they should do it again. She mentioned that maybe they should not. He came close to Theresa's face. She stopped his lips from kissing hers by softly placing her hand on his mouth.

"Good night, Father Gabriel," she said.

He kissed the palm of her hand in understanding.

"Good night, Sister Theresa."

As soon as he got home, he remembered that he had not been reciting his regular prayers every time he spent time with Theresa. Right then, he knelt by his bed and recited the night prayer of that day.

Gabriel was feeling something inside of him, as if he were getting sick, coming down with the flu or something. He did not remember the last time he was sick. It had probably been as a teenager, but he had no clear recollection of it now. He had not been sick as an adult, ever! This sensation inside of him was strange. It felt weakening, but it felt good. He was anxious and excited, tired, and ready to take on the world at the same time. He went outside to smoke a cigar and drink a glass of cognac.

"What a way to end a great day! Thank you Lord for everything you have granted me in this life. Can you give me understanding as to why Theresa is back in my life now?" he asked, looking up at the moon and the stars as though searching for an answer, but none was granted.

On other occasions, a vision or a scripture passage would come to him, but when he asked about Theresa, silence was the only answer. Gabriel gave up, finished his drink and his cigar and went to bed. Normally he was asleep quickly, but lately he had trouble falling asleep. His mind kept reliving the evening. He hugged his pillow as he recalled dancing with his beloved.

It was 1:00 a.m. when the phone rang by Gabriel's bed. He picked it up immediately suspecting it was Theresa. She told him she could not sleep either and that she had been praying for an answer as to why they had been reunited but that no hint or answer had been given to her.

"I have been asking the same question," he told her, "and I got the same answer, none!" He paused for a second and then said, "Anyway, I wanted to stay with you all night."

"Well, I really didn't want you to go. I don't even know what made me stop you when you tried to kiss me tonight, but as you were leaving, I had to lean against the door to keep myself inside and not run after you. I kissed the kiss you left in my hand as my only consolation, but I needed at least to hear your voice again," he heard Theresa say, confessing her own desire.

It felt so good to hear her say those things! For a moment Gabriel felt tempted to get up and run to her house. He could be there in five minutes. Then he decided to relax and be happy just enjoying their phone conversation.

She told him that the night before, she had had a strange dream.

"We were dancing as we were at that wedding anniversary we had a couple of weeks ago. Then we started embracing and kissing, planning a future together. As dreams go, we were suddenly walking down the aisle of a beautiful church with all our friends and relatives there. My parents and yours were present too. The celebrant was a strange priest with a sharp goatee and mustache. You were wearing a tuxedo but still had your white clerical collar; I was wearing my white religious outfit. We were married, but as soon as we were pronounced husband and wife, the candles on the side fell on the altar, which caught on fire. The priest started laughing and caught on fire as well, but he continued laughing like a maniac. We realized then that it was the devil himself that had married us! He had this horrible, deep laugh. I held on to you in fear. An alarm sounded, and you left me. I don't know where you went. The devil caught me by the arm. I felt it burning in his grasp. I pulled away from him and fell over the stairs leading to the altar. Then I woke up. I had fallen from my bed and my arm was 'asleep.' I probably had been sleeping on top of it. It was exactly four o'clock when I woke up. I called you at 4:30 when I know that you usually get up, but nobody answered the phone. I guess you had already left to go fishing."

A chill went down the priest's spine listening to the dream sequence. It was exactly the same dream he had the night before! And he woke up at four o'clock when the alarm sounded.

"Oh, my God! That was exactly the same dream I had and the same time I woke up. How can this be?" he asked Theresa.

"You are kidding, aren't you?" she gasped.

"No, Terry. I am telling you the truth. I felt a chill going down my spine hearing you relate my own dream to me and say that you also dreamt it."

"I thought you were not afraid of anything," she said.

"I am not afraid of anything, but I think I am coming down with something. The chills I get from different emotions do not necessarily mean I am afraid. I believe it is Satan who is setting a trap for us, but I don't understand what it is. Let us pray for strength to avoid falling in his trap."

They each prayed a rosary and fell asleep. A dark evil shadow ran away from the priest's window along the wall outside his house; a stray dog started barking at it and then ran away howling in fear of the invisible entity.

During the following days, Father Gabriel was preaching, managing, counseling, healing and performing miracles as usual. Sister Theresa was teaching, leading the Bible study group, playing and organizing the music for liturgies as usual. Yet when they were together, their minds became clouded and their desires were contradictory. On one hand, they wanted to continue with their ministries for the glory of God, and on the other, they wanted to abandon those ministries to spend more time with each other, to be happy together as husband and wife, to be one. Because of this both of them felt as if sick, the sweet sickness of falling in love.

Chapter VIII
The Prostitute With AIDS

On Tuesday evening, October 12th, Father Gabriel was in the home of Felipe Martinez in the heart of the barrio. Felipe had been a long time family friend. He was the man who helped Jose Arturo Infante and Maria de la Luz Negrete de Infante settle in San Antonio when they first came from Mexico. He saw Gabriel grow up. As a little boy, Gabriel had worked with Felipe and his now deceased wife, Petrita, sweeping the store and arranging the products on the shelves. They were the boy's baptismal godparents. Felipe taught Gabriel how to play chess; they had long matches that often extended for weeks. Felipe also encouraged young Gabriel to join the U.S. Army Reserves while he was still attending Catholic high school. Felipe had suggested that maybe getting some military training would help Gabriel be accepted by his girlfriend's dad, who was a general in the United States Army. He also advised him to go on and become an officer by getting an appointment to the West Point Military Academy. That was sure to impress the girlfriend's old man who was a West Point graduate himself. However, things had not worked out as planned. Gabriel ended up going to the seminary instead of the military academy. He did serve his six years of Army Reserve as a medical specialist, ending his brief, part-time military career as a sergeant.

Now, many years later, the pupil could beat the teacher in chess four out of five times. This time was the one out of five that Felipe could achieve victory against his pupil in the game. He used a deadly combination of queen, rook, bishop and knight. The priest, whose mind seemed to be on something other than the game, conceded his defeat and tried to excuse himself to go home and retire to bed early. Felipe was happy with his victory and would not let him leave.

"Why don't you stay, and sing some old songs with me?"

"Well, OK! Like in the good old days, eh, Don 'Peepy?'"

The old store owner closed the business for the night and took Father Gabriel into his house, which was located in the back of the business. Felipe pulled out his guitar and started tuning it up; he asked Gabriel to get them two beers from the fridge. He already had some nachos ready to come out of the oven. They were Gabriel's favorite kind of nachos, not only loaded with cheese and jalapeno but also with beans and bacon, plus freshly chopped onion and tomato, perfect to go with the beer!

Felipe pulled out a songbook from a bookshelf and threw it at the younger man.

"See if you can remember any of these songs, Gabe. I mean, Father."

"Watch it, old gizzard! I mean, Mr. Martinez, *mi padrino del alma* (my beloved godfather)."

Gabriel opened the book on the page containing a song for serenade, which brought him memories of twenty years before. The older man suggested that Gabriel take Felipe's mariachi group and serenade Theresa. Since the girl had spent ten years in Spanish-speaking countries when she was growing up, she was fluent in the language and the customs. She thoroughly enjoyed the serenade, but General Reynolds, her father, sent the MPs (Military Police) to escort the musicians out of the military installation. Neither the general nor his wife approved of their daughter's boyfriend because of his ethnicity and humble origin.

"Let's start with this one, 'Peepy,'" said the priest after taking a gulp of his cold beer.

When Gabriel was less than two years old and learning how to speak, he used to call his godfather "Peepy" instead of Felipe. Petrita, "Peepy's" wife, started calling her husband that nickname as well. Felipe whistled the violin introduction and started playing the huapango with his guitar.

Gabriel began singing as if he were at the foot of the window serenading his beloved, letting her know of his love and complaining about her disdain. The singer got up and danced zapateado style while Felipe gave out a scream of joy. The old man admired the way Gabriel's voice had matured and developed. His singing style gave emphasis to the feeling in the verses. He continued with the second verse expressing sadness that he was poor and undeserving of the senorita's love, but that he would achieve her love against all odds. Gabriel took advantage of the break in the song to have another nacho and some more of his beer to clear his throat and continue singing, the last verse spoke of his obsession with this woman and no other, with the hope that she will love him in return. Felipe played the guitar and whistled the violin part to close the song. He clapped for the singer, and Gabriel clapped for the guitar player. Then they both attacked the tray of nachos and their beers with gusto. Felipe looked in the book for another favorite song. They sang a few more, until the food was totally consumed between songs. The six-pack of beer also came to an end, so it was time for Gabriel to leave for sure, an hour after he initially had said he was leaving. It had been time well spent.

"Thank you for a great evening, my friend. May God bless you and keep you forever!" he said to Felipe.

"Thank you, Father. You need to come and see me more often. I can bring a couple of my friends to accompany us and have a real concert with a violin, trumpet and bass guitar."

Sharon McKenzie was a well-known prostitute of the west side. She was one of the few white girls working in that area of town; most of the others were Mexican or Mexican-American, a few blacks and some transvestites. It had not always been like that for Sharon. She graduated from a north side high school, married young, and had a family with a machinist who had a good job at a local Air Force base. They had a son and a daughter. After her children were born, she decided to work and became a truck driver. Between her husband and herself, they were bringing in about 80 grand a year. Life was good then. Her husband was a good, honest man and a loving father, but a little weak in personality. Old Steven McKenzie was easily swayed into doing things, like buying a boat to go fishing with his friends when he was not really a fisherman. He wanted to be liked, so he would throw frequent parties in their house, at least once a month, for his co-workers. At one of those parties, a new guy in the group, by the name of Fernando Galan, introduced them to using heroin.

Fernando was a man born and raised in California. No one knew his real life story, but his tattoos and rippling muscles told of some time spent in prison. Sharon was attracted to Fernando from the start. He was so different from her husband. There was something magnetic about the man, and he knew it. It was not long before Sharon was having sex with Fernando on her own bed while Steven lay, "passed out" on the floor under the effects of the heroin combined with a number of beers.

From the time Sharon first saw herself in Fernando's green eyes, things went downhill at an increasing rate of speed. Sharon got hooked on the drug. Steve divorced her when he found out she was cheating on him. The court took away her kids and gave custody to Steve because she was declared to be an unfit mother. While driving under the influence of drugs, Sharon ran over an old woman. She accumulated an ever-growing criminal record that included narcotics possession, DWI, theft, forgery and prostitution. She lost her home, her job, her commercial drivers license and her dignity; she ended up as a heroin-addicted prostitute working for Fernando. He was controlling five other women the same way. To make matters worse, Sharon had just been diagnosed to have full blown AIDS. She was scared.

The sick prostitute was drinking at a bar close to Don Felipe's store, wondering what she could do. Fernando was due to come check on her and collect his money. He took most of what Sharon made and provided her with a tiny old, rundown house. He gave her heroin, alcohol and 'protection.' She hated him!

Sharon carried in her purse the money from her last few customers. For a moment she felt guilty, wondering if they would get infected with the disease, but then she rationalized that if they got sick too, they deserved it! One of the many men she had been with had given her the disease; she was going to die because of that. They all deserved to die with her, she told herself. Sharon was not feeling well that night, and the whiskey she was drinking, straight, was not helping any.

Tears were rolling from her hazel eyes as she remembered her home, family and kids. She thought that it was all Fernando's fault. If he had never come into her life, she would still have it all. He had to pay! He did not even care about her. At first, Fernando had promised her that he was going to take good care of her. He was going to marry her after she divorced Steve. Lies! He had never intended anything other than to seduce her and humiliate her into becoming one of his whores. The drug gave him power over her and the others. It was not long after she moved in with Fernando that she woke up after a night of partying, in bed with three strange men she had never seen before. Fernando told her she had "done good" and gave her some money and a little bit of the drug. It soon dawned on her that she had become a slave to Fernando's heroin.

Sharon had met two girls, who also worked for Fernando, and who had lost their lives trying to leave him. Death was their only way out. All the women under his control knew that he had killed them, but they also knew nobody cares about another dead whore on the west side. Gina was found overdosed in an abandoned house; Shenika had "slashed her own wrists" according to the news media. Sharon was aware that it had been Fernando who injected the overdose in Gina's veins and slashed Shenika's wrists to make it appear like a suicide. He had made an example of them, to demonstrate what happened to those who tried leaving him. He had already made a small fortune with the sex and drug trade.

THE TEMPTATION OF THE MIRACLE WEAVER

Fernando never used heroin. He smoked marijuana and sporadically snorted cocaine. He cultivated a playboy image, so he worked out practicing martial arts. He owned a condo in a gated community on the north side, drove a sports car, enjoyed smoking expensive cigars, dining in exclusive places, drinking good wines and wearing designer clothes. He also always kept an eye out for other prospective "workers" to replace the ones he "lost." Fernando was also concerned about his tax report; therefore, he set up an Internet consulting business to serve him as a front to justify his "successful" lifestyle. He hired a manager to run the business because he knew very little about computer systems or Internet business. The manager had hired a group of young experts and was actually making the business progress. Soon Fernando would have problems laundering his money. Having the business also cut on his time to "supervise" his six girls. The former prison inmate had managed to stay out of jail since he had moved to Texas, and he planned on staying out.

Fernando went to the corner bar where he had told Sharon he was going to pick her up. She was there, waiting for him outside.

"Get in the car, Sharon," he said, opening the door from inside.

She came in and tried to kiss him, but he slapped her away from him so hard that she immediately started bleeding through her mouth. He got a little scratch on the back of his hand caused by her teeth when he hit her in the mouth.

"God damn it! I told you this is business. Do not try to kiss me again!"

He got a few tissues from the glove compartment, threw them at her and got one to clean his own hand.

"Clean up that mess, bitch! You are staining my car with your blood! Look at yourself. Wipe your fucking mouth!"

Sharon complied without a word. Then she reached into her purse and gave Fernando five twenty-dollar bills. He counted them and asked:

"Where is the rest of the money?"

"Business is slow," she said, "that is all I have to give you right now."

Fernando took a deep, impatient breath looking into the distance. Sharon knew that he was about to explode on her. He grabbed her by the hair and smashed her face on the dashboard, breaking her nose. She bled profusely and stained the dashboard with her blood. This situation aggravated the pimp even more. He got out of the car and went around to get Sharon out.

"Get the hell out of my car, you bleeding bitch!"

Fernando opened the passenger's side door, pulled Sharon out by the hair again, held her with one hand and punched her a couple of times with the other in her stomach, then threw her against the wall. She fell on the sidewalk gasping for air.

Fernando reached inside his sports car and grabbed Sharon's purse. He pulled out another two hundred dollars and asked her in his dominant tone:

"Why were you keeping this money away from me, Sharon? What did you want to do with this money?"

Sharon was crying and bleeding profusely through her broken nose. Her pantyhose were torn, and her knees were scraped. She tried to get up from the sidewalk.

"I need that money for medicines and to pay the bills," she stammered weakly.

Fernando kicked her in the abdomen, knocking her down on the ground again.

At that time, Father Gabriel was coming out of the store across the street when he saw a man kick a woman. The priest shouted at him:

"Stop, in the name of the Lord!"

Fernando heard the man yelling the order behind him and thought it may be a policeman saying, "Stop in the name of the law," so he jumped into his car to get away. He saw a dark silhouette crossing the street, running towards him.

"A fucking cop!" he said as he put the car in gear.

Who else would dare interfere between a pimp and his girl? The priest looked at the fallen, bloody woman on the sidewalk; she reminded him of our Lord in Calvary. The car was taking off already. Seeing such atrocious abuse, Gabriel became enraged, so he went after the fleeing pimp. There was no way the athlete could catch up with the high performance car as it zoomed down the street. Father G looked up to heaven and growled in frustration:

"Aaargh! Lord, let me put my hands on him!"

Just then, the sports car came to a screeching halt to avoid hitting a big truck that was slowly pulling out of a mechanic shop. Father Gabriel ran full speed after the stalled car. Fernando saw the angry face of the runner flashing on his rearview mirror. Still not knowing who the chaser was, Fernando saw such determination in that face that he decided to turn around and flee in the opposite direction before the man could catch up with him. As he made the quick U turn, his car came close to Father G. The priest was really charged with fury. Although he then realized that this was not an officer of the law, Fernando kept going. Gabriel punched through the driver's side window and grabbed the man by his hair. The pimp stepped on the accelerator, spinning the priest down onto the pavement. The car disappeared at the corner where it made a quick turn to the right. Father G felt pain to his right shoulder where the car had hit him.

Gabriel's right hand was cut and bleeding. He had some of Fernando's black hairs still in his hand. He thought to himself, "Oh, my God! What have I done?"

He rubbed his right shoulder and started walking back to where Sharon lay. She was gathering her things back into her purse. The priest bent down and picked up something to give it to her. He helped her to get up from the sidewalk.

"Are you O.K., Sharon?" the priest asked her.

She looked at the stranger and noticed his white clerical collar.

"Do you know me?" she said, a little surprised.

"Well," he smiled and told her, "I know your name, date of birth and address, but I don't think we have met before."

"You are a preacher. How do you know my name and...?"

"It is here, on your ID."

He handed her the ID that had fallen out of her purse. Father G touched her broken nose lightly, and she cringed in pain.

"I think he broke your pretty nose."

"He broke my whole life!" she said, crying and sobbing.

"Daughter, these wounds will heal, and your life will be whole again," the minister told her to give her hope as he gently touched her bloodied face.

He pulled out his white handkerchief and offered it to the woman.

"I am Father Gabriel," he told her, shaking her hand. "We should call an ambulance to take you to the hospital. We don't want your wounds to get infected."

"Oh, Father!" Sharon said in horror, looking at her blood on the priest's hands and shirt.

"What's the matter, child?" Gabriel asked her, noticing the alarmed tone of her voice.

At that moment, Fernando Galan came back driving his car towards them. He had told himself that a priest was no danger to him; moreover, he was angry that the man had broken his window, pulled his hair and scared the hell out of him. Fernando always had a loaded automatic 9 MM automatic pistol under the seat of his car. He had decided to teach the intruder a lesson, so he returned to the scene.

The sports car slowed down in front of the couple. The passenger side window was down. The pimp had the gun on his right hand, pointing it at them. Immediately, Gabriel shielded the woman with his body as he invoked help from God.

"Abba, protect us from the enemy!"

Fernando savored the moment as he squeezed the trigger, laughing with pleasure, but the gun did not fire! He stopped the car, and cocked the gun. A whole round came flying from the chamber. The angry pimp aimed at the couple once more and squeezed the trigger again, but the pistol did not fire either. At that moment, Father Gabriel turned around and faced the gunman; he looked at him right in the eyes and said,

"Leave!"

At the sound of the priest's authoritative tone, Fernando felt a chill in his bones and fear in his heart. He dropped the gun on the passenger's seat and took off.

Sharon saw the golden car's rear lights vanish in the distance and felt relieved. She looked at Gabriel's face. The anger had left it, and he was full of loving concern again. The woman took a deep breath before confessing:

"I have AIDS, Father. I am sorry I didn't tell you right away. Look at your hands; you have my sick blood all over you. And you have an open cut on your hand. I am so sorry!"

Sharon was crying again. Getting one of her customers infected was one thing, but infecting an innocent man who was trying to help her was quite different. The priest hugged her and leaned her head against his chest to console her.

"Always trust the Lord with your life, Sharon; He has a plan for you and for me. That's why we met here tonight."

Father G tried to encourage her, and himself, but for a second he felt his knees getting weak thinking that he may get AIDS from that encounter. Before Theresa showed up in his life for a second time, he was ready to die any day in the service of the Lord. That night, he feared that he might die and not see Theresa again. Sharon was the same size as Theresa. Gabriel held Sharon tight in his arms thinking about Theresa. A voice in his mind came out with the answer,

"Trust the Lord, always."

Meanwhile, Fernando did not stop until he got home. He had been driving as if the devil were chasing him. He got home and exited the car with the gun in his hand. He was confused and angry, so he squeezed the trigger rapidly three times pointing at the ground. The gun fired three rounds, one of which pierced the pimp's right foot. Fernando went down to the ground screaming in pain. Neighbors, who heard the shots, called the police to report a shooting in progress.

Back on Guadalupe Street, a police officer got out of his patrol car with his radio in one hand and his pistol in the other one. With his gun pointed at Father Gabriel, the cop ordered,
"Get away from the woman and put your hands up where I can see them, now!"
Gabriel recognized Officer Lara but still complied with his order.
"What the hell happened, Father G?" the officer inquired, looking at the woman's bleeding face and the priest's bloodied hands.
The priest explained to the officer while holding his hands up,
"It is not what it seems, Officer Lara."
"He didn't hit me, Officer. It was my boyfriend, Fernando Galan, who also tried to kill both of us after Father Gabriel saved me."
Sharon got in between the priest and the officer to defend her savior. The officer put his gun away. He was familiar with Fernando's name and his activities.
"Where is Fernando now?" Officer Lara asked, then, before Sharon could say anything, he told his dispatcher over the radio, "Twenty three forty, we are going to need EMS for an injured party here."
"Ten four, twenty three forty," the police dispatcher acknowledged him.
"Is he on foot, or is he driving his golden car?" the officer continued asking questions, trying to get enough information to advise other officers.
"He is driving his 'goldie.' He is probably home by now," said Sharon.
The officer put the information over the air for his colleagues to be on the look out for the golden car. He even had the license number of the car because he had dealt with the pimp before. Just the week before, Officer Lara had written Fernando up for speeding on Zarzamora Street. Everything else had been OK, so he could not arrest the pimp or search his car or his person that time. He had to let him go with only a speeding ticket. Lara was aware that once he could arrest the man, he would find the gun and drugs that he was known to carry. The patrolman thought that this might be their chance to get their hands on him and take him off the streets. Officer Lara used to go out with Gina Zamarripa, the girl to whom Fernando had given the intentional

overdose of heroin. She had been Lara's highschool sweetheart. Although they went their separate ways, Roger Lara became a policeman while Gina Zamarripa became a prostitute; Roger still had feelings for Gina. It broke his heart to hear about her death and the fact that her killer got off without being charged. There was just "not enough evidence."

On the way to the hospital, as they were sitting in the back of the ambulance, Sharon told Gabriel,

"Father, let me tell you the truth."

"You already told me, Sharon. It is not your fault; don't worry about it. I am not angry with you. Things always happen for a reason," the priest said, smiling at her, understanding her concern.

"I had heard about you," she said, looking down at the ambulance floor, searching for the right words. She continued, "I even went to one of your services one day. People say that you can do miracles. I wanted to quit using drugs, but I didn't believe in miracles."

Father Gabriel raised her face with his index finger on her chin and looked into her hazel eyes. They were part blue, part green and part light brown. Gabriel asked her to continue.

"Tonight, when I saw you come out and defend me, I remembered what you had talked about the day I went to hear your service. You told the story of a woman who had been hemorrhaging for years. She touched Jesus' garment and was cured. I saw you and imagined that it was Jesus himself that had come to my rescue. Don't ask me why. So I didn't keep you from touching me because I hoped that God could cure me through your touch. I felt so good in your arms even though I was crying; I felt as if I were back in my mother's arms as a baby. For one moment I believed with all my heart that this could happen, but later I just realized I might have instead given you a sure death for trying to save my miserable life. Father, forgive me. I know I am going to die soon, and I have been the worst of sinners."

Sharon rested her head on his shoulder, crying profusely. She reminded Gabriel of Mary Magdalene crying at the feet of Jesus. Her tears wet his pant legs; he was moved with pity as he blessed her.

"I forgive you and absolve you of all your many sins, in the name of the Father, and of the Son and of the Holy Spirit."

Gabriel kissed Sharon's head and straightened her hair with his hand. After the ambulance left them at the hospital, the priest received a couple of stitches in his right hand. A facemask was put on Sharon, and she was admitted for observation and blood studies when they learned that she had previously been diagnosed having full-blown AIDS. The medical staff also took some samples of Gabriel's blood and saliva for AIDS testing.

When he arrived home, Gabriel went to the phone to call Theresa. Then he decided not to do it, not wanting to alarm her. After all, he was not sure if he had been infected. If he were infected, his fantasy of quitting his ministry and marrying Theresa would surely vanish from the realm of possibilities. He would rather die than pass the deadly disease on to his sweetly beloved Theresa. He poured himself a glass of brandy with ice and cola, lit a cigar and sat outside the house to contemplate the starry sky. It was a warm night. He took off his bloodied shirt and threw it in a bucket with soapy water to let it soak overnight. Gabriel ran his hand on his muscular thorax and thought how useless that muscular power was in the face of an infection like AIDS.

"Lord, I need you more than ever," he prayed, "I don't understand what's going on in my life. Why did you send Theresa back to me? Am I going to die soon? Is my mission on this earth over? Do you want me to stay at your service as a priest? Are you testing me? Why is it that I don't hear your voice in my head to answer these questions when you help me in all other matters? Why do I feel this fear of death tonight?"

He drank his mixed drink, smoked his cigar and listened to the soft wind moving the tree branches and leaves. Gabriel gave up waiting for an answer and decided to go to sleep. Before going into the house, he looked up to Heaven and said,

"Good night, my Lord. Into your hands, I commend my life and my soul. Let your will be done and not mine."

The soft, warm wind caressed his face, softly moving his black hair and beard as an answer to his "good night."

The following day, Gabriel went to the hospital to visit Sharon. The doctor came to her room to talk to them. They listened with great anxiety to the doctor's words.

"Well, the rapid tests on the blood and saliva have been made, and the results were confirmed a couple of times."

Sharon and Gabriel clasped each other's hand and looked at each other for a second while the doctor continued his report.

"Neither one of you shows a sign of HIV or AIDS infection in your blood!"

Doctor Snow could not believe it himself. He was comparing Sharon's prior records, which confirmed that she had full-blown AIDS. Now her blood was perfectly normal, just like Gabriel's. The doctor tried to explain a possibility.

"It's possible that there may have been some kind of mistake on the diagnosis of your blood last time, but it doesn't seem to be obvious just looking at the records. I have no explanation for how you could have AIDS one day and nothing the next one."

"I do," said Sharon while hugging Father Gabriel, "it was a miracle! It worked! It really, really worked! Thank you Father!"

"Thank God. It was that moment of faith that you had last night, which saved you," Gabriel told her, holding her in his arms.

The doctor just smiled. He still thought a mistake had been made on the first diagnosis because he was positive the second one, showing them both healthy, was perfectly all right since he had reviewed it himself. He was happy to see that his patient was going to be OK. It would just be a matter of time for her nose to heal.

"I would still like you to come back for further testing. The results of the regular tests will not be in until two weeks, and you may not develop any symptoms until months or years later," explained the physician.

They agreed to take follow-up tests just in case, but there was no doubt in their minds that God had cleansed Sharon, and Gabriel could not have been infected since Sharon was not carrying the disease.

Relieved and inspired by the good news, Father Gabriel began to sing in the room.

"Amazing grace, how sweet the sound that saved a wretch like me."

Sharon joined him in singing, feeling that she must join in thanksgiving to God.

"I once was lost, but now I'm found was blind, but now I see. 'Twas grace that taught my heart to fear, and grace my fears relieved. How precious did that grace appear the hour I first believed!"

The old doctor could not help but be moved by their song and joined them as well.

"Through many dangers, toils and snares I have already come. 'Tis grace has brought me safe thus far, and grace will lead me home. The Lord has promised good to me. His word my hope secures; He will my shield and portion be as long as life endures."

A nurse came in after hearing their singing, but instead of stopping them, she joined them too.

"When we've been there a thousand years, bright shining like the sun, we've no less days to sing God's grace than when we first begun."

The whole improvised choir clapped as they finished their hymn.

THE TEMPTATION OF THE MIRACLE WEAVER

"Praised be the Lord!" said Sharon hugging everyone. Full of joy, Father Gabriel exclaimed,

"Amen!"

A man wearing a tan suit came into the room. Father Gabriel recognized him as a homicide detective he had dealt with in the past. Sharon was commenting to the priest in front of the nurse and the doctor.

"Father, I am definitely going to join the outreach program to get out of using heroin. I only hope Fernando doesn't find me before I get cleaned up."

"That's great, Sharon!" said the priest.

Turning to the newcomer, Gabriel greeted him,

"Welcome to the party, Detective O'Hara. We are celebrating life and praising the Lord."

He extended his bandaged hand to the officer, who smiled back and said,

"Well, I come to bring you good news and add to your celebration. Last night, we got Fernando at the condo where he lives. After Officer Lara put out the description of the man and his golden sports car, we happened to get a call in his area for a shooting in progress. Apparently Fernando shot himself in the foot accidentally while playing with his gun outside his house. When the officers responded, they found him in possession of a lot of drugs, plus the gun. Our detectives found the bullets he had attempted to fire at you, two of them were still intact inside his car. We don't know why he couldn't fire them, they were hit by the firing pin, and there was nothing wrong with them, as far as we know. You were very lucky, both of you, last night."

"You bet! Actually, the Angel of the Lord was upon us; that's why the gun didn't fire," said Sharon interrupting the detective's report.

Father Gabriel looked at her, wondering whence she got those words. She shrugged her shoulders and made a signal for the officer to continue.

"Anyway, Fernando is facing charges for the attempted capital murder of two people, the possession of the heroin and cocaine he had, unlawfully carrying a gun, and possession of Sharon's prescription medicine. The IRS was already looking into his tax reports; they are going to audit him. The Vice Unit is gathering all of his girls to put a case together for promotion of prostitution. They will need a statement from you, Sharon. The Narcotics Unit already had a couple of cases for delivery of heroin against him that they are going to file. I am sure our friend is going to spend quite a while in prison, if he survives."

"What do you mean?" asked Sharon on hearing the last part of the detective's report.

"I just learned from the hospital where he was treated for the self-inflicted gunshot wound to the foot that he tested positive for full-blown AIDS!"

Sharon looked at Father Gabriel for an explanation, but he just shrugged his shoulders.

To lighten up the atmosphere in the room, which suddenly had turned somber as they heard the sad fate of the criminal, Gabriel remembered a joke and passed it on to the group gathered in Sharon's hospital room.

"One day, a barber was talking with one of his customers as he cut his hair. The customer, a regular one, was a moderately successful insurance agent. The agent started telling the barber about one day when he had such a terrible headache that he could not work anymore. He could not talk to the customers over the phone or concentrate on any paperwork. He felt nauseated..."

"A migraine headache!" interrupted the doctor, but then covered his mouth and signaled for the priest to go on.

"Probably," Gabriel agreed with the doctor and then continued, "so the insurance agent told the barber 'I couldn't work, and decided to go home. When I got home, I found my wife in bed with another one!' The barber was shocked at the revelation but wanted more details. He asked the insurance agent, 'What were they doing when you found them in bed? Were they naked?' The insurance agent faked indignation and said, 'Hey! I found her in bed with another headache, not another man!' They both laughed. The barber said, 'That's a good one. I am going to have to remember it and use it on some of my customers.' As soon as a new client came into the barbershop, the barber laid it on him, 'You know Joe, the other day I had this terrible, migraine headache, and I just couldn't work anymore. I closed the shop and went home only to find my wife in bed with another one.' The customer responded, 'Yes, we all knew what was going on but didn't want to tell you. It's a good thing you found out yourself. What did you do to that insurance agent that you found her with?'"

The doctor and nurse left the room laughing loudly. O'Hara snickered because he had heard it before. Sharon was laughing like a child. The priest excused himself and told them he had to go.

"I still need a statement from you, Father," said Det. O'Hara, handing him a couple of forms.

"I will reduce it to writing and fax it to you from my office, like last time," Gabriel said, taking the forms with which he was very familiar.

"All right. You know what we need. I think you are writing more police reports than some of our officers. How come you get involved in so much crap?"

"Because I get involved in the community. Your business and mine involve the same people all the time," the minister reminded him.

Sharon kissed Gabriel good-bye and thanked him again. Gabriel left the hospital relieved, as if he had just dropped a ton of steel from his shoulders. He was healthy... Should he tell Theresa the story?

Another day, Gabriel and Theresa were reading a book to some children at the public library downtown. Theresa read the narrator's part and any feminine or child's parts while Father read the men's or beasts' parts. When they finished their reading, they went for a walk towards the cathedral.

"Are you going to tell me what happened to your hand, Gabe?" Theresa asked him.

"You don't want to know, Terry," he replied to pique her curiosity.

He knew that she would insist, but he liked to give her a hard time and have her speculate before actually telling her of his adventures.

"Have you been fighting again!" she inquired, acting like a mother, with her hands on her hips.

"Yes, and for a prostitute!" he answered, pretending he had actually done something wrong.

Theresa stopped walking and looked at him trying to find the truth in his face.

"You are kidding! I know you smoke your stinky cigars and drink all kinds of alcohol. You go into bars and gamble; you dance with all the women you can find. You paint nude models, get into fights, and romance religious sisters, but I did not know you were into prostitutes!" she exclaimed.

Father Gabriel smiled at an old lady who was passing by them and heard Theresa's words; then he took Theresa's arm and made her continue walking.

"You look beautiful when you are angry; however, you are angry based on assumptions. Let me explain what happened. I am not for promoting prostitution or using those services. I never have. This is a story of mercy; it was another miracle!"

Father Gabriel related the whole story to Sister Theresa. They sat down at the bench on the main plaza in front of the cathedral. Gabriel bought two shaved ice cones and came back to sit next to Theresa. He gave her one; she thanked him and said,

"Strawberry, my favorite!"

She took a bite and tasted the sweet, cold treat. Her lips turned red and wet. Gabriel stared at those lips and felt an urge to kiss and bite them.

"Well, are you going to stand there staring at me eating my ice cone, or are you going to sit down and eat yours, Gabe?"

"This ice cone is not what I really would like to put my lips on," he said looking at her red lips.

"Yeah, right! In front of the cathedral!" she said pointing at the historic landmark.

At that moment, Archbishop Rosales came out of the cathedral and, recognizing Father Gabriel, waved at them. He had never met Sister Theresa. The archbishop got in his car and went south on Main Street. The priest and sister waved good-bye and ate their cones.

A couple of days later, October the 15th, Sharon came to visit with Father Gabriel after his Friday morning Mass. He sat on one of the back pews with her.

"It is good to see you again, Sharon, how are you doing?" he asked.

"I am better, Father. I came to see you about Fernando."

"Oh, yes, you need to forgive him with all your heart for all the wrong he did to you, so you may find peace. I was thinking about going to visit with him. He should already be out of the hospital and probably sitting in jail," the priest told her.

"So you didn't hear?" Sharon said.

"Didn't hear what?" inquired Gabriel, a little puzzled.

"Fernando is dead. He tried to escape from police custody this morning as they were going to take him to jail. He always said he was never going back to prison. They say that he fought the officers who were going to transport him from the hospital to the jail. He was a black belt in tae kwan do, so he got loose and took one of the deputies' guns. The other one shot him dead before he could use the gun. Although he hurt me, I felt bad when I heard how he died," she explained containing a tear.

"I am sorry to hear that he is dead," Gabriel told her. "I didn't have a chance to go talk to him and maybe have him see the evil of his ways, invite him to change. Still, I want you to forgive him in your heart as God has forgiven you."

"You are right, Father, but it is so hard to forgive those in whom we put our trust and who then betray us."

"Those are the main people you have to be able to forgive! You have the power to forgive; exercise it! Or else you will always carry this anger against him in your heart. Forgive, and be free! Forgive and find peace!"

Father walked Sharon out the front door. She thanked him, hugged him and kissed his cheek before leaving. He waved good-bye to her and turned his eyes towards the school. Sister Theresa was watching him. He blew a kiss at her, sent her a wink and a big smile. She went back in the building wondering why she felt that rage looking at other women demonstrating their affection for the kind priest. Her possessive feelings for the pastor were getting stronger as time went by. She was losing control of her emotions regarding her former boyfriend.

Gabriel remembered what Theresa had mentioned about his "stinking" cigar-smoking habit and promised himself to quit from that moment on. He thought she would appreciate the sacrifice he was going to make for her. He had been smoking cigars for about ten years already and truly enjoyed the experience. He made a fist and hit his left palm to seal his promise to quit smoking cigars.

Chapter IX
The Revival

It was Sunday afternoon, the 17th of October. As soon as Father Gabriel finished his noon Mass, he got in his Priestmobile and headed downtown to meet Sisters Mary and Theresa for lunch at a downtown cafe. Some words of the Gospel passage kept coming back to him while driving: "Not to end in death, but it is for the glory of God." The reading had been from the Gospel of John, chapter 11, which tells of the raising of Lazarus. The priest listened to the words reverberate in his mind. He thought for a moment that this might be the answer to his confused feelings, although it was not clear. He was not physically ill, just felt a little anxious and hot. He had lost his usually good appetite and was not sleeping well. He realized that these were the symptoms of anyone who had fallen in love. The priest slapped himself and laughed, thinking he would control those feelings and be in charge of his emotions, yet he noticed that he was going 55 on a 30-miles-per-hour street, anxious to get downtown and see Theresa again. He looked at his rear-view mirror. A set of blue and red flashing lights was shining from a patrol car behind him. Gabriel pulled over right away.

"Great! This is what I get for DWD, daydreaming while driving," he mumbled.

"Good afternoon. I am Officer Calderon of the San Antonio Police Department. The reason I pulled you over is because you were doing 55 on a 30-miles-per-hour street. Let me see your driver's license and proof of insurance," the officer told him.

Gabriel complied with the officer's order and smiled at him remembering what other policemen, friends of his, had told him about keeping a good attitude when pulled over. The officer noticed his white clerical collar as he collected the documents.

"Are you the famous 'Father G' of The Holy Trinity Church?" Calderon asked.

"Yes, sir. I don't know about the 'famous' part, but some people do call me Father G instead of Father Gabriel. Have we met before?"

"Yes and no. My mom told me about you. Last year, I went to the hospital with pneumonia and a lung infection that I thought was going to kill me. Mom went to you and asked you to pray for me. It was a Friday evening when I got admitted. The doctor prescribed all kinds of medicines, but I felt just fine right before they started giving them to me. All they had been able to do was start an I.V. They checked me again and said I was perfectly all right. The doctor felt very proud that his prescription had worked so soon, until the nurses informed him they had not given me any medication up to that point. A psychologist there attributed my recovery to a psychological shock, saying that my mind probably created an overload of antibodies to prevent me from staying in the hospital. My mom came and told me that it was a miracle, and that you had prayed with her to God for my health. I personally didn't want to believe it, but it happened. I'd been wanting to go thank you in person, but I'm not much of a church-going person," the officer related.

Father Gabriel snapped his fingers remembering the incident the cop was relating.

"You are Ofelia Calderon's son! I remember your mom; she has great faith. I knew that the Lord would grant anything she asked for, and she also mentioned that you were 'not much of a church-going man.' You are very busy with your job as a policeman and all the other things you are involved with. You coach a little league team; you are involved in the Big Brothers and the Habitat for Humanity programs, right?"

The officer was amazed at how much the priest knew about him.

"I guess my mother told you everything about me, eh?"

"She was concerned that you were going to die in the hospital because you were very sick. She wanted me to know how valuable your life was, so that I would pray to God for your life to be spared then. We did pray for you that evening."

"Well, thank you Father G!" exclaimed the cop smiling and extending his hand to the priest.

"Thank God, and your mother whose faith saved you. I only joined her in prayer."

They shook hands and looked at each other smiling like new friends.

"Are you going to write that speeding ticket?" the priest asked, remembering that he still needed to get downtown to meet his friends for lunch.

"Hell, no! Excuse me, I mean, of course not! I'll tell you what; I'm going to write you a warning this time. How is that?"

"Excellent choice, Officer Calderon. I can live with that, and I promise to be more careful on keeping the speed limit in mind."

The officer wrote him the warning ticket, which he wanted to keep as a souvenir of their meeting that day. Father G signed it and told the officer:

"Now I am going to give *you* a warning for not going to church at least every once in a while. If you do all these good works that you do, without doing them for the glory of God, you are wasting your time. Come to church and be enlivened in your faith."

"You are right, Father. I will see you in church, soon."

"I still have a Mass tonight at 6 p.m."

"I'll be there! Now go on and be careful. Thank you again!" the officer said, dismissing the priest.

Gabriel drove eastbound towards downtown, happy that their encounter was a fruitful one for both of them. Even on this type of stressful situation, he could see the hand of God using him to talk to His people. He had to be speeding for the officer to pull him over and have that chat. He thought about the passage he had in his mind and wondered if that was why it reverberated in his mind: "Not to end in death, but it is for the glory of God." Gabriel checked the speedometer; it read 30 MPH at that time.

Sister Theresa and Sister Mary had to pull over to the side of the road when they heard a loud bang. Their front right tire blew up as they were heading for the downtown cafe; they were already within walking distance from the downtown area.

"We could walk from here and come back after lunch to fix the flat, Sister," said Theresa, anxious that Gabriel might already be there waiting for them.

"Oh, no, Sister. We may not find the van again if we leave it here. I heard that a bunch of car thieves live in this area, over in those apartments. I don't want Sister Magda to get mad at us because her precious stereo was stolen from the van. Let's change the tire. How hard can it be?" the younger religious said, exiting the vehicle and looking for the spare in the back.

"Have you ever changed a tire before, Mary?" asked Theresa who never had to deal with such a task herself.

"No, but we can figure it out, don't you think?"

Mary was looking at the drawing over the wheel cover and started undoing the wing nut that held the spare in place.

"Look for the owner's manual in the glove box, Theresa. I think I read some instructions there on how to change a tire."

While Theresa looked for the manual, Officer Calderon came by with his police lights flashing and pulled up behind the disabled vehicle.

"What seems to be the problem, Sister?" the officer said smiling as he approached the young religious wearing her distinctive sister's garb.

"Oh, we got a flat, and we are trying to figure how to replace it," said Mary.

"Would you like me to help you?" proposed the cop.

Mary was about to decline because she wanted to do it herself, being the self-reliant woman she was, but Theresa jumped out of the front of the van and said:

"Yes! Yes, Officer, we would be so thankful. We have a friend waiting for us downtown and we are already running late."

The officer picked up the tire from the back of the van and commented:

"All you religious people are in a hurry today. I just pulled over a priest who was speeding a few blocks from here."

Theresa and Mary looked at each other wondering, so the older sister asked:

"Who was the priest you stopped?"

"Father Gabriel. He was flying towards downtown. What is going on there?" Calderon asked.

Both of the sisters covered their mouths and snickered. Mary helped the policeman by bringing him the tools and explained:

"He is the friend we are meeting for lunch. We figured he might already be tired of waiting, but I guess you stalled him for us. How long ago did you see him?"

"I just let him go a couple of minutes ago."

The officer touched Sister Mary's hand in taking the jack from her. She pulled her hand away, feeling a little discharge of static electricity. Officer Calderon and Sister Mary were about the same age. She noticed that the policeman was handsome and polite; he noticed that the sister was pretty and vivacious. Theresa noticed the exchange of glances between them and left them by themselves. She went to look inside the police car without entering it. It had a cage in the back for the prisoners. In the front, there was a little computer and all kinds of buttons for lights and siren. The officer had a bunch of books and forms. The passenger side of the car looked like a mobile mini-library. It took only a few minutes for the officer to replace the tire for them. Just then, the dispatcher gave him a call.

"I have to go, Sisters. Have a nice day!"

"Thank you, Officer—" Theresa said as he took off in his cruiser with his lights still flashing in the direction of downtown.

Mary completed Theresa's sentence:

"—Calderon, Officer Antonio Calderon."

Theresa got in the van and said:

"He seemed to be a very nice man, and he also seemed to like you, Mary."

"Yeah, I liked him too. He taught me how to change the tires myself next time. Where did you go, leaving me all alone with that man?"

"I went to check his patrol car. I figured you wouldn't mind," Theresa told her.

The sisters laughed mischievously. They both knew that probably neither the officer nor Mary would meet again. And even if they did, their situation and that of Theresa and Gabriel were quite different. They got in the van and headed back to their destination.

"Did you ever fall in love, Sister Mary?" Theresa asked her driver,

Mary looked at her with sad eyes and responded:

"Yes. When I was in college. There was this gorgeous guy named Eric. He was a soccer player. In Greece, soccer is a big sport. He was going to become a professional player in Spain. We were in love and thinking about getting married. We decided to postpone our plans until he got his contract and I finished college. Eric was a very daring man; with the money he was advanced, he bought a motorcycle. He died in a traffic accident riding his new bike. I felt that I had died that day; all our plans were buried with him. A couple of years later, the Lord called me to his service, and here I am."

"I am sorry. I know what it feels like to lose loved ones in an accident. Both of my parents died in an airplane crash," Theresa said.

"How about you, Sister Theresa, have you ever been in love with a man?"

"Father Gabriel!" exclaimed Theresa.

"You are in love with him?" said Mary looking at Theresa.

"No! I mean, look at him in that crowd. What is he doing there? Stop the van, Mary."

Earlier, when Gabriel was at the edge of downtown, by a local university campus, a crowd of people gathering at a street corner attracted his attention. There was something serious going on there. People were gesturing for others to go get help, call an ambulance. A woman was covering her face and walking away from the group, obviously upset. The priest stopped his car and got out; he could see a body on the sidewalk. A man was using a wooden pole to move a cable away from the body. The minister approached the scene and learned that a woman had been electrocuted by stepping on a live electric cable. She was a young woman. There was a small child, no older than five, crying by her side and moving her shoulder, trying to wake his mommy up. Gabriel's heart was moved with pity for the boy. The woman did not seem to be breathing; her chest was not moving. Gabriel evaluated the situation as he moved in next to the woman's body. He knelt down and checked for a pulse; there was none. He asked an older, heavyset lady to hold the boy. The priest crossed himself and prayed to God asking for enlightenment, so he could take appropriate action in that situation. This young mother was dead already, no breath and no pulse. Her heart probably stopped beating when she received the high voltage shock. The priest thought about giving her the last rites, but immediately dismissed the idea.

Gabriel Infante had joined the Army Reserves at the age of seventeen when he was still in high school. He planned to get as much military training as he could before going to West Point. He did not know if he was going to get the appointment yet when he went to basic training. Later on he was trained as a medical specialist in the army. By then he had already turned down the appointment to West Point and was confused about his future after losing Theresa, the love of his life. His medical training in the Army led him to consider a life of service, which actually led him into the seminary. As a combat medic, he learned how to perform life-saving techniques including cardiopulmonary resuscitation or CPR.

The minister suddenly felt the energy of the Holy Spirit coming down to him as he prayed over the body and had the memory flashback of his Army medical training. He positioned the woman flat on her back and hyper extended her neck. All the noise the crowd was making around him became a blur as the he concentrated in his chosen task. For one second, he thought he saw the same woman standing among the crowd, to his right and behind the little boy who was still crying and wanting to go down beside his mommy. Gabriel undid the dead woman's front-snap bra. He put his mouth to her mouth, pinched her nose with his fingers, and blew a couple of breaths into her lungs. Then he positioned his hands interlacing them on the center of her chest and started pressing on it rhythmically, as he silently counted, "One, and two, and three, and four." When he had counted to fifteen, he moved back to blow into her lungs again. The third time he went back to breathe in her mouth, she coughed! Gabriel put his finger on her neck and found a pulse going; he was filled with excitement. The woman squinted and opened a pair of baby blue eyes filled with bewilderment. Gabriel turned to the right to see the boy. The woman he had seen behind him was no longer there. He asked the heavyset lady to let the boy come to his mother. The crowd was cheering and applauding the priest's feat. The ambulance was approaching at that moment. Father talked to the revived woman; she was still confused and trying to grasp the situation. She asked for Pedrito, her son, and complained of chest pain. The woman asked who had undone her bra. The priest advised her to stay down and to let the paramedics put her on a stretcher. They would explain everything later, he told her.

Gabriel got up and talked to the EMS technicians about what he had done so far. Just then, the sisters' van was passing by, slowly, on the street and came to a stop. Father Gabriel ran out to them.

"Sister Theresa, Sister Mary, I will catch up with you in a couple of minutes," he said.

"Father Gabriel, what are you doing?" Theresa asked, looking at him and looking in the direction of the crowd.

"Just helping a damsel in distress," he said, dismissing his actions humorously.

"Did you have to kiss the damsel to help her?" Theresa asked and threw a couple of tissues at Gabriel for him to wipe the revived woman's lipstick off his mouth.

He looked at his face in the van mirror and cleaned the red lipstick off with the tissues.

"I will explain to you later," Gabriel told her. "Go on to the restaurant and order for all of us; get me a carne guisada plate. I will be there shortly. Let me just finish here and take my car."

Officer Calderon gave them a signal for the sisters to move on. The priest went back to the side of the shocked woman and her little boy. The people were beginning to leave talking among themselves about what they had witnessed.

"I want to apologize to you, for I might have broken your ribs trying to revive you," he said.

"I don't know if they are broken, but I know that I am alive thanks to you," she replied

"Thank God who granted you a second chance. What is your name?"

"Linda, Linda Richards, and to whom do I owe my new life?" the woman asked.

"I am Father Gabriel Infante. Do you have anyone who can take care of your child while you are at the hospital?"

"No, Mr. Infante, I am new in the city, a single mother looking for a job. I have no relatives or friends here. Could you help me or refer me to someone who can?" Linda explained, not wanting to lose contact with the man who saved her life.

The paramedics placed the woman in the ambulance and got ready to take her to the nearest emergency room.

"I will take care of your son; what is his name?"

"Pedrito Sifuentes. He is a very smart boy; he is five years old."

"All right! I'll keep him with me, and we'll go see you in the hospital in a while. Has he eaten yet?" Gabriel asked the woman inside the ambulance.

"No, we were looking for a place to eat when this happened."

"Don't worry about anything, Linda, I will see that he eats and then I will take him to see you. You just get better."

The priest gave her his business card and held Pedrito in his arms. The child wanted to go with his mother. Gabriel told him, man to man, that she was hurt and needed to go to the hospital, to rest and see the doctor. The boy should come with him and let mommy get better. He was going to take him to eat and get something for mommy. Pedrito looked at his mother, who gave her approval. For some unknown reason she trusted Gabriel from the start.

"Go with our friend, honey. He will bring you to see me at the hospital. OK?"

She gave the boy a kiss and released him to the priest. Father G got out of the ambulance with the boy in his arms. Linda told the EMS technician:

"That man is good! That's just what we were looking for, and my son likes him."

Father G spoke with the police officer, the same one who had pulled him over.

"Father G, You are into something again! I thought you were going to be careful," Calderon said to him.

"Hey, I go where God needs me!"

"Yeah, I hear you. You did real good here, Father. I think that lady would be dead for sure if it had not been for you. That makes at least two of us, I guess."

"Officer Calderon, I believe you already have all my information on the warning ticket for your report. Unless you need something else from me, I would like to catch up with my friends to eat a late lunch."

"Oh, yes. I met your friends too. Say hi to Sister Mary for me. She is a very nice lady."

Gabriel walked away with his little friend's hand in his. The officer went up to the priest and gave him Linda's suitcase. Gabriel and Pedrito got in the Priestmobile and drove into the cafe parking lot. The two new friends entered the restaurant looking for the two religious sisters.

"I guess this is going to be lunch and dinner at the same time!" Father Gabriel said as he and his little friend met them at their table.

"Yes, it seems that way," said Sister Theresa looking at her birthday watch, it was already 2:30 p.m.; then, looking at the newcomer she asked, "Who is this young man?"

He was a handsome boy with black hair and his mom's blue eyes.

"Ladies, this is Pedrito Richards, five years old. His mother stepped on a live electric wire and was shocked to death, or so it seemed. I was able to bring her back by performing CPR on her, thanks to U.S. Army medical training, and, of course, to God who put me there right on time."

"My name is Pedrito Sifuentes, not Pedrito Richards," the little guest corrected the priest, and Gabriel apologized to the boy for his mistake.

"You revived the woman after she died from electrocution?" Sister Mary gasped in astonishment as the two new arrivals took their seats.

"Yes, I guess I did! The funny thing is that, in the Mass today, I had just read the Gospel passage where Jesus brought Lazarus back from the dead after four days. A portion of the scripture kept coming back to me that said, 'Not to end in death, but it is for the glory of God.' I was trying to find out why it stayed with me. I think it was a warning that this was coming. I have found it very coincidental that things like this keep happening to me. They are, somehow, usually related to the Gospel readings of the day," Gabriel told the amazed sisters.

"Wow! You did real well Father Gabriel. Praised be the Lord!" said Sister Mary on hearing his comments.

"Praised be the Lord, indeed!" Gabriel continued, "Another interesting thing that I remember about this incident was that I thought I saw the dead woman standing behind her child at the same time that she was lying on the sidewalk before I started doing CPR."

The two women looked at each other, unable to come up with a good explanation. Father Gabriel went on to give his own understanding on the incident.

"I believe her soul refused to leave this world because of her motherly duty to Pedrito. I was in one of those trances when everything seems unreal.

I knew people were around me and were saying something but I didn't understand anything they said. It was as if they were moving at a much lower speed than I was. I felt filled with energy from the Holy Spirit and had a flashback of my Army medical training days. I knew what I had to do and started doing it. To tell you the truth, I was hoping I could just lay hands on her and wake her up, but as I said before, the Lord works in mysterious ways. The woman I saw behind the boy seemed to be saying to me 'Do it, do it,' as if she knew what I was about to try."

The waiter brought the lunch the two sisters had ordered for all of them. Father Gabriel blessed the food before they began eating. They shared their plates with the boy, who ate everything they gave him as if he had not eaten in a couple of days. He was quiet and polite the whole time they ate their lunch/dinner.

The priest related to the sisters what he had learned about the single mother, that she had just arrived and was looking for a job. He also gave Sister Mary the greeting officer Calderon sent her and questioned what had happened between the two of them. Mary explained that the officer had helped them change the tire that blew up and taught her how to do it herself; she repeated that he was a nice man. Theresa conceived an idea, so she changed the conversation.

"Father, you know that Laura, the lady that works in the kitchen, is about to leave for Germany because her husband got his orders from the Army. They leave in a week. Maybe you can offer Pedrito's mom that job if it is something like the kind of job she is looking for," she suggested.

Father finished his carne guisada, leaving his plate clean, drank the last of his iced tea and agreed with Theresa.

"That's right! It sounds like a great idea. I don't really know what kind of job Linda is looking for, but we could offer her that position."

Linda Richards did start working at Holy Trinity School as soon as she recovered, Wednesday October 20th. Her ribs had been slightly bruised during CPR, but none were broken. There was nothing wrong with her, according to the doctors at the hospital. The only evidence she had of her ordeal was a burn mark from the electric cable to her right heel where she had touched the live wire. She had met the Hinojosa family when she arrived in Texas and went to their house looking for Leonardo Sifuentes, Pedrito's Father. They never heard of him, but explained that he might be a relative of the people who lived in that house five years before them.

Linda had a torrid romance with Leonardo in Milwaukee, Wisconsin, where she used to live. The Texan, Leo, had gone north in search of his fortune. He claimed to be an inventor of chemical products such as detergents, deodorants, cleaners and the like; actually, he had bought a thick book of chemical formulas for all those products. Leo was looking for a company that would manufacture his "inventions" or partners that would invest on a new chemical company. Linda liked the dreamer from Texas and gave herself entirely to him during that summer, but by the winter, Leo was gone to New York, Chicago or California in his quest for success. By the spring of the following year, Linda had their baby without hearing another word from Leo, not a phone call or a letter. The only clue she had to track Leo was a postcard he had received from Texas. A friend had sent it to Linda's address where Leo spent the summer without paying rent.

When Linda was laid off from the job she had held for ten years, because their factory was closing the plant in Milwaukee, she decided to go to Texas looking for Leo to let him meet his son. Leo's friend had lived in the house where the Hinojosas now lived, but there was no trace of him or of Leonardo Sifuentes. Fernando and Rocio Hinojosa felt pity for the single mother when she told them the reason for her visit. They had a daughter who ran away from home when she turned seventeen, and they had not heard from her in a year. Rocio offered to let Linda and Pedrito stay at their home, in their daughter's room, until Linda got her own place in San Antonio. The young mother had been honored, but could not accept their generous offer. She took her suitcase and went downtown looking for a job. The nice couple (in their early forties) heard about what happened to her and came to visit her in the hospital. She then accepted their invitation to stay at their home, which was not too far from the Holy Trinity Church and School. They introduced her to an attorney named Scott Anderson who would represent her in a lawsuit against the construction company responsible for leaving the live wire exposed to pedestrians.

Sister Theresa was very happy that things were working out for the single mother. She was a good worker and seemed content although the pay was minimal. She was able to place Pedrito in kindergarten at no charge thanks to Father Gabriel who allowed it. The only thing that began to bother Theresa was how "thankful" the Milwaukee woman was to Father Gabriel for having resuscitated her, having hired her, and having accepted her son in school without charge. Linda frequently would go and hug the priest, pressing her tall, well-formed body against the priest's in a provocative manner. Then she

THE TEMPTATION OF THE MIRACLE WEAVER

would hold his hands and kiss them a little too much in Theresa's opinion. Linda was not only tall and big busted, she was also younger, had luscious lips and a huge white smile like a toothpaste model's. She had a cascade of light brown hair and brilliant blue eyes. Father Gabriel seemed to enjoy her frequent displays of gratitude.

One day, the first grade teacher was bringing her kids into the cafeteria for lunch when she heard the distinctive voice of the principal singing in the school kitchen. It was a romantic song, a bolero that spoke of a romance that left the flavor of each other in the two lovers, a flavor that would remain in them for over a thousand years. His melodious voice resounded throughout the kitchen and the whole cafeteria. When he finished the song, Linda came to hug him and planted a big wet kiss dangerously close to his mouth. She put her arm around his neck, took his hand and placed it on her hip to announce to the rest of the ladies in the kitchen:

"This man is going to be the next Elvis! He is quitting his job as a priest to go into show business. I am going to marry him and give him six children."

Everybody laughed in the kitchen except Sister Theresa who came in with stern eyes looking at the singer. She grabbed a towel and threw it at him.

"Until you actually renounce your vows, I suggest you clean up your act in front of the children. And wipe that lipstick off your face, Father Gabriel!"

The whole crew turned away to get busy serving lunch to the children, stunned by Theresa's firmness. Linda stepped away from Gabriel and went to assist the other ladies. She had been raised without religion in her life, so she was truly ignorant of Catholic rules and traditions. She noticed that the sister was obviously jealous of her. Linda glanced in the direction of the two religious and observed how Theresa was punishing Gabriel by turning away from his supplicant gaze. No words needed to be pronounced. If she were going to get the priest, she would have to be more attractive to him than the first-grade teacher.

When they were finishing the clean up, Linda asked Mrs. Williams, the kitchen supervisor, if priests could marry only nuns. The older lady explained that priests could not marry at all. Linda had been right when she said that to marry her, Father Gabriel would have to quit his job, his ministry, his call to serve God as an ordained priest.

"Maybe he will quit, for the right woman," commented the tall Yankee.

"Not this priest. He is a saint! You don't know how many miracles he has performed," said the black lady defending her boss.

"Well I know he is a miracle worker; he brought me back to life!"

Mrs. Williams got serious looking at how excited the young woman appeared.

"Don't you dare tempt the good Father, girl. Look somewhere else!" she sternly advised.

But Linda continued talking:

"He seems to like me. I mean, he does not seem to mind my appreciation."

Mrs. Williams dismissed her saying:

"Father Gabriel loves everyone. What he has done for you, he would have done for me even if I am old, fat and ugly. For him there are no ugly people; everybody is a lovely and beautiful child of our Lord."

Mrs. Williams grabbed her sweater and walked out to her car, leaving the newcomer by herself. Linda went to the window and saw Gabriel playing soccer with the eighth-grade kids. His team had been scored on first, so they had to take off their shirts. He moved and looked "pretty good" for a 38 year old man, Linda observed. He laughed like a child and always looked people straight in the eye. Linda placed her hand on her face and let it slide down, slowly, on her neck, breast, abdomen and thigh as she was fantasizing about the athletic man playing with the kids outside.

"Gabriel, you ought to be mine. I will make your life complete. You will see!" Linda whispered to herself before getting away from the window.

At the end of the school day, Father G was at the door of the school saying good-bye to the children for the weekend. Linda sent Pedrito to kiss Father for being so good to them. The child ran towards the priest with his arms wide open; the minister picked him up and received a big kiss from the boy. Gabriel turned towards Linda and winked an eye at her to let her know the boy was getting used to his new school. She, however, interpreted his signal as something different. She thought he would make such a good father for Pedrito. He was mature, intelligent, handsome, educated, strong, full of positive energy, a teacher, an athlete, a singer, wow! And no woman had claimed him yet. Linda realized that Sister Theresa was very pretty, but she was sure Gabriel would choose Linda once she let him know her and all her charms a little better. Miss Richards decided to get more involved in all of Father Gabriel's activities to show him she was the woman he needed to be really happy. She called him on the phone inviting him to come to the Hinojosas' home that Friday evening; however, the tall lady sent Pedrito with the Hinojosas to the movies while she stayed home to "rest after a hard

THE TEMPTATION OF THE MIRACLE WEAVER

week at work."

That Friday evening, outside the Hinojosas' residence, perched on a tree branch, Satan was watching the priest as he arrived to the place. The evil one was in the form of a grackle, with shiny black feathers and red eyes. Father Gabriel turned his eyes to the dark bird after ringing the front door bell. He felt nauseated for an instant as he observed the bird on the tree. Gabriel wondered if something he ate for lunch had upset his stomach. The door opened and a familiar voice made Gabriel turn his face around. Looking at the beautiful woman who opened the door to welcome him, he forgot about the nausea and the strange bird.

"Hello, Father Gabriel! Thank you so much for accepting my invitation. Please come in," said Linda Richards taking Father Gabriel's hand and pulling him inside the home.

"No, thank you for inviting me, Linda," Gabriel responded. "Where is everybody?" he asked noticing that nobody else came to greet him.

"Oh, the Hinojosas decided to take my son to the movies tonight," she explained casually.

Linda was wearing a very soft dress that fell on her curves enhancing her figure and inviting touch. The minister felt a little uncomfortable in that situation.

"It might be better if we postpone this visit for another time, when the Hinojosa family may be present, don't you think, Linda?"

Without answering, the woman got very close to him and challenged him.

"Why do you want to leave, Father Gabriel? Do you dislike my company so much? Do I offend you? Don't you care about me wanting to become a Catholic?"

She made a disarming, little girl's face, sticking her lower lip out in feigned sadness. Father G thought that perhaps he was being overly cautious; he was sure that nothing inappropriate could happen, so he decided to stay. Linda rejoiced secretly.

"What made you decide to become Catholic, child?" he asked as he went to sit at the table.

She walked towards the kitchen swaying her hips softly as she explained the reason. Gabriel could not help but admire her voluptuous figure.

"You, of course! God sent you to me, to give me a second chance in life. It could have been someone else that revived me, or I could have died! I think that you were my message from God, that he wants me to do this. Do you care for something to drink, Reverend, something cooling and relaxing?"

She had purposefully set the thermostat at 85 degrees, so it was hot in the house.

"Yes, please!" he answered.

To break the silence, the priest related a joke to his hostess as she was getting the drink:

"A young priest was so afraid at his first Mass that he could hardly speak, so before his second week in the pulpit, he asked the monsignor, 'How can I relax?' The monsignor, a veteran of his work, said, 'My son, this Sunday it might help if you put a martini in the water pitcher instead of water. After a few sips, everything should go smoothly.' Sunday came and the young priest did as the monsignor suggested. He believed everything went very well. After the sermon, the young priest asked the monsignor how he had done. The monsignor replied, 'Just fine, except that, before addressing the congregation again, you should sip the martini rather than gulp it down. Remember there are 10 Commandments, not 12. There are 12 disciples, not 10. David 'slew' Goliath, he didn't 'kick the shit out of him.' We don't refer to the cross as the 'Big T.' We don't refer to our Savior Jesus Christ and his disciples as 'J.C. and the boys.' We don't refer to the Father, the Son and the Holy Spirit as the 'Big Daddy, Junior, and the Spook.' Next Sunday, there is a taffy-pulling contest at Saint Peters, not a 'peter-pulling contest at Saint Taffy's.' The idea of a drive-in confessional is excellent, but the sign, 'Toot-n-Tell or Go to Hell' has to go. Last, but not least, we say The Virgin Mary, not the 'Mary with the Cherry.'"

Linda was laughing her heart off in the kitchen. She really liked the priest, his sense of humor, his singing and his whole personality. She definitely had to have him, and soon.

She came back from the kitchen with a tall glass containing what appeared to be iced tea. She bent down to place the glass in front of Gabriel, and her open collar revealed most of her breasts. Gabriel began to feel hot. He grabbed his drink and took a good gulp of it to cool off. His eyes got big with surprise upon tasting the drink.

"What's this?"

He looked at the glass trying to identify the brown drink.

"Do you like it? It is a mixed drink, tamarind juice, rum, ice, mineral water and a little sugar," was her reply.

The blue-eyed beauty took a long drink to show him that it was good. He was about to say that it felt a little too strong, but decided not to since he saw that she drank it easily.

"Yes, I like it. It is really tangy and refreshing. I never had this drink before," Gabriel told her.

Linda refilled his glass and sat by his side at the table.

"What steps must I take to become a Catholic?"

She seemed to be glistening, and her perfume intoxicated Gabriel, spreading an exciting sensation all over his body.

"Well, you have to join the RCIA, which is the program that leads other denomination Christians into communion with us," Gabriel managed to explain.

The light coming from the window behind her lighted her hair. She had beautiful long, curly, thick, golden hair that fell down to her shoulders. Father Gabriel's mouth was dry because his heart throbbed with such an enticing creature next to him, invading his personal space, so he drank some more of the mysterious, strong drink. He felt the cold liquid go down his throat.

"Would you help me learn all I need?" she asked him, with her lips no farther than six inches away from his.

Her breath was like a spring breeze. Her blue eyes were pleading as if her life depended on it.

"Sure! That's my job as a pastor," he said.

He felt her breast resting on his arm as he reached for the glass to drink some more. She apologized for being so close to him and refilled his glass once more.

Linda got very close to him again and blew her words in his face looking into his dark brown eyes. Her voice was very inviting.

"Would you give me personal lessons, Father Gabriel?"

The priest felt slightly intoxicated by her perfume, her closeness, and the strong drink she had served him. With a conscious effort, he rose from his seat to break the spell.

"Well, no. We have other people who can give you that kind of personal attention. You understand, I cannot devote too much time to one of my parishioners, especially a young, beautiful woman like you."

"Why not?" Linda asked innocently.

She got up and walked close to him, looking for his eyes, trying to read his thoughts. He turned away, towards the front window. At that precise moment, he saw the sisters' vehicle passing by the front of the house. Sister Theresa was looking at his old car parked in the driveway, and then she looked towards the window. She was sitting on the passenger's side; Sister

Carmen Armienta was driving. Their house was only a few blocks away. Although she could not actually see Gabriel from the street, Theresa guessed that he was visiting someone in that house. From his vantage point, the evil grackle was still on the tree watching through the open curtains at Gabriel and Linda interacting inside the house; the Satanic black bird seemed pleased with the situation.

"Sister Theresa!" said Father Gabriel looking at the sister.

Theresa was trying to penetrate the window with her eyes, but the tree branches did not let her look inside the house.

Gabriel felt his heart jump as if he had been caught in some kind of forbidden situation.

"What does she have to do with this?" a puzzled Linda asked him, getting between him and the window.

"Nothing – I just saw her passing by. They live in this neighborhood."

Father Gabriel pointed out the window and took another sip of his drink while looking for a place to sit in the living room. He continued his explanation:

"A priest is supposed to abstain from marriage, raising a family, having love affairs, or devoting too much time to just a few people because this would cause him to leave his duties to the whole parish unattended."

"What does my being a woman have to do with it?" Linda asked pretending not to understand.

She smelled so good and looked so beautiful! Gabriel knew that she was teasing him. He sat down on the couch.

"Just imagine what the people of the parish would think if they saw me here every night, like this, just the two of us. You know how people are. They tend to make up stories even if there is nothing going on," the minister explained.

Linda moved like a cat towards him with her eyes wide open; she sat next to him, her hip touching his, her soft hand on his muscular forearm.

"Father, will you get in trouble, maybe even fired by your superiors if people started spreading gossip about you and me?"

"No, Linda, but we are public figures, living in the public eye. We are moral leaders and should not give occasion for such scandal."

"I don't want you to get in trouble for me. I'll just do what you tell me to do, anything, and I will be happy to see you at the school or in the church. I am so grateful for what you have done for me and my son. You have no idea what that means to me."

Her pretty face got closer to him; her breath caressed his lips. Those luscious lips were only inches away again whispering the words of submission to whatever he asked her to do. Gabriel had to swallow hard and close his eyes for a second to gather strength from within. Suddenly, he got up from the couch saying:

"I have to go!"

Linda was startled. She got up too and, accidentally, knocked the glass from his hand with her shoulder. The cold tamarind drink spilled on her delicate pink dress, practically turning it transparent. The fluid wet her from the neck to the waist. Both apologized at the same time. Linda excused herself to go change her now-revealing dress. He mopped up the liquid from the floor and the coffee table with some paper towels. Before Linda came back, Gabriel got in his car and fled, praying for calmness of mind. He rolled his window down and let the evening air clear his lungs that were still filled with Linda's aromatic perfume. With a trembling hand, he turned on the radio to get some musical help and erase her inviting words from his ears. He prayed:

"Thank you, Lord for helping me get away from this temptation."

After watching the priest leave the place in a hurry, the black grackle flew off the tree in front of the Hinojosas' residence and disappeared in the night apparently laughing with loud, macabre shrieks.

Gabriel continued praying as he drove to the church. Once there, he walked in and knelt in front of the altar to pray some more. He felt his weakness and sought strength. He remembered he had found willpower through prayer and meditation many times before; he had to look for it again. Alone in the church, on his knees, he prayed and prayed until the image of Linda disappeared from his mind and his body felt peace again. At times he prayed like this, so intensely and sincerely, that he lost track of time and space. It was midnight by the time he finished his prayers and went to bed. He wondered how to address the problem. Firing the temptress was not an option. Gabriel, however, promised himself to avoid similar occasions of sexual temptations. He figured he had to guide Linda's affection in the right direction. After all, she was just a woman in great need of love, he told himself. He was going to pray for God to send Linda a good man who would fill her needs.

Linda was convinced that the priest really wanted her. She noticed how disturbed he was by her closeness. He almost couldn't help himself; he really liked her! He was after all, a normal man, and she had excited him. He just needed some time to make up his mind. Once he had a chance to really know her, very intimately, he would know what to do. If Linda could only get him to have sex with her once, she was positive that he would never want to go back to his current celibate lifestyle. She would make him happier than he had ever been. She was obsessed with the man she believed that God had sent to be her partner in life. She just had to get into his heart, but very subtly.

The next Monday, November 1st, Sister Theresa saw Linda giving Father Gabriel a cake she had baked for him. Linda had actually interrupted a conference the first-grade teacher was having with the school principal in the hallway. Linda said she hoped he liked it and left. Gabriel's eyes followed the tall Yankee as she walked away, swaying her hips, towards the kitchen. He was holding the cheesecake and smiling. Theresa felt the sting of jealousy, again. She asked him in an inquisitive way:

"What's going on between you and that woman?"

"Nothing! She told me last Friday that she wants to become Catholic. Isn't that great?" Gabriel said pretending innocence.

"So, that's why you were at that house Friday," commented Theresa.

"Oh yes, I saw you and Sister Carmen drive by."

"Were you alone with her?" Theresa asked.

She had the feeling it was so but wanted him to say it was not.

"Yes, the rest of the family had gone out," he explained as if that were an unimportant point.

"How convenient! Whose idea was it?" she said, a little upset with the situation.

"What do you mean?" asked Gabriel.

"Did you just drop by to see her, alone in her house?"

"No, no, no. She had invited me to dinner at the Hinojosas' home," he said to justify it.

"When the Hinojosas were gone!"

Theresa's nostrils were flaring imagining what might have gone on between them.

"I didn't even stay for dinner!" Gabriel whispered realizing that the tone of their voices was going up as the interrogation went on.

"Why?"

Theresa lowered her tone and almost whispered the question when she saw his hand signaling for her to lower her voice. Her eyes were looking straight into his.

"Well, I thought it was inappropriate, so I left after just a few minutes."

She was not convinced, so she asked again for more details:
"What happened?"
"Nothing! We talked, had a drink, and then I left!"
Gabriel looked at her and smiled his white, mischievous smile. He then said:
"Are you jealous?"
"No, of course not!"
Theresa dismissed that suggestion but knew instantly that she was lying. She was jealous!
"You are!" Gabriel said triumphantly.
Father G was acting like a kid teasing another. Now he was the one searching her eyes, and she was the one turning them away from his.
"Why should I be? I know that you love everyone!" Theresa said defensively.
"But you feel I may be more attracted to Linda Richards," countered Gabriel.
"Well, aren't you? Who could blame any man? She is so tall, so beautiful, so sweet, so much in need of love. She even comes with a cute little kid, and she can cook!"
Father Gabriel felt great joy in confirming that Theresa really loved him and that she was being tormented by the outward appearance that he might be interested in another woman.
"Our relationship, yours and mine, is still unique. I would not exchange you for anyone," he said lowering his voice even more.
Theresa's heart felt a little relief in hearing his words, but she looked for more affirmation that there was nothing between Linda and Gabriel, which would jeopardize their relationship. He touched her hand to reassure her it was the truth.
"It doesn't seem very clear from where I am," Theresa said touching the top of the cheesecake with her finger and looking down.
"What is not clear?" asked Sister Magdalene approaching the couple after hearing the last part of their conversation and hoping to get in on it.
"Is this a pineapple or just plain cheesecake?" was Gabriel's quick response to the intruder.
Magda grabbed a piece of the cake and tasted it. Theresa and Gabriel looked at each other simultaneously and smiled as Magda closed her eyes to savor the cheesecake.
"Mmmm! Plain cheesecake, but real good! Save me a slice for my coffee

break."

Magda took Sister Theresa by the arm, and they headed towards the classrooms, talking shop. Theresa turned her head and winked at Gabriel before going into her classroom. He winked back and went into his office trying the cheesecake himself.

"It is really good!"

"Who gave you that cake, Father?" asked Mrs. Gray, the assistant principal, looking at the treat.

"Linda Richards, the new lady that works in the cafeteria. Do you want a slice?"

"No, I don't fit into my clothes anymore. I need less, not more of those treats. Just be careful with it, Father," the wise assistant advised the priest.

"You know I am not concerned about my weight; I will just burn it off at the gym," he told her.

"That's not what I am talking about," Mrs. Gray told him, adding, "You know what they say, that the way to a man's heart is by the belly. Watch out for that pretty girl. She might give you a magic potion to make you fall in love with her."

"I am already in love with her! Who wouldn't? But don't worry, my dearest Sharon, I still love you as much as before and your place in my heart is secure forever," the priest said dramatically.

Father Gabriel played a little with his assistant, grabbing her hand and putting it on his chest to feel his heart.

"Father Gabriel! I am a married woman."

"Yes, I know, but I am not jealous, my precious pearl."

He took her by the waist, danced with her in the office and guided her dancing to her desk while humming an old romantic song about two strangers who fell in love one night. The priest then picked up a rose from her desk and put it in his mouth. He danced alone towards his own office, stopped at the door and threw the rose back at the assistant principal, who was just giggling, looking at the clowning priest. Gabriel slammed his office door behind him and went to work.

Chapter X
The Winning Ticket

Linda Richards was sent to the pastor's house to help Mrs. Black clean the oven. Linda took advantage of the opportunity to snoop around the house and learn more about Father Gabriel. She entered a room that contained a number of paintings, drawings, sculptures, photos and prints. She admired the landscapes, the still life pieces, some abstractions, collages, religious themes and a good number of nude figures in action. All of the works had the initials PGI on the back of them.

"Padre Gabriel Infante!" she said his name, realizing it was all the art collection of the priest.

She was a little surprised by some of the erotic nudes. Linda left the room and asked Mrs. Black:

"When does Father Gabriel have time to paint, if he is always busy with the school and the parish?"

The old Thai lady looked at the tall Yankee woman, suspecting her of having a personal interest in the priest. The ladies in the kitchen had told her about the newcomer. There was little that escaped their gossip network.

"Father Gabriel paints when he can. Sometimes I find some of his paintings in the morning when I come in. I guess he does it late at night after business hours. He also goes to an artist's studio on Culebra Street, close to the highway. They draw and paint figures from live models every Monday evening. He goes once or twice a month."

"Have you ever modeled for him?" Linda asked the older lady as they put the oven racks back in place.

"As a matter of fact, I have. One time he did a portrait of me for one of his works. He did two, one for his collection and another one for my house. I have it in my living room."

"Did you pose nude?" Linda inquired smiling.

"Of course not! I am an old woman. Most of those models they use are young, like you. I posed with a traditional dress from Thailand."

Linda had an idea. She finished the cleaning job with the housekeeper and went back to the school to get her things. She still had a couple of hours before picking up her son from kinder, so she went looking for the artist's studio that the priest attended on Mondays. She spoke to Elizabeth Olsen, the artist that managed the studio, and Linda was hired as a model starting that same Monday evening.

Father Gabriel had a stressful day at work, plenty of problems and complaints to take care of at the school and the parish at the same time. He was looking forward to getting away for the evening and attending a figure drawing session at the art studio. He was only going to draw with charcoal on his big drawing pad, so he just took a few supplies for his work that evening. A psychologist friend of his had told him that it was a good idea to have a hobby such as art to manage stress, so he took it as a prescription and enrolled as a member of the artists circle that got together on Mondays to draw from live models. It was a good way to maintain his art skills. He had done a few frescoes for churches in different cities already. Although he did not consider himself a Michelangelo, his work was excellent, especially in the more conventional, realistic style as opposed to abstraction.

The pastor noticed a letter from Africa on his table among several others. He stopped to read it before he went to the drawing session. It was from his brother seminarian, Father Michael Frost. He had chosen to be a missionary in the black continent. He was the third of the boxing-singing seminarian group nicknamed the Archangels. He was a Louisiana native with blond hair and green eyes, the only one of the three who kept his face clean-shaven. He was also an excellent guitar player. Father Gabriel remembered him fondly. He opened his letter, hoping it would bring good news; instead, it was bad news. Michael was asking for help. His mission had been wiped out by dual calamities. First a wild jungle fire brought about by the long drought had burned most of the mission; then, when the rains came, the floods swept away what was left of it. Michael wanted to start over, but he needed some funding to be able to rebuild as quickly as possible. He had a community of a couple of thousand people already in the mission. They were in need of everything. Although he knew that Gabriel had no money himself, he trusted that he could ask his parish to send them something, anything that they could spare.

"I know that you can find a way to help us, brother," he wrote. "You were the first person that came to my mind when I prayed to God for help."

The letter ended with:

"Hoping to hear from you soon, I close sending you my love and blessings."

It was signed: "Michael Frost." There was a postscript:

"Could you also send me some hot sauce from Texas? I haven't had any in a long time. This is just for me, and it is not a priority, but if you can send me some, I will appreciate it and keep you on my heroes log."

Gabriel closed the letter and smiled remembering Michael. He raised his eyes to heaven and asked God to provide him with the means to help his brother in distress.

Elizabeth greeted the 20 artists in the warehouse, converted into a studio by her imaginative entrepreneurial vision. She announced that they had a new model named Linda that evening, which was just lucky for Linda because nobody else had been available. Linda had appeared out of nowhere and solved her problem.

"I thought I would have to pose for you tonight since I was not able to get anyone else," Elizabeth said jokingly to the class members.

She calmed them down and said:

"Please welcome Linda to our session and be gentle with her because this is her first time."

Father Gabriel heard two of the artists talking about their golf game. He remembered a golfing joke, and he shared with them as they were setting out their drawing tools.

"A world-famous golfer who used to swear a lot every time he got mad was paired up with the Pope for a charity golf tournament. The golfer was not having a good day with his swing, so without noticing it, he began letting his tongue slip. When he had a bad swing he exclaimed, 'Damn, I missed!' Then, looking at the reproving look on his partner's face, he apologized saying, 'I am sorry Father!' The Pope absolved him and moved on without saying anything else. On the next hole, the golfer had a bad shot and again let go of his expression, 'Damn, I missed!' The Holy Father admonished him, 'Son, you have to be careful with your language. God might punish you.' The golfer seemed contrite when he apologized again, 'I am sorry, Father. You are right. I will be more careful from now on.' They moved on to the next hole. The golfer messed up again and said, 'Damn, I missed!' Lightning came down from heaven and struck the pope. Then a voice was heard from above saying, 'Damn, I missed!'"

Everybody was laughing and ready to start the session. Elizabeth called Linda to place herself in the middle of the room between the artists.

There were ten male and ten female artists at the studio that night. Linda Richards looked only at Father Gabriel as she stepped out of her corner and took off her robe to stand on a wooden box that placed her on a pedestal like a living sculpture. Linda looked monumental, tall and well formed. She had piled her light brown mane on top of her head. She smiled at him standing there, totally nude, in front of the priest-artist. Gabriel was surprised to see someone familiar posing for them that night, but he smiled back at her and got ready to begin drawing. Elizabeth Olsen stopped them before they started. The teacher went and arranged the lights to enhance the figure. She told them:

"I suggest we start doing four quick gesture drawings of about 15 seconds each. Then we will double that to 30 seconds for another four poses and we will move on to one-minute drawings, four drawings too, before we take a break."

Elizabeth turned to the new model and said:

"Linda, I want you to face all four sides of the room and assume different standing positions first, then I want you to do the next four on a kneeling or sitting position, and for the last four you can lie down but make sure you move around to face all four sides of the room, OK?"

Linda acknowledged the teacher's instructions and tried to follow them. It was going to be harder than she thought. Keeping her body motionless while standing nude in a room full of people was not as easy as it seemed. They were going to give her a hundred dollars for the session. She needed the extra money to support her child. That sounded like a good excuse!

During the break, Linda put on her robe and came to Father Gabriel to see how he had sketched her. They were nice, quick drawings of the figure. She could recognize herself, although there was not much detail in them.

"Father G, what a surprise to see you here! I am embarrassed that you saw me like this," she lied to him, pretending she did not know that he was one of the artists in the group.

"Don't mind me," he told her. "You are doing a good job for your first time. You are beautiful and have such a great form. You look truly monumental up there. It is exciting to draw your figure."

"I was looking for a little extra money. You know I don't make much at the school cafeteria," Linda explained, quickly adding, "Father, could you please give me a ride home after the session?"

"Sure! I am sorry that we don't pay much in that position in the kitchen. This work is not bad. What is it? Around 30 dollars per hour for posing?" Gabriel said.

"They offered me 100 dollars per session; that ought to come in handy," she informed him.

Linda was standing next to Gabriel, her hip touching his shoulder as he sat polishing up his last drawing. The other artists were coming back from the break. Elizabeth told them they were going to do two 30-minute drawings next with a break in between each. Linda dropped her robe next to Gabriel and stepped up on the platform. The instructor changed the lighting and had her recline on a blanket. Linda was happy that the instructor had her facing the minister's side of the studio for the first pose.

Linda found herself really tired from doing "nothing" that evening. She got in Father Gabriel's car and asked him:

"Do you think I did well as a model, Father Gabriel?"

"Oh, yes!" he replied, "You did splendidly well. I think everybody was happy to have a new model."

"I am very tired. I didn't know sitting or standing still was such a hard work. I feel like having a drink. Would you care for one? My treat for the ride!"

Gabriel thought for a moment. He had nothing to do except go home and get in bed, so he accepted her invitation.

"Where would you like to have that drink?" the priest asked the model.

"I don't know any good place in town; remember I came from Milwaukee recently," Linda said.

"Then let's go for some frozen margaritas" he decided, and headed for the nearest Mexican restaurant.

Linda's plan had worked perfectly. She had shown him what she had to offer physically, although she had to show it to everybody else in the room as well, and now she was going out with him for a drink. Things were looking up!

Linda noticed that the priest was a little distant as they had their drink in the restaurant. She could not get him to look at her for more than a few seconds. He answered all her questions politely but without much enthusiasm or giving much detail. She asked him about his education and his origins, his likes and dislikes, his miracles and adventures, which he put down as unimportant. She then told him about her life, but his mind was somewhere else. She touched his shoulders and arms a few times during their conversation without his paying much attention to it. As soon as they finished their drink, he got up and led her out of the restaurant. Gabriel had another full day ahead of him starting early in the morning. He felt his heart come to a stop as they were walking out of the restaurant. A van, just like the sisters' van, was pulling into the parking lot. Then, realizing that it was not the sisters' van, Gabriel let a sigh of relief out. Linda held his arm as they walked to his car and asked him:

"What was that about?"

"It feels nice out here! Doesn't it?" he remarked, "It is incredible that we are in autumn already and it is not cold. I wonder if we are going to get any real cold weather this year."

He had changed the subject, not wanting Linda to realize that he thought Theresa had arrived and would be upset if she saw them together.

On the way home, Father G put on his favorite classical music station. Linda waited for him to say something to her, but he just drove silently, thinking about something or someone other than her. Before she knew it, they were pulling up to the Hinojosas' home. The blue-eyed girl was a little disappointed that she did not get further on this date, and realized it would take a little more time. With a surprising move, she reached towards Gabriel and kissed him on the lips to thank him for a nice time. She got out of the car and walked home, leaving the priest with the taste of her lips on his. A black evil cat with red eyes glowing in the dark was observing the scene from the top of the mailbox at the Hinojosas'. The feline seemed to smile as Linda walked by without paying attention to it; however, the woman experienced a cold chill passing by the cat. She felt goose bumps on her back but thought it was because of the kiss she had managed to give the priest. Linda turned around at the entrance to the house and, with a big smile, waved good-bye to Gabriel.

The priest waited until she went in the house before driving off. He scratched his trimmed beard and licked his lips. Linda was out to get him, he knew, but he did not want to engage in that kind of relationship with her. She was very tempting, and apparently, daring to do whatever it took to accomplish her desire. On the other hand, he did not want to hurt her by, coldly, pushing her away. He prayed for a mean of keeping her in his circle but at a safe distance. Being a flesh-and-blood man, it was not easy to turn down so much beauty. It was also very flattering to know that she wanted him. Gabriel went home and hurried to the phone to talk to Terry. She picked her phone up at the first ring.

"Where have you been tonight, my friend? I have been waiting for your call for quite a while. All the sisters are asleep already," Theresa told him.

"I am sorry to call you this late. I went to my figure drawing session; we had a new model tonight. Guess who decided to make a little extra money modeling?" Gabriel asked her.

"I have no idea who, that I know, would dare to strip in front of a bunch of strangers."

"Linda Richards!"

"Our Linda Richards that you brought back from the underworld?" Theresa asked.

"The same one. She did really well for her first time," Gabriel said.

"Did she know that you attend sessions at that place?" inquired Sister Theresa, smelling "a rat."

"I don't know. I never told her about it, but there she was. Linda said that the work of posing was harder than she thought it would be."

"I thought that once you went through an experience like that of Lazarus, you would become a great follower of Christ, filled with modesty and moral principles," commented the religious sister disapproving of Linda's behavior.

"It is not immoral for her to pose for art's sake; besides, she needs the money," Gabriel said, trying to justify her, "You know she does not make that much in the kitchen."

"I am not sure it was such a good idea to hire her after all. Did she ask you to take her home after the session?" Theresa asked.

"How do you know?"

"That's what I would do if I wanted you to know me a little better and to like me a little more. So she showed you her great body first and then went out with you."

"We just had a margarita, and then I took her straight home."

"What else happened?" she continued to interrogate Gabriel.

Theresa was getting more anxious as he confessed what she suspected already.

"She just kissed me good night and got into her house. Then I got home to call you. I missed your voice. I cannot go to sleep in peace if I do not hear it," said Gabriel to appease her.

"She kissed you! Did you kiss her back?"

The tone of her voice went up.

"Not really. She just gave me a peck without warning. It was like a 'thank you' little kiss, nothing else."

He could almost see Terry's little nose flaring, imagining the worst-case scenario.

"I am going to have a talk with that... woman!" Terry said.

Gabe was smiling at her getting upset over so little.

"What are you going to tell her, Terry?" he asked her, "Are you going to tell her, 'You better leave my man alone?'" he continued: "Remember that I am a public man, devoted to my flock. I told you already that I am not looking for an affair with Linda, no matter how inviting she is."

"Still, she is going out with you and doing things with you that I cannot do," Terry complained.

"Do you want to pose for my group?" Gabriel challenged her.

"No, would you want me to?" she shot back.

"No!" he admitted, "What else would you like to do with me that you are not already doing?"

"Well, I cannot really run at your pace because I am not used to it, but would you take me with you for a power walk in the morning when you do your workout?"

"Are you serious? Do you really want to come along and workout with me?" Gabe said, excited with the idea.

"Is that so crazy? Or are you afraid I would just slow you down?"

"No, no, no. It would be great! When do you want to start?"

"Tomorrow morning. At what time do you want me to be ready?"

"I can run to your house and pick you up at five o'clock."

"All right! Let's go to sleep. I will see you at five," Theresa almost sang.

"Good night, sweet Terry!" said Gabe in a loving tone.

"Good night, Don Juan," Terry answered playfully.

Theresa was already working on a plan to "eliminate" Linda. She was not going to let that interloper keep tempting her friend... her boyfriend, her lover? — She was just not going to let that happen. She would find a way to keep the single mother busy with something or someone else. Theresa thought about getting her a higher paying job and introducing her to an attractive bachelor. She would find something!

Meanwhile, on the opposite side of the city, a tragedy was developing. James Hickey, a young black man, was celebrating with two of his closest friends at his sister Lorraine's apartment that night. Larry and Antoine had been James's friends since they were in high school. For some reason, James invited them to have some beers with him. He was happy and told them he had broken up with his girlfriend, Ruby Maldonado.

"Man, why did you break up with her? She is a tight, hot babe!" asked Larry who considered Ruby to be the prettiest Mexican girl he ever saw.

"Larry, you just don't know how much of a bitch that doll is. I am celebrating my freedom. If you are interested in her, this is the time to make your move my man," was James's explanation and invitation to his friend.

"Hey, if James don't want her, there's gotta be something to it. I wouldn't want to get involved with her myself," said Antoine, the other friend, "I know that her family is tied to the damn Mexican Mafia. Those are some bad dudes; you don't want to mess with them. They will kill you for no reason, even if you just look at someone the wrong way. Apparently life is pretty cheap for them."

Antoine finished his warning to Larry, drank half of his beer and reached for more chips.

"So this time it's for good, brother? Or are you going to go back with her next week when she comes looking for you again?" asked Lorraine after putting her kids to sleep in their room.

James got up and hugged his sister. They were very close, the only surviving members of the Hickey family. Lorraine was twenty-four, and James, her older brother, was twenty-six. Their father died in a trucking accident; their mother died of cancer when Lorraine had her third baby. Their oldest brother, a burglar, was killed in prison. Their baby sister had run away six years before when their mother died; nobody had seen her or heard from her again. They didn't know it, but she had died in San Francisco two years earlier, among the homeless, and was buried in an unmarked pauper's grave.

"It's for good, little sis! I can guarantee you things are looking up already! I have no earthly intention of ever going back to that woman. I was thinking maybe you and the girls could go with me to live in Denver," James said.

"Did you win the lottery, James? Because I don't see how else you can take us anywhere. You are not even working anymore. Whatever happened to that job you had for years at Mr. Jackson's print shop? You left everything when you met that wench, Ruby. I knew she was no good for you from the beginning. I hope you mean it this time and never go back. Those people, Ruby and her family, give me the chills. They are killers, James, and you know it," Lorraine told him.

"I mean it, sis! And I have a little secret that you will learn in due time."

James picked his sister up and kissed her cheek. Antoine, who had feelings for Lorraine, got up and said:

"Can I get in line for one of those too?"

Antoine wanted to hug and kiss the single mother of three girls, a first, a second and a third- grader. The three different fathers of the girls were out of the picture and did not even pay child support. Antoine hoped to be the father of Lorraine's fourth kid.

"You sit your black ass down, motherfucker; this is my sister you are talking about!" James shouted, putting Lorraine down and turning to face Antoine with a menacing look on his face.

"Chill out, my man," Antoine told him. "I am just trying to be friendly, nothing else, shit!"

Antoine sat down while Larry laughed and clapped. Lorraine liked Antoine, but she was fed up with his type. All three of her last lovers had been just like him, ready to get her pregnant and then move out. She was now trying to take charge of her life. She was working as a custodian in the elementary school that all her girls attended. She had already earned her GED and was attending night classes at a community college.

"Hey, Antoine, if you really want some of this, you have to change your ways a little," Lorraine teased her friend pointing at her exuberant body.

"I will become a born-again Christian for you, baby!" he said enthusiastically.

Antoine looked at her and then at James to make sure he was not going to jump him. James let his sister manage the situation.

"That is the first thing, but you also need to get yourself a job," the woman said.

"Hey, I work! Whenever I can, but I work. You know I am a self-employed entrepreneur."

"I wouldn't call a twenty-five-year-old man with a lawn mower an entrepreneur. You still live with your mamma 'cause you can't even pay for a place of your own. I am tired of living in this goddamn public housing," she told Antoine.

"OK, all right. I promise to get me a job. They're always hiring at the barbecue place or the burger joints. Is that all you want? Man, women are just interested in money, money, money," said Antoine thinking he had some chance to get into Lorraine's pants.

He drank his beer after clinking Larry's. James was still looking at him with a serious face.

"Well, let's see. You become a good Christian, get yourself a college degree, a good job, a nice place and a car, then get me a wedding ring, and I am yours forever," Lorraine declared.

"Shit! You dreaming now, girl. You know I wa'no good at school. I flunked out of the ninth grade after my third try, and you want me to get a college degree. Who can do that?"

"I am doing it. I want to show my girls the way. You know I got a job and am attending college at night. I don't want to be a burger flipper; I am going to have my very own business," she announced.

"Well, you right baby. If I say I'll give it a try, can I get a little 'advance'?"

Antoine reached for Lorraine's hand. James grabbed Antoine's wrist and threw it back to his lap. They were sitting around the coffee table in the living room. James started threatening Antoine, who was trying to defend his position. Lorraine was talking loudly to both of them. Larry just laughed and clapped, amused by their quarreling.

"All right, cut it out! You are going to wake my babies up. I am going to bed now. I know neither one of you bums have to get up early, but I do. You better clean up any mess you make in my home, or I will never let you back in," Lorraine warned them as she walked to her bedroom.

"Can I go too?" asked Antoine.

The beers he had already drunk had lowered his inhibitions, so he felt brave enough to challenge the tougher James.

"Only if you do what I told you," the woman reminded Antoine from her bedroom door.

Lorraine went in, closed the door and locked it.

James moved his head from side to side; he was happy that his sister had handled Antoine's advances well. It was not that he did not like Antoine, but James was the man of the house. He was the only male figure in his nieces' lives. He had big plans for all of them. James got up, went to the fridge and grabbed three more beers. He brought the cards out and invited his two friends to play a little poker.

The three friends were playing and reminiscing of their high school days. James was the only one of the three who had actually graduated. He had been a great athlete in school, playing football and as a member of the track and field team. He won a city 10 K race when he was a senior; his school won the state championship with him as a wide receiver. At the time of his graduation, James felt responsible for Lorraine, his only sister left. Natalie, the youngest, had run away and their mother had died, so instead of going to college, he decided to stay in the city and get himself a job to help Lorraine support her three girls, as if he were their father.

"James, ain't you afraid of Ruby's brother — what's his name?" asked Larry after they finished their poker game and decided to put on a movie.

"Julian Maldonado, he thinks he is a bad ass, but I ain't afraid of him," said James, but without much conviction.

He knew Julian had killed a few men and that he had pistoleros (hit men) under his command that had murdered others.

"What'd Ruby say when you left?" asked Antoine, leaning back on the recliner.

He wished he had been in James's place when Ruby met him. She first liked James because he was a great dancer. They were at a mutual friend's wedding. After dancing once with James, Ruby danced the night away with him. Antoine figured that he could have hooked up with the Mexican beauty if Ruby had started dancing with him instead of James. Antoine, however, was not quite as good a dancer as James.

"She cussed me out and threatened that she was going to tell her brother that I beat her and raped her and that I was gonna talk to the cops," James explained.

"Oh, man! What you gonna do if she actually tells him?"

Antoine got up from the armchair and went looking out the window to check out the apartments parking area.

"I ain't worried about it. Sit your black ass down and watch the movie," was the relaxed answer by James.

The beers had worked their magic and were dissolving James's real concern of retaliation from the Maldonado family.

They watched the movie, but at the end of it, some gangsters killed the main guy. The possibility of retaliation came back to their minds.

"James, you got any guns here?" asked Larry from his position, lying down on the sofa.

He realized that things might get serious if the girl actually told her brother those lies.

"Shit, no! You know how my sister is. She wants nothing to do with guns in her house because of her kids. I sold the one my dad left me and ain't bought one since," James said.

James put on another movie and went back to the love seat to continue drinking his sixth beer. Things might get a little rough if Ruby did lie to her brother about him. For a year he had an up-and-down kind of relationship with the beautiful Mexican girl. She had taken him as a trophy. James was a nice looking specimen of a man, deep voiced, tall, muscular, handsome, honest, with a good sense of humor and great rhythm on the dance floor. She, however, was into drug dealing and got James involved in the business. That was the reason he had left the printer job he had since graduating from high school.

"Beep, beep, beep, beep!" James's pager went off.

He looked at it. It was Ruby's mobile phone number.

"I guess this woman didn't believe me when I told her I didn't want nothing to do with her no more," said James heading for the phone.

He was going to put her in her place once and for all. He quickly dialed her number. As soon as he heard her voice, James told her:

"I told you we were through, Ruby... What?"

The ex-girlfriend interrupted his statement saying:

"And I told you we were not through, lover boy. I told my brother that you beat me up, raped me in front of your friends and threatened that you were talking to the narcotics task force about us. Needless to say, he got a little pissed off at you. I think he already sent some of his friends to deliver a message to you," she informed him.

James dropped on to a stool in the bar between the kitchen and the dining room. His legs felt weak. He knew what that meant, and it left him speechless.

"Good-bye, Jimmy-boy. You are dead meat, motherfucker!" Ruby said laughing.

His two friends looked at him and understood what was going on just by looking at his body language. Ruby laughed out louder before hanging up on James.

"Shit! I guess I'm in trouble now. I better get out of here and go some place where they cannot find me. Larry, your truck running?" James asked.

"Man, that truck's been broke for a month," was the answer from Larry. "I ain't got no money to fix it. It needs a new transmission and shit."

A sudden knocking at the door startled them all. The three friends looked at each other fearfully, with eyes wide open. The knocking was repeated, louder that time.

"Bam, bam, bam, bam!"

Lorraine came out of her room, tying on her robe.

"Hell! Why don't you get the door?" she yelled at them.

She stopped and understood what the situation was just by looking at the faces of the three men's standing still in the living room area looking at each other.

"I gotta go! They want me. Just stall them for me. I don't think they will do anything to you if I'm gone. Tell'em you ain't seen me today," James whispered to his sister and friends.

He then ran to the back bedroom window. Lorraine lived on a second floor apartment, which had only one door. As soon as James jumped from the second floor window, Lorraine opened the door. Three Hispanic men barged in with guns in their hands.

"Where is James?" one of them demanded.

He pushed Lorraine down on the sofa next to Antoine and Larry. They pretended to have been awakened by their knocking on the door.

"We ain't seen'im," Lorraine said, trembling.

The guy who pushed her slapped her hard.

"Lying bitch! We know he is here. *Muchachos, busquen en los cuartos!* (Guys, search the bedrooms!)" he ordered his men.

Antoine tried to do something to defend Lorraine, but he fell back down on the sofa with the point of the gun between his eyes.

"Do you want to die tonight, nigger?" threatened the pistolero.

"No, sir," he mumbled.

"Good! I may decide not to kill you if you just tell us where he is."

"He already left," Lorraine told him, adding, "I think he was going to Corpus Christi."

The mobile phone rang on the pistolero's waist. He picked it up and listened to the caller; it was Ruby. She told him James had left the location.

"Let's go, guys. The bird flew through the back window. We got to catch up with him," the oldest of the three gunmen called the other two.

Lorraine's girls woke up and started crying, startled by the two strangers in their room. Lorraine got up from the sofa to see what was going on. The older mafioso grabbed her by the neck, put the gun to her temple and said:

"We're leaving now. If you call the cops, we'll be back. We know where you live."

All three men bolted out the door and got in a car. James had "borrowed" a car he found with the engine running. It had been left by a man who was dropping off his girlfriend in the apartments. When the man finished kissing his girlfriend good night, he turned and saw James fleeing in his sports sedan. The man yelled and ran after him but was unable to stop James. His girlfriend let him in her apartment to call the police.

Ruby was alerting the Mexican Mafia hitmen by phone that James had gotten into a red sports sedan. They saw the car speeding by and started chasing it with their big luxury car. James took a street to an interstate highway with the intention of losing them. He gained speed in the sporty car; before he realized it, he was doing a hundred miles an hour. He took the exit to the loop, hoping the hitmen would go straight on the expressway. Unfortunately for him, they did see him and followed him onto the loop. The luxury car gained on the sporty car as they approached the next interchange. James slowed down a little because he wanted to turn onto the road going west hoping to let them go south on the loop. One of the gunmen fired a couple of rounds as their white car approached the red car. James ducked and jerked the steering wheel to the right. The car got onto the access ramp west as he planned, but he was going on the left two wheels. The vehicle fell on all four wheels again. Immediately, James stepped on the gas and headed towards downtown. Looking in the rearview mirror, he saw smoke coming out of the tires of the white car; the mafiosos had decided to stop and back up instead of going all the way around.

James took the next exit he found. He turned south on it and hid under the overpass for a couple of minutes. It was 4:15 in the morning. He could hear the speeding white car going away, trying to locate him going west. He drove away from the overpass thinking where he could go. He thought about going to the East Side Police Substation, but he realized he would be arrested for driving a stolen car. He did not want to go to jail. It would not be safe there for him. Julian had guys in jail that could do what these three gangsters were trying to do out there. He decided to turn east instead, to get out of the area. The big car seemed to have vanished.

James went to his old high school, thinking it would be safe for him to hide there at that time of the morning; however, Ruby figured out where he went. She drove over to the school to confirm. She was evil and smart. Once she saw the red two-door, she concealed her own silver convertible and called Miguel Salinas, the hitman with the big luxury sedan.

"I found your man, Mike," Ruby told Miguel on her cell phone. "He is hiding behind the high school stadium, come and finish the job. I want to go to bed."

In 15 minutes, the white car arrived. James was able to spot them before they found him, so he drove away quickly. The chase was on again!

"How in the hell did they find me?" exclaimed James frustrated.

James took a highway going into town to get away from them, but the hit men kept chasing him back to the loop doing over a hundred miles an hour. The traffic was sparse that Tuesday morning; the smell of death was in the air. The red car did not have much gas left in the tank; the warning light announcing "empty" came on as James drove into the downtown area with his enemies tailing him. Every time they got close enough to the sporty car, one of the pistoleros would pop out and shoot at James. He was forced to drive from side to side to avoid getting hit. The condemned man got out of the highway. He did not want his car to run out of gas on the open road, where he would be an easy target. He turned west as soon as he exited the freeway. He hit another car at the first intersection, but kept on going. The impact slowed him down a little. The front tire was rubbing the metal and blew up. Now the Mexican Mafia men were already next to him. They fired a couple of shots at the car. James ducked inside and lost control of the vehicle. The red car flipped over and fell into a creek bed. Everything went black for James upon impact with the base of the bridge.

The twenty-six-year-old man felt no pain; It was as though he were floating in the air. James pulled out the lottery ticket he had been carrying in his shirt pocket and laughed. He then saw himself running scared. How could he be in two places at once? From his floating-up-in-the-air position, he followed his other self, running through dark alleys, followed by the barking of many dogs. He also saw that the white car was catching up with him. At the end of the alley he saw it approaching. Someone fired three shots and said something to him. His running self fell to the ground like a rag doll.

His survival instinct woke James Hickey from his stupor as he heard some men talking in Spanish to each other and coming down to the bottom of the almost-dry creek. He crawled out of the window of the car and ran as if he were going for a deep pass in a football game. His life depended on it. Miguel spotted him first and fired a shot in his direction, but the bridge provided James with some cover from the bullets. The hitmen climbed back up to their car to catch up with him. They were very familiar with that side of town. James still had the vision of his death and was running faster than he ever had. Before he got to the downtown area, he saw the white car approaching him. He thought about God at that moment. A period of his life flashed through his eyes in that brief instant.

The Hickeys had converted to Catholicism while living in Chicago. All the children had been baptized, celebrated penance, first communion and confirmation. James had even been an altar boy when he was eleven and twelve years old. He had been a sporadically practicing Catholic until he met Ruby a year back. Now he prayed:

"Lord, help me!"

The luxury sedan was already in front of him, blocking his way. All three men fired at the same time at a range no farther than three feet away. Miguel told James:

"This is Julian's message for what you did to his sister, motherfucker!"

James fell like a rag doll on the pavement feeling life escaping him. The gangsters took off, burning rubber, and disappeared down the street. It was 5:30 a.m.

That morning, when Gabriel got to the sisters' house, Theresa was already stretching in the front porch. She was wearing tennis shoes, shorts and T-shirt. She came out yawning but determined to go for a power walk. It was 5:00 o'clock as he had promised.

"Good morning, Gabe. Are you ready for this?" she asked.

"Let's do it, Terry!"

They took off walking towards downtown at a good pace. Theresa was doing a lot of the talking while he just listened and enjoyed her voice and her company. This was better than talking on the phone. He could see her and enjoy her presence. She looked so lovely even that early in the morning. Gabriel was surprised that he was already sweating while Theresa was cool as a cucumber. She told him some of the things that she had gone through in Europe, in Latin America and in Africa. Gabriel looked at Theresa's body; she was becoming a middle-age woman with a fuller figure. He remembered a joke and shared it with her as they walked.

"A little four-year-old girl was eating a Twinkie in the barbershop while watching the barber cutting her dad's hair. She was standing too close to the chair, so the barber looked at her and told her with a kind smile, 'You are going to get hair on your Twinkie, sweetie.' The little girl smiled back and told the old man, 'I know. I am getting boobs too!'"

Theresa laughed at his joke and slapped his shoulder knowing that they were free of any intrusion as they walked in the dark, early morning. Before they realized it, they were next to the downtown area. They were about to turn back home when they heard three shots and a car speeding away. It was 5:30 a.m.

"Let's go back, Gabe! Those were gunshots!" said Sister Theresa alarmed.

"No, let's go check it out!" Gabriel tried to convince her to go with him. "Listen," he said. "Whoever fired those shots is apparently gone. I cannot even hear the car that took off. I think it happened around the block over here. I hear someone crying for help. Can you hear?"

He took her by the hand and kept walking in the direction of the sound he heard.

"Yes, I hear someone moaning, there, in the alley!" said Theresa walking fast hand-in-hand with Gabriel.

There was a black man moaning and rolling on his own blood in the alley a block away from the homeless shelter, and just about three blocks from the hospital. Father G turned him over and noticed that the man had been shot three times and looked as though he was going to die. The priest placed his hands on the fallen man; Theresa looked at Gabriel wondering if he was going to perform a miracle and save the man's life. The minister looked at her and shook his head indicating he would not. Instead, he picked the dying man up in his strong arms and said:

"The hospital is only three blocks away. Let's take him there. It'd be faster than calling an ambulance."

Theresa just followed him, praying that they might be able to get medical help for the man soon enough to save his life. He was still alive and started talking when they got to the emergency room. The priest asked for a stretcher to place the gunshot victim. While they waited for the medical staff to come and look at him, the injured man thanked them for their help and asked them in a weak voice:

"Who are you anyway that would care to help a stranger?"

"I am Father Gabriel, and this is Sister Theresa."

"Ah, two servants of the Lord! I guess He sent you to see me on my last breath."

The man knew he was dying, but Theresa tried to give him courage.

"Don't say that. You are in the hospital now. As long as there is life, there is hope."

The dying man laughed painfully and kept talking to them.

"I — had a vision — last night. I saw the winning lottery numbers in that vision, 1, 3, 7, 12, 40 — and 50. I went and bought a quick pick — and I got exactly those numbers! — I was — excited — because I just knew that I had the winning — ticket."

Sister Theresa saw that he was struggling. He coughed some blood. She looked around.

"You should save your strength. Where are the doctors or the nurses?" she exclaimed.

Gabriel put his hand on the man's shoulder and signaled for him to continue his story.

"I was sure I was going to be rich — I broke up with my girlfriend — She was no good — Has a brother — in the Mexican — Mafia. She is beautiful but has — an evil heart. Father, I was a good Catholic — until I got together with Ruby — She is the one that set me up. Julian Maldonado, her — brother, he was the one that sent his pistoleros — to kill me. They told me — before firing the shots — 'Julian sent you this — moth...' cough, cough!"

It seemed as if no one was available in the emergency room while the man's life slipped away. Father Gabriel got closer to James listening to his faltering voice. The man had his eyes closed and was talking very low, as in a confession. Theresa stepped back.

The emergency medical team finally came and took over the stretcher as the priest blessed James and absolved him of his sins. They hooked him up to a monitor and started an IV. The monitor read only a flat line. The patient's heart had stopped beating. The emergency team went to work trying to revive him. They set up their equipment around the victim and were ready to act. The trauma specialist there, Dr. Solis, told them to stop, not try anything else. He pointed to the man's injuries.

"This man received three fatal shots, to the heart, the liver and the right kidney. I don't know how he made it to the hospital still alive. He should have died where he fell. There is nothing we can do to bring him back. He is gone!" the doctor declared.

Gabriel and Theresa were still there watching the scene. Then, they went to sit down for a moment. Theresa was curious to know what else the dying man had told Gabriel. She sat next to him and asked:

"Can you relate to me what the man was telling you?"

"Yes, I can," Gabriel replied. "I am surprised that he got to tell me so much in so little time. I feel as though I knew him from the few flashes he gave me about his short life. His name was James Hickey. Apparently Ruby Maldonado, his girlfriend, was very upset that he dumped her, so she called her brother, Julian Maldonado, the guy in the Mexican Mafia that he mentioned. She accused James of beating her and raping her before leaving her apartment. James allegedly was going to turn the Maldonados over to the police, which was not true. All James wanted was to get away from them and live to collect the lottery prize. He has a sister, Lorraine Hickey, living on the east side, whom he planned to help with the money. He gave me the ticket."

Father Gabriel showed Sister Theresa the ticket James had given him.

"Yes, I saw him handing you something. What did he say about it?" she asked.

"He told me to take his half for my needs and give the other half to Lorraine. He trusted that I would do so. He also told me he had foreseen his end exactly as it happened."

"Ten Million dollars is the estimated price for this Wednesday!" exclaimed Theresa reading the ticket.

"Half of that would help Father Michael rebuild his mission in Africa very nicely!" commented Father G, wondering if that was why they found the dying man.

"Who is Father Michael?" asked the religious sister.

"He was in the seminary with me. We were ordained together. He and Father Raphael, whom I told you about before, were very close to me. We have a lot in common. Raphael went to Los Angeles to work in the inner city. I came back home to preach to my people and Michael decided to be like you and become a missionary in the black continent. You should meet both of them one of these days; they are like brothers to me. We practiced boxing together while in the seminary; they are both very tough and very sweet at the same time," Gabriel related to her.

"Like you," Terry said, adding, "I really ought to meet those guys."

A police officer came in to get a report on the shooting victim. After talking to the two religious, Officer Vaughn told them they would have to go to the Homicide office and give a statement. Father Gabriel looked at his watch. He had to get back to celebrate his morning Mass and take Sister Theresa home to get ready for school.

"Officer, we will go to the Homicide office later on. We have to get back to our parish now," he said.

"I am sorry, Reverend. It is really important that you talk to the detectives now," the officer insisted.

"I already told you all the information we have. I understand about the statement to the detectives; however, I must be back for the morning Mass. Check with the Homicide supervisor. They know me and will tell you that you can trust me. I will come back later and bring Sister Theresa with me."

The officer called Homicide and talked to Sergeant Villanueva who told him it was OK to let the religious go. Father Gabriel had helped them before in several cases and was familiar with the procedures. Officer Vaughn took the two religious home in his patrol car. They dropped off Theresa first and then went to the priest's house.

During the reading of the Gospel in the Mass, Gabriel remembered James Hickey because the section he read was from Luke 12:13-20. It was about a rich man who had the best harvest year and was concerned about what to do with so much wealth. He decided to expand his barns to store his riches, then to eat drink and be merry, but the Angel of the Lord appeared to him and called him a fool because his life was going to be taken that same night.

Father G thought about the lottery prize, ten million dollars! If James's first vision of winning the lottery were as right as the vision of his own death, Gabriel could become a millionaire, take Theresa with him and disappear to a remote paradisiacal island in the Caribbean. He shook his head to erase that tempting vision and pronounced his friend's name in his mind.

"Michael, Michael, I believe God will provide what you asked of Him through me."

He continued the celebration without further interruption.

As soon as he was able to go to the police station to give his statement about the shooting, Gabriel went and took Theresa with him. It was a good excuse to go downtown with "his girl." When they got there, a homicide detective welcomed them and took Theresa in for her statement. While Father waited, he saw a black girl coming into the police station in tears. He assumed she was Lorraine; there was a certain resemblance in her face to that of James.

"Are you Lorraine Hickey?" the priest asked her.

"Yes, who are you?" she said looking at the stranger.

"I am Father Gabriel. Did the police explain to you—?"

"Yes, yes, I can't believe it! Are they sure they have the right man?"

"Unfortunately, I think they do," Gabriel told her.

He paused for a moment and then said:

"I was there when James passed away. He loved you very much and his last words were precisely of the love he had for you and your girls."

Father Gabriel grabbed her hands to lend her moral support. She was devastated. Lorraine hugged the priest seeking comfort as she broke down crying again.

"James is now with the Lord. I am sure that he will continue watching over you. Think that he has gone ahead to prepare a place for you in heaven when you two meet again. I know that you are a woman of faith."

Lorraine stepped away from the priest and sat down, wiping her eyes with a tissue.

"How long did you know James? He never mentioned you," Lorraine said.

"Long enough to be sure that he did not live in vain. I helped him make his peace with our Lord before his last breath."

Another detective was assigned to take Lorraine's statement and also to take her to identify her brother's body. Before she left the waiting area, she asked Father Gabriel:

"Would you help me with the funeral, Father?"

The minister held her hands tight, smiled at her and told her:

"Of course, Lorraine. You can count on me."

A third detective came out and invited the priest to go into his office to give his statement. Detective Joe Fernandez not only shook his hand but also hugged the priest like an old friend. Gabriel had officiated at the detective's marriage earlier that year. The detective was very polite; he was also very efficient and finished the statement before the other detective completed Sister Theresa's statement.

When the Gabriel came out to wait for Theresa, there was a beautiful Mexican woman in the waiting room. He was sure she was Ruby, so he called her name.

"Ruby Maldonado?"

Her attorney was by her side. Both the woman, who looked like a movie star, and her attorney turned to see the priest with a puzzled look.

"Who are you?" asked the attorney looking at Gabriel's clerical collar and getting between them.

"I am Father Gabriel, but that's not important. I have a message for Ruby," he announced.

Gabriel sidestepped the attorney to face his client and tell her:

"James told me that he loved you very much. It is very sad that you will have to go on for the rest of your life knowing that you caused his death."

"Wait a second! I object to this baseless accusation against my client. Who the hell are you? And under whose authority do you make this accusation?"

Ruby's attorney protested immediately and got in between them again. Father G placed his powerful hands on the attorney's shoulders, looked into his eyes and told him:

"I work under the authority of the Almighty. What I say is the truth!"

Then, effortlessly, he moved him out of the way to face Ruby once more. He told her:

"Come and talk to me, alone, when you feel you are ready to talk about this, Ruby."

The woman reached out to place her hand on his chest, and smiled at him seductively.

"Are you interested in the 'opening' left by the unfortunate death of my boyfriend?"

He took her hand off his chest and responded:

"I am more interested in the vacuum in your life than in any 'openings' you have. May God forgive you!"

Then Gabriel quickly stepped out of the room, leaving them puzzled. The attorney realized the reason they were at the police station because Detective Fernandez came to get Ruby for her statement. The attorney started questioning the policeman.

"Is there a warrant for my client? Why do you want to question her when she is a victim herself? Her boyfriend was killed this morning by some thugs, and you are wasting your time questioning innocent people when you should be out looking for the culprits," he ranted.

Fernandez looked at both of them, shook his head and took them in for her statement. He knew that the attorney would not let her answer any questions other than her identity and personal information. Like a consummate actress, Ruby went in crying, playing the distressed damsel.

Gabriel was outside the police station waiting for Theresa. He saw her come out, laughing with the detective. They stopped at the door to say goodbye. Sister Theresa hugged the detective; he gave her a kiss on the cheek.

"What was that all about?" questioned Gabriel, a little bothered by the policeman's demonstration of affection.

"What?" Theresa asked, feigning ignorance.

"You just met that guy, and you let him hug and kiss you like—"

"—Like every other woman hugs and kisses you?"

"Well, that's different!" Gabriel said defensively.

"No, it is not!" Theresa argued.

"Who is he, anyway?" Gabriel asked.

"He is Charlie, Charles Ross. His older sister, Alice, used to go to school with me. She is married to a banker and has six children now. I spent the night at her house a few times. That's how I know Charlie. He was a little boy then. When we started talking, he asked me if I had been in his sister's high school. That was how we found out that we already knew each other. He confessed that he had a crush on me back then."

"Oh, yeah?" said Father G smiling as they walked to his car.

"Yeah! He was about ten at the time. Are you a little jealous?"

"No!" he lied, but then admitted, "Well, maybe. This is strange. I never felt this way before, that I remember."

"Oh, get over it! He is married and has two babies. Now if he got divorced or suddenly became a widower—" Theresa said, playfully.

"Get in the car and stop torturing me, woman!"

Gabriel opened the car door for Theresa and spanked her on the way in as her punishment.

"Hey, that hurt!" she protested, but got in the car with a big grin in her face.

"Are you mad at me?" asked Theresa, as Gabriel drove out of the parking lot.

"I cannot get mad at you; I love you too much," he declared.

"Could you then sing me a song on the way home?"

Gabriel thought about a song, took a deep breath and began singing. The composer of the song asks for God's forgiveness for loving so passionately that even killing someone does not matter. He is tormented when someone else speaks, sees or touches his beloved. She has become his hell and his heaven.

"How do you manage to come up with the right song at the right time?" Theresa asked him.

"I don't know," he confessed, and then added, "Inspiration combined with a wide repertoire, I guess."

He really did not know, but songs would come to him from memories of his youth. He knew several hundred songs, so there was plenty to choose from. Usually a single word was enough to trigger a song from his repertoire.

On Thursday morning, November the 4th, Father Gabriel was reading the newspaper and remembered the ticket he had in his shirt pocket He had not mentioned it to anybody else. Only Sister Theresa and he knew about the ticket. The winning numbers were 1, 3, 7, 12, 40 and 50; all were meaningful biblical numbers, the same numbers that were on James's ticket! Gabriel opened his eyes wide in amazement and checked the numbers on the paper twice against those of the ticket. James was right: he had a 10 million dollar winning ticket! The priest sat back on his desk chair in his office. He felt a kind of dark power come upon him. He had never experienced this feeling before; he had never cared about money before. God always provided him with everything he ever needed. The scene he had during the Mass on Tuesday morning came back to him. Theresa had been in his arms wearing a small bikini, playing with him in the clear and warm waters of the Caribbean. Gabriel closed his eyes and enjoyed the vision in his mind. The dark power surrounding him moved to the window and took the shape of a black cat with eyes red as lit charcoals. The feline seemed to smile watching the priest rubbing the multi-million-dollar winning lottery ticket between his thumb and index finger.

"What are you daydreaming of, Father Gabriel?"

Sister Theresa brought him back to reality as she entered his office unannounced.

"Close the door, Sister, and have a seat."

Gabriel smiled at her and showed her the ticket. She understood what that meant.

"Oh, my God! A winner?"

"Yes, James was right!"

"What are you going to do now, Gabriel?"

"There are two options, my friend: Option number one," the priest said getting up from his chair and coming around the desk to say it in a whisper and look closely at her pretty face. "We keep the ten million and elope to the Caribbean where no one will ever find us, and live happily ever after."

Sister Theresa opened her eyes wide and blushed considering that idea.

"Or?" she said to interrupt the silence Gabriel had created.

"Or we tell Lorraine about her brother's last wish. This would make her and her children millionaires, a whole mission in Africa prosperous for many families, Father Michael very happy, and you and me to remain as we are."

"Definitely the second option!" said Theresa, thrilled that a miracle had taken place again.

"Of course! Blessed be the Lord who always provides to those who trust in Him!" exclaimed the priest, going back to his seat as if her words had freed him from the spell of the dark power that had taken over when he learned about the winning numbers.

"We will tell her after the burial today. But — what brought you to my office?" he inquired.

"I came to— I am sorry— I totally forgot why I came!"

"Well, I think you accomplished your mission, Sister," Gabriel told her, adding in a fake authoritative tone, "now get your...self back to your class."

Once Theresa left, he turned around and looked at his crucifix on the wall.

"Thank you Lord, for sending Theresa to help me make the right decision."

Outside the principal's office, the black cat with the red eyes jumped off the window where it had been watching the couple. The creature disappeared before hitting the ground and changed into the foul-smelling whirlwind. It picked up speed and dirt, running across the soccer field and knocking down a couple of children on its way. The whirlwind vanished as the soccer players wondered what had happened and helped the fallen children get up. There was a strange and strong odor in the air. The kids started teasing each other about being responsible for the smell.

After all the people left the cemetery, Father Gabriel and Sister Theresa walked with Lorraine back to the limo that would take her home. Theresa took the three kids to the side while Gabriel talked to Lorraine alone for a moment. He explained what happened in James's last minutes of life and the visions he had. The priest gave the winning ticket to the single mother after describing her brother's last wish.

"James told me to keep his half for my needs and to give the other half to you and your girls. I don't need anything, thank God! But I have a friend who needs all the help he can get in Africa, Father Michael. He is a missionary over there. His mission was destroyed by fire and flood; they have to start the whole thing over. He had asked for our help just before I met your brother."

Lorraine found it hard to believe the priest would hand over ten million dollars and not want to keep any of the money for himself. Gabriel gave her a letter with the information on Father Michael's Mission.

"Father, you can count on that money for your friend's African mission. As a matter of fact, I will go over there personally and see that he gets all the help he needs even if it is more than half of what James left us. I was thinking about leaving town to protect my girls anyway, and I always wanted to go to Africa!"

They called the girls and embraced each other in a group hug. Then they formed a circle and started dancing around, singing praise to the Lord. Lorraine hugged the priest tightly; he picked her up and spun her around with her feet off the ground. When he put her back down, she kissed him on both cheeks and called her daughters to kiss him too. Lorraine went and kissed Theresa while the three little girls mugged Gabriel with kisses. The mother and her three daughters boarded the limo to go home. The limo driver was amazed at how happy these people were after just burying a relative, but he said nothing.

"Oh, wait! Lorraine," Gabriel called out, "Could you also please take Father Michael, on my behalf, a big jar of the hottest picante sauce you can find?"

"Sure, Father Gabriel," she responded from the open window of the limo, "I'll take a whole box of different sauces and see which one he likes the best.

Will we ever see you over there, in Father Michael's mission?"

"Maybe! Just keep me informed on its progress. Sister Theresa has worked in Africa before; she could be my guide over there."

"Sounds like a good plan!" agreed Theresa, imagining they could travel together. The limo drove away with the new millionaires.

Gabriel and Theresa stood by themselves looking at the limo disappear as it left the cemetery. Theresa hugged him and kissed him on both cheeks. He held her in his arms for a moment remembering the vision of what he could have done with the money if he had decided to keep it.

"You did the right thing, and I am very proud of you!" she told him.

He offered her his left arm and took her to his Priestmobile. It felt good to walk side by side with his beloved friend. Satan in the form of a grackle with red eyes was watching them from the top of an electric pole outside the cemetery as they drove out. He growled:

"You are not so good, Gabriel. You will fall sooner or later."

Chapter XI
The Exorcism

Don Pedro Mireles went to Father Gabriel's morning Mass on Wednesday to invite him to breakfast. The priest agreed to go with his old friend, but first he had to talk to a couple with a three-year-old boy he saw staying inside the church after the Mass.

"Shalom! How are you folks doing?" said the pastor approaching them as they finished their prayers.

"We are OK thank you, Father. It is our little boy who is sick, very sick. We heard that miracles happen in this church. That's why we came today. Benito, our baby boy here, needs a heart transplant. He was born with a defective heart. The doctors say that he can only be cured with an operation. We would need half a million dollars for such an operation; we have no way of getting that much money. I am self-employed; I own a small tire repair shop; we don't even have health insurance. If Benito doesn't have the operation, he'll surely die soon. He is our only son," the boy's father, Leopoldo Cardenas, explained to the pastor.

Father G felt great compassion and approached the boy. He placed his hands on him and prayed. Instead of feeling the healing energy of the Holy Spirit, Gabriel felt that he was having a vision. He saw a golden demon sticking his hand in the little boy's chest to squeeze it. The demon looked at the priest and laughed.

"Do you want this boy, Gabriel? You will have to fight me if you want to help him."

Gabriel looked at the boy in his vision. The little guy started to cry in pain and terror. The cry of the child brought the priest back from his vision. He let go of the child's head, squatted down to his level and looked into his big, scared eyes. The boy had seen his vision too. Gabriel touched the boy's face and told him:

"Don't worry, Benito. I will protect you from the big, bad, Golden Demon."

Benito's mother looked at her husband in amazement and then asked Father Gabriel:

"How did you know about the Golden Demon? Benito had spoken to us about him, but we thought it had been that he got scared one day while watching wrestling on TV. There was a masked wrestler called the Golden Demon who beat up another wrestler," she explained.

Father G found himself trembling and sweating after the terrible vision. He did not know what to do at that point, but he told them:

"Go in peace. God will provide the means to save your son. I am going to pray for Benito. Come back Sunday. By then, I should have more information for you."

The couple did as they were told and did not question the priest. He gave them his blessing and kissed Benito on the top of his head.

Gabriel was shaken by the strange experience. He walked to the restaurant with Pedro but declined to have breakfast. He only drank a little of his water to wet his tongue and throat. The older guy disposed of some huevos rancheros with bacon, flour tortillas and coffee. Father G was reviewing his little New Testament pocket book while Pedro ate.

"Prayer and fasting!" he mumbled closing the book as if he had found what he was looking for.

"What are you talking about, Father?" Pedro asked.

The priest opened the book again and read from chapter 17 of Matthew's Gospel. The passage speaks of a possessed man whom the disciples could not cure. They brought him the man and Jesus exorcized him. When the disciples asked him how come they could not do it, Jesus explained that it was because of their lack of faith adding that those demons could only be expelled through prayer and fasting. Pedro looked at his religious friend not understanding what he was talking about since the priest had not shared with him the problem of the Cardenas family, nor the vision he experienced that morning. Instead, Pedro changed the subject to something he found in the paper at that moment.

"Isn't this, Jorge Ramirez, one of your boys?"

The old man showed him a picture of the county's most wanted criminal. The young man had been an altar boy, bible student, cantor, lector, seminary candidate, good high school student and pride of his family. That same young man was wanted on warrants for aggravated sexual assault of a child, aggravated robbery, and aggravated assault on a police officer. He was also suspected in several other similar crimes.

"The paper says he should be considered armed and dangerous because he took an officer's weapon and has been using it in the robberies. There is a 50,000 dollars reward for the capture or information leading to his capture,"

Pedro read out.

The police force was hot after him. Apparently he had sexually assaulted a member of his family but the paper gave no details on that case. Father Gabriel rubbed his forehead in disbelief.

"Oh, my God! How can this be?" he exclaimed.

Pedro noticed that the priest was saddened by the news of his young friend, so he looked for a different theme to discuss with him. He opened the sports page.

"Look at this, Father. They are offering 500,000.00 dollars to the man who can defeat the Golden Demon in the ring. The contest is open to all, professional or amateur fighters, wrestlers, boxers, judo or karate fighters, or any other man tough enough who dares to face this giant."

The title of the wrestler caught the minister's attention. He started pondering on the coincidence of the advertisement, the amount of money, and the vision he had. Don Pedro took another gulp of hot coffee and related to his friend.

"You know, Father, I used to be a good professional wrestler long ago. If I were 20 years younger, I would fight this guy. He is known to have killed several men in the ring and left some others disabled for life."

The priest seemed to be in a trance, but he heard the old man. Gabriel was saying:

"500,000 dollars— Golden Demon— Fight— Heart operation— Prayer and fasting."

Thinking about Jorge Ramirez's family, Father G shook his head and told his friend:

"I have to go, Pedro, thank you for inviting me to breakfast."

"You only had a drink of water, Father!"

"The intention is what counts, my friend. I will see you later."

The priest almost ran out of the restaurant after shaking Pedro's hand and headed for his office.

Mrs. Greene, the parish secretary, told him the Ramirez family had just called for him. They wanted him to go to their house immediately.

"Jorge?" said Father G, guessing what the call was about.

"Yes, apparently he came back home. They also called the police," explained Mrs. Greene while Father gathered some of his things, crucifix, holy water, prayer book and his stole. The secretary had seen Jorge's picture in the paper that morning too.

"I will be back as soon as I can. Tell Deacon Garcia to take any appointments I have this morning, and notify Mrs. Gray that I am out so that she can take charge at the school."

The priest got in his old car and drove to the Ramirez's family home. A couple of patrol cars and an unmarked detective's car were there already. Lupe Ramirez, Jorge's mother came out crying to receive the pastor with a hug. Raul Ramirez, the father, took off his hat and shook the priest's hand. The policemen were searching the house and the immediate vicinity, but Jorge was gone already. Gabriel noticed that both parents had some recent injuries. Raul had a black eye and a busted lip; Lupe had bruises on both sides of her neck. The officers holstered their weapons and informed the parents that the boy was not around anymore. They put out the description of the wanted man advising officers in the area be on the look out for him.

The patrolmen left, but the detectives, one from Sex Crimes and one from Robbery, stayed to talk to the parents. The Ramirezes were very distraught; they had obviously been crying a lot. Father G asked them to sit down and tell him what had happened. They went into the living room to talk. The detectives asked the priest if they could sit in and listen to what they had to say. The priest asked the Ramirezes if they had a problem with that. They agreed to let the detectives come in and listen.

"Everything had been going so well for Jorge. He was more sure every day that he wanted to become a priest like you, Father Gabriel. Then he started hanging out with a small group of students at his high school, and he began to change. All of a sudden, he started staying up late, smoking, drinking, probably started experimenting with drugs and sex," the mother was telling the priest, who was holding her hand to comfort her.

"That group of boys and girls were interested in witchcraft, Santeria, devil worshiping, heavy metal music, horror movies and black clothing. They would get together and go to the cemetery at night."

At that moment, someone was coming through the front door. The detectives automatically reached for their guns ready to confront the suspect they were looking for; however, it was a girl, Cindy Lowe, who was asking if anyone was home. Lupe said:

"Cindy, come in. We are in the living room."

Jorge's father went and got the young girl. She had been the closest to Jorge, his "girlfriend" in the group. She had bruises on her face and arms too.

"Where is he?" asked the recently arrived girl.

"He is gone again, Cindy. Sit down and help us try to sort things out,"

Lupe told her, bringing her to sit by her side on the sofa.

"What did you do in that group that made Jorge change so much? He is not my son anymore. I don't recognize him at all!" the mother questioned the girl in front of her husband, the detectives and the priest.

"At first it was all fun and games, we were looking for thrills and deep sensations," the girl confessed. "We got into heavy metal music and horror movies. Then somebody brought cigarettes and someone else alcohol; we thought we were really cool then. From there, we tried sniffing glue and paint, smoking marijuana; one of the guys had a friend that could get us crack and even heroin or cocaine. We tried it all. Of course, with all these things, we also started having sex with all of the members. There were six boys and six girls; we called ourselves 'Satan's Apostles' to scare the bullies in school. We would go and have orgies in the cemetery, chanting to the evil spirits and getting high."

The distraught parents lowered their heads and covered their faces hearing what they had suspected that was going on. The girl continued with her story.

"It was on one of those nights at the cemetery when it happened."

Cindy's face reflected the terror of that night as she tried to explain.

"We had gone to the library earlier that day looking for books on the occult, chants, witchcraft, Satanism and ancient religions. Each one of us signed out a book. Jorge found the one we all agreed was the coolest. It had a cover that looked and felt like human skin and was written in red ink, like blood. It seemed to be very old and was as thick as a Bible. That was the book we used to invoke Satan that night."

Now it was Father Gabriel who was shaking his head hearing about that aberration.

"What was the name of that book, Cindy?" asked the priest.

"I cannot remember, I think it was a foreign name of a Middle Eastern language, but I cannot recall what it was."

"OK, please continue telling us what happened that night." Gabriel urged Cindy.

"We made some designs on the ground in the cemetery, a circle, a six-pointed star and some symbols we copied from the book. Jorge got in the middle of the circle and began leading the prayer from the book; we were repeating every word he said. We were outside the circle. The moon got covered by clouds— An electric storm began approaching as we continued our chanting. We freaked out, but we continued the prayer even though we didn't know what we were saying. Then a strong wind with dust involved us in darkness. Lightning hit Jorge. The circle and the star caught fire, so we could see what was happening to him. We stopped chanting and could not make a sound even if we tried. We saw something like a claw of fire holding Jorge. He could not move but was screaming in terrible pain. It chilled us to the bone to see him like that. The giant fire claw rotated his body around. Then he fell on his knees with his face looking up. Something or someone invisible opened his mouth wide. We heard a deep, sinister laughter all around us and a voice that said, 'Eat me!' All the dust, fire and wind collected into a stream that went in through Jorge's mouth, and the voice said, 'You are mine now!'"

The girl had tears rolling down her cheeks and was moving her body back and forth anxiously, just rocking on the sofa as she remembered the terrible scene. Lupe put her arm around her to give her courage. Cindy continued telling her story:

"Jorge jumped up after all the fire went into his mouth. His voice had changed, and his eyes were lit like burning charcoals. We all got scared and ran away, but Jorge grabbed me by the ankle to keep me from escaping. He slapped me around, hard, tore all my clothes off and sodomized me right there. He then threw me naked in an open tomb and left me there. I don't know where he went. I was more scared than I had ever been in my life. That was the last time I saw him. He was not himself anymore."

The girl looked around the room for support. Jorge's parents were covering their faces in shame; the detectives were looking at Cindy incredulously. The only one that seemed to believe what she said was the priest who took her hand and squeezed it lightly to let her know he understood.

"What kind of drugs were you doing that night, Cindy?" asked Detective Donald Garcia from the Sex Crimes unit.

"I don't remember using any drugs that night. It was the book we had been reading that placed us under a spell."

"What happened to the book?" asked Father Gabriel.

"When lightning came down and hit Jorge, the book caught fire and was burnt to ashes, but even the ashes were picked up by the strong wind and went into Jorge's mouth. I think he was possessed by the devil!" Cindy said, almost whispering the last sentence.

"Did you make a police report about what happened, about you being raped?" asked Detective Garcia, still not believing the girl.

"Who was going to believe me?" shot the girl back to the incredulous detective.

"I just went home and took a bath. I haven't been able to sleep much since that night," she said.

"How about the rest of your friends?" continued questioning Detective Garcia.

"We haven't gotten together again. Two of the girls left town. Two of the boys are in a mental clinic under therapy. The others are staying with relatives, thinking that the devil is looking for them. Two boys and a girl went to their church looking for safety," the girl explained.

"We are going to need statements from everybody. I want you to give me their names, addresses and phone numbers for me to go and talk to them," Garcia told Cindy.

After the girl finished with her story, it was time for the Ramirezes to describe to the priest and the officers what they knew. Lupe began telling them:

"That night, I heard Rosita, our thirteen-year-old daughter, crying, so I got up from bed and went to see what was wrong. When I opened the door to her room, I saw— Jorge was— raping his little sister."

Lupe choked and could not continue describing the scene. Raul took over the story.

"I jumped on him to get him off his sister, but the boy hit me so hard that he threw me clear across the room. I crashed against the wall and got knocked out."

Lupe took a deep breath and related what happened next.

"I was stunned, Jorge— or whatever that was, continued sodomizing Rosita and looking at me with his eyes bright red. He told me, 'You are next, bitch.' I was unable to move a finger, just looking at that beast molesting my girl. When he finished with her, he came to me and grabbed me by the neck, almost choking me. All I could think was 'God help me.' I grabbed my rosary from around my neck and pulled it out of my robe. The beast moved back and released me when he saw the crucifix on it."

Lupe pulled out the rosary from inside her blouse to show them, and she continued:

"He ran away, out of the room; he seemed to have been scared. I helped my husband get up and together we checked on Rosita. She was really hurting and frightened to death. We decided to call the police."

"I went and called them," said Raul. "I felt that Jorge had cracked my head when he hit me so hard. He was as strong as ten men. That was not my son. He loved his little sister and would never let anyone hurt her. Something

THE TEMPTATION OF THE MIRACLE WEAVER

got into him."

Raul Ramirez was a good 6 feet 2 inches tall, a 250 lb. man.

Detective Ronald Cooper of the Robbery unit mentioned:

"Sometimes the drugs make people much stronger than they normally are and make them display really abnormal behavior."

The parents heard his explanation, but they did not want to believe it was any drug that altered their son's personality to that extreme. Lupe told them what happened next.

"When the policemen came, they searched for Jorge, but they couldn't find him. I took my daughter to the hospital for a medical exam."

Raul took over the story to relate what happened after the women left.

"I wanted to have myself checked at the hospital too and needed to pick up Lupe and Rosita. When Officer Scott and I were about to leave the house, we heard some noises on the roof. I ran to the backyard to yell at Jorge to come down. Officer Scott went to the front. The boy jumped from the roof on the officer in the driveway and beat him unconscious. When I came around, Jorge had taken the officer's gun and was about to shoot him. The officer was lying on the driveway, unconscious and bleeding. I screamed at Jorge not to shoot the cop. Jorge was laughing like a maniac. He said to himself, 'Take him out, now!' but it was not his voice or his laughter I heard. I thought quickly and did what my wife told me she had done. I pulled out my rosary with the crucifix and came close to him. I didn't want him to kill the officer but didn't even anticipate that he could have killed me too. I heard a deep voice say, 'Come on, Jorge, do it!' I noticed that his hand was trembling, but it began to pull the trigger. I said, 'In the name of God, Jorge, don't do it!' and showed him the crucifix. He ran away, got into the officer's patrol car and drove off."

The two detectives were rubbing their foreheads, obviously affected by the story. Raul went on with what happened after.

"More officers came. They searched for the boy all night but the only thing they found was the police car abandoned in a creek."

"Which library did you get the book from, Cindy?" Gabriel asked.

The girl said she would show them the place. The detectives decided to go their own way, not finding any value in searching for the book in question.

The priest took Raul, Lupe and Cindy to the public library where they had signed the books out. A nice older librarian attended them and remembered that the strange looking group of kids had checked out a number of weird books. She said she remembered the book in question, a thick one, like a

Bible, with a tan cover and written in red ink. A very old book indeed, she agreed, but she could not remember its name. She checked the records of all the kids that had signed books out; all but Jorge's were listed. The librarian blamed herself for probably not making the proper entry that day, so there was no record of the book being signed out by Jorge. Also since she didn't remember the name of the book, she couldn't look it up to verify it existed. Father Gabriel thanked her for her help, and all of them went back to the Ramirez's home. The Catholic minister dropped them off after giving them some moral support and advice. He assured them of his prayers and promised to try and help them as much as he could.

Once he got back to his parish office, Gabriel thought about the best way to deal with the serious problem at hand and decided to go to the church to pray. The place was empty, so the priest knelt in front of the altar and submerged himself in deep prayer. He truly believed that the evil one was involved in this matter. He could feel the demonic presence in the Ramirezes' house. The stories those people had related were not made up. Gabriel just wondered how all the recent events were tied up, Benito, operation, Jorge, possession, the Golden Demon, money, faith, fasting, prayer and fighting evil. He needed strength, faith, courage, understanding and guidance from above. He prayed for hours without feeling the passing of time.
Timmy Bravo, the adoptive son of James Bravo, the gym owner, came out of the Holy Trinity School and peeked inside the church on his way home. He decided to go in and pray as he usually did before a big test. Sometimes the pastor had found Timmy there praying alone and had always managed to give him a treat, a candy, a fruit, a toy or something else that he got from God-knows-where; the boy suspected that his godfather-priest was actually a magician. The third grader came in from the sunny daylight into the darkness of the church and saw his godfather praying in silence. Timmy took a long look at the kneeling priest. There was something different about him; he had a halo around his entire body as if he were fluorescent. The thing that amazed the boy the most was the fact that the praying priest was floating in the air! His knees were a good foot off the floor. Timmy smiled, approached Father G and asked him:
"Father G, how do you do that?"
The minister opened his eyes and turned to the boy. Gabriel smiled at his godson and looked into his innocent eyes. Timmy gave him a big smile back. Father G looked up towards the image of Christ and crossed himself, ending

his prayer. Timmy looked at the priest's knees again but found them resting on the steps to the altar.

"What was your question, my old friend, Don Timoteo El Bravo?" asked the priest, putting his arm around the boy's shoulders and walking out of the church with him.

"I want to know how you can fly," said Timmy, adding, "I saw you flying up in the air when you were praying. Your knees were off the ground like this much."

Timmy showed with his hands a space close to a foot apart.

"Ha, ha, ha, you have quite an imagination, my old friend! I would say that you could not see very well since you came from the sun into a dark church; however, I have a question for you too. How come you don't wash your ears well?"

"What do you mean, Father G?" asked the puzzled boy.

The priest rubbed the boy's ear and pretended to pull a one-dollar coin from it. He had actually found it under the altar when he finished praying, and he picked it up when Timmy was looking at his knees on the steps. Timmy was amazed at the magical powers of his friend; and concluded Father was definitely a magician as he always suspected.

"Look, Timmy, you don't tell anyone that you saw me flying, and I won't tell anyone that you have dollar coins stuck in your ears. Plus, you get to keep the dollar!" Gabriel told him.

Timmy smiled and winked at him. The boy placed the dollar in his pocket and shook his godfather's hand, then took off running to his home, only three blocks away. The priest sent his blessings behind the sprinting boy.

He then remembered Jorge. About nine years before, Jorge was like Timmy. Father Gabriel had been assigned to that same parish as an associate pastor for a year back then. Jorge was an altar boy as Timmy was now. Both boys admired the priest and took him as a role model. They always said they wanted to be like him. Now the older boy was in mortal danger. All that goodness he had shown growing up went to the trash in a brief time. He had committed the greatest sin in the book, betraying God by calling on Satan to worship the Prince of Darkness. Gabriel wondered what went wrong and still hoped that it was not too late to save the young man from eternal damnation.

Gabriel was hungry, but he gave instructions to his housekeeper, Mrs. Black, to give the food she had prepared for him to the poor family down the street from where she lived. He also asked her to continue giving them his food until he told her otherwise. Mrs. Black wondered what got into him, so she asked him:

"What is the matter, Father G, don't you like my food anymore?"

"No, I mean yes, I love the food you so graciously prepare for me, but trust me on this request. You continue doing what you are doing as if you were feeding me, but take the food to those neighbors of yours, the young widow and her kids."

"You mean Maricela and her three children?"

The Thai lady, who was a widow herself, made a face of disgust because Maricela Alva was known on the entire block to be of loose reputation.

"Yes. I think that's where my food should go for a few days," Gabriel declared.

"What are you going to eat then?" the cook asked.

"God will provide, my dear friend, God will provide. You don't have to worry about me, but just help me in this mission, OK?"

"OK, you are the boss, but that slut does not deserve that you worry about her."

"Come on, daughter, what have we learned about judging others?" the priest reminded her.

"I am sorry, Father, you are right. I will do as you asked," she replied.

Father Gabriel massaged his stomach to keep it from growling. He was sure his hunger would go away. He then thought about the instructions he gave to the housekeeper; they had been spontaneously blurted in an attempt to keep her from knowing that he was going to be fasting for some time. He had seen Maricela once and had heard a lot about her and her questionable morals. He did not know why he suggested Mrs. Black take the food to her but trusted it had been by divine inspiration.

That evening, Father Gabriel was visiting with the members of the Bible Study Group, which was led by Sister Theresa since she took over Sister Katherine's duties in the parish. They had finished their meeting and were having coffee and pastries in the library. They had read the parable of the lost sheep and were making comments on it. An old gentleman invited the pastor to join them in eating.

"Come on, Father, eat some of these delicious pastries that my wife prepared for us tonight. We have to finish them all, and you've got to help us do so."

The man put a cookie in his mouth and closed his eyes with pleasure to show the priest how good they were. The delicious smell of fresh coffee tempted Gabriel's empty stomach. He prayed for strength to resist temptation and keep his fasting. He had not eaten or drunk anything since the last drink of water he had that morning with Pedro.

"I am sure they are delicious, but I have to pass on them tonight, thank you!"

The priest moved on to hug and greet Grace Jones, a long time parishioner.

"Father Gabriel, how good it is to see you here with us tonight. You are always so busy. When are you coming to have dinner with me? You know my house is always open for you. When was the last time you came over, a year or two ago?"

"I am sorry. I think we should make it formal and put it on my appointment book tomorrow. That way I will not forget to visit your home for such a long time, Grace. Just call Mrs. Greene and tell her to give you the day that I am available. She is the one that guides me doing all the things I have to do through the day."

Gabriel stepped back and bumped onto a soft body behind him. He turned around apologizing and found himself face to face with Theresa.

"I am sorry for bumping you, Father, I was getting some cake and didn't see you," she apologized in return.

Theresa took a bite of her piece of cake. He found himself fascinated by watching her eat it. She drank some coffee as he kept staring at her. He had not thought of those actions as sexy until then. Theresa also had a beautiful smile, which was then adorned by a little smear of chocolate on her pink lips. Gabriel imagined himself licking the chocolate off those lips.

"Father!" Grace called out, noticing that he had not returned to face her after exchanging apologies with the sister.

"Yes, Grace," said the startled priest turning around to look at Grace.

"Did Jesus actually have long hair and a beard? Or did he look like the good shepherd image of the early church, you know, with short hair and no beard?"

"What do you think he should have looked like, Grace?" he asked.

"I personally think that he had the long hair and the beard like the actor in the movie about Jesus of Nazareth," Grace told him.

"I agree with you, my friend," the pastor wisely said.

He made the rounds talking to most of the people at the meeting. They seemed to be happy with Sister Theresa leading their group. It was a cordial and decent bunch of people sharing their faith and learning more about the word of God. By 9:30 they were ending their session and heading to their homes.

After all the members of the Bible study group left the rectory, the two religious ended up alone in the house. Theresa collected all the trash and put it in a bag to take out. Father G turned on the TV to watch the ten o'clock news. Theresa came to the living room and sat with him to watch the TV; he offered to take her home. She said Sister Carmen was probably on the way to pick her up already. Gabe took Terry's hands as they sat alone in the couch. They look into each other's eyes without saying a word for a little while. Gabriel sang part of the song he had sung at the twenty-fifth wedding anniversary, the part that spoke about the two old lovers face to face looking at each other as if they were two adolescents, unable to say a word.

"Beeeeeep, beeeeep!"

The horn of the sisters' van warned them that Sister Carmen was outside waiting for Theresa. Terry and Gabe jumped a little, startled by the horn. Then they exchanged silent, understanding glances before getting to the door. She kissed his hands; he kissed hers. They hugged to say good night, and Theresa left with Carmen. Gabriel watched the van disappear in the night down the street.

"Good night, my love," he said softly and then closed the door.

When he got back to the living room, he noticed that Theresa had purposefully left him half a cup of her coffee and half a slice of her cake. He knew exactly what that meant.

When they were dating in high school, money was never enough to do all the things they wished to do, go to the movies, dinner, dancing, go on rides or concerts. One of those times, when they were walking downtown after a high-school football home game, they went into a restaurant to have some coffee and cake. It was not a cheap place, and Gabriel realized that he had only enough money to buy one piece of cake and one expensive cup of coffee. Also, Theresa had left her purse in her best friend's car. They decided to stay and split the coffee and cake in half; they thought that was more romantic than each having his and her own. Obviously, she still remembered that night.

That evening, Gabriel had scored the winning touchdown on a defensive play. He was playing corner back and intercepted the ball; then he ran 80 yards for a touch down. At that time, he thought he was in heaven, the hero of the game, and sharing a little pleasure with an angel named Theresa. She had promised him he would "score" with her for sure next time they had coffee and cake just like that evening. That was then, now he had another chance at sharing time with the angelical Theresa. The best part was that she felt the same way about him; however, "scoring" with her was quite a different proposition now, easier but harder at the same time.

The newscast started on the TV and pulled him from his thoughts.

"The most wanted criminal in the city is a young man named Jorge Ramirez. He is only a high school senior but is already wanted on several felony warrants. If you know where he is, call the police or sheriff's department. This individual is on a one-man crime spree involving robberies, assaults and rapes on the west side of the city. Do not confront this young man yourself because he is armed and extremely dangerous," the grim-faced announcer warned the viewers.

Father G sniffed the cake and the coffee. He looked around him. There was no one to see him eat a little piece and drink a little gulp, but then his eyes rested on the crucifix on the wall. Gabriel went and dumped the cake in the trash and the coffee in the sink.

"Fast and pray. Fast and pray!" he reminded himself out loud.

Gabriel sat down and continued hearing the news about the wanted criminal.

"Some people in the city believe that this criminal is possessed by a demon. We interviewed some of them to ask them why."

They showed a girl in darkness, to avoid revealing her identity. Father recognized her figure and her voice as that of Cindy.

"Jorge Ramirez is possessed by a demon. He would never do what he has done if he were not. I was there when he was taken by the devil himself. I saw it happening!"

The TV then switched to show Detective Cooper making his comments on the case.

"This young man was a member of a drug-using group interested in the occult. They experimented with different drugs and then used the possession claim to try and avoid responsibility for their criminal behavior. The only devil here is the drug they were using to get high," the detective said decisively.

The screen then showed the father, Raul Ramirez, also in darkness to protect his identity.

"I can tell you that my son was possessed. The only thing that stopped him from killing all of us was the crucifix that my wife and I have on our rosaries. He is not afraid of any man, only of God Almighty. Why would someone on drugs run away from the image of Christ?" Raul asked.

The news reporter, Linda McCoy, faced the camera and told the audience:

"Demonic possession or another criminal on drugs? You decide if this young man who is letting his animal instincts run wild by raping, robbing and hurting people is a victim of demonic possession or another depraved predator loosened by the use of illegal drugs."

Gabriel meditated for a moment. He somehow knew that he would have to face the devil in Jorge sooner or later. He wondered if he would be ready for the encounter. The priest looked at the crucifix again and felt confident he would. The TV news broadcaster continued:

"There is a demon in San Antonio these days, indeed, a golden demon who is challenging any and all men in the area to fight him in the ring for a nationally televised fight, 'mano a mano.' There is a prize of 500,000 dollars for the man who dares to face this masked demon in the ring and beat him, but so far there are no takers, and for good reason."

Father G paid attention to what they had to say about the wrestler. There was a connection between this event and the crimes that were taking place. He just needed to figure out how they were related.

"This 6 foot 6 inches, 330-pound hulk of a man has already killed two men and sent to the hospital dozens of others around the nation who dared to take him on. Some of his opponents have ended up with broken backs, brain damage or other similarly permanent disabilities."

The TV showed some video spots of the wrestler in action, mangling one opponent after another without mercy.

"Some people suspect the mysterious masked demon used to be a professional football player. Others say that he was a trained killer from Delta Force. We went around town following the phenomenon to see him train. He can bench press 500 lbs. He can run the 100 yards in 12 seconds. He is said to have never lost a fight in his life. He is a destroyer! Boxers, wrestlers, karate or Judo fighters cannot stop him," the announcer said.

The TV showed the Golden Demon flexing his huge muscles surrounded by four beautiful women, a blonde, a redhead, an Asian, and a black girl. The giant shouted into the microphone with a raspy voice:

"I am the most dangerous man in the world! I am the best! I am looking for a man to beat me, but I don't think you got any real man, like me, here! This is a town full of chickens, bunch of cowards! But I got to tell you, I do like your women a lot!"

He took a hold of each of the girls and kissed them in front of the camera. Then he finished his interview with a demonstration of his power. He broke a number of cement blocks with a karate chop and another with a head butt.

He walked away with all four women on his arms, two on his wide shoulders and one on each forearm.

"No way!" said a man the reporter interviewed in the street, when asked if he would fight the Demon, "I would not fight him even for 100 million dollars!"

They then showed a voluptuous woman in her thirties saying:

"I think he is sexy. I would take him on any time, but in my bedroom, not in the ring!"

Last, they showed an old man walking with the support of a cane.

"Sure, I would get in the ring with that Golden Demon. I am not afraid of him."

The old guy lifted his cane as if to hit some imaginary opponent, swung it in the air in front of him and fell on the grass. His cane flew up in the air.

"I'll take him on... as soon as I get out of the hospital," he said as he was being helped to get up from the grass outside the nursing home.

The news anchor gave the information on how to contact the promoters if anyone was interested in facing the Golden Demon for half a million dollars. Gabriel wondered if that was the money Benito needed for his heart operation. He was going to sleep on it and decide later. There were too many things going on at the same time.

The next day, Father Gabriel called Detective Garcia and asked him if he could be notified if Jorge was located. He offered his help since he was so close to the boy. The detective told him they still had no good leads but that he would keep him informed if they needed his help. Timmy was sitting outside the principal's office listening to the priest's conversation with the police officer because the door was only half closed. Mrs. White came in when she noticed Father was off the phone.

"Father, Sister Magdalene sent you one of her third graders with a discipline problem. Apparently this boy, Timmy Bravo, hit another boy, John Clark, with his fist in class."

"Bring the defendant in!" said the principal in a solemn voice so that Timmy would hear him.

Mrs. White told the boy to go in, and she closed the door behind him. When Timmy came in, Father G was tapping his palm on the desk and looking up to the ceiling wondering what the little rascal had done this time. Before the principal could say anything, the accused spoke first.

"Father G, do you believe Jorge has the devil inside of him?"

"Where did you hear that?" Gabriel inquired.

"I saw it in the news."

"Well, I don't know about him, but tell me about you. Did the devil get inside of you to make you hit little Johnnie?"

"Oh no, Father, that was just me. I punched him because he disobeyed me," the boy explained.

"How is that?" asked the priest, puzzled by Timmy's quick response.

"He was cheating," the little fellow said, adding, "Remember I went to pray in church yesterday because we had a big test today? Well I was doing good, and then I caught Johnnie copying my answers. I told him to stop, but he kept copying from my test. I just had to discipline the little boy!"

The principal pretended to cough and covered his face to conceal his smile. He regained his composure and explained to Timmy that it was not his place to execute justice in the classroom. He would have to apologize to Johnnie for hitting him and would write: "I will love my neighbor as myself; I will not punish my neighbor" a hundred times on a paper to be turned in the next day into the office.

"Did you explain to Sister Magda why you hit Johnnie?" Gabriel asked.

"Yes, and she already gave him a zero on the test and a note for his parents."

"Good! That was all that was needed in this case to begin with."

Father Gabriel scribbled a note and sent it back with the boy to the classroom. Before leaving the office, Timmy turned around and told the principal:

"I will keep an eye out for Jorge and let you know if he comes to the neighborhood."

"You do that, after you do your assignment this evening," he told the boy.

The principal watched the little rascal heading back to his classroom; Gabriel just shook his head and smiled recalling his words, "I just had to discipline the little boy!"

Timmy was a player on the basketball team that Jorge Ramirez had been assisting his father to coach, so the little boy was concerned that his assistant coach and friend might be possessed. The priest did not want Timmy involved in that matter.

On Friday, Father Gabriel remained in the church in prayer after the morning Mass. He had not eaten anything except the Eucharist since Wednesday morning. His hunger and thirst were beginning to be painful that third day of fasting, but his prayer seemed to help him ignore his bodily needs. Gabriel got up from his prayers and crossed himself. He looked at his watch; it was 12:30 p.m., and he thought he had prayed for only ten minutes. He had actually been there for four hours! Sister Theresa came in the church looking for him.

"Father, where have you been all morning?"

"Here."

"Since the Mass?"

"Yes."

"What did you do all morning?"

"Pray."

"Have you eaten lunch yet?"

"No."

"Let's go to your house and I will give you something to eat. You look hungry," Theresa said.

"I don't— "

"You don't want me around during my break? Come on, I have a little time while the children are out doing P.E."

Theresa grabbed him by the arm and pulled him towards the door.

"OK!" Gabriel said, yielding to her playful pulling.

The priest wondered what he could do to keep Theresa from forcing him to eat, but without telling her he was fasting.

Mrs. Black had left to take his lunch to Maricela and her children. They were becoming friends quickly after the old lady started taking them Father's food. Maricela had just been laid off from the topless club where she worked as a dancer; the city authorities had closed the establishment by a community initiative. The unemployed mother of three had no savings and was not in any government program. The kindness of the messenger who brought them the food at the most appropriate time made Maricela think about changing the direction of her life. Mrs. Black told her she might ask her brother-in-law if he could hire Maricela in his construction business as a receptionist. Gabriel was delighted to hear the good news from Mrs. Black, and the old housekeeper felt proud she was making a difference too.

As Gabriel and Theresa entered the rectory, he asked her:

"Theresa, you said you would pose for me alone, right?"

"Right here? Right now? Nude?" a surprised Theresa exclaimed.

"Yes, yes, and no. Let me make a portrait of you as my lunch, right here, right now, but you don't have to take off your clothes. All kinds of people come in during the day, and we wouldn't want to shock them. What do you say? Will you indulge me for lunch by letting me eat and drink your image, please?"

"OK, how long will it take?"

"Let's do a 30-minute portrait. Sit there on the sofa in a comfortable reclining pose while I get my pencil and pad."

Theresa went and arranged herself on the sofa in a position she thought she could hold for half an hour, one that would let her face him as he drew her. Gabriel came back running like a kid with a new toy and placed two chairs in front of the new model, one for his drawing pad and one for himself. He turned the radio on to listen to a conservative talk show while he worked on the portrait. Theresa commented:

"Why do you listen to that man? He has an annoying voice and sounds very full of himself."

"I agree with a lot of things that he says. He gives a different take on the news than the regular media, which is obviously slanted to the left. Many people don't like him, but I think he is a man of truth. He preaches self-reliance and self-responsibility," Gabriel said.

"Well, at least for this time, could you put on some music instead? I don't want to get too interested in what they are talking about in his show because I do have to go back to my class."

"You are the boss, Terry. I want my models to be as comfortable as possible."

He switched the station to classical music on FM and began the drawing. His hunger did not matter while he was doing something so exciting, talking to God in prayer or drawing Theresa's beloved image. He worked fast because he wanted to get as much detail as possible in the time available. Theresa was enjoying the experience, having his eyes run up and down her whole figure, absorbing every detail. Theresa also enjoyed seeing him without anyone else to interrupt, watching him working and smiling at her.

"Would you like to watch a basketball game with me tonight?" the artist asked the reclining model.

"Are the San Antonio Latigos playing again?"

"No, I was invited to watch our CYO (Catholic Youth Organization) team of third graders take on Holy Cross. Do you remember Timmy, the boy at the gym who called me out when you were looking for me the first day?"

"Oh yes, he is in Sister Magda's class isn't he?"

"Right, he is on the team and wants me to go watch him play tonight."

"Sure, will you pick me up? Theresa asked.

"Of course!" he exclaimed. "Our time is up. I think I got enough detail; I will work on it a little more, later tonight. Look," he invited her to see the drawing, "Do you like it?"

"It's beautiful, but that does not look like me. It looks as though you drew an angel, not a middle-aged religious sister."

"That's because I see you almost as an angel and not as a religious sister, Terry."

"Let me see it when you finish it. I'll talk to you later. At what time do you want me to be ready for the game?"

"I will be at your house at 6:30. Will Sister Magda object to it?"

"I will invite them all to come along, but I doubt that any will. They are into baseball, not basketball," said Theresa.

"Thank you for this excellent lunch, my dear friend," Gabriel told her, placing his hand on her back.

"It was my pleasure," she replied.

He walked her out to the door and watched her walk across the street to the school. Then the pastor got busy with his work. He made a few phone calls and opened some correspondence. He sorted out the things that needed to be done, the ones that could be delegated, and the ones that could be left for other times. He worked fast and furiously trying to do as much as possible before going out with Theresa that evening. The good thing was that he had enough time because he was going to skip dinner; the bad thing was that he was really starving. He went back to praying in his room when dinnertime came and his stomach started growling for food again.

Father Gabriel and Sister Theresa went to the game alone, as she had predicted. All the other religious sisters were busy with their own schedules and decided to pass on the invitation. Magda had noticed that her new subordinate had become very good friends with the pastor, but there was nothing wrong with that. All the sisters were a little in love with him anyway, and he continued to carry out his duties without any indication that things had changed in his life. He was definitely a man of God; they all figured that if Jesus walked the earth in our days, He would be like Father Gabriel.

"Have you been fasting?" Theresa asked her friend.

"Why do you say that?" Gabriel answered with a question to avoid hers.

"You look a little thinner. I heard your stomach growling like a lion, and you refused to let me feed you lunch. Plus, I see that you washed your face and combed your hair. I have read the Gospel too, and I know that's what Jesus told us to do when we fast."

"Yes," he admitted.

"Why? Are you tormented by something specific?"

"I have some devils to fight. I need more prayer and fasting to gain strength in faith."

"Wow! Can I help you with anything?"

"Pray for me," he told her.

"You got it, but I already do, all the time," she assured him.

"I was wondering where all this new extra energy was coming from. That explains it!"

She just smiled back at him. He was a man of great faith. Theresa wondered what he meant by "fighting devils" but decided to let him tell her when he was ready. She had learned that he did not like to boast about his supernatural contacts. It was so good to spend time with him; alone in his car, or in his house, anywhere with him was great. She would go to the end of the world and back holding his hand. It was great to be in love again although this relationship of theirs was somewhat unusual and perplexing but still enjoyable.

James Bravo welcomed Father Gabriel with a hug when they arrived to Holy Cross Gym. He shook Sister Theresa's hand and thanked her for coming to lend her support to their team. James had taken over coaching his adoptive son's team because Raul Ramirez was having a tough time with the situation with Jorge at home. Little Timmy and his teammates came to hug Father G chanting:

"Father G, Father G, we're going to win because you're here!"

"You better play well or else you will lose, even if I came to watch you," Gabriel warned them.

Theresa was observing the priest shaking hands with all his little players. James went to the other coach and said something to him; then he came back and talked to Father Gabriel.

"Father, could you lead us in prayer to start the game?" James asked.

"Sure!" Gabriel agreed.

The priest went to the middle of the court and thought about a prayer. Before he started, one of his kids shouted:

"Sing us a song, Father G!"

"OK let's do both. Did you know that when you sing to God you are praying twice?" he announced.

The priest signaled for everybody to sit down. The two teams sat around him with their coaches. The referees sat at the bench and watched to see what he was going to do. He started by reciting the first part of a song in

English and Spanish. The verses described Jesus of Nazareth, his age, origin, profession and so on; then the actual song spoke of the love of Christ and invited the listeners to seek him to find true peace. He finished the song and said:

"Let's play some basketball!"

Gabriel took his seat by Theresa's side. His song had moved her.

"I still don't know how you can just stand up there and, all of a sudden, sing a song that can touch our hearts so easily."

"Your company helps me to come up with the right song at the right time. You inspire me to sing from the bottom of my heart," he whispered in her ear.

Timmy's team did win, but it was a close game. Holy Trinity led first, but then Holy Cross took the lead. The visitors regained the top only to lose it again in a minute or two. It was that way the entire game, which kept the parents on both sides on the edge of their seats, cheering for their kids. The score was in favor of Holy Cross, 36 to 35 with only five seconds to go in the last quarter. Timmy dribbled the ball between three opponents and went all the way in for a lay up that went in at the buzzer to give Holy Trinity the win 37 - 36.

Gabriel took Theresa home and walked her all the way in to hear her relate the game to the other sisters. They turned to see him and accuse him of praying to God for their team to win.

"I would say that is cheating, Father," said Sister Mary Daskalos in a playful manner.

"I disagree! What happened is that our team had greater faith than theirs," Sister Carmen said.

"You got a point, because the Lord would not show favoritism for one church over another. We are all Christians, children of the same God. I think He let the best team win," conceded Mary.

"I don't think God intervenes in these games at all!" exclaimed Sister Magdalene.

Father Gabriel related another joke to the sisters.

"Speaking of faith. There was a man of very deep faith living close to the Mississippi River. One time the rains were so heavy, that they caused the river to overflow and flood the whole area. The forecasters told everyone that the rain was going to continue, so they were advising the people of that valley to evacuate their homes and move to higher ground. Our faithful man, called Joshua, decided to stay home. All his neighbors left when the water was coming to their ankles. The fire department sent a truck to get the only man left in the valley when the water was up to his knees, but he told them to go away. They explained to him that the rains were going to continue and that the river was going to swell up even more. Joshua said, 'The Lord will take care of me,' and refused to go with them. Later on, a rescue crew came on a boat when the man was already with the water up to his neck. They told him to get on the boat with them, that the rain was going to continue and the river would keep rising. He told them the same thing, 'The Lord will take care of me,' and sent them away. The water kept rising as predicted. Joshua climbed on top of his roof to stay above the water. He was standing on his chimney, on the tips of his toes, with the water splashing on his face. A rescue crew from the National Guard in a helicopter came by and found him. They threw down a ladder and told him to come aboard because the rain was going to continue and the river would not stop swelling. Joshua yelled at them, 'Go away. The Lord will take care of me!' They left him there, so he drowned, died and, of course, went to heaven. When he got to the pearly gates, he talked to St. Peter, a little "ticked off," 'Where is the Lord, St. Peter? I must talk to him right now!' St. Peter led him to the Lord for an audience. Joshua addressed the Lord saying, 'Lord, I was always faithful to you. Why did you let me die? What happened there?' The Lord told him, 'I don't know. I sent you a truck, a boat and a helicopter.'"

The sisters broke down in laughter. Father wished them a good night and went home.

When the priest got home, he was surprised to find the beautiful Linda Richards in his bed, under the covers, waiting for him.

"What are you doing here, Linda? How did you get in?"

"You left the door unlocked. I came here to talk to you. Since you were not in, I decided to wait for you. I was a little tired, so I got in your bed."

She was right. He did not care to lock the door although he knew he should lock it at all times. He normally left it unlocked.

"What did you want to talk to me about, child?" he asked her.

"Well, it is very personal, but I feel that I can trust you with anything. You know how priests are supposed to be celibate?"

"Yes, that's right."

"Well, I have been in the same boat as you since Pedrito's father left me pregnant six years ago. It has been a long time since I made love to anyone. I know how you must feel having to restrain yourself for years without sex."

"So?" Gabriel asked, guessing where she was going with that conversation.

"So, I have come for both of us to get a little relief. I know you are a very discreet person, and I know how to keep a secret. Come in, your bed is nice and warm already. I am not wearing anything at all."

She smiled and stretched her arms out, inviting him to embrace her. Father Gabriel just stood there, frozen, wondering what to do. The offer was quite tempting. He would be doing her a favor and providing her with some physical comfort. He himself could use a little relief as she said. She was so beautiful.

"What's the matter? You don't like me?" Linda said in a sad tone.

"It's not that."

The priest sat on the bed next to her. She pretended to be hurt by his hesitation and sat up to get out of the bed.

"I am sorry. You must think I am a slut, coming on to you like this. I should've known better."

She was actually beginning to shed some tears as she reached for her clothes and began getting dressed. Gabriel walked around the bed and touched her pretty face.

"I am really flattered that a woman like you would want to share her body with me, but this would not be right."

"Who would get hurt, Gabriel? You? Me? God? Sister Theresa?" Linda shot back at him.

"Riiiinnnngggg— Riiiinnnngggg— Riiiinnnngggg!"

The personal phone on Gabriel's night table rang insistently. This was a number that few people had. The minister felt that it must be important, so he picked it up.

"Father G. it's me, Timmy. Jorge is robbing the store at the corner right now!"

The priest looked at Linda and hung up the phone in a hurry.

"I am sorry, Linda. I've got to go now!"

He grabbed his stole, crucifix and a little bottle with holy water that he had on top of his chest of drawers before walking quickly out of the room and the house. Linda was perplexed, having no idea why he rushed off as if someone's life depended on him. She decided to go back home. Although she was frustrated, Linda thought she would try again later, in a different way.

The athletic priest ran the three blocks to the corner store in less than 30 seconds. He could see a man that looked like Jorge inside the store, arguing with the store manager while pointing the gun at his head. Jorge had signs of the rough week he had gone through all over his body. His clothes were dirty and torn; he had dry blood and some infected injuries; his hair was a mess. His eyes looked like two lit charcoals; his face, unshaven for many days, was scratched and swollen. It was Jorge, all right, and he might be high on drugs or — possessed. The priest entered the store and shouted:

"Jorge! In the name of God, drop the gun and leave that man alone!"

The horrible creature turned his red eyes to see the intruder.

"Padre Gabriel Infante, favored child of God, at last you come to me! I have been waiting for this opportunity to have a little chat with you. Are you finished with that slut, Linda Richards, so soon? — Oh, I see that you didn't have time, but she was very tempting wasn't she? You should have taken her and made her happy. Where is your mercy for the poor, needy woman?"

How in the world did Jorge know? The priest tried to gain control of the situation.

"Jorge, come outside with me and let's have a talk."

"Jorge is dead and burning in hell!" the beast told him in a loud, raspy voice, then trying to sound sweet he added, "He says 'hi.'"

"Let's go outside. Let the man go; this is between you and me," the priest told the creature.

Father G looked into those lit eyes; they were not human! Gabriel knew he was in the presence of real evil: everything seemed to be very confusing and he felt nauseated.

"Ah, Gabriel, tonight Jorge has to kill somebody. I thought it would be this store clerk, but a pious priest like you will be a much better start. Ha-ha-ha-ha-ha-ha!"

Jorge pistol-whipped the store clerk who fell like a sack of potatoes to the store floor. Gabriel reacted by jumping on the gunman, trying to disarm him. The beast swung his arm with amazing power and threw the priest clear across the store knocking down a magazine rack and some groceries off the shelf upon impact. Jorge got in a crouching position like a beast about to lounge at his prey. Father G got up from the floor and looked into the beast's eyes. Looking into those evil red eyes, he had a vision. He saw Jorge trying to stay afloat in a sea of lava, screaming helplessly and in deep pain. The priest trembled realizing he was facing pure evil.

"Jorge found power, pleasure and wisdom in me, Gabriel," the beast told him sounding just like Gabriel's own Father.

The minister began to pray:

"The Lord is my shepherd. There is nothing I shall want!"

THE TEMPTATION OF THE MIRACLE WEAVER

"If you bow before me, you will have anything you want, Gabriel."

The beast pointed at the counter of the store by the register. Gabriel saw Theresa there, sitting on the counter wearing a short red dress and made up to look like a super model. She was smiling at him sending him a kiss and stretching her arms out.

"The Lord is my rock in whom I trust!"

Gabriel closed his eyes to erase the sinful vision of temptation.

"Bow, priest, or you will surely die tonight!"

The possessed man pulled his gun up and pointed it at the priest who was praying:

"Lord Jesus Christ, son of the living God, have mercy on me, a sinner!"

Gabriel pulled out his crucifix from inside his shirt and started walking towards the gunman. The beast grimaced at the audacity of the minister. The presence of the large crucifix had an effect on him. He covered his face with the left hand and squeezed the trigger with the right hand. Father G stepped on some spilled mustard and lost his balance at the time the gun was fired. The bullet missed his chest by a hair. He regained his balance and continued advancing and praying. The prayers were giving him confidence; he stopped trembling.

"The Lord, creator of the universe, will deliver me from all my foes because my trust rests on Him alone!" he prayed louder.

The demon fired another shot as the priest advanced closer to him. Gabriel felt the impact on his chest and almost fell backwards. The crucifix had taken the direct hit and had protected his body. Father Gabriel recovered his balance and continued getting closer to the demon. The beast fired a third round. Time seemed to slow down. Gabriel saw the bullet spinning out of the gun and coming at his head. He leaned to the left and felt the round zooming by his right ear. The glowing red eyes were wide open in fury and disbelief. The possessed man tried to fire again, but Gabriel was already on top of him. The priest grabbed the gun with his left hand and twisted it away from the startled demon. With his right fist, the boxer/priest punched Jorge right under the chin, knocking him down on his back. The gun fell on the floor away from Jorge. With great aplomb, Father Gabriel pulled out his bottle of holy water and threw some, forming a cross, on the body of the fallen man.

"In the name of the Father, and of the Son, and of the Holy Spirit."

The creature began to writhe on the floor and cried out in a loud voice. "Noooooo!"

Father G knelt next to Jorge pressing down on his chest with the metal crucifix.

"Glory to the Father, and to the Son, and to the Holy Spirit. As it was in the beginning is now and will be forever, Amen, Alleluia!"

The lights of the store flickered and went out. The merchandise shelves started shaking and falling down. A terrible, inhuman voice yelled from inside of Jorge:

"Get away from me!"

The exorcist made the sign of the cross on the possessed man who was beginning to go into convulsions.

"The power of the eternal God, your Lord, commands you, Satan!" Gabriel called out.

Jorge's left hand seemed to acquire a life of its own and started crawling like a big spider towards the gun on the floor, not far from them. The hand grabbed the gun and placed its index finger into the trigger hole. Gabriel looked at it and commanded in a thunderous voice:

"In the name of our Lord, Jesus Christ, I command you, Satan, Leave this man at once and return to hell! It is the Father who commands you. It is the Son who commands you. It is the Holy Spirit who commands you, and you cannot refuse Him. Leave this child of God in the name of Jesus!"

All the windows of the store blew out at once as the evil spirit, with a horrifying scream, left the body of the young man. At once, the lights of the store came back on.

The store clerk "came to" and got his own revolver from under the cash register. He got up from behind the counter and saw Jorge with the gun on his left hand pointed at the priest. Gabriel was on his knees praying and looking at Jorge as the boy was getting up a little dazed and unsteady on his feet. The clerk, Walter Simmons, did not hesitate. To defend the priest, he pulled up his .357 magnum and fired two shots in the direction of the armed bandit. Walter's eyes turned reddish for an instant and an evil smile appeared in his face. The shots hit the robber in the chest and the abdomen.

"Noooooo!" screamed Gabriel, receiving the mortally wounded body of Jorge in his arms.

The priest felt the warm blood of the young man running down his chest and abdomen. Jorge's eyes were brown now and looked at the priest with a myriad questions. Both the priest and the young man knew there was no time for questions. Jorge's life was slipping away as quickly as the blood was leaving his body.

"Faa—ther Gabriel, wh—why?"

THE TEMPTATION OF THE MIRACLE WEAVER

"My son, we don't have much time," Gabriel told the dying boy.

He placed the young man's head on his lap while kneeling on the floor.

"Father G are you all right?" asked Walter, the store clerk, seeing that the priest was bathed in blood.

"I am O.K., but call an ambulance for him," the priest told him, so that he would leave them alone.

"Jorge, I know that you sinned by betraying our Lord, but you still have time to repent and come back to Him. He is waiting for you, like the father of the prodigal son. Do you remember?"

"Yess," Jorge said, as his voice grew faint.

"Do you accept Jesus Christ as your savior and reject Satan?"

"I— do."

Jorge's neck went limp and he exhaled. Father Gabriel made the sign of the cross over the dead boy, absolving him from all his sins. Gabriel saw his own tears falling on Jorge's face. He closed the boy's eyes with his hand and gently laid him on the store floor as if he were putting a baby in a crib to sleep. At that time the police arrived with their guns in their hands; the EMS technicians followed them into the store upon their signal. The priest got up with his hands open and reaching up in the air.

Father G let the paramedics check him out. He had some minor bruises on his face and back, but he had not been hit by any bullet. His thoughts were on Jorge's family and what to tell them about the events of that night. Walter was telling the officers what he could remember, but there was much that remained unexplained. Detective Cooper came over to the scene despite the fact that he was already off duty.

"Well, Father, what do you think?" Cooper asked, "Was Jorge possessed as that girl, Cindy, claimed?"

Father G looked at him straight in the eye and said:

"Yes."

The detective did not expect the priest to answer so decisively.

"Well, I guess that doesn't matter now since the poor bastard is dead!"

The priest was bothered by the detective's callous comment.

"Listen, Detective, Jorge Ramirez was a very good young man until he sought friendship with evil. He was responsible for summoning a demon, yes, but all the crimes you are investigating were committed while he was possessed by an entity much more powerful than he. When I expelled the demon that was in him, Jorge had no knowledge of what he had done while he was possessed. At least he had a chance to repent of his sin before he passed away."

"You mean he is going to heaven after all he did, raping, assaulting and robbing?"

"I am sure he is," Gabriel affirmed.

"Goddamn! Oh, excuse me Father, but how fair is that?"

Father Gabriel smiled at him and placed his hand on the detective's big shoulder.

"Have you ever heard the parable of the workers?" he asked.

The huge detective admitted he had not and sat in the ambulance while the minister paraphrased the parable for him and how it applied to the case.

"There was a landowner who went out to get workers for his vineyard at dawn. They agreed on the usual wages for the day and went to work. The man found other workers at midmorning and sent them into his vineyard as well, then others at noon and yet others in the afternoon, whom he also sent to work in his vineyard. At the end of the day, the landowner had the workers come to him to receive their pay, starting with the ones that came last. When the workers hired first saw that the ones hired last were getting a full day's wages, even though they had only worked about an hour, they were expecting to get paid more because they had done a lot more work. When they saw that they got the same as the others, they complained to the landowner. The man heard their grumbling and told them he was not doing them any injustice as they claimed and asked them if he was not free to do with his money as he wished. They had worked as long as they had agreed, for the amount for which they had agreed to work. He questioned if they were envious because the landowner was generous. So it is with the Kingdom of Heaven: the last shall be first and the first shall be last. Jorge had a chance to change his sinful condition before his death, and I am sure that he was welcome in Heaven because he repented from his sins before his death."

"Well, now that you put it that way, I can understand it, Father Gabriel."

Then priest and policeman agreed to go together to notify the family of the incident and the death of their son. Although he was deeply saddened by the turn of the events, Gabriel felt relieved that it was over. He had learned to accept God's will and not question it when something like that happened.

Chapter XII
The Big Fight

The next morning, Saturday November 13th, Father Gabriel got up at 4:30 a.m., as usual, after only one hour of very deep sleep. He went running a few miles and got to the gym where he hit the heavy bag until he became exhausted. Then he took a cold shower and returned to the church to celebrate the Saturday morning Mass. Theresa met him at the sacristy.

"Good morning, Father."

"Good morning, Sister. Shalom!"

"Did you have a good night?"

"It was an exciting, incredible night; but I only got to sleep about an hour," he said, smiling.

"Yeah, I bet it was an exciting night!" Sister Theresa nodded, adding, "I went to your house to see if you wanted me to go running with you, but you were already gone. I found these by the side of your bed."

Theresa showed him a pair of pink lace, silky panties.

"Oh! —Well, they are not mine. They probably belong to Linda Richards."

"That's what I suspected. I smelled her perfume on your bed."

Theresa turned around to avoid looking at his face, crossed her arms and tapped her foot waiting for his story to explain how Linda's panties ended up under his bed.

"It is not what you think— well, almost, but not quite," Gabriel declared with a mischievous grin.

"Didn't you say it was an 'exciting, incredible night?' Now you are going to deny you went to bed with Linda?"

Gabriel loved to see Theresa jealous over him. It was time to celebrate the Mass, so he bent towards Theresa's ear from behind her and whispered softly:

"I will explain to you after Mass. Will you play some music for the celebration?"

"No!" she snapped, "I will just sit here and wait for you."

Father Gabriel smiled at her little tantrum and kissed the top of her head before heading to the altar to start the Mass. Theresa knelt in front of the cross in the sacristy and prayed that it was not true. She did not want Gabriel to have spent the night with Linda. Then she stopped and realized that she wanted Gabriel for herself and for no one else. Their love affair was becoming more and more physical; she wanted to have him and be in his arms. Theresa changed her prayer to ask for wisdom in deciding what to do with the man of her life. She needed to know if God was now calling her and Gabriel to married life, or if it was just a temptation.

After the Mass, the priest came back to the sacristy with a big wide smile to face the still-serious religious sister.

"Well—?" she said, helping him to change out of his religious vestments.

"Linda was waiting for me in bed when I got home last night. Apparently she wanted to be of service to me, to 'relieve the pressures of celibate life.' She said that she herself had been celibate for the last six years, so it would be good for both of us. She is very aggressive and was quite tempting," he said matter-of-factly.

"And—?"

"I got a call from a little 'angel of the Lord,' Timmy, who informed me that at that very moment Jorge was robbing the corner store! So I ran out of the house and confronted the demon that possessed Jorge. Linda stayed behind. I guess she left, thinking that she scared me off."

"Why did she leave her panties?"

"I don't know. She may have lost them, or maybe she wanted me to have a souvenir of last night to reconsider her offer."

"Are you going to?" Theresa asked with a concerned look.

"I don't know," Gabriel replied. "She is beautiful; you should have seen her."

Theresa's lower lip was sticking out like an angry little girl's. Father Gabriel hugged her and reassured her.

"No, no, no, no, and no. I told you before that I don't intend to engage in an intimate relationship with Linda. You are the only one I want to keep as my partner for life. You know how much I love you, Terry."

"Would you be willing to quit being a priest for me?" she challenged him.

"Would you be willing to quit being a religious sister for me?" he answered in kind.

"Yes, I would," she said firmly, "If you are willing to come along and join me. I have been praying for wisdom to decide what we should do with our love. I am beginning to think that maybe we should consider marriage as an option."

"Why don't we let things run their course and look for a few more signs on the road before taking the plunge into that decision? I have been very happy so far the way we are right now," Gabriel told her.

"Yes, I am happy too, but don't you wish you could have more?" she replied.

Theresa walked closer to him with her lips half-open, ready to be kissed. She reached up with her mouth, looking for his. He held her face and, to her surprise, blew into her eye.

"There, Sister! I think I got it out."

At that moment, Sister Magdalene came into the sacristy looking for Theresa. The others were in the van waiting to go to a friend's house out in the country; Francis Schott, the restaurant owner, had invited them all to breakfast. Theresa wiped her eye and understood what Gabriel had done to cover the appearances. Magda would have caught them in the act if he had kissed her, but Theresa had wanted him to kiss her, even if they got caught. She actually wished they had been caught!

"Thank you, Father Gabriel. I have to go now. We'll see you later."

The priest walked them out and waved good-bye to all of them. Then he started walking briskly to Don Pedro's pawnshop.

The two friends went back to the restaurant they had been in the previous Wednesday, but this time, Father G ate a hearty breakfast, steak and eggs, hash browns, juice, pancakes, coffee and a fruit salad. The old man looked at him eating like a castaway just rescued several days after a shipwreck in the high seas.

"My God! When was the last time you ate, Father?" Pedro asked him.

"Tuesday evening. Do you remember I told you about fasting and praying last Wednesday morning?"

"Yes, I would have died if I had not eaten anything since last Tuesday," said Don Pedro.

"I almost died, not for lack of food but for lack of faith," commented Gabriel, looking back into the events of the last few days.

"Lack of faith— you? Get out of here!" scoffed the older guy, pushing Gabriel's shoulder, dismissing the statement as a big lie.

"I had a test of faith last night, my old friend."

"How did you do, Father?"

"I passed!"

"What happened?"

The friend got curious. Some of the things the priest went through were truly incredible, so he figured this was one of those.

"Jorge was possessed by a demon, but with the help of the Almighty, I was able to expel it."

"Great! So Jorge is OK now?"

"Well, he is dead, but I trust that he is now resting in the Lord. I was able to give him absolution after the demon left him. Jorge was killed by the store clerk he was robbing. I guess it was better that way. Nobody wants to believe in demonic possession nowadays. He would have had a tough time with the judicial system," the priest said.

Pedro thought for a moment pondering if it actually was better to be dead than alive with all the problems the boy would have faced for the things he did while possessed. Pedro shook his head, not wanting to think about it. He opened the newspaper as the priest continued devouring his big meal.

"Speaking of demons, nobody has accepted the Golden Demon's challenge to fight. Today is the deadline to accept it. They will have to go to Houston next," Pedro read aloud from the newspaper.

Gabriel's heart jumped in his chest; he told Pedro:

"Would you help me fight the Golden Demon, my friend?"

"You mean the two of us, together against him?"

For a moment Pedro's expression became lively, but then he looked at the picture of the giant and decided to pass on the offer. He put the paper on the table to show Gabriel the photo.

"Look at him. He weighs as much as both of us rolled in one. It is impossible to beat an animal like that in the ring," declared the old man, pointing at the picture of the huge muscle man.

"With God, nothing is impossible!" Gabriel affirmed.

"But, Father, you are 6 feet by 200 pounds. This killer is 6 inches taller, 130 pounds heavier and twice as strong as you!" Don Pedro reminded Gabriel.

The old man thought it was his duty to stop the priest from even considering the deadly proposition any longer. He asked the priest:

"Do you want to die young? Is that it?"

"Last night, with the help of God, I faced and defeated real evil. This other one is only a man like you and I."

The priest finished the last gulp of his cup of coffee. His plates were all clean. He seemed to be confident that he could do it.

"Would you really, really dare to fight this giant?"

The old friend put his hand on the priest's shoulder and looked into his eyes.

"Yes!" Father G exclaimed with a big smile while rubbing his satisfied stomach.

"But, Father, why?" asked Pedro, shrugging his shoulders.

The minister pointed at the newspaper where it said "$500,000.00 Prize." Pedro could not believe it.

"You want money? Listen I could lend you, give you if necessary, some cash if you need the money that badly —Maybe not so much, but— How much do you need?"

"I need it all, but not for me. It is to pay for a miracle."

"Miracle? I thought you always did those for free."

"The Lord works in mysterious ways, Don Pedro. I know that I am going to fight this Golden Demon, and I am sure I am going to defeat him, but I feel that I need your help for some reason. I think you can tell me how to beat him in the ring."

The friend felt privileged by the priest's comment, but he joked around a little.

"Father, I am sorry, but I don't want any part in your death."

Pedro finished his own cup of coffee to end their breakfast.

"Earlier, you said that if you were twenty years younger, you could take him, well I am you, twenty years younger! Tell me, what would you do, as a wrestler, to beat such a formidable enemy?"

They left the restaurant and walked back to Pedro's business. The old man said:

"I got it! You have to get an edge. Physically he is superior, and we cannot change that. Psychologically, he has also placed himself on top, with his mask and his records and his shows of invincibility. I say we throw him a psychological curve, which combined with your great determination, will bring him down!"

Pedro got excited as he thought of the details of his plan.

"I have a brilliant idea. Let's get a mask to put you at the same level as him, incognito, but since he is a demon, you should be an angel— a saint— or— an exorcist! Yes, that's it. I am going to get you a silver mask like that of the famous Mexican wrestler, 'El Santo.' Then we will add a nice blue cross on it to make you 'The Silver Exorcist.' I am going to do some surfing on the web to get as much intelligence information on this man as I can; he has got to have a weakness somewhere."

"Women!" said the priest joining in the enthusiastic plan his friend was developing.

"No, well yes, but I am looking for something like his Achilles heel. He must have a physical weakness that we can exploit, but we need to find out where he comes from first."

The old man went into his office and turned his computer on to start his research. Father Gabriel was going to leave the shop when the friend asked him:

"Are you sure about this?"

Father G stopped smiling and said:

"Do you remember those people in the church on Wednesday morning that I stopped to talk to before we went to breakfast?"

"Yeah, a young couple with a cute little boy," Pedro said, recalling the family.

"They need as much money for their son's operation as I can make beating this guy, so the answer is not 'yes' but 'hell yes!' I am sure I will do it!"

"Amen!" said Pedro, as the priest left, slamming the door behind him.

The old man laughed and clapped although he was not sure it would be possible to accomplish what the priest wanted. He decided he would follow the plan he had just conceived to help the Miracle Weaver.

Pedro loved Gabriel as if the priest were his own son. The old man had a son, Rogelio, who died in Vietnam. Gabriel seemed to have the same spirit. The new wrestling-star-manager called the fight promoter to accept the challenge and set up a meeting to sign a contract. He left his employees in charge of the pawnshop while he hurried to get the silver mask tailored to look as he wanted. He also was able to gain a lot of helpful information on the Internet about the mysterious Golden Demon. It was a matter of knowing where to search and be willing to throw a few dollars for the information to go into the right web sites and chat rooms.

The Golden Demon had indeed been in the Delta Force after a few years with Special Forces at Ft. Bragg, North Carolina. When he left the military, he had been cut by the Centaurs of the professional football league because he hurt his right knee during training just before the season started, so he never got to play professionally. He was known in the power-lifting and bodybuilding circles to have gained 50 lbs. of muscle using steroids. He was huge already when he came out of Delta Force, but he added those extra pounds trying to make it in the professional football market. His real name was Charles O'Hara. His father was an alcoholic who abused him physically when he was a child; the father was killed in a traffic accident driving while intoxicated. His mother was a very strict disciplinarian who took 'Charlie' to church everyday. She never allowed him to date or go out until he finished school and joined the military. His former acquaintances did not know him as the Golden Demon because he had changed so much and had not associated with them anymore, but they had a wealth of information on Charles O'Hara, from Manhattan, New York. Charlie's mother was found dead mysteriously one day. She broke her neck on what seemed to have been a fall from the second floor. Rumor had it that Charlie killed her and made it look like an accident. Pedro got a lot of personal information on the giant from women who had dated the wrestler. He then had enough material to use, physically as well as psychologically, against the opponent. Now he had more confidence they would triumph.

Theresa Reynolds made a couple of phone calls over the weekend to some old family friends; retired General McKennan was one of them. Theresa arranged for a job offer from a big insurance and investments company for Linda Richards. If she accepted it, the single mother would be making triple the salary she was earning in the kitchen job at the school. Theresa also asked Scott Anderson, Linda's attorney, to meet with her after school on Monday. During the meeting, Theresa questioned the attorney and learned that he was single and prosperous. He liked Linda, but, as her attorney, he kept a professional relationship with her. Theresa told the lawyer that Linda was showing great interest in someone she 'had just met' and that it would be just a matter of time before Linda could actually 'be open' with that man. The astute sister did not elaborate on Linda's love interest in Gabriel, instead, she made it sound as if it were her attorney that Linda was interested in. Theresa suggested Scott appear at Linda's second job in the artist studio and that he offer her a ride because 'the poor girl had to walk all the way home after the session, unless she caught a ride.' Theresa shared her admiration for Linda for her dedication to the support of her little boy to the point of having to work as a model to make ends meet. The attorney obviously got excited at the possibilities and thanked Theresa for all her help. She also told him that she had found Linda a much better job offer, but that she would prefer Scott gave her the news and not mention her part in it. He promised her he would let Linda know about the job opportunity without revealing his source.

That same Monday evening, the 15th of November, Don Pedro called for a press conference to announce the big fight. By his side, sat a dark-shrouded figure, like a monk, with a silver mask. The media ate up the story of a fight between the Golden Devil and the Silver Exorcist. All was set for the event that would take place the following Sunday evening at the local coliseum. The Demon put on an act, as expected, at the press conference.

"I will torture this puny opponent until he prays and begs his God to take him away to ease his pain. He is daring, but he will regret it once we get in the ring!" he boasted.

Father G was silent listening to the giant run his big mouth. The priest was holding a large wooden cross in his hands, as if praying. He was not even looking at his opponent. The wrestler mocked him, but without getting a reaction from the mysterious challenger.

"You see? He is already making peace with his God, but it is too late for him. Not even God can help a man who dares to challenge The Champion Of The Universe!"

The giant approached the side of the table where Gabriel was sitting in prayer while Pedro spoke to the media. The Golden Demon wanted to intimidate the challenger by getting close to him as he said:

"This is just a puny coward who does not even have the courage to speak in the presence of The Champion Of The Universe."

The golden masked wrestler slapped the priest in the back of the head to get his attention. The sitting man responded quickly by hitting the brute on the right knee with his wooden cross. The sharp pain on the weak knee made the masked giant lose his balance. He slapped the table with both hands, hard, to regain his balance and pretend ferocity. He growled half in pain and half in anger:

"Aaahrgh! I may not wait until Sunday to tear you apart. Come on, coward. Get up! Right here, right now, and let's see what you've got!"

Four security officers came to restrain the big man. His four glamour girls joined the security force to pull him away from the challenger who still remained in his chair. Don Pedro got in front of Gabriel to protect him from the attack of the Golden Devil, knowing full well the giant was not going to do anything there. It was mostly a publicity stunt; however, the knee check confirmed what Pedro had told Gabriel. The Golden Devil had experienced a career-ending knee injury while training for the Centaurs, and it was still his weak spot. They would have to use that in the actual fight.

"What kind of unprofessional behavior is this? I demand more respect and protection for my fighter who is a true professional — not a brawling clown like that yellow devil," Pedro announced, adding, "His days in the ring are numbered! He needs to start looking at his retirement options now!"

THE TEMPTATION OF THE MIRACLE WEAVER

The TV crew captured Pedro Mireles's entire protest and then followed the Golden Demon being escorted out of the room. Pedro and Gabriel exited through another door and got in the limousine that took them back to the Wild West Side boxing gym. The event was well set and awakened the interest of the public. A news crew followed the limo all the way to the gym despite their attempts to lose them; James Bravo let the masked challenger and his manager come in but closed the door to the news crew, protecting the identity of the Silver Exorcist. Gabriel changed out of his outfit, got on the roof of the place and left through the back alley. Pedro came out and met the news crew asking for their understanding in keeping the fighter's identity secret. They agreed and left the location. Pedro knew they would try to find out who the challenger was but vowed not to let them know.

The Holy Trinity pastor went to Leopoldo and Alma Cardenas's home to inform them about the plan.
"I want you to trust me. Let Benito watch this fight," he told them, "He may get a little scared, but ultimately, it will help him overcome his nightmares once he sees me defeat the Golden Demon. If he does not want to watch, don't force him."
"God bless you, Father, but do you really think you can beat that giant?" asked Alma. She had her doubts that it could be done.
"There is nothing impossible with God, Alma. This way you will get the money you need for Benito's operation."
"You are going to fight that killer and then give us all the money for the operation?" said Leopoldo in surprise. He was sure it could not be done.
"Yes. It is just a matter of faith, time — and maybe some pain," explained the priest, picking Benito up in his arms.
The boy hugged him tightly and kissed his cheek as if he understood what the man was going to do for him.
"We will pray for you Father," said Alma taking her boy out of the priest's arms.
"Thank you, my friends. Just remember to keep faith in your hearts."
The minister left them with a glimpse of hope after he warned them not to tell anyone he was the masked Silver Exorcist. Once he drove away, Leopoldo told his wife:
"We went to the church praying for a miracle to cure Benito. If Father Gabriel can beat that demon, it will truly be a miracle."
"I feel confident that he can do it. I hear that God is always by Father

Gabriel's side. Do you remember the story of David against Goliath?" Alma reminded her husband while hugging her little son.

"Yes, I remember that story. Let's hope God is with Father Gabriel as he was with David, honey," Leopoldo said, joining them in a family hug.

On Tuesday, the 16th of November, Father Gabriel called Sister Theresa into his office after school. He was physically tired after training hard in the gym the whole day. Pedro had shown him some wrestling tricks and had him practice holds and throws, falls and rolls. They made a large canvas training dummy stuffed with sand and weighing 350 lbs. Gabriel had been manipulating the bag, hitting it, rolling with it and picking it up. He lost several pounds from the unusual workout but felt he had profited from the experience. He had only four more days to prepare for the big fight. Although he had faith that he would prevail, he sensed that he also had to do his part. Fortunately he was in great shape; he just needed to practice some wrestling moves. The principal told his first grade teacher his plan and asked her to keep it a secret.

"That's crazy, Gabe; I think you should call it off. What if you get seriously hurt?"

She placed her little hands on his muscular chest.

"I can assure you that not only am I going to be all right, I am going to win and get the money little Benito Cardenas needs for his operation."

There was not even a shadow of doubt in his determined face. Theresa stood there, very close to him. All the others had gone home for the evening.

"You are so brave and so good, Gabe," she told him.

"I want you to pray for me," he begged her.

"I always do."

"Thanks, Terry!"

"You are most welcome!"

They were getting closer to each other with every exchange, lost inside each other's eyes. With her hand on his chest, she could feel his heart beating harder and faster. He placed his hands on her shoulders. She broke the silence expressing her concern.

"Gabriel, you could die fighting this man."

"If I do, remember that I loved you forever!"

His hands slipped down to her waist to pull her close to him; she grabbed his shirt and pulled him down to her. Their mouths met in a warm, long, deep, forbidden kiss. Gabriel opened his eyes, let go of her, stepped back and went around his desk to sit down.

"Oh, my God! That was so — good, yet it seems so — wrong!" Gabriel whispered.

He covered his face refusing to believe it had actually happened. Theresa sat down on the couch and said:

"I agree — on both counts."

He changed the subject of the conversation to avoid dwelling on it.

"Would you like to help me in this fight, Theresa?"

"Do you want me at your corner in a bikini like the Golden Demon's girls?" she asked mockingly.

"That would be great, but actually I want you to recruit some people to attend the fight with you and distribute some posters I am going to give you. Who can you trust to keep this matter a secret?"

"Keep what matter a secret, the fight — or us?"

"The fight, my secret identity as the masked 'Silver Exorcist,'" Gabriel replied.

"I think some members of my Bible study group are trustworthy, but I know that everybody already suspects what's going on between us. It's becoming a source of gossip, a scandal!"

"A scandal!"

"Yes! We may have to come to a decision sooner than you think," Theresa said.

Gabriel looked at her. He remembered what she had told him in the sacristy the previous Saturday. A melody came to his mind with the word she gave him, so he began to sing another old romantic song in which a love affair is said to be a scandal, but the poet encourages his beloved not to pay attention to what people say and to love him even more because the real scandal is being incapable to love. She clapped in approval of his song and reassured him of her support in anything and everything he wanted from her.

Little Timmy came over looking for Father Gabriel, so the two religious had to say good-bye for the evening.

Father Gabriel walked Sister Theresa all the way to the front door with Timmy following close behind them, watching them look at each other.

"Are you in love with Sister Theresa, Father G?" asked Timmy, looking up to his godfather after the woman left.

"Of course, my little friend. I love you too. I love everybody!" the priest said, feeling exposed by the little guy.

"You know what I mean. Are you going out with her?" the curious youth continued his inquiry.

"What do you think?"

Father sat down on a bench and faced his inquisitor.

"Yes! Everybody has seen you two. One day I even saw you on TV singing and dancing and kissing at a restaurant downtown. It was on the news last week. They said that you got mad and pushed the cameraman down. I didn't know priests could do that. Are you allowed to go out with nuns only?" asked the child.

"They are lying. I didn't get mad; it was an accident. The cameraman tripped and fell," said the priest, "We priests can go out with our friends just like everybody else. We can dance, sing, have fun, skate, and bowl — everything. We just don't have time to get married and have our own families."

"So you get to fool around with the nuns and don't have to marry them?" said the little boy smiling devilishly and winking an eye at his friend.

"Hey, I didn't say that! What do you know about fooling around anyway?" Gabriel exclaimed, slapping him lightly over the head.

"You know Susan, the redheaded girl in my class?" Timmy asked him.

"Yes —"

The priest moved forward to hear what the boy had to say about her.

"I kissed her the other day!"

Father Gabriel smiled at Timmy and decided to change the subject of their conversation there. He remembered a joke he could tell him instead.

"You know, Tim, you reminded me of a story. There was a man once in a plaza selling a dog. When another man approached him, the first man offered to sell him his dog, which was sitting next to his foot. 'How much do you want for your dog?' the second man asked. '1,000 dollars!' was the owner's answer. 'Why so much money for a common-looking mutt?' the second man inquired looking at the canine. 'This dog can talk,' answered the seller. 'I can't believe that. If it were true, a thousand dollars wouldn't be much, for a talking dog.' Just then, the dog talked to the prospective buyer, 'Please, sir, buy me from this horrible man. He is selling me because he is jealous of me. I won a medal of honor in combat and a Nobel Prize for literature. I have a Ph.D. in physics, and the Queen of England made me a knight. Buy me and take me away from this rotten excuse for a man!' The second guy was truly amazed and said to the owner, 'This is incredible! Why are you selling such a wonderful animal?' The owner of the dog told him, 'I am tired of all his lying!'"

Timmy cracked up in loud laughter, imagining the talking, lying dog.

THE TEMPTATION OF THE MIRACLE WEAVER

Father remembered that Timmy had come looking for him before they got into their conversation.

"OK, my laughing friend, why were you looking for me?"

"Oops, I forgot! Don Pedro sent me to get you because he wants you to go to his shop. He wants to show you something."

"All right. I'll be there. You may now go home and do your homework. Keep the things I told you to yourself, and I won't tell Susan's parents you are fooling around with their daughter."

"Can I tell the joke about the dog to my friends?" Timmy asked.

"Sure, but only the joke. Deal?"

"Deal!"

The boy shook hands with the priest and took off running towards his house.

On Sunday evening, November 21st, at the Coliseum, the arena was full. Gabriel was amazed at how many people were attracted to watching a man (possibly) be mangled by a giant. The promoter of the event had organized some preliminary fights to create the proper mood for the main event. The first fight was a sumo-wrestling match between two oriental wrestlers. Theresa wondered why such large men had to wrestle with almost no clothes on, but she watched the match with interest. There was some animal magnetism to that ancient, oriental martial art. The second fight of the evening was a full contact karate match. These fighters were of normal size but seemed to be able to fly. They exchanged punches and kicks throughout the six rounds they had scheduled. One was given the victory, but both ended up bloody and swollen.

The third fight was an Olympic style Greco-Roman wrestling match between two college-age boys. They had the speed and grace of the karate fighters but pushed and held each other a little like the huge sumo wrestlers. At least in this match there was no blood drawn by either one of the wrestlers. It was a cleaner fight involving skill and strength. One of the wrestlers was black while the other was white; both were about the same size in muscular development. The match was visually attractive, almost like a dance to Theresa's eyes. She had never attended an event like this, but she was having a good time watching the brutish sports. The last preliminary fight was between two middleweight local boxers, a black man against a Hispanic man. They punched each other as if they were trying to kill the opponent. They, like the karate fighters before them, ended up bloody and swollen. The judges called it a draw to the disgust of parts of the public who thought either the black guy or the Hispanic guy had won, depending on their own racial or ethnic background. A fight broke between two dissenting spectators. The security guards from the Sheriff's Office descended on the unscheduled fighters and threw them out of the arena. A man who was sitting behind Theresa offered her a beer, noticing that she was a very attractive lady and that she was alone. Theresa politely turned him down explaining she was actually on duty doing some work for the upcoming main event. Another woman who was behind the drinker jumped in on the conversation and accepted the beer he was giving away, so the man had someone to share his beer and conversation with. Theresa looked up to heaven and thanked God for the intervention.

Suddenly, the main lights were turned off. An organ started playing, and a choir sang a church hymn. Then a blue light flooded the arena while the announcer said:

"Ladies and gentleman! Welcome to The Texas Coliseum! Cartwright Productions has the honor and pleasure of bringing you the main event of the evening, a battle that promises to be apocalyptic in nature. We are about to witness the forces of good versus the forces of evil, in the ring, in front of our very own eyes, a fight for the title of Champion Fighter of the Universe. Ladies and Gentlemen, join me in welcoming, first the challenger, from this great city of San Antonio, Texas, standing 6 feet even and weighing 200 pounds of stainless steel muscles. He is the representative of good and righteousness, the enigmatic, 'The Silver Exorcist!'"

An ovation resounded throughout the coliseum for the unknown local challenger as people stood and clapped in welcoming the wrestler into the arena. The choir sang again their angelical hymn until The Exorcist got on top of the ring and greeted the audience.

Again, the lights went out for a moment. Then, red lights illumined the arena. A series of gas burners were turned on, creating a fiery path from the dressing rooms ramp to the ring. The sound system started playing a foreboding heavy metal overture as the announcer went on to welcome the champion.

"Ladies and gentleman! Hold on to your souls. With us tonight, from the depths of the underworld, at 6 feet 6 inches, weighing 330 pounds of pure fury, the undefeated, the incredible, the powerful Champion of the Universe, 'The Golden Demon!'"

Some people clapped, some booed, some screamed obscenities, some cheered to welcome the champion all the way into the ring. A teenager tried to get his autograph as the masked wrestler made his way to the ring; the choir played something like a satanic hymn. The giant picked up the teen and threw him over some of the fans; the Golden Demon growled at the daring fan and threatened the audience that disapproved of his treatment of the boy. The security guards advised the wrestler to keep moving as they kept the angry fans away from him. The rejected fan got up in the middle of the crowd and noticed he was bleeding through the nose after crashing against someone's head.

"Way cool, dude, awesome!" he exclaimed.

The Golden Demon got in the ring and strutted around, ignoring his opponent. His four girls escorted him as he paraded in the ring with his powerful arms raised high. One of the girls stopped and got close to the challenger. Although Father Gabriel looked very athletic when he took of his black poncho, he seemed to be quite small compared to the giant who had just arrived. The Exorcist was wearing an all silver outfit, mask, Speedo and wrestling lace up boots with blue trimming and a blue cross on the mask. The Demon's black girl approached him and put her hands on his muscular torso.

"If you can defeat my man, you can take me as part of the prize too," she whispered.

She licked her lips and looked at him with lusty eyes. Then she turned around and walked away swaying her ample hips and swinging the 'devil's tail' attached to her bikini bottom. Gabriel followed her with his eyes and then turned to the public. His eyes met those of Theresa's not too far to his left. He winked at her; she gave him a 'thumbs up' signal.

"Father, I can help you with that evil woman after you finish with her boyfriend," whispered Don Pedro who fancied the exuberant black woman.

"Yeah, you do that for me, my friend, although, she could be your granddaughter," Gabriel joked in a whisper. Pedro raised his eyebrows and nodded in agreement.

Theresa trembled a little when she saw the two wrestlers side by side. The Golden Demon looked huge in comparison to Gabriel (or anyone else). Then she noticed something like a halo around the whole body of the challenger. Theresa remembered that some saints were said to have that halo. She dismissed the idea as probably a reflection of the lights on the silvery outfit of the Exorcist. Theresa made eye contact with the seven other parishioners she had recruited to help Father G with his plan. There were two parishioners on each side around the ring on the third row by ringside. Finally when the match was about to start, the referee called the two fighters to the center of the ring to hear him relate the rules of the fight.

"I will call the end of this fight. It will only be stopped if one of you surrenders or is unable to fight anymore. There is no time limit. I will call for any time-out by ringing the bell. No weapons may be used. If I see anyone of you two introducing a weapon, I will stop the fight and disqualify the fighter. Is that understood?"

Both fighters agreed on the rules. The Silver Exorcist stretched his hand out to the Golden Demon, who just slapped his hand away with a growl. The challenger went to his corner to wait for the start bell and knelt to pray one last time. As soon as the bell rang, the masked demon charged towards the challenger like a raging bull. Father G was barely getting up.

The Demon hit the Exorcist on the back of the head with both hands forming a hammer, then grabbed Gabriel's forearm and swung the religious against the ropes across the ring. When the challenger bounced off the ropes, the champion received him with an extended arm like a clothesline. Father G saw his feet go up in the air and fell flat on his back on the white canvas. He looked to his side and saw Theresa's worried expression, with her hands on the sides of her face. He turned his attention to the giant who was climbing the corner of the ring apparently to dive on top of his fallen challenger. People were shouting. Gabriel took a deep breath to regain his composure and rolled quickly to the side, out of the way of the flying demon. The bigger guy landed on his butt on the canvas while the smaller guy got up and jumped on him getting him in a chokehold, to the delight of the crowd. The giant got up with the challenger on his neck. Father G felt his feet leave the canvas as the huge wrestler stood up struggling to get the pesky challenger off his neck. The Exorcist tightened up on the big neck. The Golden Demon intentionally fell backwards and crushed the Silver Exorcist against the canvas with all his weight. Gabriel lost his wind with the impact, so he let the enemy go. Both fighters rolled away from each other to regain their strength. They got up and circled around the ring. The giant began growling again.

The Demon reached out and grabbed the Exorcist's wrist. Gabriel got under the giant and flipped him over his shoulder with a judo movement. The golden masked warrior bounced on the canvas and got up. He was furious! He jumped forward and tackled the silver masked gladiator. Gabriel slipped out of the grasp of the opponent and rolled all the way out of the ring. The Demon growled louder and challenged him to get back in. The Exorcist looked

THE TEMPTATION OF THE MIRACLE WEAVER

at the screaming public. His eyes searched for Theresa's in the third row. He winked and smiled at her, with a 'thumbs up' signal, to let her know he was OK. Theresa and an elderly lady who was next to her got up and raised their signs which, when put together read, "REPENT CHARLIE!" The giant looked at the signs and cussed at the two women holding them. It worked! Father G took advantage of the distraction and got in the ring behind the demon to tackle him by the knees. The Golden Demon fell on his face and slapped the canvas with both hands.

The Exorcist quickly unzipped the opponent's right boot and took it off. He got up and away from the tackled champion who was puzzled by the challenger's actions. Father G threw the boot towards the public, to the right of where Theresa had raised the first two signs. The giant saw where his boot ended up and noticed two more people raising signs that together read, "CHARLIE, MOM LOVES YOU." The giant looked at the Exorcist realizing this was probably his doing. He grabbed the challenger by the neck and thigh and raised him up high over his head as if he were weightless. The Golden Demon threw the Silver Exorcist towards the audience and ordered him to get his boot back.

Father G got up from among the people and asked for the big boot. When he got it, he threw it farther out, to another section of the arena. When the devilish fighter's eyes followed his boot, he met another set of raised signs that read, "REPENT, MURDERER!" The Golden Demon grabbed the ropes, obviously upset, and threatened the two young men holding the signs. He did not notice that the challenger was on him again. This time, the Exorcist kicked the Demon on the side of his exposed, bootless right knee. During the preparation for the fight Pedro and Gabriel had noticed that the Golden Devil used quite a heavy padding on his long boots to protect his weak knee, so they had come up with the plan of exposing the knee to hit him there. A loud scream of pain silenced the crowd as the giant went down onto his left knee and held on to his right knee. The furious champion lunged forward and grabbed the challenger by an ankle. He twisted Gabriel's foot and made him fall on the canvas. The Demon crawled on top of the Exorcist quickly and they began wrestling and rolling on the mat. The golden masked fighter got on top of the silver masked fighter and choked him with his gigantic hands. Father started praying out loud:

"The Lord is my rock in whom I trust!"

Although he was trying hard to get the huge hands off his neck, he couldn't. His vision started dimming for lack of oxygen. He let his arms fall to his sides, limp, as if he had passed out. The Golden Demon smiled triumphantly and relaxed his grip a little. Theresa watched in horror thinking that Gabriel was dead. The Silver Exorcist suddenly slapped the Golden Demon as hard as he could with both hands on the ears with his little reserve of energy. The giant released him and covered his ears in pain. Father G took a deep breath and rolled backwards to get away from the giant. The Golden Demon was down on his left knee with both hands on his hurting ears. Then the Exorcist launched his attack, kicking the demon right on the face as if his head were a soccer ball. The Giant fell back; his mask turned bloody. He managed to pull himself up holding on to the ropes and turned around to face the daring challenger.

With a furious scream, the champion charged towards the priest. Gabriel quickly sidestepped out of his way but kicked him on the right knee again as he passed. The giant growled in pain once more and went down to his left knee asking for mercy with his hand raised. Their eyes met. The priest pointed at the last set of signs that read, "MOMMY FORGIVES YOU, CHARLIE." The giant got mad again and jumped up on his good leg. Limping a little, he pushed the smaller opponent hard against the ropes and tried to punch him on the bounce back. The master boxer ducked and avoided the high punch; however, he got under and quickly punched the giant's body ten times. With the wind knocked out of him the Golden Demon hugged the priest and leaned on him. They both went to the mat, but the giant had lost strength. Gabriel slipped away from him and climbed on top of the corner post of the ring. The Golden Demon managed to get off the canvas still trying to catch his breath. As the big man was standing in the middle of the ring, the Exorcist launched himself like a rocket and hit the giant between the chest and abdomen. Any other man would have been knocked unconscious by the impact, but the Golden Demon got up once more and faced the Exorcist.

They started circling around. Father G gave the signal with both hands for the signs to come up again, all together this time, as he made the Golden Demon look around the four sides of the ring. "REPENT, CHARLIE." "CHARLIE, MOM FORGIVES YOU." "REPENT, MURDERER." "MOMMY FORGIVES YOU, CHARLIE." The priest was pointing at the signs.

"I know who you are, Charles O'Hara, and I know what you did to your mother," Gabriel whispered as they continued circling around each other.

"Shut up! I will kill you too!" his opponent warned him.

The Golden Demon lunged towards the Silver Exorcist who moved out

THE TEMPTATION OF THE MIRACLE WEAVER

of the way and tripped him, sending him onto the ropes.

"Killing me will not give you the peace you seek, my son!" the priest shot back.

Gabriel crouched and circled around again to keep the conversation going with the signs up.

"You are nothing! You know nothing!"

The big man attacked, swinging a powerful punch at the Exorcist's head. Father G moved back, out of the reach of the big fist, but stepped quickly in to counter with two punches to the body and two to the head. He was much faster than the giant. The Exorcist stepped back on the tips of his boots, like a boxer, to start circling again and show him the signs once more. He raised both arms to have his assistants raise the signs again.

"This is the end of the Golden Demon! It is time for Charlie O'Hara to come back and face justice. That's the only way you can find forgiveness and peace!" the priest pronounced solemnly.

With an intimidating growl, the wrestler reached out and grabbed Father G's head. He put the Exorcist in a headlock under his right arm. The priest was more confident now, so he relaxed in his grip and punched him on the exposed, tender right knee again. The giant let him go and went down in pain holding his right knee. He was kneeling on his left knee and protecting his right with both hands. The Exorcist walked confidently in front of the kneeling giant and said in a loud voice:

"I exorcise you, Charles O'Hara, in the name of the Father, and of the Son, and of the Holy Spirit!"

He was making the sign of the cross over the puzzled wrestler. As his hand descended, a chorus from the audience responded:

"Amen!"

Father Gabriel's right hand came back up as a powerful fist and met the chin of the Golden Demon in a demolishing punch. The giant fell on his back knocked out. The Silver Exorcist flipped him on his chest and removed his golden mask. He got up and showed it around to the ovation of the public. The referee came and raised his arm declaring him the winner.

The four girls came over to help the fallen giant who was slowly coming back

"Who— are you?" the unmasked wrestler asked his now triumphant opponent.

"I am a messenger from the Lord. He has sent me to tell you that forgiveness is yours if you ask for it, from the bottom of your heart!"

"Are you a minister or something?" was the wrestler's next question.

"What difference does it make what or who I am? You are the one who needs to deal with your life and your relationship with your God. What matters to you now, Charles O'Hara, is that you are no longer a demon, just a man."

"You are right! But I still need to know who I am writing the check to for the half million bucks you won."

"Make it out to a couple named Leopoldo and Alma Cardenas. I already promised it to them."

Father G approached the huge wrestler and hugged him, shook his hand and told him:

"You don't realize it, but tonight you became an instrument of the Lord in performing a miracle. Make your peace with Him and do what is right, my son."

The giant stood listening to the words, not knowing what to make of them. The Silver Exorcist turned around and raised his arms to say good-bye to the crowd. Theresa sent him a discreet kiss; Gabriel smiled at her in return.

Several reporters approached the Silver Exorcist as he descended from the ring, but he referred them to his manager, Don Pedro. The Golden Demon sat down in his corner and realized that he had to turn himself in to the police for the murder of his mother. The Exorcist had a strange effect on him. That fight had changed Charles, as if the demon within him was actually gone. He felt strangely relieved and believed that there was hope in his life. He began crying. His girls were surprised by the extraordinary outburst of tears. They put a towel over his head, and he asked them to lead him to his dressing room.

Pedro and Gabriel rode in the limousine for their disappearing act at the gym, to prevent the media from finding out who the Silver Exorcist was. Pedro gave them a brief interview at the gym and went home. Once he was sure the media people were gone, he headed for the rectory to celebrate with his fighter.

Father Gabriel was surprised to find a party at the rectory. Sister Theresa and the poster holders were there to congratulate the Silver Exorcist for the victory over the Golden Demon. Theresa hugged him and kissed him on the cheek. Then all the others came and hugged him too. Don Pedro came just in time for the party. They opened a bottle of champagne and toasted the new Champion of the Universe, Father Gabriel, "The Silver Exorcist." He told them:

"I want to thank each and every one of you. This was great teamwork, and everyone contributed. Above all, let us thank our God who helped us and protected me, allowing me to be of service to Benito Cardenas. You know? Mother Theresa of Calcutta once said that charity, to be true charity, has to hurt… I can attest to that tonight. I am hurting in places I was not aware I had in my body, but we are here to celebrate our victory. Would you join me in singing a song to our Lord, the true Champion of the Universe?"

Sister Theresa went to the piano and started playing for the group to sing. The song was one of trust in God despite all odds. The words were a reminder not to ever be afraid of anything because God goes ahead of us always; all we have to do is follow Him.

A dark shadow crossed the window, peering inside the rectory. The dirty whirlwind ran down the alley and a low, angry voice uttered a warning.

"I am not done with you Gabriel! You will fall! You are not that strong!"

A white cat with gray stripes watching the dirty whirlwind, arched her back with her hairs straight up, and ran away so scared, she was unable to make any sound. The feline disappeared behind a house. The evil entity in the whirlwind went down to the creek, and the night became peaceful again.

Chapter XIII
The Seduction

It was December already. Everything was looking rosy for Gabriel and Theresa. They were working out together in the mornings; Theresa had started running in addition to their walking. She also did some light weights at the gym while Gabriel lifted heavy weights or punched the bag. They shared lunch at the school during working days. She played the music for several Masses. They went out bowling with all the sisters. Either Gabriel would call her or Theresa would call him at night to chat on the phone. They even entered and won a dance competition on December 5th. They had to practice several different rhythms, which was a good excuse for them to get together a couple of evenings a week to practice the dance and hold each other in their arms. Theresa posed for the artist a few more times; she cooked for him some Sundays. Linda seemed to have lost her obsession with the priest. The fall felt as if it were still summer in South Texas. The nights were cooling down but the days were still warm. The gossip about the priest and the religious sister had spread throughout the parish and beyond; however, there were no specific complaints against either one.

Their love affair had evolved from the moment they had their encounter at the gym on September 5th to the time when they kissed in the principal's office on November 16th. They found themselves intensely in love with each other and growing more physically passionate. Their dreams became more sexual in nature. The time to make a decision was approaching faster than they had expected. While Theresa was becoming more secure that this was a sign from God for them to engage in married life, Gabriel was tortured with the idea of abandoning his ministry, as much as his body was demanding it of him. He wanted to believe what Theresa was saying, that all the signs were there for them to enjoy their love, but he still had a doubt. All he asked of her was to be patient and give him a little more time. He was waiting for a definite sign that would tell him it was the right thing to do. It was then that a figure from their past came to enter their lives again.

It was Saturday morning, December 11th. Theresa challenged Gabriel to a tennis match. He had not played the sport since his high school days but accepted her challenge just to be with her again. Saturday was a good day to meet. There were only two Masses, one early in the morning and the other one in the evening, and no school activities.

"Where is Sister Mary? I thought she was coming with you," said Gabriel, welcoming Theresa to the tennis courts with a hug and a little kiss.

"She decided to stay on the computer instead. She said it was too hot to be outside."

"Well, what are we playing for?" he asked his rival in the tennis court.

"What would you like to lose?" replied the woman confidently.

"To you? I could lose anything and not regret it," Gabriel declared.

"I am not so sure of that anymore! Let's bet lunch. How is that?" Theresa told him.

"I think I could handle either paying your lunch or having you pay for mine."

"Let's do it then," Theresa said. "We'll see if you are as good in the tennis court as you are up in the pulpit, or the ring, or in the basketball court, or in the soccer field, or— "

"I get the picture! You may stop now," Gabriel begged her, "I am sure that you are about to give me a reverend spanking, but I'll defend my honor to the best of my ability, with the help of God."

"Leave God out of this, and see how well you fare by yourself."

"I am doomed then." Gabriel called out, going to take his position in the tennis court.

They started warming up. Gabriel thought it would not be so hard after all. He could chase the ball and hit it back with moderate skill. He noticed, however, that he had to do a lot more running than Theresa. Although he was in good shape, he started breaking a sweat quickly while she remained cool and relaxed, hitting the ball consistently well, over the net and in bounds, without much difficulty. The game was one sided in Theresa's favor. She beat her friend in both sets, 6-0 and 6-0.

"Game for Ms. Theresa 'Navratilova!'" exclaimed Gabriel after swinging hopelessly for an out-of-reach ball she sent to finish him off on the last game.

"You know, you really are very good!"

The priest congratulated his tennis rival shaking her hand over the net.

"Thank you, Gabriel. You are as gracious in defeat as you are in victory."

"Where do you want me to take you for lunch?" Gabriel asked the winner.

"Do you know any fresh seafood places around here?" Theresa asked him.

"There is a good restaurant in the heart of the west side where you can have some fresh shrimp and oysters cocktail with a cold beer."

"Sounds good. Let's go take a shower first," the lady said, picking up her racket cover.

"That sounds even 'gooder!'" Gabriel exclaimed. "My place or yours?"

"I will take my shower at my place, and you will take yours at your place until you make up your mind as to what you really want with me," Theresa told him pointing at his chest with the racket handle.

She bumped him with her hip as she was getting in the car; he was holding the door open for her. Gabriel just laughed and said no more. He was still not sure he was ready to abandon his ministry and seek married life with his lovely friend, but it was more tempting every day.

"Guess whom I found the other day at the mall?" Theresa asked while Gabriel drove her home.

"Barbara Ann Williams?"

"Yes! How'd you know?"

She turned to see him truly surprised.

"Some people say that I am psychic," Gabriel explained, then after a brief pause he confessed, "But to tell you the truth, Barbara called me to invite us both over to her place tomorrow. She is having a small reception at her place in the Hill Country to preview an exhibition of twenty years of her works."

"That— girl! I told her I would be the one to invite you!" said Theresa, feigning anger. "Can you come?"

"I already put it on my calendar," Gabriel told her, "Do you think I would pass on this opportunity for free wine and cheese?"

Gabriel dropped Theresa off at her place and promised to come back and get her in an hour. They went out and had their lunch as planned. He had no idea what the presence of Barbara Ann Williams meant for both of them at that stage of their relationship.

Barbara was a very creative person. She had never been able to conceive a baby, but she explored her artistic creativity in poetry, dance, painting, photography and music. She played the piano from an early age and took dance lessons throughout her formative years. She became a beautiful, creative, mature woman who had grown accustomed to getting everything she wanted. She was rich, famous, and wise in the ways of the world. Barbara had a master's degree in Literature and another one in Fine Arts. She had divorced her first husband and buried her second one, who left her much richer than she would have been otherwise. Barbie had been Theresa's best friend in high school. Although Barbie had a crush on Gabriel when they met at a school dance, she never tried to get between her best friend and him.

After Theresa left the city, the two girls lost contact. Theresa wrote to her after reading the first of Barbara's published poetry books. Theresa was already a religious sister by then. They wrote back and forth to each other sporadically, perhaps a couple of times a year. When Barbie moved back to Texas with her second husband, she met Gabriel at an opening of an exhibition by a local artist. Gabriel was already a priest in the diocese. Barbie assumed that Gabriel, being a priest, knew that Theresa was a religious sister and that she would know about him because they all belonged to the same church. At the time Barbie saw Gabriel, she did not mention Theresa and when she wrote to Theresa, Barbie did not mention she had found their friend as a priest in Texas. She had lost contact with both of them since then until Theresa and Barbie met at one of the local malls.

The other three religious sisters took Theresa to that mall to get her a little gift after they learned that she had a birthday in their house without letting them know. Barbie was shopping for a new wardrobe for the season. The sisters bought Theresa a pair of nice athletic shoes since they knew that she was walking and running in the mornings on some older, well-worn shoes she had. After their encounter with the beautiful black artist, the sisters decided to let Barbie take over and keep Theresa in her company while they went to do their own activities. The two old high school girlfriends went to eat at an expensive steakhouse reminiscing about years of friendship.

When Terry told Barbie about the situation she was in with her former-boyfriend-turned-priest, Barbie convinced her that this was a clear sign that they were meant for each other. She wondered why Terry had not already jumped at the opportunity and snatched Gabriel in marriage. Barbie assured her she would already have done so if she were in Terry's shoes. Barbie encouraged Terry to do what she wanted so badly; furthermore, she promised her she would help her make it happen. It was not too late for both of them; Terry could still give Gabriel a child or two. Barbie concocted a plan to get them together at her ranch, "The Garden of Eden," the following Sunday evening. That was when she told her about her "private party" idea with the excuse of having the art show preview. Gabriel would be interested in something like that. Barbara did not wait for Theresa to invite him; she was afraid Terry would back out of their plan. That was why she invited their friend herself. Gabriel was excited about the opportunity to see Barbie's art and share some time with the friend out in the Hill Country.

The Garden of Eden Ranch in the Texas Hill Country, about an hour's drive from the parish, was, indeed, an earthly paradise. It had a lot of fruit trees, among them peach, orange, tangerine, grapefruit, banana, coconut, pineapple, papaya, pecan, even grapevines. The fields around the main house were carefully tended like a golf course. In the very center of the property, there was an artificial lake with an island in the middle. The mansion was built on that island, completely surrounded by water. The trees on the perimeter of the property formed a forest that enclosed the paradise inside. Barbara Williams had a staff of twenty men, all of them personally handpicked by her. They were between twenty-one and forty years old. They shared a dorm in the forest outside the island. Her ranch hands, cooks, butlers, drivers, gardeners, guards, secretaries, and a manager constituted a small army of admirers working for her. It made her feel like a little goddess some times. Her staff cut her hair, filed her nails, massaged her, fed her, protected her and responded to her smallest desire. She had been heard telling her friends she did not need to remarry because she had twenty men at her service. She, however, kept a wedge between herself and her staff. Although she treated all her staff well in pay and benefits, she warned them they had to agree never to attempt owning or marrying her. As soon as one felt he was in love with her, he had to leave the job. She had already bedded all of them and did not want any of them fighting over jealousy. She claimed to love them all the same when she actually just used them all. She felt like a female sultan with a harem of male slaves. Barbie thought of herself as a modern, liberated, independent woman; however, deep inside, she felt unhappy despite all her success.

Sunday afternoon Father Gabriel left his house right after the twelve o'clock Mass. A passage from scripture resonated in his mind; it was the promise of God to Abraham after he agreed to sacrifice his own son in obedience to the Almighty. God was going to bless him abundantly and give him numerous descendants, all because he obeyed God's command. The priest recalled he had a little discussion with a high school student before the noon Mass about a school paper she was writing on Lorenzo Ghiberti's "The Sacrifice Of Isaac," a famous bronze relief from the beginning of the XV century in Florence, Italy. Gabriel told the girl the place in the Bible where she could find the passage depicted in that masterpiece. "It was created by Donatello's teacher," he told her and also gave her some pointers as to the artistic importance of the work. Gabriel pondered on the significance of the passage, but his thoughts were interrupted by the presence of a young deer crossing the highway in front of his car. Father G stepped on the brakes and swerved to the right to avoid hitting the animal. He was relieved after looking in the rearview mirror and seeing that the deer was OK as the young animal joined his mother on the other side of the road. The priest forgot what he was thinking about and turned the radio on to the classical station.

Gabriel arrived at Barbara's ranch at 2:30 p.m. She buzzed him in through the main gate. Barbie came to receive him on a boat after he drove along a winding paved road to the edge of the lake. The priest parked his old car in a parking area by the little jetty and admired the beauty of the man-made paradise. It was another rather warm fall day with a few clouds providing relief from the hot sun. As Gabriel walked towards the boat, he noticed there were several luxurious cars parked in the covered parking area where he left his Priestmobile, a limousine, an expensive high performance sports car, an exclusive four-door sedan, a luxury sports utility vehicle and a big brand-new truck. The priest admired the artificial lake and smiled at Barbie who was waving at him from the boat. When he got on board, the black woman hugged and kissed him. He noticed she was wearing a long red dress of very thin and soft material, which revealed that she was not wearing anything else underneath it. Father Gabriel turned around to admire the scenery and commented on it.

"This is a beautiful place you have here, Barb."

"Thank you, Gabe. My late husband and I designed it and made it just the way we wanted it. It's sad that he didn't get to enjoy it," his hostess commented.

"Are you short on help? Why didn't you send someone to get me?" Gabriel inquired.

"Oh, I let all my staff off for the whole weekend. I wanted this party to be very private."

"Is everybody else here already?" asked Gabriel, wondering who else had been invited.

"Yes, sir. You are the last guest on the list."

The trip to the island was brief. The priest jumped off the boat and offered his hand to Barbie. When she stepped out of the boat, her dress opened up and exposed most of her thighs. Father G turned his eyes discreetly to the mansion and its gardens. She held his hand and walked up the hill with him.

"What do you think of my little home?" she asked with obvious pride.

"Magnificent! This is a palace in the middle of paradise!" he admitted.

"That's why we named it the 'Garden of Eden.' We have lots of different fruits and flowers, and little animals, lots of water — only the best."

She pointed to examples as they climbed an easy cobblestone path with a creek running down by its side. There was a white rabbit in the shade of a tree by the creek. Barbie would not let go of his hand as they walked towards the house. The minister heard music coming from the mansion. There was also a delicious fragrance in the air, and the view all around was beautiful. The sexy woman holding Gabriel's hand was gorgeous too; her hand was soft and warm. The priest could not help but be aware of so much sensual beauty.

Suddenly, Father Gabriel stopped for a second because he had a vision. A man was shooting himself inside the mouth and then collapsed on a table next to a note he had left explaining his suicide. The note had Barbara's name on it.

"What's wrong, Gabriel?" asked Barbara seeing that he stopped walking and seemed suddenly far away.

"How did your husband die?" Gabriel asked, trying to interpret the vision.

"He developed a cancerous tumor in his brain. He retired from his business as stockbroker and came with me to Texas to build this place where he could live his last days. He lived for two years after the tumor was found, but his condition got worse after he suffered a stroke. Three months later, he passed away in his sleep. I learned later that you perform miracles. It is too bad I didn't know, or I would have asked you to heal him," Barbie said.

"I only do God's will," Gabriel explained. "He is the healer. I am a mere instrument of His divine love and mercy, but the things that have to happen will take place regardless of how much we try to change them. We must learn to interpret the signs we find on our way and be willing to fulfill our destiny."

They continued their walk and got to the entrance of the mansion.

"Speaking of destiny —" Barbara commented as they entered the sumptuous interior.

"Hello, Gabe!"

Terry was already there, wearing a white dress of the same daring style and material as the revealing red one Barbie had on. The religious sister looked like a beautiful bride in that dress; she had her reddish brown hair piled casually on top of her head, exposing her creamy neck. Even from a few steps away Gabe noticed that Terry smelled as if she had been anointed with expensive perfume. She even had some makeup on!

"Hello, Terry! You look great!"

Barbara noticed how they looked at each other, and she smiled devilishly. It seemed as if she had been erased from the scene at that moment, so she cleared her throat to break the spell Terry had cast on Gabe.

"Hummm — hummm!"

Both, Gabriel and Theresa turned to see Barbara.

"Would you please take your shoes and socks off, mister — Father Gabriel Infante?"

Barbie showed him her bare black feet and Theresa's bare white feet on the white carpet. He immediately complied with her request.

"Oh, sure! I didn't realize you observed that oriental custom."

"Also, take off his black coat and his clerical collar, will you, Terry? While I get us something to drink," said Barbie, heading for the bar.

Terry approached Gabe to get his coat and collar.

"Where is everybody else?" asked Gabriel as Terry placed his clothes in an open closet.

"This is it, my friend!" Barbie announced, offering him a glass of red wine. "It's just my two best friends in the world, and me, the artiste!" Barbie said, smiling broadly as she handed a glass of wine to Terry.

Father Gabriel looked at his glass of wine and recalled that he already had some consecrated wine in the three Masses that morning. Fewer people than usual had partaken of the cup, so he ended up drinking what was left over. He always was aware of his alcohol intake, but he thought it would be fine to have a little more.

"Cheers! To old friends reunited, that we might remain friends forever!"

Barbie offered the toast as they clinked their raised glasses. How could Gabriel refuse to have a drink with such lovely company? He tasted the wine and found it to be excellent. The stereo system was playing Mozart's "A Little Night Music." Gabriel closed his eyes to savor the wine and listen to the music. The sweet perfume from both women engulfed him and harmonized with the music and the taste of the wine. He opened his eyes again and saw the two beautiful women waiting for him to say something. He smiled, filled with sensual pleasure, and looked around the richly decorated interior of the mansion.

"This is just great! Thank you God for giving us life that we may enjoy all things, especially the love of our friends!" he said.

Sister Theresa touched his glass and said:

"Amen!"

"Listen, you guys, lighten up on the religious stuff," said Barbie as she began walking to another room signaling for them to follow her.

"You are here to have a good time," Barbie continued, "I know both of you are professional religious people, but for right now, limit yourselves to being simply a man and a woman, Gabe and Terry, my dearest old friends. We are fixing to take a trip together in time. We have lots to talk about, and I have a very nice evening prepared for you."

The hostess stopped at the threshold of another spacious room to tell them:

"Let me be your guide. Welcome to the Garden of Eden, where dreams come true."

They clinked their glasses in agreement and drank more of the inviting red wine.

In the room, there was a table set up with crackers, cold cuts, cheeses, fruit, more wine, ice water, glasses, napkins, and silver utensils. The priest grabbed some crackers, meat and cheese because he had not eaten lunch, and he was really hungry.

Barbie showed them a gallery filled with twenty years of artistic works, drawings, paintings, photographs, sculptures, poems, and a series of nude pictures of her taken for a popular men's magazine some years before. Barbie's artistic style was sensuous and very rich in contrasting arrangements. Her compositions were sharp and full of energy. She explained some of her favorite pieces in detail while the music of Chopin, Beethoven and Brahms played on the stereo system. When she finished her presentation, Barbie turned to face her minute, selected audience and took a bow.

"Bravo!" Gabriel clapped to let her know he had truly been impressed by her artistry and her many achievements. Theresa joined him in the applause and said:

"You are really good, Barbie!"

Gabe looked at Terry and shook his head in disagreement.

"Good? She is great!"

He walked towards the wall and showed Terry a large close-up painting of a flower up that reminded him of another famous great American female artist's work.

"Look at this! I sometimes wish I had the sensitivity of a woman and could paint like that, and those poems — My God! I cannot even imagine myself trying to create such beauty."

THE TEMPTATION OF THE MIRACLE WEAVER

Barbie was obviously pleased with his comments and filled their glasses with more wine. The ambiance was exciting as they drank and ate merrily. Then they moved on to the music room.

Barbie turned the stereo system off. Father Gabriel stood close to Sister Theresa to whisper:

"You really look fantastic this evening, love."

"Thank you!" she said, blushing slightly. Then she sat down at the piano to play a lively tune from memory.

Barbie came in exclaiming, "Yes!" in approval of the piece Terry was playing. Barbara took Gabriel's right hand and placed it around her waist, she then took his left hand saying:

"Shall we dance?"

Gabriel looked at Terry. She nodded in approval and kept playing energetically throughout the whole piece while the two friends danced. At the end of the piece, Gabriel spun Barbie, held her by the waist and leaned her back for a grand finale. She laughed and said:

"I like that position. It is so — dramatic!"

As Gabriel drank some of his wine, he remembered a joke and shared it with them.

"A woman went to the dentist with a toothache. The doctor examined the terrible cavity and informed her, 'I am afraid we are going to have to pull that tooth out.' The woman, who was terrified at the prospect of a painful extraction said, 'Oh, no. I'd much rather have a baby.' So the dentist told her, 'Well, make up your mind because I have to adjust the chair.'"

The two women covered their mouths but laughed out loud at his joke. Then Terry asked Barbie to switch places with her. Terry approached Gabe and curtsied prior to dancing with him; he bowed to her and held her by the hand and waist waiting for the music. Barbie started playing a romantic tune. Gabriel recognized the melody and began to sing. The acoustics in the room were so good even he was impressed with the sound of his own voice. It was a romantic song about two strangers who become lovers one night, during "a warm, embracing dance."

Barbie played with passion, excited to see them dancing as if they were the only two people in the world, lost in each other's eyes. They looked so good together! She felt a little envious of their obviously deep love for one another. Gabriel breathed in Theresa's perfume and felt her soft flesh in his hands as he enjoyed the music and the dance. The wine had already had an effect on his thinking; he felt happy and relaxed. Gabriel continued the song until the end. Theresa rested her head on his chest as their dance came to an end.

"Thank you, Gabe. That was beautiful," Theresa told him.

"Let us thank Barbie for the music and the great setting," Gabriel suggested, bringing his dance partner to the piano player.

The three friends hugged and kissed each other.

"I think I died and came to heaven!" Gabe exclaimed.

"You haven't died, my friend, and you ain't seen nuthin' yet!" Barbie remarked, walking out of the music room with her friends following her.

The hostess smiled devilishly, walking in front of the couple. All three seemed to be enjoying themselves.

"Is it just me, or is it hot?" Barbara said as she opened a double door to a patio in the back.

"I feel just fine!" claimed Gabe, gulping the last of his third, or fourth glass of wine.

"Me too!" Terry told them, imitating Gabriel in gulping the rest of her wine.

Barbie came with the bottle to refill their glasses. The priest refused because he was feeling "a little too happy;" Terry did take a refill. Gabe asked Barbie for some water instead.

"Can you transform the water into wine?" asked Barbara, giving him a glass of iced water.

"No! What kind of question is that?" Gabriel said, drinking some of the water to erase the taste of the wine.

"Didn't Jesus do that at a party?" asked the hostess in a playful mood.

"Yes, at a wedding in Cana, but there was a need to avoid embarrassment to the family at that time. Plus, there is more to the significance of his actions in transforming the water into wine. It was not just to show off," the minister explained as they walked out into a pretty space outside with a small waterfall, a sparkling swimming pool, a bubbling Jacuzzi and a beautiful patio filled with flowers.

"Well, I'm hot, so I'm going to take a dip. Come on and join me!"

Barbie unbuttoned her long red dress and let it fall on the floor. She turned around, totally nude, and encouraged them:

"Come on, you guys! What are you afraid of? The water's fine and there is no one else to see you go skinny-dipping."

Theresa took another gulp of her wine and began to undo her white dress. Gabriel looked at her dropping her dress just like Barbie had done and then diving gracefully into the pool. He put his glass down on a patio table and excused himself.

"Where is the nearest bathroom?" asked Gabriel, heading into the house.

"There is one on the left door as you enter," Barbie informed him walking into the heated pool, "Hurry up; the water is just fine!"

Terry was swimming lazily across the pool.

The priest went into the bathroom for a few minutes. When he came back, he had only a towel wrapped around his waist.

"Come on, Gabe! You are an artist. Don't tell me you have a problem with nudity?" said Barbara, teasing the friend.

He took off his towel and took his glass from the table to walk into the pool using the steps. He told the hostess:

"No. You are absolutely right. It is just that—"

"—You have never done this before," guessed the hostess, completing his sentence.

The two women laughed in a playful mood. They were standing with the water up to their shoulders on opposite sides of the pool watching him coming into the water. Father G walked in and stopped when the water level came to his chest. He said:

"Actually, I did it once before."

The women laughed, surprised by his statement. Terry asked him:

"When was that?"

"One time I was in Munich, Germany. I was held over for a day. My plane would not leave until evening, so I went around town to see the sights, walking. It was an unusually hot day; therefore, I decided to freshen up by going to a public bathhouse. To my surprise, it was a co-ed bath. I did not realize it until I was already in and noticed all the women there. I don't speak German, so I didn't understand the sign up front. I have to admit I was a little shocked at first, but then I realized that everyone else was acting very cool and collected. I decided to blend in with the crowd. I got me a massage, a bath, a shave, got my clothes dry cleaned and walked out of there refreshed and enriched. Let me tell you; it was quite an experience!"

They all laughed.

"You are right!" Barbie said, to lend credibility to Gabe's story, "I have been to those places in Europe. People over there are a lot more liberal about nudity, sex and the human body."

"What about you, Terry?" asked Barbie turning to her friend with curiosity.

"Well, yes! Kind of— It was in Europe too, in Spain."

Terry blushed and smiled, a little embarrassed. Father took a gulp of his drink and waited to hear her story. He noticed that his water tasted suspiciously like wine. He looked at his glass and said:

"Hey! This is not water; it is white wine!"

"A miracle!" exclaimed Barbie with a devilish smile, "I thought you said you couldn't change water into wine."

Gabriel tasted it again and looked around looking for an answer. His eyes rested on an open bottle of white wine sitting on the table where he had left his glass before going to the bathroom. Barbie had obviously switched his water for the white wine while he was gone.

"You — mischievous little wench!" he yelled splashing water on Barbie's face, "You were the one who changed my water for white wine. You—"

They all laughed at the trick she had played on him.

"It is a wonderful wine though!" Gabriel admitted, having a little more of it, "I'm sorry, Terry! You were about to tell us about your Spain escapade."

"Oh, yes! Well, it happened a long time ago. I was still a young woman," Terry said.

She paused for a moment and felt both of her friends' eyes fixed on her, waiting for the rest of the details. She went on with her story.

"I decided to go to a topless beach in Barcelona. I felt really weird. I am not an artist like you two. I had a big beach towel wrapped around me. I put it down on the beach and ran into the water. The beach was full of people; I didn't think anyone noticed me, but a handsome Spaniard swam towards me and started a conversation. He invited me to go out with him, but I showed him my ring and told him I couldn't do it. He was very nice and complimented me before he swam away looking for another available girl on the beach."

Barbie smiled, looked at her and asked her:

"That's it?"

"Were you totally nude then, like you are now?" intervened Gabriel before Theresa said anything.

"No, only topless," Terry answered nonchalantly.

Theresa started swimming to the deep side of the pool.

"What was his name?" Gabriel asked in a loud voice.

Terry stopped swimming, looked back and asked him:

"Who?"

"The creep, the Spaniard," Gabe said.

"Rodrigo!" Terry answered, amazed at the jealous tone of Gabe's inquiry.

"Rodrigo is a nice name!" Barbara commented.

THE TEMPTATION OF THE MIRACLE WEAVER

Terry was already on the deep side of the pool.

"I didn't say he was a creep. He was quite a gentleman!"

Terry pulled herself out of the pool, took a few steps, and dove back in. Gabriel finished his white wine. Terry swam under water and surfaced next to him to ask:

"What was the name of the girl that massaged you in Munich?"

"Monika."

"I've heard things about those Monikas," Terry told him half-closing her eyes.

"It was just a massage!" he protested, with a wide smile of pretended innocence.

Gabriel took her face in his hands and pulled her close to him.

"You are so beautiful, Terry," he whispered.

Barbara interrupted their moment because, again, she felt ignored. She told them:

"I thought you had said that Gabe could walk on water. How come he sunk just like us in the swimming pool?"

Gabriel turned to Terry, surprised that she had shared that incident with Barbie. Theresa shrugged her shoulders in response to his look.

"Only Jesus could walk on water, Barbie. I had to run on it not to sink," Gabe declared.

They all laughed again and drank some more.

"You guys look so good together!" said Barbie, finishing her wine, "I am getting inspired just looking at you two. Would you pose for me? I think I can do a series of images mixed with poetry— about everlasting love, timeless love, invincible, passionate, tender love, but I need your help. Please, please, please?" she begged them when she noticed they were hesitating to do it.

The lovers looked at each other and smiled in agreement.

"Let's do it!" announced Terry with a big smile. She was feeling extremely relaxed by then.

"We are yours," said Gabe in agreement with Terry. "What do you want us to do?"

Barbie got out of the pool looking for the right location.

"This is not the right setting. Yes! I got it! Let's go down to the lake," she said as her eyes followed the path of the little creek from the waterfall to the artificial lake.

"I want only nature in the picture. No man-made objects, only water and trees and flowers, sun, clouds, birds and you two. Let me get my camera.

Don't go anywhere."

Barbara took Gabriel's towel to dry herself off before going in the house. Terry hugged Gabriel and, while they were still in the water, asked him:

"What do you think?"

"Too late to go back! But she is a great artist. I am sure she will do something nice."

Gabriel caressed Theresa's little face; she ran her hands over his shoulders. Barbie came back wearing a hat and a canvas bag strapped across her chest but still without any clothes on. She threw an apple to Gabe and another one to Terry.

"That's all the equipment and props that you will need for this shoot."

They all went down to the lakeshore to work on her project.

"I feel like Eve in the Garden of Eden," said Theresa holding on to Gabriel's hand.

"Yeah, and I feel like Adam. It must have been nice to be there," Gabriel said, trying to stay relaxed.

"Where does that leave me, guys?" asked Barbie, overhearing their conversation, "I guess I am the serpent in the garden offering you to eat of the forbidden fruit, eh?"

"I have to tell you, though. You are a good-looking snake, Barbie!" joked Gabriel watching her descend to the edge of the water, still searching for some place to start shooting pictures.

There were three horses already tied to a tree by the water, one white, one black and one golden. Barbie invited her guests to go truly "bare" horseback riding. The animals had no saddles but were prepared with bridles to control them. The two lovers looked at each other and decided to "go for it" under the guidance of their friend. Barbie mounted the white stallion because he was the most spirited one and only listened to his master's voice. Terry rode the older black mare and Gabe the young golden mare. They went on a sightseeing tour of the estate. Terry was a little apprehensive that someone might see them like that, but Barbie reassured her that there was no other human being in her property. The whole staff was out for the weekend. The place was truly incredible; and the colors of fall made the sights more exciting. That was going to be the last of the warm days of fall. The cooler weather was already forecasted for the next week. The water was cold, but they endured it calling it "refreshing."

The artist shot several rolls of film that afternoon. She made the couple hug and kiss and touch each other in many ways. They ran and rolled on the grass like children. Then she took them to a place where the soil was soft, and she made them cover each other with mud until they ended up like two clay figures. They later went into the cold water and washed most of the mud off playing in the lake before returning to the mansion. The sun was setting in the horizon when Barbie ran out of film. She told them:

"Let's go to the house and take a good bath; then we will have dinner!"

They let the horses run free, knowing that they would return to the barn for their food. The two friends started the climb up to the mansion holding hands and following Barbie. From the house, the view of the evening sky was breathtaking. Automatic lights came on throughout the estate controlled by electronic eyes as night came upon the property in the Texas Hill Country.

Barbara took the couple into a luxurious guest room with a huge bathroom equipped with a Jacuzzi and shower. She told them to use anything they needed and meet her for dinner downstairs in an hour. She left them alone and went to her own master bedroom to take a relaxing bath. Gabe and Terry looked at each other. They were alone in a bedroom, half-drunk, nude and a little muddy. He picked her up in his strong arms and said:

"It's time for your bath, dirty girl!"

She kicked and screamed like a little brat, playing along with him.

"No, no, I don't want to!"

"Oh yes, you will take a good shower!"

He put her down in the shower stall and opened the cold water.

"Aaaaaah!" Terry screamed, feeling the cold water on her chest. She grabbed him by the beard and pulled him in with her.

"Aaaaaah!" he screamed, feeling the cold water on his back. Barbie could hear them laughing and screaming, having a good time. She smiled devilishly, thinking how well her plan had worked. She toasted to her own image in front of the mirror before going in the hot tub. She closed her eyes and imagined the two were making love by then. Outside, the wind gathered in a thick, dark and dirty whirlwind, which approached the mansion. Barbara got out of the tub and closed her window. She made a disgusted face smelling the putrid odor carried in by the whirlwind. She closed the curtains and went back to the tub; she had goose bumps all over her skin and felt nauseated, but just shrugged her shoulders and had some more wine.

Gabriel and Theresa were very relaxed, enjoying the new experience of showering each other, washing each other's hair, then slowly drying each other's body. When they were finished, Terry went to the closet and got a couple of bathrobes. They put them on, sat on the king-size bed and stared into each other's eyes for a long, silent moment. Gabriel was the first one to speak.

"Thank you for letting me bathe you, Terry. It was great!"

"I am yours, and you know it, Gabe," she said, offering him her lips.

He kissed her mouth with passion. They lay down on the bed, and she caressed his face. He looked into her eyes and held her hand. She had put her ring back on without thinking. The ring that indicated that she had committed herself to God. His eyes rested on the ring. The window was open, and the moonlight was reflected on the simple golden ring. His eyes focused on the ring; he could see the moon and the stars shining on it. He felt something like an electric bolt run up and down his spine realizing this was God's woman he was about to take. He suddenly jumped up and walked away from the bed.

"No!"

Gabriel put his hands on his ears where words still echoed, "I am yours." He turned around and looked at her getting up from the bed.

"You promised your life to our Lord. You cannot be mine," he said slowly.

He looked deeply tormented.

"But I love you, and you love me. What's wrong with that, honey?" Theresa asked.

She followed him. He turned away from her. She hugged him from behind. He was crying as he had not cried since the time she disappeared from his life.

"I am committed to our Lord first, and so are you! We may love each other, but we cannot have each other, not this way — It would be a betrayal to God," he told her firmly and fell to his knees.

"But He wants us to love one another," she argued, coming around and holding his face in her hands.

"It is not the same as to have sex with one another," he explained in anguish.

She released his face and dropped her hands to her sides; then she walked away from him, showing her frustration. She snapped at him saying:

"What do we do then, my love? I mean, what are we doing here?"

"We are being tempted by the devil!" he declared.

Terry walked back to face him; he stayed on his knees.

"Oh, come on, Gabe! This was all planned by Barbie after I told her we had found each other and still loved each other as much, or more, than we did twenty years ago. What's wrong with trying to be happy? Barb says it is not too late for us! Many others have given up religious life for lesser reasons— We could get married like we dreamt, and have children of our own! You can do all kinds of things; I am a teacher. We would manage and make it work. We would not abandon our faith in God. Maybe He is the one that brought us back together for that purpose."

Theresa was pleading with him, her eyes were reddish and wet, partly because of the wine and partly because she was ready to cry seeing her opportunity slip away.

"Barbie set this trap?" he asked, sitting on his legs on the carpet, shocked by the information.

"Well, she came up with the plan, but I agreed to do it— because I love you so much. I am convinced that I want to live with you the rest of my life, even if it means giving up my vows."

She sat on the carpet next to him; he kissed her forehead.

"You would be giving up God for a worthless man," he whispered.

"The man I love with all my heart!" she declared.

"I am not worthy of such love, but I am concerned that you have been taking advice from the enemy."

"Barbie is my best friend; she is not Satan!"

"I am not talking about Barbie, although I am afraid she has been used as its instrument," Gabriel explained.

At this, the whirlwind hiding the evil entity moved away from the mansion furiously and knocked down a tangerine tree and a peach tree on the way towards the lake. The whirlwind died down at the water's edge with a low grumble.

Father Gabriel put his hands on Sister Theresa's shoulders and looked into her eyes. He was very serious and continued explaining to her.

"When I first arrived and was holding Barbie's hand on the way up to the house, I had a vision of a man's death. Then I noticed that, subtly, Barbie was mocking me about possibly saving her husband from his death, transforming water to wine and about walking on water. Why did you tell her I ran over the river the other night?"

"I didn't tell her!" Theresa said, remembering Barbie's comment in the pool.

"I feel some evil presence in this place, Theresa. Pray with me my evening prayer, so we may finish this trial without surrendering to the enemy's plan," he begged her.

They arose, walked through the balcony's double doors and knelt together facing the starry night sky. The whirlwind had vanished.

"In the name of the Father, and of the Son, and of the Holy Spirit," prayed Father Gabriel making the sign of the cross.

"Amen!" answered Sister Theresa.

They prayed under the light of the full moon, asking for God's protection, asking Him to bless their mutual friend and also for Him to guide them in making the right decision about their loving relationship.

The voice of Barbara came through an intercom system as they were finishing their prayers.

"Hey, you guys, dinner is ready; come down and get it while it's hot!"

They felt a little better after the prayer, so they came down holding hands wearing their white bathrobes. The words from the Bible passage he had remembered earlier, about the obedience of Abraham, returned to his mind. Barbie was wearing a black silk robe and gave each of them one like it to change into. Then, all wearing the black silk robes, they sat at the table already set with china, sterling silverware, candlelights and elegant crystal glasses.

Dinner consisted of brisket, corn on the cob, mashed potatoes, green salad, black bread, red wine, cheesecake with strawberries, and coffee. Barbie was very talkative. Apparently she had also had more than her fair share of the fine wine. She related to the friends how she left Texas after high school to study art in Chicago. She married a jock in college, a black basketball player named James Jackson, but that marriage did not last. It ended in divorce after three years. Barb went on to New York where she got a degree in Literature. There she met Brian Fleming who was as old as her father; however, he was an intelligent, sweet and successful Wall Street stockbroker who convinced her to marry him. She told them about her success as an artist and poet, about her circle of rich friends, the death of her beloved husband, her pride of her beautiful estate. Theresa asked Barbara about her parents, brother and sister.

"My folks still have their barbecue restaurant and catering business on the east side of San Antonio. My sister, Laura, is happily married to a serviceman; they are living in Germany right now. My brother, Leonard, is a psychologist; he lives in Portland with his wife. They have a boy and a girl. I used to go see my parents about once a month, but I have been staying away now because they are too critical of my lifestyle. You know, they are always trying to get me to go with them to church. They are very strong Baptists and want me to 'give my life to Jesus.' That is one sure way of asking me to leave, trying to impose religion on me!"

Theresa finished her coffee and tried to focus on the good things Barbie had shared with them.

"Wow! You are such a success! Look at you, a mature, liberated, independent woman, smart, talented, beautiful, healthy, rich, famous. You have been blessed girl!" Theresa told her.

"Then how come I am not happy?" Barbie asked, looking for an answer from her friends.

"You have a good heart, Barbara Ann Williams, and the Lord has a plan for you. I can see that what's missing in your life is God," Gabriel said.

Barbie raised her hand to stop Gabriel from expanding on that point.

"Wait, Gabriel, I asked you earlier to leave your profession at the door. I get enough of that type of sermon from my folks."

She got up and walked away from the table. Gabriel got up and walked after her. They stopped out in the hallway. The priest placed his hand on her shoulder and said:

"OK, I am sorry I insulted you with my comments, but I am talking to you as your friend."

Barbara placed her hand on top of his and responded:

"I know, and you are right. This is just not the time. You guys wanna see a movie?"

When Barb placed her hand on top of his, Father Gabriel had another vision. He saw the spirited white stallion rearing and kicking. He knocked down a bar on a gate and jumped over the lower bar, escaping from the estate.

"What's wrong, Gabriel? This is the second time you blackout on me when I am talking to you," Barbie inquired.

Gabriel opened his eyes wide trying to focus on Barbie's question. He had not heard it.

"What?"

She smiled, thinking the wine had gotten to her friend, so she asked him again:

"Do you want to watch a movie with us? It's a chick flick, so I don't know if you like those."

Gabriel smiled and hugged Barbie with his left arm and Terry with his right arm. Inside his mind he was trying to interpret his second vision and wondering what it had to do with the first one, but he managed to say:

"I love chick flicks! Especially in the company of such lovely chicks!"

Barbara guided them to a small auditorium for private concerts, plays, movies and other social and artistic events. The women were holding to his arms on each side.

"Gabe, you have muscles of steel! How do you manage to stay in shape being so busy as a priest and school principal?" asked Barbie, feeling Gabe's muscular arm and rubbing his chest and shoulder.

"He runs, swims, lifts weights and practices boxing," explained Terry.

"When do you have time for all that?" wondered Barbara.

"At five o'clock in the morning, between my morning prayer and breakfast," was Gabriel's answer.

"Ugh! Who wants to get up that early? I am a night person and do not get up before 10 a.m., ever!" commented the hostess, sitting her friends in some comfortable seats to watch the movie.

"Terry has already started getting up early to work out with me," Gabriel boasted.

"You guys knock yourselves up at five in the morning. Just don't wake me up before ten, OK?" Barbie told them, "Let's enjoy this movie."

Barbara pushed a button on a remote. The lights dimmed. A red curtain opened up revealing a silver screen, and the movie started rolling. The auditorium had an excellent surround system; it was like being in a theater. They relaxed and enjoyed the show. Since Gabriel was sitting between the two women, he could feel their hands on his alternately during the movie. Every time Barbara touched his left hand, he would get a new vision, a funeral, a tall, dark, handsome black man, a wedding, and a baby. When Terry squeezed his right hand, Gabriel felt goose bumps all over his right side. By the time the movie was over, it was midnight. Barbara was bright and alert while Gabriel and Theresa were yawning, beginning to get tired.

The hostess led them out of the auditorium and into a cozy living room to listen to old records, look at pictures from her albums and talk some more. Barbie pulled out some pictures she had of Terry and Gabe at the zoo and the Municipal Park, evidence of a day on which all three of them skipped school. They had been in detention the following Saturday for that, but they thought it had been worth serving detention to have had one whole free day to spend together.

"You know, I remember that on that day I wanted to tell you guys we should move up north, to Utah, and become Mormons. That way Gabriel could have both of us as wives and all three could live happily ever after."

They laughed about it. Barbara continued her confession.

"I had a big crush on you, Gabriel, but Terry was, and still is, my best friend, so I gave up on you for my friend to be happy with you. Then we all went our separate ways, and you see what happened. Fortunately we are back together again, and we are going to make it come true this time, right girlfriend?" She winked at Terry and continued, "I will be your maid of honor at the wedding, but if you have a baby girl, you have to promise you will name her Barbara."

The hostess was filled with enthusiasm and anticipation. Gabriel stopped her, saying:

"There will be no wedding, my friend. We are already married to our ministries."

Barbara was surprised to hear his answer. She asked:

"After what happened here today, you are still going to continue with your present jobs? Will you be only — secret lovers? Hey, you can count on my silence; my lips are sealed! And you are welcome to use my house anytime, but what if Terry gets pregnant? Will that change things?"

"If I get pregnant, it would be an act of the Holy Spirit, an immaculate conception!" Theresa said lightheartedly.

"Do you mean—?" a surprised Barbie began.

"Nothing happened in that room," Terry told her, placing her hand on Barbie's. "Gabriel was quite a man to resist temptation, but he made me see my error in trying to pull him away from his ministry and also in giving up mine."

"I don't understand, Terry," Barbara said, unable to believe what she was hearing.

"Neither do I Barb, but this is the way it is going to be for us," Theresa told her shrugging her shoulders, "I will tell you one thing though — We had a blast today!"

Then, Terry reached out and hugged her friend for providing them such an exciting day.

"Don't you agree, honey?" Theresa said as she turned to see Gabriel

"This was without a doubt, the most sensually satisfying day of my life," he answered, "I think I got 'high' from so much beauty around me today. I really enjoyed every minute of it. I wouldn't change a thing if we had to do it over, but I know that will never happen. I will always be grateful to both of you for the pleasure, the joy, the friendship and the love you have given me."

They continued talking, listening to music and looking at pictures. Terry fell asleep on Gabe's arms as they were reclining on the sofa. Barbara got a blanket to keep her warm.

"You guys can sleep in that guest bedroom if you want to, Gabe," she told him, pointing to the room where they had bathed.

"I don't think so, Barbie. I've got to get back to my parish. I have a morning Mass to celebrate and school business to take care of. I better get going because I still have a long drive home."

Theresa looked like a sleeping angel. She probably had consumed more wine that day than on any other day in her life. Gabriel kissed her lips softly and laid her head on a pillow as he got up from the sofa. Barbara covered Theresa and tucked her in with the blanket. She seemed to be warm and comfortable there. Retrieving his clerical collar and black coat, Gabriel went to the bathroom and changed back into his clothes. He came out looking like a priest once more. Barbara rose from the floor and came to walk her friend out of the mansion. At the door, they stopped and looked at each other. Gabriel held both of Barbara's hands in his and kissed them. He thanked her again for a great day. She pulled him down to her and kissed him more as a lover than a friend. He was surprised by her action and attempted to resist but began having another vision at the contact of her lips and her tongue.

Father Gabriel came back to his senses and pulled away from Barbie's kiss. She seemed to be looking for his reaction to her display of affection, instead he informed her about the visions.

"I have bad and good news for you, Barbara. Sometimes I get these visions about different things. Let me tell you what I just saw. Your manager, Larry, is dead; he took his own life. He was really in love with you and could not accept your position any longer. He could not be happy with just a part of you, but he knew he could never have you entirely for himself. He shot a bullet through his mouth and left you a note."

Barbie looked at him in disbelief and stammered:

"You are kidding — Right?"

The priest looked at her with a serious look on his face. He asked her:

"Do you have a manager named Larry?"

"Yes, but how do you know that he shot himself or is going to shoot himself?"

"That doesn't matter. The police'll notify you this morning. You'll be suspected of murdering him until it's verified that he took his own life."

"You are not kidding!" Barbie exclaimed, realizing that Gabriel was dead serious.

She felt her legs trembling and getting weak. Gabriel supported her and walked her to a patio bench, under a lighted pole, near the entrance of the mansion.

"It's my fault that Larry is dead!" she mumbled.

"No, Barbie. He made his decision because of what was in his own mind. Do not blame yourself for someone else's actions."

Father Gabriel stopped short of advising her to reflect on her relationship with her the men in her staff, which created that situation. It was just not the time to talk about that.

"Listen; let me give you the good news. Your prayers have been heard!"

"I never pray!" protested the woman.

"Maybe it was your parents' prayers then, or your brother or sister's. I think in your subconscious you did pray, in your own way, and those prayers were heard in heaven. You will conceive a child next year!"

He smiled at her and put his hand on her abdomen. She sneered at him saying:

"Friend, you've had too much wine tonight!"

Gabriel told her the rest of the vision:

"Your white stallion, Rocky, escaped from your estate. A tall, dark and handsome man will bring him back to you. Do not let that man go away because he will father your child and fill your life with the happiness you are missing right now. Your kingdom, this 'Garden of Eden,' will be sold, and your life will change completely."

Barbara laughed out loud, pretending she did not believe a single word the priest had told her, but deep down, a small spark of hope appeared in her soul.

"Stay out here and talk to your God, daughter, He is, and has been, waiting for you to come back to Him. I will find my way out."

The minister disappeared downhill while Barbie stayed seated in the bench and repeated his prophetic words:

"A tall, dark and handsome man will father my child. God, may that be true!"

Then she realized that Gabriel would need to be taken on the boat across the lake. She got up and walked down the hill to catch up with him. He had already disappeared from her sight; she thought he would have to wait for her at the dock anyway.

"Gabe! Wait up, my friend. I'll take you back to your car!"

She walked along the cobblestone path by the creek towards the little dock where the boat was tied. She did not hear him answer, but she noticed he had cut across some wet grass. She could see his footprints leading to the dock as if he had taken off running. The last footprint was at the edge of the dock, but away from the boat. He had not boarded the boat to wait for her. Where was he?

She then heard the engine of his Priestmobile start. He was already on the other side! He could not have swum across that fast, unless he had run over the water! Barbara saw the Priestmobile headlights lighting the way as it went out of her estate. She dismissed the whole incident and decided to go to bed, but Gabriel's predictions kept resounding in her mind throughout the night. She got on her knees and prayed to God, as she had when she was a little girl, and fell into a deep sleep.

Chapter XIV
The Conclusion

Father Gabriel went out for a run after he recited his morning prayers. It was five o'clock in the morning on the 13th of December. Very few people were already up and going, some newspaper delivery persons, a few store employees preparing for the business day or some poor people waiting for the bus that would take them on a long ride to their jobs. There was always something going on in the big city, and the priest seemed to have the weird luck of stumbling onto things when he just went out for a little run. Most of the time, he enjoyed running because it was a time alone to meditate on the prayers of that day and to be in touch with himself and God's world. Sometimes, he would be back in his house without knowing how far he went or which route he took. His run usually lasted from 30 minutes to a whole hour. His favorite running experience was when on a warm summer morning a light rain would shower and cool him; that happened once every other year or so. It felt as if the hand of God was holding him those mornings. This time, he was thinking more and more about Theresa and less about the prayers of the day; actually, he had already forgotten the prayers of the day. It was a rather cool December morning; the warm season was over, but the cold did not bother him.

The rabid barking of a loose, large dog persuaded him to avoid a street and run instead towards the highway. He was wondering if he had made the right decision in turning down Theresa at Barbara's mansion. The woman practically had already given up her vows, to give herself to him, and he had turned her down. That had probably hurt her, and he hated thinking that he could hurt the woman he loved so much. As usual, he consoled himself thinking God would provide them with the right path to follow and the relief to his torment, and hers. Suddenly, the sound of screeching tires pulled him out of his thoughts, a terrible metal crashing sound mixed with breaking glass, screams of pain, and a car horn blaring, as though crying out for help. An accident had occurred on the highway, not far from where he was; he ran faster to get there quickly.

Gabriel saw a man stumbling, and trying to run away from the highway exit ramp. The man threw away a bottle and held on to his arm in obvious pain as he fled the scene. The lights of a passing truck lighted the man's face as the priest looked at him. He was a man in his twenties who was bleeding through the mouth and had a terrified look on his face. The only distinguishable feature Father G noticed on him was a relatively big mole on his cheekbone. The man covered his face and ran away from the priest. Then, Gabriel heard a woman moaning for help from inside one of the cars involved in the collision. He ran towards her. It was clear that there was no chance of survival for either of the car occupants. Their small car had been crushed by the head-on collision with the other man's big sport utility vehicle. After they were hit, their car flipped over the railing of the exit ramp and landed upside down. It had obviously been the fault of the utility vehicle drunk driver because he had entered an exit ramp driving the wrong way. The minister kneeled by the woman's side of the car. She was still conscious and in great pain. She asked him to get her out of the car; it was not possible without equipment because the car was smashed out of shape. The two occupants were trapped inside. She asked him to check on her husband. Gabriel went around and looked at the driver. He was a man in his forties, unconscious and with a pale color on his face. The priest felt for a pulse on his neck. There was a faint and slow pulse still beating in him. The priest talked to the man in his ear; he was unresponsive. Gabriel prayed for him that he might be forgiven and allowed to go into heaven. He went back to the woman who was still moaning.

Father Gabriel told her that he was a priest and asked her if she wanted to make confession. The dying woman looked at him with tears in her eyes; she agreed to make a confession right then and there. The priest absolved her of her sins and blessed her. She asked him for a favor. He promised he would try to do whatever she asked of him. The woman begged him to take care of her only son who was born blind and was at home. The horn of the utility vehicle languished and died out. Silence surrounded the scene as both husband and wife left the world of the living. Father Gabriel was praying over their bodies, still trapped in the car. He felt the presence of death; a chilling wind from the north caressed his face and gave him goose bumps. He thanked God for the opportunity to have helped the couple to die well. The police cruiser, ambulance and fire department truck came over. Father G talked to the responding officer and asked to have the information on the owners of the vehicles. The plates of the utility vehicle reflected that it had been stolen in another state. The officer gave the priest the name and address of the owner of the small car.

Frank and Elizabeth Parker had an address on the northwest part of the city. Father Gabriel asked the investigator sent to the scene if he could go with him to notify the next of kin. Detective Anthony Walker agreed to take him along. The priest remembered that the man had thrown a bottle in the grassy area, so he led the detective to it. Walker had it processed for fingerprints. They also collected some blood from the utility vehicle for DNA testing. Gabriel said the man with the mole may have a broken arm and might be looking for medical attention, so the police were going to check the area hospitals. Father Gabriel ran back to his house to take a shower and change into his religious clothes. Det. Walker came over to the church a little later on and picked him up.

John Paul Parker had been named after Pope John Paul I, who had only reigned for a month in the Catholic Church before dying. The boy had been born blind, as his mother had told Father Gabriel, the same day that the pontiff passed away in Rome. Parker was now a grown and handsome man, yet his handicap had kept him from a normal life. His parents had sheltered him all his life. He was left alone in the world; there were no other known relatives around that could take care of the young man. Father told Walker that he would stay with John and help him with the funeral. John Paul's blind blue eyes shed tears of pain when he learned about the accident. He seemed truly hopeless, desolate, wondering what was going to happen to him now that his parents were not there to assist him. He needed them everyday for many things. He had learned to read Braille, so he was better educated than most people his age. Not having a real social life, he had devoted a lot of his time to study a great variety of subjects. He listened to talk radio, enjoyed classical music and played the piano by memory. He had a strong faith in Jesus based on what his mother had taught him. Inside his home, John Paul could move easily because he already knew where everything was, but he had never been outside his home by himself. He never went to school. He had only one friend that was allowed to come and visit with him when he was a boy, but he had moved away with his family. Gabriel talked with John and listened to his story. He reassured the youth that he would accompany him through the whole process. The priest emphasized the fact that God had allowed him to assist John's parents to die well, insuring that they would be received in heaven. They would be there, waiting, when it was John Paul's time to go meet them.

There was an older lady at the house, Mrs. Martinez, who had been hired to take care of the son that weekend while his parents went out of town. Frank had to attend a conference in New Orleans Saturday and Sunday for his work. He wanted to take Liz and their son along, but John Paul suggested they go alone. He volunteered to stay home and let them go by themselves to have "the time of their lives." They did have a lot of fun in New Orleans till Sunday night. They left New Orleans at 10 p.m. and got to their hometown on time to meet their death. Father G asked John Paul to concentrate on the positive, all the good times they had and all the love they shared. The minister let John mourn his parents that day while he went and took care of all the necessary arrangements for the funeral. Mrs. Martinez agreed to extend her stay a few days to assist the young man with the house chores.

Gabriel went to his office. There was a message from Archbishop Rosales to see him. Gabriel knew it was about his relationship with Theresa. The scandalous report shown in one of the local channels had gotten the Archbishop's attention. They had blown the incident at the restaurant out of proportion; now other people were giving the Archbishop suspicious reports about the priest and the religious sister. Theresa called Gabriel, apologizing for not being there to take care of her class. He told her he had already made arrangements that morning for a substitute to take her place for that day. He also told the other sisters that Theresa was not feeling well and had stayed at her friend Barbara's house. It was true because she was not feeling well at all. Not only did she have a royal hangover from all the wine she had the day before, but also she felt really sad that she had tried to trap Gabriel (and that the plan had failed). Theresa declared herself to have acted selfish and foolishly. She was crying over the phone. To make things worse, the police were there. They had informed Barbara that her manager, Larry Samson, had been found dead, just as Gabriel predicted. Barbara was shocked. He had left her a letter. Apparently he had been broken-hearted because he loved Barbara but knew that she would never have him as anything else but her employee. They had agreed that as soon as any of her employees felt that way toward Barbie, they had to resign, for she did not want any complications. Barbie was blaming herself for Larry's death, and she told Theresa that Gabriel had already foretold her about this. She just had not believed it at the time.

The eighth grade teacher, a lady named Mrs. Nogarelli for her second husband (her maiden name was Esther Jones), was in the office picking up some papers and having a coffee break. She was known to be always interested in other people's business. She was able to hear that Father G was talking to

Theresa on the phone, so she sat down as if she were reading the paper by Father's office door to listen in.

"I don't know about you, Terry, but I had the best time of my life yesterday with you in Barbara's Garden of Eden," Gabriel said.

Esther wondered what kind of a 'good time' he was talking about.

"Please don't feel bad about what happened between us," the priest continued.

Mrs. Nogarelli raised her eyebrows and took a little sip of her coffee imagining what might have happened.

"I am sure that things will work out one way or another," Father Gabriel claimed.

The teacher smiled devilishly. Her suspicion was proving to be correct about the two religious.

"I think I am in trouble now," Father Gabriel declared next.

Esther leaned closer to the door to hear better.

"Apparently the archbishop knows about us and wants to see me today."

Esther almost fell off her place in the bench from leaning so close to the door. She looked around, but there was no one else in the room to see her listening to the priest's private conversation.

"No, I am not afraid of anything— What do you think can happen? That I get kicked out of the church? Let me tell you, if I have learned one thing in my life is this: I have a destiny to fulfill, and I will do it with gladness because that's what God has planned for me, and for you too, yes! I will always love you, no matter what happens— Listen, you take your time over there and let me know if you need another day or two off for that problem."

Mrs. Nogarelli covered her mouth. She suspected Theresa was pregnant and was probably going to have an abortion.

"I have a young blind man that was entrusted to me by his dying mother this morning. I also have to make arrangements for a double funeral."

Mrs. White came back in the office, so Mrs. Nogarelli stood up and folded the paper. She gulped the rest of her cup of coffee nervously and dripped some on her white blouse; she also scalded her tongue with the hot liquid in her rush to get out of the office. Mrs. White made no comment.

The archbishop had a long talk with Father Gabriel. On one hand, he had to take action on the allegations of misconduct brought against his subordinate; on the other hand, he did not want to lose the most charismatic priest in his archdioceses. Gabriel admitted he was having a love affair with Theresa and explained about their former relationship. All the allegations against him were true as related to the religious sister; they did go out on a date. They did dance and played together; they did love each other in a very intense way. The assumptions about them having sex were wrong, and the gossip about her being pregnant by him was also wrong. Gabriel claimed to still be as effective in his ministry as he was before; however, he had to admit that he was spending more time with Theresa than with any other single person. The priest told the Archbishop how they had agreed to be faithful to their vows without having to give up on their love. The superior reminded Gabriel about the public position of a minister of the church and how this type of scandal brought problems for the whole community of believers. He advised the subordinate to distance himself from the sister and occupy his time with his ministry more evenly distributed among his parishioners. Of course Gabriel had to pray for strength to accomplish this, but he needed to distance himself from all opportunity for temptation. The archbishop offered to reassign him somewhere else in the archdioceses if that would help, at least temporarily. Gabriel refused emphatically to be moved, but then moderated his tone of voice and predicted God would provide with a timely solution. The archbishop agreed, thinking he might just give God a little help in that matter.

Although he came out of the archbishop's office in one piece, Gabriel still had a little doubt in his mind if his decision to remain a celibate priest was better than marrying Theresa. Every time he remembered her face, her smile, her figure, he felt a burning desire to follow his passion for her and abandon his ministry. He would not stop being a Christian, he could even later become a Catholic deacon or a Protestant preacher to still serve the Lord, and make the woman he loved very happy. He had never felt this way before. He raised his eyes to heaven, opened his arms and asked for clarity of mind to be sure of what he should do. Then he remembered he had a task at hand involving the burial of John Paul's parents. Also, what was he going to do with the young man? He had promised his mother he would look after his welfare.

"God will provide the way!" he told himself, and began walking briskly towards his car.

When he was back in his office, Father Gabriel got a call from Det. Walker of the Traffic Investigations Unit. The suspect in the intoxicated double manslaughter case was nowhere to be found. They were able to locate the hospital where he was attended under a fictitious name, but he was already gone. The fingerprints lifted from the bottle were legible, but there were no similar prints on record. The detective asked the priest:

"Do you think you would be able to identify the man if you saw him again?"

"Yes, Tony. I am positive I can," affirmed Gabriel.

"All right, I will let you know if anything develops on my side. I am going to try and get pictures of possible suspects for you to view. Keep your eyes open in case you come across the man."

"Sure. I will let you know if I see him or find out anything about him on my side, Detective."

The priest hung up and wondered why in the world he had to be involved in that case when he had enough to worry on his own. He repeated in his mind that God has a plan for everything even when we don't understand it, so he could continue his daily activities in good spirits.

Monday night, Gabriel had a dream. A man was beating a couple to death with a big bottle. Although it was a clear glass bottle, it wouldn't break as the heartless assailant kept pounding on the man and woman. Gabriel tried to run and stop the man, but his feet were too heavy. He was moving in slow motion, trying to reach the scene. Even his scream for the attacker to stop was low and distorted. The killer laughed, looking at the two bodies lying in a pool of blood. He took a drink from the bottle he used to kill them. Then he turned around to see Gabriel in the face and told him in an evil tone:

"You are too late, Gabriel. You are just too late. Ha, ha, ha, ha, ha!"

The killer's face was imprinted vividly in Gabriel's mind. It was the face of the man with a mole. He threw the bottle stained with his bloody fingerprints to a grassy area, and then ran away. Gabriel turned his eyes to the bodies. A little blind child, around ten years old, was crying over them, just feeling their unresponsive bodies and with his face turned up to heaven.

"Help, please, someone help me, Oh God, please — Someone help me!"

Father picked him up and looked into his blind blue eyes; he saw the reflection of his own face in them. The priest woke up with the sound of an ambulance passing by. It was midnight.

Gabriel got off his bed and went to his desk. He pulled out a drawing pad and pen and began sketching the face from his memory and his dream, the man with a mole on his cheekbone. He typed up a letter explaining that this was a picture of the suspect in the DWI case Det. Walker was investigating. He faxed the letter and the picture to the Traffic Investigation Unit, so the detective would have the information as he arrived to work that morning.

Satisfied with his work, he went back to bed to continue sleeping for a few hours. His dreams changed directions. He was nude in the Garden of Eden. The day was as pleasant as could be. He walked alone by the water, admiring the landscape and all the life around him. A colorful bird came to rest on his shoulder. He picked up a white rabbit that was eating alfalfa. On the other side of the lake, he saw Theresa, also nude, waving at him. He put down the rabbit; the bird flew off his shoulder. Theresa crossed the water running over it without sinking. He waited for her with his arms wide open. She jumped out of the lake and into his arms. They embraced and kissed. Music started sounding from above, so they began dancing and looking into each other's eyes, declaring their love for each other. A warm drizzle surrounded them and got them wet. They danced into the water and made love on the grassy lakeshore.

Suddenly, lightning flashed in the distance and they heard the thunder. The warm drizzle became a cold rain. The sunny day became gray, filled with clouds and rain. The pleasant lake became a turbulent river. They slipped into the water and the current separated them. Their hands slipped away from each other. The river took Theresa away. The heavy rain, thunder and lightning continued. Gabriel was yelling her name. Theresa emerged on the other side of the river. She turned around, waved good-bye and sent him a kiss. Gabriel sat on the shore crying helplessly. The music continued amid the thunder and rain. Theresa was out of sight on the other side of the lake. The taste of her last kiss was still on his lips. He heard the words from Genesis again, reminding him about the reward to Abraham for obeying God's command. The rain was mixing with his tears as he looked up to heaven and saw the light returning to the sky. He opened his eyes and came back from dreamland into reality.

His alarm clock radio was on. It was raining outside, and he had overslept. It was 7:00 a.m. instead of the usual 4:00 when he normally got up to start his days. Gabriel stretched and popped his back, grabbed his "Liturgy of the Hours" and knelt by his crucifix to recite his morning prayer. He wondered if the dream had a meaning or was just a sexual fantasy of his, but he trembled remembering how real it had felt. Gabriel asked himself if Theresa might have shared that dream as well; he decided to open his prayer book and tried concentrating on the prayers instead.

The archbishop paid Gabriel a visit in school that morning. He wanted to talk to Sister Theresa and hear her side of the story. The pastor explained that Theresa was helping her friend, Barbara Williams, who had to bury her business manager in Fredericksburg. She needed a few days to comfort her friend because Barbara felt responsible for his suicide. Archbishop Rosales asked Father Infante to have Sister Reynolds visit with him when she returned to the parish. Mrs. Nogarelli asked to have a word with the archbishop. They talked privately; then the Archbishop left. The woman told the church official what she knew about the romance. Esther had not approved of the new religious sister from the beginning; moreover, if the principal were removed, she would take over control of the school.

Father Gabriel had a meeting with his deacon, Andres Garcia, and his assistant principal, Sharon Gray. He asked them if they had noticed him not paying enough attention to his duties as pastor of the parish and principal of the school. They both agreed that he had been a little more absent than usual and not as involved with the day-to-day operations, which had given both of them an opportunity to exercise their decision-making power. They also agreed that everyone knew Father was paying special considerations to Theresa, and that everybody was talking about them. They said the people suspected they were going to leave the church and that sister was pregnant. However, they also had noticed that Father had been glowing and seemed to be the happiest he had ever been. He had performed more miracles that semester than any other similar period of time. Things had become more intense! Neither the deacon nor the assistant principal had a problem with supporting the priest whatever his decision was. As a matter of fact, they commented that he and Theresa made a lovely couple. Father thanked them for their support and understanding. He wanted to have a meeting with the whole staff to put rumors to rest the following Monday. Before he dismissed them, he told them a joke:

"There was a priest, Father John, who got tired of the parish work and decided to go into a monastery seeking solitude and peace. He presented himself to the superior of the monastery, Father Frank, and was admitted to the congregation. The only requirement he had to contend with was the bow of silence all of them had to take in order to remain in the monastery. 'You will not speak at all, unless I authorize you to do so,' said the superior. Father John nodded in understanding and did not speak a single word anymore. Upon completing five years in the monastery, Frank called John to his office and told him, 'Father John, since you are celebrating five years with us, I will allow you to say two words.' John thought about it for a moment and said, 'Cold food.' Frank raised his eyebrows and said, 'Oh, I'm sorry that we have been giving you cold food. I will see to it that you get hot food from now on. Go in peace.' Five more years went by, upon completing ten years in the place, Frank called John again into his office and allowed him to speak two more words. 'Hard bed,' said John that time. Father Frank apologized again and promised he would see to it that Father John got a mattress for his bed. 'Go in peace,' said Frank, dismissing John. Five more years went by, upon completing fifteen years in the monastery, as was customary, Frank called John into his office and allowed him to speak two more words. 'I quit,' said Father John that time. Father Frank looked at him for a moment and then told him, 'You know, Father John, it will probably be the best thing to do. All I've heard from you for the past years has only been bitching and complaining!'"

Andres and Sharon headed out of his office laughing at his joke.

"Now, you two go in peace," Gabriel told them.

Thursday, December 16th, was the day of the double funeral. Few people came, no other family members, only Frank's co-workers from the department store where he had been working as manager of the electronics department, and a few friends of Elizabeth's from the neighborhood. She had a degree in English, but she had chosen to stay home for the last twenty years and take care of their blind son. After the burial, Father Gabriel took John Paul with him back to the church. The priest was riding with John in the limousine, so he asked the driver to drop them off at the church. He had some business to attend to before the end of the school day. The priest asked the young man to wait for him in the church. John Paul agreed and opened his Braille Bible to read while he waited for his new friend to finish his work in the school. John Paul was very impressed with Father Gabriel and trusted him from the beginning. He felt peace when the priest led him by the hand; he was no longer afraid.

Detective Walker called Father Gabriel to thank him for his help in the case. He had the news media publicize his sketch of the suspect. A few clues had been received that led the detective to a big supermarket chain warehouse on the northeast part of the city. He found a guy matching the description there. When the detective approached him, the man took off running and a foot chase ensued. The suspect, a Mexican national by the name of Rogelio Ramirez-Esparza, ran to the street in front of the business and pulled an old lady out of her car, dumped her on the median, and then sped off with her vehicle onto the highway to get away from the detective. Walker requested back up but had to give chase in his small, unmarked vehicle. Rogelio lost control of the little sedan on the curve where the loop turns west. He got off the road, and could not get the car going again because the front-right tire was broken. The suspect ran on foot but was tackled by the traffic investigations detective in the grassy area. He was booked in jail and demanded a lawyer. His fingerprints matched those on the bottle; his face was as the priest/artist had described in his drawing, with the big mole on his cheekbone. He was facing several other criminal charges on top of the two intoxication /manslaughter cases for which Walker had been investigating him.

There was a man waiting to see Father Gabriel when he got off the phone with the police, a Marco Antonio Galan, who claimed to be a friend of the Parker family. He had read the obituaries and wanted to know at what time the funeral service was going to be held. Father Gabriel met him at the entrance of the school and informed him the funeral had already concluded. The young man was disappointed to hear that. He explained he had been a friend of the family; he used to go play with their son, John Paul, when they were kids. Now Marco had recently returned to the city to work for a local business after completing his college degree in computer sciences in another state. Father told him John was there in the church and would be happy to see him.

"Do you mean he is not blind anymore?" asked Marco Antonio.

"I am sorry— He will be happy to know you are here. He told me about you when we met," said the priest.

They walked together to the church; Gabriel signaled to Marco Antonio not to talk so that they could surprise his friend.

"John Paul!" Father G pronounced his name loudly in the otherwise empty church.

"Yes, Father Gabriel. I am right here," replied the young man from his seat in the front row.

"I got good news for you, son."

"Well, let me first read you my favorite part of the Good News: the Holy Gospel according to John, Chapter nine," John Paul said.

"OK, go ahead."

"As He was walking along, He saw a man who had been blind from birth. His disciples asked Him, 'Rabbi, was it his sin or that of his parents that caused him to be born blind?' 'Neither,' answered Jesus, 'It was no sin, either of this man or of his parents. Rather, it was to let God's works show forth in him.'"

Father Gabriel was moved by his reading and felt the Holy Spirit coming onto him.

"Get up, John Paul!" the priest told him.

Father was already there and took him by the arm. He made a sign to Marco Antonio to be quiet and wait where he was. He walked John Paul out through the side door.

"How did Jesus cure the man born blind?" Gabriel asked John as he walked him outside of the church into a patio.

"Well, Jesus— it was kind of nasty. He made mud with his saliva and some dirt to rub it in the poor guy's eyes. Then He sent him to wash in a pool of water," John related.

Father put his hands on the young man's shoulders.

"Do you believe that could actually happen?"

"Yes, but where is Jesus when you need Him? I wish I had met him 2000 years ago that I may see," the blind man told the priest.

Gabriel bent down and spat at the soil where rows of colorful flowers were planted. He made some mud, blessed it, and saying a prayer unto heaven, he rubbed the mud unto John's eyes.

"Hey! What are you doing to me?" the startled young man complained as the priest covered both eyes with the sticky mud, "It hurts!" he shouted.

John grabbed the priest's hand to get it away from his eyes.

"It was the power of God that healed the blind man in the Gospel of John. Although Jesus left us to go back to His Heavenly Father, He sent us the Holy Spirit to empower us and do the things He did while He lived among us. You say you believe in him; what I do I am doing in His name. Now, go wash your eyes in the church. I will give you some holy water," Gabriel explained.

Marco Antonio was looking from a distance in disbelief, moving his head from side to side, and expecting nothing to happen. John Paul knelt in front of the altar with Gabriel's help and started washing the mud off his eyes with the bowl of blessed water the priest handed to him. Father Gabriel stood over John, his hands raised in thankful prayer. Marco Antonio noticed that the priest seemed to glow as he stood like a Christ over the blind man. Then the priest handed John Paul a towel to dry his face.

"Ah! —Oh, my—God— I see— I can see!"

A squinting John stood up and stumbled onto the priest. Gabriel held him in his arms.

"Thank you, God Father Almighty! Thank you, Jesus! Thank you, Holy Spirit!" said Gabriel.

The young man opened his eyes wide and saw the face of the priest; he thought Jesus must have looked like that when he was on this earth. John kissed the priest on both cheeks and went down on his knees in front of the altar to thank God from the depth of his heart. Gabriel had tears of emotion in his own brown eyes. He turned to see where Marco Antonio was waiting. He was on his knees too, crossing himself after witnessing the miracle. Father signaled for him to come over; the young man stood up and hurried to the altar.

Gabriel swallowed hard to overcome his emotion.

"John Paul, don't you want to hear my good news yet?" he told the formerly blind friend, putting his hand on John's shoulder.

"What could be better news than being able to see for the first time in my life, Father?"

John turned around and looked up to see his healer.

"Being able to see the goodness of the Lord is more important than the power of seeing with your eyes, my son. Let me introduce you to your old friend Marco Antonio Galan," explained Father Gabriel pulling the visitor closer to John.

"Matony! Is it you?" exclaimed John Paul as he stood up to embrace his old friend.

"Yes, Jopal! It is me!" was the reply.

They called each other by their nicknames, Matony and Jopal, a combination of their own two names. They embraced very tightly in front of the priest.

"I got back in town and read in the paper about your parents, my friend. I am sorry!" said Marco.

"Thank you, my friend. You cannot imagine what your presence means to me today. This is the saddest day of my life, when I had to bury both of my parents, yet it has become the happiest day too. I have been given sight and you have come back!" John Paul informed him.

Father Gabriel walked them out the door and told them:

"You guys must have a lifetime of things to catch up on with each other. Why don't you, 'Matony', take 'Jopal' here and show him the world?"

Marco hugged the priest and took the assignment with great excitement and joy.

"Oh, I had forgotten to tell you, John. The police already arrested the driver who caused the accident."

Gabriel looked into the new eyes of the young man. They had turned a dark green color.

"Father, I don't hate the man anymore. I have forgiven him in my heart. May God also have mercy on him for what he did."

The priest hugged the young man and praised God for giving him the grace and peace that forgiveness grants.

"Let us allow the judicial system to take care of him as they see fit then," said the priest in closing.

Gabriel turned around and went into the church. The two friends walked with an arm around each other to Marco Antonio's car, a midnight blue sporty convertible. John kept looking around and taking deep breaths as if he wanted to take the image of all creation into himself. The priest looked out and saw them drive away, euphoric. He sent them his blessing from the main door, turned his eyes to the image of the risen Christ in the center and winked at Him.

"Now I see, my Lord. I now can see too, 'Let God's works show forth.'"

Gabriel felt inspired by the friendship between the two young men and his own friendship with the Lord, so he started singing a song to God, it was a happy Spanish song of friendship that can be directed to a human friend or to God Himself. The powerful and melodious voice of the priest filled the church as he sang at the door. Several people passing by smiled and waved at him. He responded to their greetings smiling and waving back, but continued singing until he finished the song. Gabriel felt that he was doing what God meant for him to do. He had to continue his ministry and renounce his own human desires to devote his life to Theresa.

"Faithfulness to God must prevail! That's what the passage about Abraham was telling me!" he said to himself.

Friday was a regular day of work, morning Mass, school and parish appointments. Linda Richards quit her job in the school cafeteria and came to thank Father Gabriel for all his help. She apologized for trying to make him get into an intimate relationship with her. The pastor told her he had been flattered that such a beautiful woman would consider him for a partner, but that they indeed had an intimate relationship as it was. Linda explained that he could probably make any woman in the world happy with his goodness, integrity, his positive attitude, wisdom, voice and hot looks. He was the sexiest priest she had ever seen, and she still owed him her life.

"It was God who gave you life to begin with, and He gave you a second chance too," Gabriel told her, trying to shift attention away from him, "What are you going to do with your new life now, girl?" he asked her.

They were sitting down at his desk. He was holding her hand.

"Well, I got that new job in public relations with a big insurance and finance company. Also my attorney, Scott Anderson, got me a 250,000 dollars settlement with the power company, but he seems to be truly interested in me. He likes my son very much, and my son likes him back. Scott refused to take his part of the money, unusual for any attorney, and he let me have all the money for me to settle down on my own. We started dating after the settlement, and he is just a wonderful man," the woman confided to the priest.

"I am sure you will be happy with him. I know Scott and think he will be an excellent role model and father for your child, lucky him!"

Father Gabriel closed his eyes as if he were seeing the future; then he went on to say:

"You will give him twin daughters by this time next year."

Gabriel let her hand go and admired her figure, imagining her pregnant.

"Come on, Father, I am just beginning to date this man, and you are already loading me with two kids of his," she said.

Gabriel came around his desk to hug her and assured her:

"You will be very happy with your new family."

Linda kissed him and left his office. The priest raised his eyes to heaven and thanked the Lord for the happy outcome.

Before the end of the school day, the eighth grade boys organized themselves to play a game of volleyball against the eighth grade girls. They were short one player, so they asked Father G to join them. The girls complained that it was unfair for them to have God on their side, if Father G played with their team. The pastor laughed out loud and guaranteed them that it was not the case. One of the girls pulled Theresa from the hallway and asked her to join their team to make things even. Theresa looked at Gabriel sweetly from the doorway; he was already in the volleyball court with a ball in his hands. He signaled for her to come on over and join the game. She said she would be back in a minute, to go ahead and start warming up.

She came back wearing shorts and a school T-shirt ready to play. Her hair was tied in a ponytail; she looked like a college girl. Theresa began serving for her team. Father's boys were not as good as they bragged to be, so they began losing one point after another. A serve by the sister cleared the net and hit one of the boys on the head to bounce out of bounds. It was already seven to nothing. The next one landed in between two of the backcourt players who just looked at each other, eight to zero!

Finally, the boys picked up the serve and set Father G up for a spike. He rose above the net and hit it nicely, but Theresa picked it up before it hit the floor and set her girls up. The girls placed the ball easily on the other side of the net. The two boys that reached for it collided and just bounced the ball on the net to lose another point. Gabriel was running all over the court trying to lend support to his players, but even he was hitting the ball out of bounds. The final serve was uncontested for a score of fifteen to nothing.

The bell rang to indicate the end of the school day. The boys conceded their defeat to the girls and promised to do better on a rematch the following week. Theresa told them they would probably do better because she was not going to be with them any longer. Sister Kathryn was back from Ireland, so Theresa was going to return to Europe that night. Gabriel felt his heart sink in his chest upon hearing the news. He already knew this was going to happen as was revealed in his dream, but it was still painful to go through it. He recalled how in his dream Theresa waved good-bye from the other side of the lake.

Gabriel and Theresa walked into his office. Mrs. White, the secretary, was leaving for the day. Theresa sat on the couch. Gabriel was going to sit behind his desk but changed his mind and came to sit next to her on the couch. They looked into each other's eyes, not knowing what to say. Both started talking at the same time, and both stopped and asked the other one to go on. They laughed a little. Father G held her hands in his.

"Terry, I had a dream—" Gabriel told her.

She looked at him puzzled, but then said:

"We were in the garden?"

"Yes! How did you know?" he asked her.

"Apparently we had the same dream again," Theresa exclaimed in amazement.

"I was on one side of the lake—" Gabriel began.

"—And I came from the other side of the lake to meet you. We danced to some music from above and actually made love. It was the greatest experience I had ever had in my life. It felt so real!" she completed describing the dream sequence.

"It started raining, hard—" continued Gabriel.

"—Thunder and lightning came suddenly. I was swept by the current, and we ended up back on our separate sides of the lake," she told him, verifying that it was exactly the same dream.

They looked at each other with eyes wide open.

"Where did you go, love?" he asked her.

"I don't know. I woke up, and it was—" she shrugged her shoulders.

"—Seven O'clock?" he completed her sentence.

"Yes! I overslept, but that was the sweetest, and saddest, dream."

"I knew then this was coming to an end, and that you were going back to Europe."

"Do you want me to go, honey?" Terry asked him.

"It is God's will, love. Who are we to oppose it? He has given us all this time to enjoy together, and he also has given us the opportunity to meet in dreams!" he answered full of confidence then.

"You are right. We should be thankful, faithful and obedient to our Father's will," Theresa nodded, "I had the time of my life these past few months that I shared with you. I will always keep you in my heart next to our Lord."

She wiped her tears off her eyes and smiled at him. They hugged for a moment; then she told him she had to go home and get ready for her departure. He offered to take her to the airport.

Father Gabriel went to the sisters' house to pick Sister Theresa up that evening. All the sisters were emotional as they said good-bye to their friend. They had gotten to love Theresa in the time she shared with them. Terry gave Sister Magdalene a cheesecake she had baked exclusively for her; she knew of her love for food. To Sister Mary she gave a recent book on the great religions of the world because she had learned how curious the young religious sister was about knowledge. To Sister Carmen, who was always cold in the classroom but never complained, Theresa gave her long wool sweater. Even for Sister Kathryn whom she had just met, Theresa got a CD with meditating music. She hugged them all and said good-bye expressing her wish to stay in touch with them. The religious sisters saw the couple leave for the airport and commented how good they looked together. Sister Kathryn dismissed their comments as sacrilegious; the other sister took her in the house to fill her in on all the little things they had seen while she was gone. Theresa was looking all around as Gabriel drove to the airport. She asked him not to get on the highway and take the side streets instead. She wanted to see the city for the last time and fill her eyes with the images where she had found romantic love, twice, in her life.

"I am already missing this place, Gabriel!"

He said nothing in reply; he felt like a golf ball was stuck in his throat.

"Say something to me, Gabe. Fill my ears with your voice," she pleaded.

"I can't say anything right now," he explained.

"Then sing me a song, for the last time," Terry begged him.

"A song— a song! What song can I sing when I feel like dying?" Gabe asked himself out loud.

Gabriel remembered an old tango that spoke about the sadness of not having one's lover near anymore; he started to sing it as they approached the international airport. The poet laments having to wander throughout the world alone while his beloved will be out of his reach. He prays to the Miraculous Virgin for forgiveness if in his song he demands to have his beloved return to him, but he claims that he will surely die without his cherished love. The poet says he found her singing and singing too he lost her, so he is resigned to die singing. Theresa listened to every word and enjoyed the bitter-sweetness of the song. She treasured her beloved Gabriel's voice in her heart promising never to forget it. She took into herself his image as he drove on, his hair, his profile, and his powerful hands. Terry got close to him, leaned her face on his shoulder and breathed in deeply trying to record his aroma in her lungs forever. Gabriel felt his shoulder getting wet with her tears as she rested her little face on him.

The woman ran her hands over his face. They had stopped in the airport parking lot. He said nothing as she let her hands slip from his face to his neck, his shoulders and chest. She pulled his face a little towards her and kissed him desperately. He responded with the same passion. Their kiss lasted for a moment that seemed to stop time. The roaring of a landing airplane brought them to open their eyes and sit there, silently looking at each other. Gabriel got out of the car and came around to get her door. They walked in silence carrying her luggage into the terminal.

The time for departure came as scheduled. Those last minutes ran as fast as sand through one's fingers in the ocean when a wave hits one's hand. Father Gabriel was wearing his black pullover shirt without the clerical collar and gray pants. Sister Theresa had a conservative beige two-piece suit with a brown silk blouse. No one could tell they were religious people just by their appearance. Boarding time was announced for Theresa's flight. They shook hands as principal and temporary teacher would. He thanked her for a good job; she thanked him for a good time. They could not hold it anymore, so they embraced in a tight hug and kissed each other, knowing full well that there was no tomorrow for them.

A very old lady dressed in red turned around to see them engaged in their long, passionate kiss and smiled. Gabriel looked at Theresa with great anxiety, trying to remember every part of her face. She turned to see that the rest of the passengers were all inside the tunnel going into the plane. He kissed her hands; she kissed his. They walked to the boarding tunnel. She gave her ticket to the attendant. He let her hand go softly. She waved good-bye and started walking into the tunnel. He stepped to the side to see her go. She turned around and blew him a kiss. He caught it in his hand and placed it in his heart.

That was the last view he had of her. He proceeded to the window to see the plane take off. The old lady in red saw him standing there and asked him:

"Is that your wife you were sending off? It's just beautiful to see how you two love each other."

He could not see her face clearly; his eyes were clouded with contained tears. She looked as if she were eighty years old and had some black sunglasses covering a pair of strangely red eyes.

"Yes, we love each other very much!" he told her.

Gabriel pulled out his handkerchief and wiped his eyes to see the plane take off. He turned around after the plane disappeared from sight in the night sky, but the old lady was gone as if she had never been there.

Suddenly Gabriel experienced a great rage and felt an urge to hit someone. He clenched his fists and tensed all the muscles in his body. He could see the reflection of his own image on the glass window looking out onto the airstrip. His face was getting distorted; his eyes turning red like lit charcoals. He felt trapped inside himself. Everything around him had stopped moving. He heard something like a scream and did not know if it was from his own throat, but the sound was not human, like a never-ending cry of sorrow. The smell of evil and the nausea he experienced warned him about Satan trying to possess him. He fought from the deepest recess of his mind and heart by calling on the name of the Lord:

"Lord Jesus Christ! Son of the living God! Have Mercy on me, a sinner!"

He felt a little relief from the pressure on his chest, so he repeated the name:

"Jesus! Jesus! Jesus! Jesus!"

The suffocating pressure was lifted, and Gabriel fell to a seat in the waiting area. The noise of the crowd of people returned to his ears and he could see clearly his surroundings.

"Thank you God! Thank you Lord! Thank you Jesus Christ!"

Gabriel crossed himself and started walking out of the airport not wanting to look at anyone. He could not identify if he was happy, sad, afraid, mad or indifferent; he just knew he had to get out of there and go home.

Father Gabriel felt numb all over. He did not know how he made it home. The priest went into the church to pray. As he went deep into his prayer and meditation, he started glowing all around. His body, kneeling in front of the altar began levitating. Peace came into his heart as he surrendered his life to his God and found the joy of true friendship with the Lord. It was clear that his greatest temptation was over now. Gabriel had been wounded and now carried a scar in his heart, but he had survived and felt stronger in his faith because of the experience. The words from Genesis came back to his mind about the reward to Abraham for being obedient to God. When he walked out of the church, it was already the dawn of a new day. He had been in deep prayer all night but had lost sense of time.

THE END

Also available from PublishAmerica

DOVIE
A TRIBUTE WRITTEN BY HER SON

by B. Harrison Campbell

Paperback, 142 pages
5.5" x 8.5"
ISBN 1-60672-171-2

My first recollections of my life was when I had just turned three. I was in an orphanage and my mama was crying. I didn't know why. She was just crying and I wanted her to feel better. As I grew a little older in the orphanage, I realized what it was all about. I had become three and the rules were that a child could no longer stay in the room with their mother after that. They had to be transferred to a dormitory with other children of about the same age and sex. I believe that was when my mama firmly made up her mind to leave the orphanage to seek a new husband and a new home where we could all live together again. It didn't exactly work out that way and it was a crushing blow to Mama. But that had become the norm for my mama and grandparents. They all had lived their lives from birth in dirty, dark and dangerous mining camps, going through one mine explosion that killed 30 of their friends and acquaintances. And shortly thereafter, losing several loved ones to a national and worldwide devastating disease. And traumatic deaths followed my mama and grandma throughout their lives, even my daddy, who died at the age of 40 of bee stings that left my mama with six small children, including me at the age of three weeks. But we had a Savior that led us to the greatest fraternal organizations in the world, and still the greatest ones in existence today—The Masonic Fraternity and The Order of the Eastern Star. A large part of my story deals with our lives and experiences in the Home they built for us, as well as the lives and experiences of hundreds more who came there to live with us. My mama and my grandma spent almost a lifetime in abject poverty and grief when, except for fate, they would have been among the wealthy and aristocratic families in Birmingham and Jefferson County. I have often wondered: what, exactly, went wrong?

Available to all bookstores nationwide.
www.publishamerica.com